James Fitzmaurice-Kelly

The Life of Miguel de Cervantes Saavedra

James Fitzmaurice-Kelly

The Life of Miguel de Cervantes Saavedra

ISBN/EAN: 9783337098612

Printed in Europe, USA, Canada, Australia, Japan

Cover: Foto ©Raphael Reischuk / pixelio.de

More available books at **www.hansebooks.com**

THE LIFE OF
MIGUEL DE CERVANTES SAAVEDRA.

A BIOGRAPHICAL, LITERARY, AND HISTORICAL STUDY

WITH

A Tentative Bibliography from 1585 to 1892,

AND

An Annotated Appendix

ON THE

CANTO DE CALÍOPE.

BY

(JAS.) FITZMAURICE-KELLY.

Det ädla landet här en tid dem hyste;
Så ger det sin Cervantes, sin Murillo
Och återgår till skaparslummerns ro.

CARL SNOILSKY, *España.*

LONDON: CHAPMAN AND HALL, Ld.

1892.

A MON AMI.

Bien tard, hélas! trop tard peut-être,
Après maints chagrins survenus,
Le destin ouvre une fenêtre
Et tout à coup nous fait connaître
Un de ces amis inconnus.

H.-F. AMIEL.

J'ai des songes, fort bleus, bien roses,
D'une beauté claire et caressée ;
Les portes en ne sont tout-closes
Jamais !

PREFACE.

It has long been my desire to write a Life of Cervantes. When this book was first begun, there existed in English, so far as I know, only the *pastiche* of Roscoe and the trifling monograph by Mrs. Oliphant; the former merely a rough translation, patched and boggled, from Navarrete; the latter too slight and sketchy for any but very young readers. While correcting the last chapter of the present volume, I have seen — *vidi tantum* — the more recent work of Mr. Henry Watt, at a period, however, too late to be of any service to me. I have, therefore, contented myself with glancing hurriedly through his pages: and, differing as I do from some of his opinions, I venture to hope that there may be room for the two volumes side by side.

My materials, like those of my predecessors, have been derived in great measure from the exhaustive and invaluable *Vida de Miguel de Cervantes Saavedra*, by Martín Fernández de Navarrete, whose whole-hearted devotion and minute general accuracy are beyond all praise. His monumental labour and untiring industry have met with but scant recognition from his successors. I gladly avail myself of this opportunity of saying that it would be impossible for me, at least, to exaggerate the immense extent of my obligations to him. From the later contributions of D. Jerónimo Morán and D. Ramón León Máinez I have derived some suggestions, which are, I trust, duly recorded elsewhere. I have conscientiously endeavoured in each case to indicate the exact source of my indebtedness, and any absence of such reference on my part must be taken as being purely accidental. I can only most earnestly say with Alonso de Ercilla that

> Si de todos aquí mención no hago
> No culpen la intención, sino la mano.

I have greatly regretted my inability to accept, in at least one instance, the conclusions arrived at by D. Pascual de Gayangos; and it may well be imagined with how much hesitation and reluctance I presume to place on record my dissent from the opinion of that ripe scholar and judicious critic.

The bibliography is, I believe, on a larger scale than anything on the same subject which has preceded it. I would fain hope that it may be found useful by many Cervantistas. I am painfully aware of the numerous deficiencies of my modest little appendix;

and I shall be happy to acknowledge any additions and corrections, however unimportant or minute, from those students of Spanish literature who may do me the honour to examine it critically. It would be singular indeed if, in the treatment of a topic which extends over a space of time so considerable, I should not have fallen into many heinous errors both of commission and oversight. But, incomplete and imperfect as this essay undoubtedly is, its blemishes would have been still more marked without the assistance of Dr. Richard Garnett and that of my friend Mr. G. K. Fortescue, to both of whom my thanks are very gratefully rendered. To M. Alfred Morel-Fatio, whose authority as a bibliographer is widely known, I am indebted for service in this matter, as in many others. The death of the accomplished Dr. Pieter Anton Tiele, of the University of Utrecht, who had kindly undertaken to place at my disposal his ample knowledge of Dutch bibliography, has been to me a matter for extreme regret. I am highly sensible of the loss which that portion of the work has sustained in being deprived of his efficient co-operation. M. Jean Théophile Naaké has given me much needful help in the transliteration of the entries in the Slavonic sections; and to the advice of Professor Johan Storm, of Kristiania, I am obliged for direction on points of Scandinavian scholarship. My sincere thanks are likewise due to my friend Mr. Charles Liddell for the leading he has ungrudgingly

lent me on all questions of Italian and Provençal learning. M. R. Foulché-Delbosc, Mr. Gregory W. Eccles,
Mr. R. Nisbet Bain, Mr. J. P. Anderson, and Mr. Henri
van Laun have aided me in many matters of precise
detail. Lastly, let me profess my deep sense of obli-
gation to the learned D. Marcelino Menéndez y Pelayo
and to the illustrious orator D. Emilio Castelar.

The name of one friend, without whose counsel,
encouragement, interest, and unfailing sympathy this
book would probably never have been completed, I am
compelled to omit ; but the omission is in every way
against my own inclination.

> No cantefable prent fin.
> N'en sai plus dire.

Yet my gratitude is none the less profound because
of my compulsory silence.

JAS. FITZMAURICE-KELLY.

October, 1892.

GENEALOGICAL TABLE.

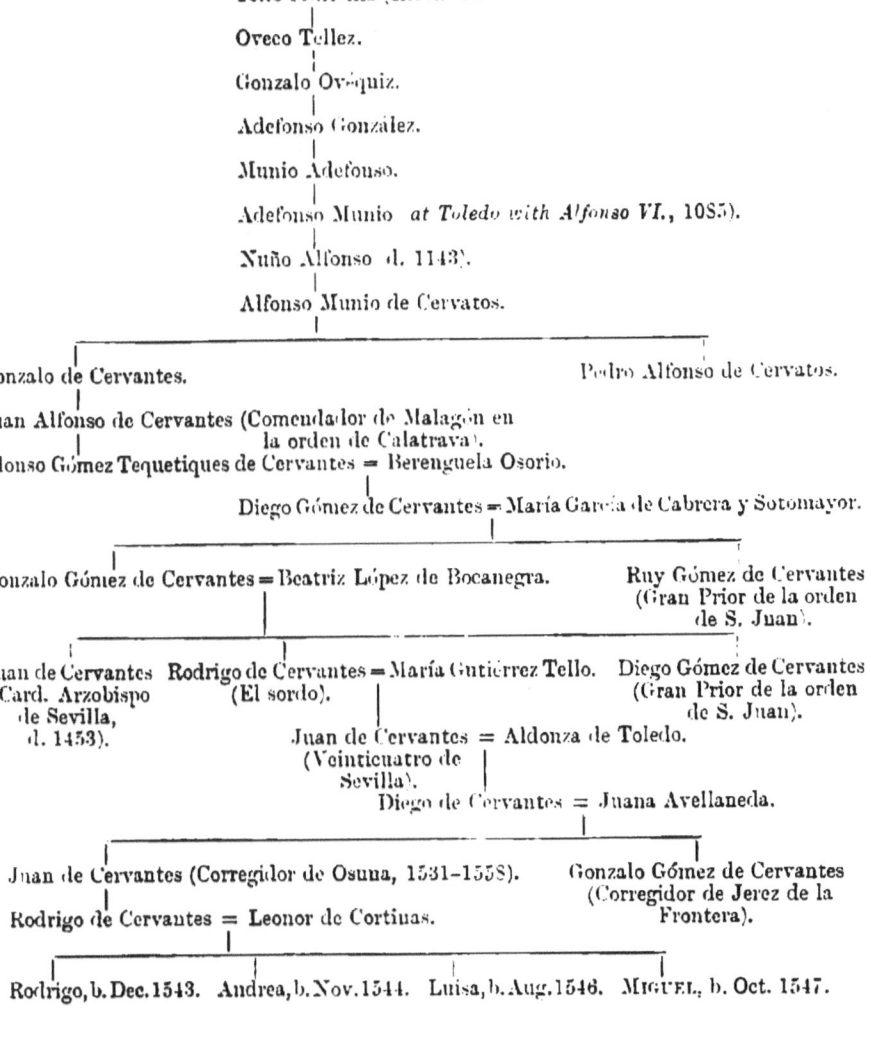

Tello Murielliz (Ricohome de Castilla *cerca* 988).

Oveco Tellez.

Gonzalo Ovequiz.

Adefonso González.

Munio Adefonso.

Adefonso Munio (at *Toledo with Alfonso VI.*, 1085).

Nuño Alfonso (d. 1143).

Alfonso Munio de Cervatos.

Gonzalo de Cervantes.

Pedro Alfonso de Cervatos.

Juan Alfonso de Cervantes (Comendador de Malagón en la orden de Calatrava).

Alonso Gómez Tequetiques de Cervantes = Berenguela Osorio.

Diego Gómez de Cervantes = María García de Cabrera y Sotomayor.

Gonzalo Gómez de Cervantes = Beatriz López de Bocanegra.

Ruy Gómez de Cervantes (Gran Prior de la orden de S. Juan).

Juan de Cervantes (Card. Arzobispo de Sevilla, d. 1453).

Rodrigo de Cervantes (El sordo). = María Gutiérrez Tello.

Diego Gómez de Cervantes (Gran Prior de la orden de S. Juan).

Juan de Cervantes = Aldonza de Toledo. (Veinticuatro de Sevilla).

Diego de Cervantes = Juana Avellaneda.

Juan de Cervantes (Corregidor de Osuna, 1531-1558).

Gonzalo Gómez de Cervantes (Corregidor de Jerez de la Frontera).

Rodrigo de Cervantes = Leonor de Cortinas.

Rodrigo, b. Dec. 1543. Andrea, b. Nov. 1544. Luisa, b. Aug. 1546. MIGUEL, b. Oct. 1547.

CONTENTS.

CHAPTER V.

CHAPTER VI.

CHAPTER VII.

CHAPTER VIII.

CHAPTER IX.

CHAPTER X.

THE LIFE OF CERVANTES.

CHAPTER I.

THE YOUTH OF CERVANTES.

Antiquitas sæculi, juventus mundi.

TELLO MURIÉLLIZ, Ricohome of Castile, who died towards the end of the tenth century, may be looked upon as the founder of the family of Cervantes. His grandson in the fifth generation was the famous Nuño Alfonso, whose reputation is only less than that of the Cid Campeador, and of whose half-fabulous achievements an elaborate record, based on the manuscript genealogy of Juan de Mena, has been left by Rodrigo Méndez Silva.[1] Nuño Alfonso was born in Galicia (probably at Celanova) in 1090, and, after being appointed Alcaide of Toledo, a post of honour first occupied by the Cid himself, died fighting against the Moors under Farax at Peña del Ciervo, on August 1,

---

[1] "Ascendencia Ilustre, Gloriosos Hechos, y Posteridad Noble del Famoso Nuño Alfonso. . . . Que escrive Rodrigo Mendez Silva" (Madrid, 1648).

1143.[1]   His first wife was Doña Fronilde, by whom he
had a son, Pelay Munio, and a daughter, Fronilde—an
unhappy girl whom he afterwards killed on suspicion
of an intrigue.[2]   His second wife was a widow, Doña
Teresa Barroso, who bore him five sons and several
("*algunas*") daughters,[3] one of whom, Ximena Múñiz,
wedded the Count D. Pedro Gutiérrez de Toledo from
whom Charles V. traced his descent.   The third son of
Nuño Alfonso, Alfonso Munio, assumed the territorial
surname of Cervatos on inheriting the castle of Cervatos
built by his father on a strip of land near Toledo
granted to him by Alfonso VII.   On the death of
Alfonso Munio, his elder son, Pedro Alfonso Cervatos,
succeeded to the estate, while the younger son, Gonzalo,
in order to distinguish himself from his brother, changed
the family arms and took the surname of Cervantes,[4] the

---

[1] Méndez Silva, f. 18. See also "Origen de las dignidades seglares
de Castilla y Leon, por el Doctor Salazar de Mendoça" (Toledo, 1618),
f. 32.

[2] . . . "se arrojó Nuño Alfonso à matar à doña Fronilde su
hija del primer matrimonio, por hallarla hablando cõ vn Cauallero ;
y lo mismo hiziera del, si la industria de escaparse no le valiera,"
Méndez Silva, f. 14. See also Nuño Alfonso's will : " Yten, mando
se digan otras docientas Missas por la desdichada de mi hija Fronilde,
que yo maté." Ibid. f. 21.

[3] The sons of Nuño Alfonso by his second marriage were
Fernando Munio, Pedro Munio, Alfonso Munio, Telle Munio, and
Juan Munio. Ibid. f. 4.

[4] The arms of the Cervatos family were : Azure, two stags in
pale, trippant to the left, or ; a bordure gules charged with eight
saltires or. These Gonzalo de Cervantes changed to : Vert, two hinds
in pale or, the upper one at gaze, the lower pascant.

The castle was probably restored by Alfonso VI. soon after his
occupation of Toledo in 1085, and was named after San Servando,

name of a fortress on the Tagus, in the restoration of which by Alfonso VI., Adefonso Munio, Gonzalo's great-grandfather, had assisted. From Gonzalo was descended Diego de Cervantes, Commander of the Order of Santiago, who settled in Andalusia and married Juana Avellaneda, daughter of Juan Arias de Saavedra, *El Famoso.* One of Diego's sons, Gonzalo Gómez de Cervantes, from whom the American branches derived, became Corregidor of Jerez de la Frontera, and, later, Corregidor of Cartagena; while another son, Juan de Cervantes, became Corregidor of Osuna (1531–1558). Juan's son, Rodrigo de Cervantes, married, about 1540, Leonor de Cortinas, of Barrajas; their offspring were four children, Andrés, Andrea, Luisa, and Miguel.

Miguel de Cervantes Saavedra was born, probably on St. Michael's Day, at Alcalá de Henares, and was baptised in the church of Santa María la Mayor, on Sunday, October 9, 1547.[1] It seems strange that any

a Spanish martyr of the fourth century. There is a reference to San Servando (or San Servan) in the "Poema del Cid":

> "Essa noch Myo Cid Taio no quiso passar.
> Merçed ya rey, si el Criador nos salue.
> Penssad sennor de entrar a la çibdad:
> E yo con los myos posaré a San Seruan."
> (v. 3045–3049.)

Calderón likewise mentions it in "Cada uno para sí," Act II. sc. xx.

[1] The following is a copy of the baptismal certificate: "Año de 1547. Domingo nueve dias del mes de Otubre, año de mil é quinientos é cuarenta é siete años, fue baptizado Miguel, hijo de Rodrigo de Carvantes é su muger Doña Leonor; fueron sus compadres Juan Pardo, baptizóle el reverendo Sr. Br. Serrano cura de

doubt should ever have arisen as to his birthplace;
but nothing can be more certain than that many of
his contemporaries were ignorant of it, and Lope de
Vega, to whom Cervantes was personally known, speaks
of him in terms which imply that his birthplace was
presumed to be Madrid. As the years passed by, and
the fame of Cervantes grew, the most baseless surmises
were made; and, a century after his death, Madrid,
Seville, Toledo, Esquivias, Lucena, Consuegra, and Alcázar de San Juan each claimed him as her own. Diego
de Haedo's *Topographia é Historia General de Argel*,
published during the lifetime of Cervantes, states his
birthplace accurately enough, and Méndez Silva, writing
some thirty years later, confirms the statement of the
Abbot of Fromesta, whose work, though of primary
importance in many respects, appears to have been
almost entirely overlooked by Cervantistas till Juan
de Iriarte and the Benedictine monk, Martín Sarmiento, called attention to it nearly a century and a
half after the date of its publication.[1] In 1752 the

nuestra Señora: testigos Baltasar Vazquez Sacristan, ó yo que le
bapticé é firmé de mi nombre = El Br Serrano."
It will be noted that the surname is given as Carvantes, and the
same form is used in the case of Andrea, Miguel's sister; but this is
obviously a clerical error, the form of Cervantes being used in the
certificates of Andrés and Luisa. Cervantes' elder brother Andrés
assumed later on the name Rodrigo.

[1] "Topographia é Historia General de Argel . . . por Maestro fray
Diego de Haedo, Abad de Fromesta, de la Orden del Patriarca San
Benito, natural del Valle de Carrança" (Valladolid, 1612).
In a pamphlet entitled "Remarks on the Proposals lately pub-
lished for a new translation of Don Quixote. . . . In a letter from a
Gentleman in the Country to a Friend in Town" (London, 1755), it

discovery of Cervantes' baptismal certificate by Agustín de Montiano y Luyando finally set the question beyond dispute.[1]

The Alcalá de Henares of Cervantes' boyhood was a very different place from the decaying, stagnant Alcalá of to-day, whose grass-grown, silent streets gently echo the muffled footfall of the infrequent traveller.[2] Some fifty years earlier the great Cardinal Ximenes had there laid the foundations of his University, had called around him some of the most accomplished scholars of the time, and within a brief space had made

is pointed out that the Cervantes mentioned by Haedo must be the author of "Don Quixote." The reference (p. 30) is to a "passage out of Haedo, a Portuguese writer, which has hitherto been unobserved by all the writers which I have seen, that mention Cervantes, but can belong to no other person," etc. Colonel W. Windham, to whom the pamphlet is attributed, had not, apparently, read Haedo's original, but relied on the summary given by Joseph Morgan in his "Complete History of Algiers" (London, 1728), ii. pp. 563–566. Morgan ends by saying: "It is Pity, methinks, that Haedo is here so succinct in what regards this enterprising captive." Colonel Windham may be fairly held to divide with Sarmiento the honour of discovering the great writer's birthplace.

[1] The matter was much complicated by the discovery, at Alcázar de San Juan, of the baptismal certificate of a Miguel de Cervantes, son of Blas Cervantes Saavedra, baptized November 9, 1558 ; and, further, by the discovery, at Consuegra, of the baptismal certificate (dated September 1, 1556) of another Miguel de Cervantes. On the margin of the first was written: "Este fué el autor de la historia de Don Quixote"; and on the margin of the second: "El autor de los Quijotes." It is, however, improbable that either of these could have fought at Lepanto.

[2] Alcalá de Henares is also mentioned in the "Poema del Cid" (vv. 444–446). The reputation of the theological faculty in the University of Alcalá survived until a comparatively recent date. Questions relating to the temporal and dispensing power of the Pope

Alcalá, where he himself had once been a student at the grammar school, the rival of Salamanca and of Basel. Here the celebrated Lebrija lectured, and here Núñez de Guzmán laboured with Demetrius Cretensis and Juan de Vergara on that Complutensian Polyglot which, through the munificence of Ximenes, spread the reputation of Alcalá throughout the world. In this busy, thronged University town, with its seven thousand students beneath the shadow of its college towers, the young Cervantes probably passed his youth. In Spain, as in the rest of Europe, it was a period of transition. The old Spain, the ancient order of things, was passing away; the long struggle of seven hundred years begun by Roderick on the banks of the Guadalete was ended by the conquest of Granada from Boabdil; the unity of the country and the destruction of her infidel enemies were at last accomplished. Spain was now at the topmost pinnacle of human glory. Columbus had added to her trophies a new world in which Hernando Cortés, equalling the legendary achievements of the early paladins, had with eight hundred men shattered the empire of the Aztecs. Only the splendour

were referred to it, at the suggestion of Pitt, in 1788, when it still ranked with the Sorbonne, Löwen, and Douay faculties. See Charles Butler's "Historical Memoirs respecting the English, Irish, and Scottish Catholics" (London, 1819–1821), ii. p. 110; and "The History of Catholic Emancipation," by W. J. Amherst, S.J. (London, 1886), i. p. 163.

For a sketch of the foundation of the University, cp. "Der Cardinal Ximenes und die Kirlichen Zustände Spaniens am Ende des 15 und Anfange des 16 Jahrhunderts," von Carl Joseph Hefele (Tübingen, 1851), pp. 94 et seq.

of their successes flashed across the Atlantic ; only the
triumphs of Spanish valour and discipline stirred
men's hearts in Valladolid and in Valencia. The groans
of Guatamozin, the tortured king of Mexico, passed un-
heeded, and the murder of the Inca of Peru was forgotten amid the successes of Pizarro. In an earlier
generation, Gonzalvo de Córdoba at Atella, at Tarento,
in the island of Cephalonia, and on the banks of the
Garigliano—the crowning victory of the Great Captain—
had established the reputation of that terrible Spanish
infantry which for a century carried everything before
it. Charles V., tired of the unending struggle against
the Lutherans, against Francis I. and Henry II. of France,
had, like Diocletian, abdicated the throne, had placed
the sceptre in the younger hands of Philip, and had
retired to die near those peaceful cloisters of the
monastery of the Jeromite monks at Yuste, which, with its
orange groves and cool streams in the still shadow of the
Estremaduran hills, had been, through many troubled
years, a part of his imperial dream. The age of printing
had come, and had brought with it new influences and
forces into literature.[1] The great Renaissance of letters
in Italy reacted on the Spanish students who thronged
the Universities of Naples and Bologna. Even the
iron-hearted Spanish soldiery who crushed the power
of Francis at Pavia had felt the new tendencies ; and
in many a country town were little groups of veterans
who, ceasing to study war, had hung the trumpet in the

---

[1] See the interesting note in the "History of Spanish Literature,"
by George Ticknor (Boston, 1888), i. p. 355.

hall and formed provincial centres of that new learning,
that new appreciation of foreign rhythms to which
Boscán had lent the first impulse. In that golden age
of Spain, as in the old Greek republics, the man of
letters was also either a man of affairs, like Hurtado de
Mendoza, or a man of arms, like Alonso de Ercilla.[1]
One of the most potent foreign influences at this critical
moment in the history of Spanish literature is to be found
in the person of the Italian Jacopo Sannazzaro, himself
of Spanish descent, whose *Arcadia*, with its train of
shepherds, nymphs, fauns, and satyrs, became the parent
of the modern idyllic romance. Among those who
adopted the new methods was the great Garcilaso de la
Vega, whose exquisite Theocritean pastorals show the
profound influence of Sannazzaro, and, more indirectly,
of Petrarch. Here and there, no doubt, some Castillejo
or Villegas would stand fast in the old paths, vainly
fighting the battle against the introduction of the new
Italian methods. But the cause was lost. Garcilaso
had so stamped the impress of his genius upon the
borrowed forms that Spain, for good or evil, received
them from his hands and took them to herself as part
of her intellectual heritage. Rarely, indeed, in the
history of letters has the genius of an individual so
altered the channel and the current of a nation's
literary expression. Yet at first the influence of
Garcilaso was confined to a comparatively narrow

---

[1] See A. W. von Schlegel's " Vorlesungen über dramatische Kunst
und Litteratur. Sämmtliche Werke " (Leipzig, 1846), vi. pp. 391–
392 ; and Friedrich von Schlegel's " Geschichte der alten und neuen
Litteratur. Sämmtliche Werke " (Wien, 1846), ii. p. 61.

circle which took years to widen. The popular taste of the day turned with insatiable enthusiasm to the fantastic romances of chivalry which celebrated the impossible exploits and prowess of Amadis and Palmerin, of Esplandian and Felixmarte. The *picaresco* novel was just springing into life, and while Cervantes was still a boy, sauntering idly by the river,—"*nuestro famoso Henares*," as he fondly calls it — there appeared *Lazarillo de Tormes*, the predecessor of *Guzmán de Alfarache*, of the *Pícara Justina*, and the long line of *picaresco* tales which Europe knows chiefly through the intermediary genius of René Alain Le Sage.

In such an awakening world, amid such contending influences, the young Cervantes grew up to manhood. Of his youth we know little beyond what we can deduce from casual phrases scattered over his own writings. He probably picked up what knowledge he could in a haphazard way, since the smallness of his father's means would make systematic education almost out of question for him. It has indeed been asserted that he studied for some time in the University of Salamanca; but this statement rests solely on the unsupported authority of a certain Tomás González, who declared that he had found the name of Miguel de Cervantes in the matriculation lists of the University. No subsequent seeker has been successful in verifying this entry, and the statement of González seems almost unworthy of discussion. It is by no means unlikely that one of the other Miguel de Cervantes, whose names have been mentioned earlier, may have studied

at Salamanca; but there is something like mockery in
assuming that a poor man like Rodrigo de Cervantes
would send his son to the ancient, distant University
of Salamanca, rather than to the younger but not less
famous University of the town in which he lived. In
Alcalá, then, though not an University student, we
may assume that Cervantes passed his early youth,
noting with keen eyes whatever his little world could
show him — noting with interest, for example, the
figures of two distant kinsmen of his own, Don Carlos,
the hero of Schiller's play, and Don John of Austria,
the future hero of Lepanto; both of whom came into
residence at Alcalá in the November of 1561. Among
the pleasantest memories of these boyish days were the
performances of Lope de Rueda, the father of the
Spanish theatre, whom he probably saw in some provincial town—perhaps Segovia—and of whom, thirty
years later, he still speaks with enthusiastic admiration.
Lope de Rueda died in 1567, having perhaps contributed as much as any one to the education of
Cervantes, whom we find at Madrid in 1568, in his
twenty-first year.

Don Carlos, the heir to the Spanish throne, had died
on July 24, 1568. On October 3, his stepmother,
Isabel of Valois, third wife of Philip II., died in child-
bed. The coincidence of their premature deaths gave
rise to sinister suspicions in the age in which they
lived—suspicions which seem to have lurked in the
dark imagination of Isabel's mother, Catherine de
Medici; but it is safe to assert that, so far as concerns

the death of Isabel, these suspicions were without the least foundation.[1] History, remorselessly shattering the airy, uncurbed imagination of the dramatist, reveals Don Carlos to us as a sombre, brutal, malignant, half-insane spirit, differing vastly from the gallant passionate lover immortalised by the genius of Alfieri and Schiller, Otway and Chenier. Isabel, who has the rare distinction of escaping the slanderous banter of the amusing, malignant Brantôme, so far from having conceived an incestuous passion for her stepson, appears to have felt for the crack-brained boy no other feeling than that of affectionate pity. But however the malicious tongues might wag in the market-place, condolences, official and officious, were not wanting to the widowed King. Amongst others, Juan López de Hoyos, professor of humanities in Madrid, published, early in 1569, a collection of verses by different hands, to which we find Cervantes contributing, thus making his first appearance as an author.[2] Juan López de Hoyos directs special

---

[1] In M. Gachard's "Don Carlos et Philippe II." (Paris, 1867) the relations between the pair are minutely and ably discussed. Philip's more or less deliberate neglect of proper precautions no doubt contributed to the death of Carlos, but that he had any more direct part in bringing about his son's death has never been proved. Those who maintain that Don Carlos was murdered by his father have never been able to agree as to the exact manner of his death, which Llorente attributes to a slow poison. Other writers declare that he died by suffocation, strangling, decapitation, etc.

Cp. Catherine de Medici's letter to Fourquevaulx in Friedrich von Raumer's "Briefe aus Paris zur Erläuterung der Geschichte des sechzehnten und siebzehnten Jahrhunderts" (Leipzig, 1831), i. p. 155.

[2] "Historia y relación verdadera de la enfermedad, felicísimo tránsito, y suntuosas exequias fúnebres de la serenísima Reina de

attention to the verses of Cervantes, whom he calls his
" dear and beloved pupil." It assuredly needed an
infallible literary instinct to detect in the crude stanzas
of the young man the least foreshadowing of the unrevealed powers of the future author of *Don Quixote,*
for it must be owned that Cervantes' dirges are of
no remarkable excellence. But no one expects that
a *Lycidas,* an *Adonais,* an *In Memoriam,* or a
Thyrsis should be forthcoming whenever a Royal personage dies; and one may fairly say that Cervantes'
juvenile lines are no worse than the bulk of official
elegies, and are infinitely better than some of the astounding verses called forth in our own century by the
very similar occasion of the death of the Princess
Charlotte. Apart from the *Cancioneros,* Boscán and
Garcilaso, comparatively little verse had been published, and the little that had been given to the world
was so little read that a high standard of taste was
scarcely possible. It may therefore be assumed that
Cervantes met with even more than the usual large
indulgence which, on similar occasions, cynical contemporaries have agreed in according to courtly versi-
fiers. In the autumn of 1568, Monsignore Giulio
Acquaviva, *Camarero* of Pius V., came to Spain on a
special embassy to settle some outstanding difficulties
between the Holy See and Philip II., with regard to the
state of affairs in Milan, and also as the bearer of the
official condolences of the Pope to the King on the

España Doña Isabel de Valois, nuestra señora, con los sermones, letras,
y epitafios á su túmulo," etc. (Madrid, 1569).

death of Don Carlos. His task was no easy one, and probably Philip's ear caught something hollow in the formal phrases of sympathy on his son's death—a subject which was highly distasteful to him. The young Monsignore—he was only in his twenty-third year—appears to have failed in the object of his diplomatic mission, and early in the month of December the passport for his return journey to Italy was made out.[1] With him went the young Cervantes, before the volume containing his juvenile verses had appeared. Much ingenious discussion has taken place with regard to the cause of this abrupt departure, and, as usual, the amount of speculation seems out of all proportion to the extremely slender evidence. There is a vague legend that Cervantes held some minor post at Court, where in his early youth he is said to have been a page. No positive evidence in support of this tradition can be brought forward; but a document discovered at Simancas, by the indefatigable industry of D. Jerónimo Morán, has an indirect bearing upon it.[2] From this paper (dated September 15, 1569) it appears that one Miguel de Cervantes had been previously condemned for wounding Antonio de Sigura in the neigh-

---

[1] Philip had written to Zúñiga, his minister in Rome, on August 27, 1568, that His Holiness need "not feel under the necessity of sending him letters of condolence."—W. H. Prescott's "History of the Reign of Philip the Second" (London, 1873), ii. p. 449.

[2] "Vida de Miguel de Cervantes Saavedra, por Don Jerónimo Morán" (Madrid, 1863), pp. 26–27. "Para que un alguazil vaya aprender á Myguel de Zerbantes." The said Myguel de Zerbantes, having wounded Antonio de Sigura, "fue condenado á que con berguenza publica le fuese cortado la mano derecha."

bourhood of the Court, and, having escaped from justice, was supposed to be in hiding not far off. Few offences, according to the cruel ordinances of the old Spanish code, were visited with penalties more terrible than those meted out to brawlers within the precincts of the Court ; nor was Spain peculiar in a statute which in our country existed to a period within the remembrance of men still living. Philip, who held the threads of every question, however minute, in his own hands, was the last man in the world to abate by one jot or tittle the debt due to the outraged majesty of the Crown. Diego Hurtado de Mendoza, a man of ancient family, an official of the highest rank and most eminent distinction, one of the glorious galaxy during the morning of Spanish letters, incurred professional degradation, if not absolute ruin, through a similar outbreak. But the long list of distinguished offenders whose names are included in his *pièce justificative* shows that in Spain such sallies of tempestuous passion were by no means rare.[1] The law, in Spain as in England, based primarily not on popular approval but on the personal will of the sovereign, might single out one offence for the special reprobation of the courts of justice ; but the private citizen, especially in Spain, where the current of

---

[1] "Historia de la Literatura española, por M. G. Tickuor, traducida al castellano, con adiciones y notas críticas, por D. Pascual de Gayangos y D. Enrique de Vedia" (Madrid, 1851–1856), ii. pp. 501–504.

The English procedure in similar cases, with its ghastly ceremonial involving the presence of the Sergeant of the Woodyard, Master Cook, Sergeant of the Poultry, Yeoman of the Scullery,

men's blood flows faster than in other latitudes, took little heed of the saws of the courtly legislator. Court or no Court, the fiery Spaniard had no idea of meekly pocketing an affront ; and, in his twenty-second year, we may be very sure that discretion was the smallest factor in the valour of Cervantes. It is, indeed, by no means certain that the Miguel de Cervantes referred to in the above-mentioned document, is actually the youngest son of Rodrigo de Cervantes of Alcalá de Henares : but nothing in the subsequent career of Cervantes is inconsistent with the hypothesis. The Miguel de Cervantes who was flying from justice had assuredly every possible reason for keeping out of reach of Philip's alguazils, for he had been sentenced to have his right hand cut off previous to being exiled for ten years. A faint tradition has long existed to the effect that at this time Cervantes had some love passages with one of the ladies about the Court. If so, this in itself might well condemn him to exile. For a similar act of presumption, Camoens, twenty-five years previously, had been sent first to Constancia, and afterwards to Ceuta. A mere poet must not lightly lift his eyes to a high *Dama de Paço*, be she Caterina de Atayde or another. The name of Cervantes' goddess has not come down to us, as

Sergeant Farrier, Groom of the Salcery, etc., is stated in Luke Owen Pike's " History of Crime in England " (London, 1876), ii. pp. 83–84.

For Mendoza's case see D. Eloy Señán y Alonso's " D. Diego Hurtado de Mendoza, apuntes biográfico-críticos " (Granada, 1886). Those who doubtfully attribute " Lazarillo de Tormes " to Mendoza will be confirmed in their doubts after reading M. A. Morel-Fatio's conscientious examination of the question in his " Études sur l'Espagne " (Paris, 1888), pp. 115–177.

in the case of Camoens, but her existence is only too
probable.

And in this place, as well as in any other, attention
may be drawn to the strange parallelism which exists
between the chequered destinies of Cervantes, the
greatest of Spaniards, and Camoens, the *fine fleur* of
the Lusitanian genius.   As in the case of Cervantes, the
very day on which Camoens was born is unknown ; and,
in the case of the latter, the year of his death is still a
matter of dispute.   As Cervantes fled to Italy in half-
voluntary, half-compulsory exile, so Camoens was interned at Ceuta to escape a still worse thing.   Camoens,
in passing through the Straits of Gibraltar, came into
conflict with a squadron of Moorish pirates, and lost the
use of his right eye ; Cervantes, a generation later, was
maimed for life in the battle of Lepanto.   Camoens
served as a simple soldier in North Africa ; Cervantes,
likewise, took part in the occupation of Tunis and La
Goletta.   Camoens, returning unpromoted to Portugal,
fell into a street brawl at Lisbon in the defence of a
couple of maskers, and a wound inflicted by him on
Gonçalo Borges—fortunately not in such a sacrosanct
spot as that where Cervantes and Sigura had crossed
swords — cost him some three years' imprisonment.
Cervantes, returning unpromoted to Spain, but with
recommendatory letters in his pocket, met with a fleet
of Algerine pirates, was taken prisoner and kept in captivity for five years.   It would be easy to prolong the
parallel, but, for the present, we may leave it.[1]

[1] John Adamson's " Life and Writings of Luis de Camoens "
(London, 1820), i. pp. 231-236.

. Whatever the motives of Cervantes may have been, there is absolutely no doubt that he did join the household of the young Papal legate, who, himself a patron of letters, may be supposed to have sympathised all the more readily with the young poet, after his own very recent and unpleasant experience of the unbending nature of the King.[1] From Valencia, the city of the Cid, the charms of which are celebrated in a characteristic passage in his last book, *Pérsiles y Sigismunda*, Cervantes, with his patron, passed to Italy, not to return for twelve years. In an imperfect way, the decree of the Court was to be accomplished on board the *Marquesa*, and in the Algerine galleys.

[1] Acquaviva's recommendatory letter from Zúñiga, the Spanish Minister in Rome, is dated September 19, 1568. His return passport is dated December 2, 1568. His failure does not seem to have been discreditable to him, as he was created Cardinal in 1570 at the age of twenty-four. He died on July 21, 1574, and is buried in St. John Lateran. He was the second son of the Duke of Atri, and nephew of the celebrated General of the Jesuits. A slight sketch of his brief career may be found in Baldassare Storace's "Istoria della Famiglia Acquaviva" (Roma, 1738), and an engraving of his tomb is given in Pompeo Litta's "Celebri Famiglie Italiane" (Milano, 1819). Cervantes refers to his position as *camarero* to Acquaviva in the dedication of "Galatea" to Ascanio Colonna.

CHAPTER II.

HIS CAMPAIGNS.

No creo que cosa hay mas lastimera,
Qu' el miserable officio del soldado,
Siempre armas, nunca paga, y por su suerte
O gran infamia ó sentenciado á muerte.

LUÍS ZAPATA, *Carlo Famoso*, Can. vii.

WE can form some idea of the route taken by Acquaviva and his train by tracing the path of Periandro
in *Pérsiles* from the city of those fair Valencians who
betrayed Cervantes into the unpardonable heresy of
ranking their dialect above his native *propio toledano*.
Only the Portuguese tongue, he declares, can vie with
it in grace and sweetness ; but, as we shall see later,
his leaning towards Portugal had a basis so purely
personal that a very large deduction must be made from
his somewhat florid eulogies. Barcelona and Perpignan
are left behind ; the land of Guillem de Cabestanh and
Peire Vidal, the Provençal country where " every man
and woman learns Spanish," fades away in the west till
at last Milan is reached, the half-Spanish town of Lucca
is passed, and after a final halt at Acquapendente the
cavalcade rides into Rome through the Porta del Popolo.

Cervantes arrived in Rome in the spring of 1569 and remained there for some fifteen months. It was probably during this time that his *Filena*, now lost to us, was written, and that he laid the foundation of his knowledge of Italian literature. For the young Monsignore Acquaviva, whose protection had been so opportunely extended, he seems to have retained the kindliest memory, but to a young man of his temperament the monotonous duties of *camarero* would inevitably become more and more unendurable. Chinese Gordon regulating the length of ladies' trains at Calcutta was scarcely more grotesquely out of place than the impetuous Cervantes murmuring agreeable nothings to the importunate crew who throng the antechambers of a prospective Cardinal. In the summer of 1570, he resigned his post and enlisted as a private soldier in Diego de Urbina's company of Miguel de Moncada's regiment, which at that time formed part of the force under the command of Marc Antonio Colonna.

It was a critical moment in the history of Europe, and, as Cervantes played some small part—" *Tuve, aunque humilde, parte* "—in most of the important events which followed, a few paragraphs may be spared here to a rough outline of the state of affairs. When Selim II., son of Solyman the Magnificent, ascended his father's throne, a peace of nearly thirty years' duration had existed between the Turkish Empire and the Venetian Republic. The political tendencies of heirs-apparent are seldom a profound secret, even in Turkey, and as Selim was believed to be bitterly hostile to Venice, the

news of his accession was received in the Palace of the
Doges with the gravest anxiety. Selim's powers of
dissimulation were, however, Oriental in their complete-
ness, and one of his first acts, on assuming the reins of
government, was to renew the existing treaty. The
earlier part of his reign was devoted to the administration of domestic affairs, and to the crushing of a
formidable revolt among the wild tribes of Yemen.
Previous to ascending the throne he had for many
years cast a longing eye upon the island of Cyprus, and
when he felt himself sufficiently secure at home he at
once turned to the accomplishment of his old desire.[1]
The autumn of 1569 found him free to act. The winter
was spent in amassing warlike stores, and in the silent,
stealthy equipment of army and of fleet, with such
success that in the spring of 1570 the preparations of
the Turkish armament were practically complete. In
the month of April, 1570, Cubat Caius was sent to
Venice as a special ambassador with instructions to
complain that Cyprus had for some time past become
the head-quarters of the Levantine corsairs, who preyed
on the peaceful merchantmen of Turkey and molested
the free passage of the Moslem pilgrims on their road to
Mecca. With a view to remedying these evils Cubat
was directed to call upon the octogenarian Doge, Pietro
Loredano, for the peremptory surrender of Cyprus to

---

[1] "Della Historia Vinetiana di Paolo Paruta" (Parte Seconda,
"Della Guerra di Cipro"), (Vinetia, 1645), p. 7. . . . "lassciauassi
publicamente intendere che quanto primo succedesse nell' Imperio del
padre, hauerebbe cerca'o di farsene Signore," etc.

the Ottoman Empire. A more barefaced request has
seldom fallen even from ambassadorial lips, and Cubat,
as he passed in ominous silence up the steps of the
Giants' Staircase between Sansovino's noble statues of
Mars and Neptune, must have anticipated the inevitable
reply. Only one response was possible, and the demands of the Turkish envoy were unanimously rejected
by the assembled senators in the Chamber of the Great
Council.[1] Within a few days of the rejection of the
Turkish proposal the aged Doge Loredano died, and
was succeeded by the brilliant, eloquent, shifty Mocenigo.
The question could now be settled only by the arbitrament of arms, and it remained for Venice to seek
assistance in the imminent, unequal struggle. Allies
were not easily to be found. No power desired to
enter into alliance with a state convicted of unexampled
perfidy in its relations towards its neighbours. Old
grudges still rankled; old envies, engendered by the
commercial supremacy of the Adriatic Republic, still
flourished; nor was it forgotten that to the calculating
neutrality of the Venetian oligarchy some of the most
disastrous defeats sustained by European arms in previous conflicts with the Turks were attributable. Venice,
however, left no stone unturned, and her envoys were
sent forth in all directions. Paolo Paruta, the historian
of the war, tells the story of the failure of the Venetian
ambassadors with a quiet humour which is irresistible.[2]

---

[1] "Della Historia Vinetiana di Paolo Paruta" (Parte Seconda,
"Della Guerra di Cipro"), (Vinetia, 1645), p. 31.

[2] Ibid. pp. 9-26.

Luís de Torres, a Spanish prelate of great diplomatic
astuteness, after a tolerably reassuring interview with
Philip II., passed on to visit Sebastian I., King of
Portugal, a pious youth who would gladly have lent
his aid; but the prosperity and the armament of his
country had been arrested and temporarily destroyed
by a recent epidemic of the plague, and the Portuguese
galleys lay disused and unarmed in the harbour of
Lisbon.   Charles IX., the Most Christian King of
France, could not afford to quarrel with the Sultan.
He had his own difficulties nearer home with Gaspard de
Coligny and his Huguenots, and was forced to content
himself with profuse promises that he would use all his
influence at Constantinople on behalf of his excellent
friends from Venice.   The Nuncio at Vienna made a
despairing appeal for help to Maximilian II., but that
weak, good-natured successor of the Cæsars was in a
high state of dudgeon and resentment with the Pope
for having presumed to confer the title of Grand Duke
on Cosimo of Florence without any reference to th
Imperial susceptibilities.   Under these circumstar ed
Maximilian declined to enter upon a campaign ag ted
a great military empire, the frontier of whic! d to
practically co-terminous with his own.   Eliza' Jubat
England was not likely to enter into any ras! ; Pietro
ments, but great hopes were entertained th yprus to
might be found in the sovereign of Pers'-
Odyssey of adventurous wandering throug' arte Seconda,
Wallachia, the travelled Thane, Vicenzo .   " lassciauassi
returned with the news that he had   ell' Imperio del

endeavours to enter the presence-chamber of the Great
King, and that Caidar, the Regent of the aged Tamas,
would anxiously await the successes of the Venetian
arms before committing himself by entering into any
compromising covenants. Fortunately for Venice she
found an ally in an unexpected quarter. The chair
of Peter was filled at this time by Michele Ghislieri,
under the title of Pius V., and, to the delight of
Suriano, the Venetian Minister in Rome, the Pope
declared that he looked upon the matter as a final
struggle for supremacy between Christianity and
Islamism. Alexander VI. might invoke the aid of a
Mahometan dynasty against a Catholic Emperor; but
Pius V. was of different stuff, and, while he wore the
Fisherman's ring, the Vicar of Christ would not join
hands with the Commander of the Faithful. He rallied
to the side of the Republic, and, adopting the idea
from Cosimo, Grand Duke of Tuscany, called upon the
Catholic sovereigns of Europe to unite with him in a
ᴸᵛ'Holy League which should wage another crusade against
neᴜₑₑ Turk.[1] On July 1, 1570, the representatives of
disa…nice, Spain, and Rome met in the Vatican to draw
vious the bases of an agreement. There at once began a
howeve of interminable wrangles on almost every point
sent forᴜ especially with regard to the division of ex-
of the waᵢ'n which, considering that their existence was
ambassador…the Venetians conducted themselves with a
want of generosity which surprised even

[1] " Della Hi
" Della Guerra ᵈli Cosimo Medici, Gran Duca di Toscana, discritta da
[2] Ibid. pp. ᶨldini " (Firenze, 1578), pp. 75–76.

their most hostile critics. When the spring of 1571 was reached, the Catholic delegates were still word-chopping and arguing on comparatively unimportant points of detail.

In the meantime, the drunken barbarian on the Bosporus had not been idle. The triumphs of dialectics he left to his Christian enemies to award among themselves. While the Vatican resounded with the echoes of diplomatic controversy, Selim, careless of the academic laurels which he might have gained against Zúñiga, devoted himself to the more practical task of superintending the final preparations of his armament. On August 1, 1570, a month after the opening meeting of the Christian representatives in Rome, more than three hundred Turkish ships of war, under the command of Piali Pasha, a Hungarian renegade, appeared off the coast of Cyprus, and anchored in the bay of Limasol. The Ottoman troops were at once disembarked and advanced on Nicosia, which was carried by storm on September 9. The fall of Nicosia placed Cyprus at the mercy of the invading force and, with the exception of Famagosta, the whole island submitted to the conqueror. Mustafa Pasha, the commander of the land forces, then formally called upon the garrison of Famagosta—some seven thousand men under the command of Astor Baglione and Marc Antonio Bragadino—to surrender. The summons was rejected, and on September 15 the systematic investment of the fortress began.

While the Christian envoys in Rome were engaged

in their ingenious diplomacy, a futile attempt was made
to relieve the beleaguered garrison. Marc Antonio
Colonna, Duke of Paliano, with the Genoese Giovanni
Andrea Doria and the Venetian Girolamo Zane under
his orders, was entrusted with the supreme command;
but the old mutual distrust and hatred of Venetian
and Genoese foredoomed the expedition to failure,
and Colonna found himself paralysed again and again
by the malignant recalcitrancy of his lieutenants.
On September 21 the allied fleet lay off the island
of Castelrosso; and, after being scattered by a heavy
storm, the ships of the three admirals met once more
in one of the harbours of Scarpanto, where the
smouldering quarrels broke out afresh, and the galleys of
the combined forces returned without taking one serious
step towards the relief of Cyprus. It would be difficult
to exaggerate the angry disappointment with which
the news of the return of the abortive expedition was
received in the Vatican and in the Piazza of St.
Mark. Some scapegoat had to be found, and the
unlucky Zane, who of the three admirals deserved
the least censure, was at once placed in close arrest,
and ultimately died in prison. The failure of the
relieving squadron had its result. The tedious steps
of the wrangling diplomatists were quickened, their
petty differences arranged, and on May 25, 1571, the
treaty of the Holy League was formally proclaimed in
St. Peter's. Eight months had passed since Baglione's
garrison had been hemmed in by Mustafa; but the
indomitable spirit of the defenders of Famagosta re-

mained unabated, and the month of May found them still repulsing the attacks of the besiegers. The divided leadership and the conflicting personal pretensions of the chiefs had wrecked the autumnal expedition of the previous year. It was now hoped that under happier auspices, and beneath the standard of a more illustrious name, the heroic defenders of Famagosta might be relieved, and a deadly blow be synchronously struck at the increasing power of the Ottoman Empire. Don John, the natural son of Charles V. (and, through Ximena Múñiz, the distant kinsman of Cervantes), was appointed Generalissimo of the combined armaments of the League, and on September 15 and 16, 1571, the three hundred caravels of the Christian fleet sailed from Messina under his command. Cervantes embarked on board the *Marquesa* (commanded by Sancto Pietro), one of the ships of Giovanni Andrea Doria's division. On October 5 the fleet lay off Cephalonia, when a Candian brigantine brought Don John the depressing tidings of the fall of Famagosta. The commander of the allies learned with amazement that as far back as August 1, six weeks previous to the assembling of his forces at Messina, Famagosta had surrendered. It speaks volumes for the sleepless vigilance of the Turkish corsairs, or for the characteristic remissness of the Venetian scouts, that two months should have elapsed before any tidings of the disaster reached the allies. Terms highly favourable to the gallant garrison, which had kept an overwhelming force at bay for nearly eleven months, had been ob-

tained from Mustafa Pasha by Baglione and Bragadino.
These conditions were completely disregarded by the
Turkish general as soon as the Venetian officers were
in his power. On August 5, a discussion between
Bragadino and Mustafa, with regard to one of the
minor articles of the capitulation, ended in an angry
dispute. Bragadino and his officers were at once
arrested. Baglione, the soul of the heroic defence,
and his chief lieutenants, Martinengo, Quirini, Rago-
nasco, and Straco, were hacked to pieces by the
scimitars of the Turkish janissaries, while Bragadino,
drenched with the blood of his comrades, was reserved
by the vindictive barbarian for a fate infinitely more
horrible. His ears and nose were cut off, and on
August 17, after suffering unspeakable outrages, he
was flayed alive. His body, filled with straw, was
mounted on a cow and treated with nameless indignities,
while the crimson umbrella of state was borne before
him with ceremonious mockery. Finally, his stuffed
skin was swung up to the yard-arm of the Turkish
Pasha's galiot. Famagosta underwent all the horrors
of a place carried by storm. The churches of the
Christians were rifled, their tombs outraged, their
homes violated; and those survivors who escaped
the minor misfortune of massacre were sent to the
slow martyrdom of the Turkish galleys.[1] Such tidings,
of the class "that turns the coward's heart to steel,

[1] Paruta, pp. 139–144. "Chronica y Recopilacion de varios successos de Guerra, etc. Compuesta por Hieronymo de Torres y Aguilera" (Çaragoça, 1579), ff. 42–45.

the sluggard's blood to flame," ran round the fleet
and fanned the fierce desire of the Christian troops to
meet their enemy.   At sunrise on Sunday, October 7,
their galleons lay off the rocky Curzolarian group—
the holy Echinean Isles of Homer, whence Meges led
his forty black ships to the siege of Troy.   The look-
out in the maintop of the *Real*, Don John's flagship,
sighted on the horizon two strange sail, the vanguard
of the Turkish fleet under Ali Pasha, one of the most
able and humane officers in the service of the Sultan.
The standard of the League, blessed by the Pontiff,
and bearing upon it a representation of the Redeemer,
was hoisted, and the report of a gun fired from the
Real, which gave the signal for battle, called forth a
burst of cheers from the allied fleet.   Adverse winds
delayed the actual conflict for some hours, and when,
soon after noon, the first cannon was fired and the
action began, Cervantes lay below, ill with fever.   He
at once sprang up and, replying to the remonstrances
of his comrades, Mateo de Santisteban and Gabriel de
Castañeda, with a touch of Quixotic extravagance, left
his sick-bed to take his share of the fighting.[1]   Some
Cervantistas, suffering from a more than ordinarily
severe attack of *lues boswelliana*, would almost have
us believe that Christendom, on that great day, was
saved by the single arm of their hero.   But it may
at least be claimed for him that he quitted himself
like a man, and when the night fell, when the battle

---

[1] "Vida de Miguel de Cervantes Saavedra, por D. Martín
Fernández de Navarrete" (Madrid, 1819), pp. 317–318.

was ended, the pursuit finished, and the enemy scattered, the sinister lightning flashed upon the face of Cervantes stretched upon the deck, with two severe gunshot wounds in the breast, and one in the left hand which was destined to cripple him for life. The *Marquesa*, originally part of Giovanni Andrea Doria's command, had been in the thickest of the fight with the right wing of the fleet, under Barbarigo. Doria himself commanded the left wing of the fleet as the armada came into action. His manœuvres during the earlier part of the engagement appear to have been of a somewhat dubious character, and the Venetians, who were distinctly of Dante's opinion that the Genoese were

> uomini diversi
> D' ogni costume, e pien' d' ogni magagna,

maintained, with all the obstinacy of incurable prejudice, that he dexterously kept out of action till the battle was practically over. This is doubtless an exaggeration; nor was the specious Italian lacking in plausible explanations of his peculiar seamanship. His explanations, however, do not appear to have carried conviction to every mind. The Pontiff, indeed, when he heard of Doria's strange tactics, expressed himself with the primitive fervour of an apostle, declaring them to be more worthy of a bandit than anything else; but Genoa herself was more than satisfied. She hailed her distinguished son with enthusiasm, and the shattered fragments of an immense statue of Gianandrea which once stood before the Ducal Palace in the Piazza Nuova,

and which may now be seen in the cloister of San
Matteo, remain to show us how

> widowed Genoa wan
> By moonlight spells ancestral epitaphs,
> Murmuring—"where is Doria?"

To us who live three centuries and more after the
event, it is difficult indeed to understand the immense
effect produced by the victory of Don John. To us
Lepanto is of scarcely more importance than the
capture of Ochakov by Potemkin, or that carrying of
Ismail by Suvorov with which most English readers are
familiar through *Don Juan.* Lepanto is to us but the
first ominous symptom in the clinical history of that
Sick Man whose steps become more feeble every day.
Even as a mere feat of arms, the heroic deliverance of
Vienna by Sobieski has somewhat dimmed the splendour of Don John's achievement. But contemporary
judgment is ever prone to exaggerate the historic value
of contemporary exploits and, to Cervantes and the men
of the sixteenth century, Lepanto was what Salamis was
to Æschylus. The philosophic inquirer, who seeks to
know the consequences as well as the causes of things,
may ask, in his embarrassing way, to be informed of the
advantages reaped after so brilliant an exhibition of
desperate valour, and the candid admission must be
made that few victories so complete produced immediate
results so inadequate. Lepanto was in truth but one
incident in the development of a long series of events,
the first ebb in the tide of victorious advance. But to

Don John, to Pius V., and their contemporaries, Lepanto was the crowning victory of the world. To the last day of his long life, Cervantes was proud of his share in it. He bragged of it with an innocent, simple pride that has in it something profoundly pathetic. To have been there was for him in some sort an assurance of immortality. Like most veterans he loved to fight his battles over again, and we may be very certain that he turned as fondly to the story of Lepanto, as Mr. Bright referred to Peel and Cobden and the Corn Laws. The legend is never old for him, nor can the lapse of forty haggard years wither its infinite variety. Page after page of his writings is covered with allusions to it; nor is prose a vehicle stately enough for the conveyance of his impassioned reminiscence. Verse and the gods alone can expound the full significance of his enthusiasm, as where in the *Viaje del Parnaso* we find Mercury saying :

Bien sé que en la naval dura palestra
Perdiste el movimiento de la mano
Izquierda, para la gloria de la diestra.

And so forth, through all his volumes, are heard the notes of his own pæan in which he sings of that unique battle, in which, as he believed, he had helped to save the world.

The victorious fleet steered for Sicily, and on October 31, 1571, it cast anchor in the bay of Messina. The returning heroes were everywhere hailed with extraordinary enthusiasm. The Pontiff, when the news of the triumph reached him, exclaimed : "*Fuit homo*

missus a Deo cui nomen erat Johannes." The brush
of the painter and the pen of the poet were both
devoted to the celebration of the victory. The mighty
Titian, then in his ninety-first year, spent his last days
on the unfinished picture of Philip offering Fernando to
Victory which now hangs in the noble *Museo* of Madrid,
among the masterpieces of Velázquez. Vicentino's
commemorative painting still decorates the Hall of
Scrutiny in Venice ; but the more celebrated picture of
Tintoretto has mysteriously disappeared. Cristóbal de
Virués, a personal friend of Cervantes, and himself a
sharer in the triumph, celebrated Lepanto in *El Monserrate* ; its glories were sung in Catalan by Puyol,
and Herrera's noble ode was followed by a superb rival
in the twenty-fourth canto of Ercilla's *Araucana*. One
word of notice may be given to Juan Latino, the negro
poet mentioned in the prefatory *versos cortados* in *Don
Quixote*, who published, amongst other courtly verses, a
laudatory poem on Don John. Philip II., listening to
the solemn vesper anthems, received the news with
characteristic self-control ; it is not too much to say
that in Rome, Venice, and Madrid, no other man was
so icily unmoved.[1]

---

[1] D. Cayetano Rosell's "Historia del Combate Naval de Lepanto "
(Madrid, 1853) contains an admirably careful account of the battle
and of the events which led up to it. It is worth noting that Torres
y Aguilera, so far from agreeing with the Venetian estimate of Doria's
behaviour, speaks in the highest terms of his seamanship and valour
(ff. 71–72). Doria, however, held a Spanish commission. Cp. in
this relation P. Alberto Guglielmotti's "Marcantonio Colonna alla
bataglia di Lepanto " (Firenze, 1862).

Cervantes remained in hospital for nearly six months before his wounds were sufficiently healed to allow of his joining the colours once more. In the April of 1572, he had so far recovered that he could enrol himself in Manuel Ponce de León's company in Lope de Figueroa's regiment, then quartered at Corfu, and, later in the year, a component part of the expeditionary force engaged in the fiasco of Navarino. Figueroa's regiment was probably among the troops landed on October 2, under the command of the Prince of Parma, with a view to operating against the Castle of Navarino. On October 7, Don John, fired by the recollection of the combat of the previous year, and anxious to repeat, if not to excel, the immortal victory on its first anniversary, vainly strove to induce the Calabrian renegade, Aluch. Ali Pasha, the wary commander of the Turkish forces, to give battle. But that skilful leader, who, alone among the Ottoman officers, had secured distinction at Lepanto by the annihilation of the ships manned by the Order of St. John, had no intention of imperilling his reputation or his safety by entering upon any conflict under conditions disadvantageous to himself. Only one of Aluch Ali's galleys fell into the hands of the allies—that commanded by Hamet, the nephew (or son) of Barbarossa. The story of Hamet's death—his being torn to pieces by the teeth of his galley-slaves—is placed in the mouth of the Captive in *Don Quixote*. Meanwhile, the stores of the allies were rapidly becoming exhausted, and Don John, tired of being a mere pawn on the diplomatic chess-board, seeing that success under the given con-

D

ditions was as impossible to him as to Aluch Ali, resolved in the bitterness of his soul to return to Italy. On October 8, the fleet of the allies sailed back towards Corfu, and on October 25, the forces of Don John disembarked at Messina. The contrast between the triumphant return of the previous year and the fruitless expedition of 1572 is mournfully obvious.

> The painful warrior, famoused for fight,
> After a thousand victories once foiled,
> Is from the book of honour razèd quite,
> And all the rest forgot for which he toiled.

One or two sentences will suffice to tell the last chapters in the history of the League. Throughout the spring of 1572, the Venetian envoy at Rome earnestly urged the necessity of the most strenuous exertions in continuance of the war. At the same moment, the Venetian representative at Constantinople was secretly engaged in independent negotiations for terms of peace, without the consent or even the knowledge of the Spanish and Roman Courts. On March 7, 1573, the Venetian envoy at the Golden Horn signed a treaty by which Venice resigned all claim to Cyprus, undertook to surrender the port of Sopoto in Albania— the one Venetian success under Veniero in the abortive autumnal expedition of 1570 — and, furthermore, engaged to pay into the coffers of the Sultan the sum of 300,000 ducats. Voltaire's caustic remark that one might imagine Lepanto to have been a Turkish victory finds full justification in the action of the Venetian

Republic.[1] On the same day, March 7, 1573, on which these terms of peace were signed by Marc Antonio Barbaro in Constantinople, Tiepolo, the Venetian Minister in Rome, solemnly pledged himself to adhere to the covenant of the League. The suspicions which had kept aloof so many states when Torres and d'Allessandri were wandering over the world in search of allies proved too well founded. It is needless to dwell on the good faith of the state which pledged itself to one line of policy in the presence of the Vicar of Christ, in the chambers of the Vatican, while at the same time a diametrically opposite pledge was given to the Grand Vizier at the Porte. Venice had deserved her reputation only too well. The pages of mediæval history are rich in examples of every kind of infamy ; but it is at least doubtful whether any civilised state can show an instance of political turpitude and dishonour more disgraceful than the perfidious abandonment by Venice of that League which her abject terror had called into existence for her own protection. The League was practically dissolved on April 7, 1573, and with its dissolution vanished the last hope of uniting the forces of Christendom against those of Islamism. The action of Venice in deserting the League called forth a storm of execration from the allies. Fierce anger blazed in the hearts of the new Pontiff, Gregory XIII., and Don John. Philip, when the news reached him, kept his usual impassive calm, and contented

[1] "Essai sur les mœurs et l'esprit des nations," ch. clx. : "Il semblait que les Turcs eussent gagné la bataille de Lepante."

himself with a remark of caustic irony on the policy of the Venetian Republic and his own disinterestedness.[1]

For a year Cervantes led the humdrum garrison life of a Spanish soldier at Messina, while copious despatch writers—"miserable creatures having the honour to be"—in Madrid, Rome, and Venice, followed that tortuous policy of chicane which is dignified by the name of diplomacy. The retirement of Venice from the League had, of course, destroyed the projects previously matured on the hypothesis of her adherence, and the summer of 1573 was passed in the discussion of the new plan of campaign involved by the altered condition of affairs. A resolution to send a force against Tunis was the final outcome of the deliberations in Madrid, and in this expedition Cervantes took part. On October 7, the second anniversary of Lepanto, the fleet, under Don John, with more than twenty thousand men on board, put out from Favignana, and, on the evening of

---

[1] The policy of Venice is discussed with much moderation in the third volume of Mr. Prescott's "History of the Reign of Philip II." Most students of the period will probably censure her dishonourable tactics with more severity than is displayed by the American historian. The secrecy of the independent negotiations at Constantinople was in flagrant violation of the twenty-second paragraph of the tripartite treaty (see Rosell, p. 186, "Eadem ratione," etc.). Some such step was, probably, expected from Venice and provided against beforehand. The Venetian aspect of the matter may be found in the letters of M. du Ferrier, printed in M. E. Charrière's "Négociations du Levant," etc. (vol. iii. p. 375 *et seq.*). There is something highly amusing in the solemn impertinence of Mocenigo's speech to the Senators: "la compagnia d' altri, che douerebbe esserci d' aiuto et solleuamente, conosciamo per proua, che ci è di peso o d' impedimento."

October 8, sailed in between the promontories of
Mercury and Apollo, past the white Arab town of Ras-
Sidi-bu-Said, under the hill of Byrsa, where, three
hundred years previously, amid the fig-trees and the
date-palms, the saintly Louis had breathed his last.[1]
The troops were landed near the palm-trees and
tamarind-shrubs of Goletta, which was occupied without
resistance ; and on October 10, two thousand soldiers
picked from the garrison of Goletta advanced on Tunis,
under the command of Santa Cruz, " the thunderbolt of
war," who had captured Hamet's galley at Navarino.
At nightfall the allied forces were in possession of the
town, the Turkish troops, under Hyder Pasha, having
retired on the approach of the enemy to that sacred city
of Kairwân, where three hairs from the beard of the
Prophet sanctify the mosque of Abdullah-el-Belawi, and
where the Djâma 'l Kebir, the model of the celebrated
mezquita of Córdoba, attracts the Moslem devotee to
the tomb of Sidi Alba, the companion of Mahomet.[2]
Don John had received instructions from Philip to
dismantle and destroy the fortifications of Goletta ; but

[1] See M. Francisque Michel's admirable edition of Guillem
Anelier, the Provençal poet, for a touching account of the death
of Louis:

> "Et esdevenc s' apres que vole lo Salvador
> Que mori 'l rei Frances, dont perderon color
> Totz aquels de la ost, e' n agron grant dolor," etc. (p. 32).

[2] "Don Juan de Austria, por Don Lorenzo Vanderhammen,"
ff. 169–173. Torres y Aguilera, ff. 101–105. I fail to see anything
exceptional in the "rapacity" of Don John's troops which so horrified
Mr. Prescott. They seem to have behaved as all soldiers in all
countries still behave under similar circumstances.

these instructions were studiously disregarded. Dreams
of a vast African empire, first suggested by the Pope
before Lepanto, and sedulously fostered by his private
secretary Escovedo, floated before the vain, ambitious
imagination of Don John. So far from dismantling
or destroying, he appointed the celebrated Gabriel
Sorbellone, who with Pacioti had designed the almost
impregnable defences of Antwerp, to the post of Captain-General of Tunis, with instructions to fortify the
military position by the strengthening of the old works
and by the building of a new fortress with all possible
speed.[1]   During the last week in October, Don John
sailed for Europe, leaving behind him a considerable
force under Sorbellone and Portocarrero, the military
governor of Goletta. Lope de Figueroa's regiment
was quartered in Sardinia. In the April of 1574,
Marcello Doria suddenly removed this corps to
Genoa, where, owing to the internecine jealousies between the Portici of St. Luke and St. Peter,
serious disturbances, bordering almost on civil war,
had broken out with such acuteness as to call for
the personal intervention of Don John. In the
Galatea and the *Novelas*, Cervantes has left many
a trace of his wanderings—many a sketch of Genoa's
gleaming walls, of Ancona's silent bay, of Bologna's
half-Spanish University, of Florentine palaces and
Venetian splendour. The disturbances in Genoa were
scarcely quelled when rumours of a Turkish descent on

---

[1] Torres y Aguilera and Vanderhammen, *passim*. See also the
"Relaciones, etc., de Antonio Pérez" (Paris, 1598), pp. 270-275.

Tunis caused Don John to sail from Spezia, with Figueroa's regiment and other troops, for Naples, where he landed on August 24, 1574. On July 12, his old enemy Aluch Ali Pasha, with a fleet of three hundred sail and forty thousand men, had appeared before Tunis, while a vast cloud of Arab horsemen and Turkish irregulars from Fez and Tripoli, advanced along the right bank of the Medjerdah. Aluch Ali's Chief of the Staff was an engineer, Jacopo Zitolomini, an Italian renegade who had formerly served at Tunis in the Spanish legion. Zitolomini had once been a hanger-on at the Court of Philip : one of the needy, threadbare gentlemen who haunted the ante-chambers of the palace with requests for employment. In an unfortunate hour for Spain, Zitolomini was cudgelled by one of the alguazils at Philip's Court, and, unable to obtain redress from King or Ministers, the exasperated adventurer had betaken himself to Constantinople, abjured Christianity, entered the service of the Sultan, and, assuming the name of Mustafa, had risen to dignity and fortune. His hour had at last arrived ; his " vigil long " was over. His minute and exact knowledge of the position and defensive works of Goletta and Tunis stood him in good stead. On August 23, Goletta was taken by storm, and on September 13, the position of Tunis was carried at a cost of thirty thousand lives, Mustafa falling dead in the breach as he led on his troops against his countrymen. The miserable tragi-comedy of Famagosta was practically repeated. Don John had sailed with his fleet from Naples to Messina, and thence to Palermo, where the news of the fall of Goletta reached him during the last days of September. There was, however, still hope of relieving Tunis itself; but all Don John's efforts were frustrated by a storm which forced him to put into Trapani, where he lay land-locked and tempest-bound when, on October 3, he received the news of the loss of Tunis and the capture of the gallant Sorbellone, just as, three years previously, he learned at Cephalonia the loss of Famagosta and the capture of Bragadino. With the force at his disposal any attempt to retrieve the disaster was impossible, and nothing remained for him but to accept with sullen acquiescence the annihilation of his vague ambitions and golden dreams, and to return with his galleons to Naples.[1] Here Cervantes remained for almost a year, under the command of the Duque de Sesa, Viceroy of Sicily, and it is doubtless to this long sojourn that we owe the enthusiastic reference in the *Viaje del Parnaso* :

> Esta ciudad es Nápoles la ilustre,
> Que yo pisé sus ruas mas de un año :
> De Italia gloria, y aun del mundo lustre.

And here Cervantes' campaigning days are practically over. In September, 1575, he obtained leave to return to Spain, and, armed with recommendatory letters from

---

[1] Torres y Aguilera, ff. 110–123. Vanderhammen, ff. 175–189. Sorbellone (the Gabrio Cerbelló of the Spanish writers) was ultimately ransomed. For a brief sketch of his career see "Scena d' huomini illustri d' Italia del Co. Galeazzo Gualdo Priorato" (Venezia, 1659). The pages of this volume are not numbered, but what relates to Sorbellone may be found under the letter G.

Don John himself (who, in June, had returned from a visit to Philip) and the Sicilian Viceroy, he embarked on board the *Sol* with his brother Rodrigo, Juan de Valcázar, and Pedro Carillo de Quesada, once Governor of Goletta, and now indirectly the godfather of Don Quixote himself. On the morning of September 26, the *Sol* was sighted by a squadron of Algerine pirates who swooped down upon her, captured the crew after a desperate resistance, and carried them into Algiers. For the present, then, Cervantes' fighting days are ended. He had had his desires. He had kept safely out of range of Philip's alguazils; he had drunk deep of the fountain of Italian letters; he had seen life and men and cities. He had served in Italy and Sardinia, at Lepanto, at Corfu, at Navarino, Goletta, and Tunis. He had borne arms for five years; he was a crippled man, and had found promotion's path a slow one. He was twenty-eight years old, and had touched the period when the faint penumbra of retrospect first darkens the disk of life. Some of the best part of youth lay behind him, and all his glory, his battles, and his hard blows had left him still a simple soldier. But fortune seemed about to smile on him at last. Some little prospect of advancement seemed about to dawn when the young warrior, crowned with his Carthaginian laurels, stepped on board the *Sol*. That vision faded into the painful distance as Arnaut Mamí led him into his Babylonian captivity.

CHAPTER III.

THE CAPTIVITY.

The city is of night, perchance of death. . . .

Her subjects often look up to her there:
The strong to gain new strength of iron endurance,
The weak new terrors; all, renewed assurance
And confirmation of the old despair.

JAMES THOMSON, *The City of Dreadful Night.*

IN the modern Gallicised Algiers few indeed are the remains of those bad old Moorish times when the imprisonment of Cervantes began and ended.[1] In those days the ill-paved streets of the nine-gated town wound their narrow length along in serpentine folds so much more close than the tortuous by-ways of Toledo and Granada, that two men could scarcely walk abreast with ease. The low, deep, confronting houses, with the emblematic aloe-plant above each door, approximated so closely that an active lad could leap from a balcony

---

[1] The chief authorities which I have followed in writing this chapter are Haedo's " Topographia é Historia General de Argel," and Pierre Dan's " Histoire de Barbarie et de ses Corsaires" (Paris, 1649). I have also made free use of the documents found in Seville in 1808 by Juan Agustín Ceán Bermúdez, reprinted and condensed by Navarrete, pp. 312–349.

on one side of the footpath to a balcony on the opposite
side.   He could promenade almost the whole town by
means of the terraces and roofs of the buildings—a circumstance, says the old monkish chronicler, with a touch
of quiet humour, of which the light-footed thieves take
every advantage.   The white, one-storeyed houses, viewed
from the Mediterranean, seemed to rise above each other
like the tier on tier of some vast Roman amphitheatre.
Five times each day, from the minaret galleries of a
hundred mosques, the voice of the blind muezzin
chaunted his *adán*—his call to prayer, with its solemn
refrain of *Aláhu akbar.*   To-day the entire province of
Algiers possesses but two genuine specimens of representative Oriental architecture—the Grand Mosque and
the mosque at Sidi Okba, beyond Biskra.   The combined
influences of the Zouave, the Chasseur d'Afrique, and the
cosmopolite tourist have murdered the Eastern interest
of Algiers; but, at least, the relentless extinction of
the picturesque by these exacting vagabonds has been
accompanied by an improvement in the material conditions of existence for which Cervantes and his unhappy
fellow prisoners must have often sighed.

The population at that time was divided into the
two exhaustive classes of freemen and slaves.   The
slaves, some twenty-five thousand in number, were
mostly Christians, while the bulk of the freemen consisted chiefly of Turks, Moors, and Jews.   Among the
Turks were enrolled the renegades of all sects and
climes, and these, after the manner of their kind,
proved the sternest, harshest taskmasters.   The lot of

the galley-slaves was so unutterably wretched that exaggeration can scarcely misrepresent it, and, with a characteristic refinement of cruelty, the logical minds of their captors led them to treat most harshly those slaves who by social rank or previous education were likely to be able to endure least. But it would be unjust to deny to the Algerine satrap the possession of the faculty of judicious discrimination. Those who were fortunate enough to have the easier, lighter tasks apportioned to them sold water in the streets, and were soundly flogged if their own remissness, or the absence of thirst on the part of the passers-by, caused their receipts to fall below the minimum sum appointed by the peremptory fiat of their owners. They washed linen, calcined walls, cleansed the putrid streets, acted as nurses to the Moorish children, and tended the flocks and herds. Such were the unlaborious tasks allotted by the thoughtful humanity of the slave-owners to the enfeebled victims of decrepitude and old age. The unhappy beings who laboured under the fatal disadvantages of youth and vigour were yoked with horse, ass, or ox, and forced to drag the primitive Moorish plough over the sterile plains. When their labours in the quarries were ended they were harnessed to carts, while the whip was freely used to quicken the faint steps of the wretched victims as they carried the vast, rough blocks of stone to the site where they were to erect the harem of some debauched pro-consul. In the last resort they were compelled to carry out the hideous duties of the public executioner. The code of punishment existing in this realm of Azrael was as cruel as it was summary. Slaves were stoned, tied to a horse's tail and whirled over rugged pebble pavements against the sharp edges of projecting walls; they were impaled, buried alive, bastinadoed to death, broken on the wheel, torn asunder by boats, or hung up by the ankles with their ears and noses slit.[1]

If the destiny of the Christian slave was one of the most aggravated cruelty, the lot of the Jewish freeman—though a common hatred of the Christian dogs might have been expected to unite the Israelite and the Mahometan—was not without its trials and degradations. Rightly or wrongly, the Jews had acquired an infamous reputation as coiners of false money, and Turks, Moors, and Christians joined in treating the supposed criminals with the most brutal manifestations of arrogant contempt. A Moorish boy meeting a wealthy, elderly Rabbi in the open street would order him to remove his cap, and make him humbly lift his hand to his bared head in token of submission. The unfortunate Hebrew crying his wares for sale would occasionally be brought to a halt at midday and ordered to take off his sandals, with which some white-burnoused young Turk would strike the wretched Israelite upon the mouth amid the jeers of the bystanders. So great was the contemptuous hatred with which the Jew was regarded that, when any dispute arose between a Christian and a Jew, the sympathies of the Moslem were always with the

[1] Dan, pp. 405–407. Haedo, f. 8.

Frankish slave.[1] But for all his ignominy and humilia-
tion the Israelite received the recompense which was
sweetest to him. The commerce of the province was
almost entirely in his hands. The trading vessels from
far-off lands, armed with the protection of a safe-
conduct, thronged the ports with cargoes for him.
England sent her tons of ore, her miles of cloth;
French galleons supplied the harems with lace and
veil-cloths; Valencian brigantines brought pearls and
wine and specie, and Catalonian argosies filled the
air with the voluptuous odours of rich scents and
perfumed waters; Genoa unrolled her bales of velvets,
of silks and damasks, while her Venetian rival displayed her wealth of inlaid coffers, brazen tripods,
and coloured glasses. As the middlemen in all this
traffic the long-suffering children of Abraham found
their account.

It seems strange indeed that this nest of corsairs
should have been the centre of a flourishing trade, while
away on the Mediterranean their galleys struck terror
into the crews of peaceful merchantmen. Christian
and ex-Christian brains and hands created and sustained the prosperity of Algiers. Christian slaves
worked at the oar while Christian renegades directed
the policy of the State. All posts of high authority
among the ruling class were filled by renegades. It

---

[1] Haedo, ff. 19 and 23. His estimate of the Jews is highly
characteristic, especially in the little touch of self-complacency with
which he says: "Todos muy ignorantes, y grandemente pertinazes en
sus ceremonias y sueños ludaycos, porque lo he esperimētado y
disputado con algunos, no pocas vezes."

is not needful to believe unquestioningly the odious
details set out with so much minuteness by Haedo;
nor will the indulgent student of human infirmity
mete out to these unfortunates the stern judgment
of that moralising chronicler. Yet it must be admitted
that if the motives of their conversion were not beyond
suspicion, their subsequent lives touched the nadir of
infamy and social degradation. Abandoned to the
most loathsome and disgusting vices, their open disregard of morality and their flagrant violation of the
elementary principles of common decency would have
scandalised the inhabitants of the Cities of the Plain.
But the very nature of their crimes forms a protection
against exposure.[1]

No inns existed in the town, and the trading
Christians who entered Algiers were compelled, since no
true believer would suffer their shadows to pollute his
threshold, to seek lodging in the houses of the detested
Jews. The Moslem pilgrims on the road to holy Kairwân slept in the mosques, which still throughout the
East afford the poorer wayfarer that shelter which in
the Iceland of to-day the wealthier traveller finds in the
village chapel. But though inns were wanting, there
was a superabundance of drinking taverns where food
and wine were sold. These houses were usually managed
by Christians. " O ye that believe! Verily wine, and
the casting of lots, and images, and divining arrows, are
an abomination from the works of Satan: shun them,

---

[1] Haedo, ff. 9–10, 27–28, 32–39. Dan, pp. 332, 336, 338, 343,
345–347.

therefore, that ye may prosper." The true believer, mindful of this last injunction of the Prophet, left the selling of wine to the mere Christian dogs ; so also did the renegade, still hankering after the flesh-pots and good things of Egypt. But unfortunately observance of the law ceased at this point. Conscience might prevent the Moslem selling the accursed liquid, but the curious elasticity of interpretation which characterises the Laodiceans of every sect came to his aid. Judged by the result, it allowed him to enter the Christian cabarets, drink more than was good for him, and maltreat the "infidel" owner.[1]

Three languages were current in this inferno— Turkish, Arabic, and *franca*—"un barragouin facile et plaisant," says Pierre Dan—a gibberish of Spanish, Italian, and Portuguese, of which probably some idea

---

[1] "Quant aux hostelleries, ils n'en ont point. . . . Mais au lieu de ces hostelleries, il y a quantité de tauernes & de cabarets, qui ne peuuent estre tenus que par les Chrestiens captifs. Ils y vendent d'ordinaire du pain, du vin, & des viandes de toutes les sortes. Là se rendent pesle-mesle les Turcs & les Renegats, pour y faire leurs débauches," etc.—Dan, p. 89.

The views of Mahomet with regard to wine-drinking appear to have undergone some development. The passage in the text (Koran, chap. v.) is distinctly stronger than a previous passage in chap. ii. On the other hand, the well-known verse in chap. xvi., "And of the fruits of palm-trees and of grapes ye obtain an inebriating liquor and also good nourishment," appears almost to sanction the use of wine. But in all probability the reference is to *zebeeb*, an infusion of dry grapes or dates of which the Prophet himself drank at times. The prohibition does not appear to extend to Paradise, where there are, apparently, "rivers of milk, whose taste changeth not : and rivers of wine, delicious to those who quaff it."

may be formed from the grotesque song of the Mufti in
Le Bourgeois Gentilhomme :

> Se ti sabir,
> Ti respondir,
> Se no sabir,
> Tazir, tazir.
> Mi star Mufti:
> Ti qui star ti?
> Non intendir:
> Tazir, tazir.

This may perhaps be taken as a fair example of the
bastarda lengua of Zoraida in *Don Quixote*.

Away up in the stately palaces of the Pashas, where
the weird Moorish music of *kemengeh* and of *ood*
floated past the porphyry pillars, through the cool
arcade, while the Ghawazi and the Almahs trod their
lascivious measures on the mosaic pavement of the *patio*,
near the perfumed waters of the bright, clear fountain,
the problem of existence may have seemed easy and
pleasant enough. The life of the prisoners in the galleys
is summed up in Dan's trenchant phrase : "S'il y a
quelque lieu dans le monde qui puisse auecque raison
estre appellé l'Enfer des Chrestiens, c'est assurément
la malheureuse contrée des Turcs & de ceux de
Barbarie." [1] The town was a town of palaces and jails,
the latter greatly preponderating. The *Baño de la
bastarda* contained some two thousand captives, to
whom at least the shadow of liberty was conceded.
These prisoners were chiefly employed on the public

---

[1] Dan, p. 411.

E

works, and could wander about the streets without
hindrance so long as their owners did not need their
services.   Assuredly life was less hard for them than for
their manacled brethren in the *Baño del Rey*, which was
guarded by a corps of janissaries. Here stood the
Christian church ; and as there were always some priests—
occasionally as many as forty—among the prisoners, the
Turk took a cynical pride in the spiritual accommodation
so copiously provided by his benevolent foresight. Some
of the senior prisoners had exceptional privileges granted
them ; for example, one Pedro, a Catalan, a great
benefactor of the captives, was permitted to erect a
private altar in the house where he lived, at which Mass
was daily celebrated till with seven other masters of the
galleys he escaped to Valencia in 1582.[1]

In this world of corruption and degradation Cervantes
passed five years. He had become the slave of Dali
Mamí, a Greek renegade surnamed *El Cojo*, who had
commanded one of the Algerine galleys on that unlucky
September morning in 1575. In this kingdom of Eblis,
where the Spirit of Despair seemed to brood for ever, the
intrepid young Spaniard soon became the acknowledged
leader of the prisoners and the centre of their wavering
hopes. Every plan of escape was matured in that busy,
fertile, ingenious brain, and carried into execution by
that brave heart. While his captors found their pleasure
in watching two tattooed Moors oiled from head to foot
wrestle amid the clash of cymbals and of drum, he may
have stolen down to the market-place with his brother

[1] Haedo, f. 41–43.

Rodrigo, and with Luís de Pedrosa—a native of Osuna, whose father had been a friend of Cervantes' grandfather, the old-time Corregidor of Osuna—to hear the *ráwí*, the Arab *trouvère*, tell the "Tale of King Omar bin al Nu'uman and his Sons," in which Kanmakan and Sabbáh seem the Oriental analogues of Don Quixote and Sancho Panza. So also he buoyed up the spirits of his desponding brethren by improvising dramatic representations—playing perhaps in some of his own lost plays, or in some of those comedies of his old favourite, Lope de Rueda, to which Osorio alludes in *Los Baños de Argel.* [1]

But on the whole his opportunities for diversion must have been few. Haedo, in one of his dialogues between Doctor Antonio Sosa and Antonio González de Torres, places in the mouth of the former a ludicrous account of one of the practices of the Algerine corsairs

[1] "Antes que más gente acuda,
El coloquio se comience,
Que es del gran Lope de Rueda,
Impreso por Timoneda,
Que en vejez al tiempo vence.
No pude hallar otra cosa
Que poder representar
Más breve, y sé que ha de dar
Gusto, por ser muy curiosa
Su manera de decir
En el pastoril lenguaje."

Jornada Tercera.

For the reference to the "Tale of King Omar bin al Nu'uman and his Sons," and the probability of Cervantes having heard it in some Algerine bazaar, I am indebted to the late Sir Richard Burton, whose varied accomplishments it would be an impertinence to praise.

E 2

with regard to their newly captured prisoners. It was
no uncommon thing for them, he says, to address the
captive, some poor Estremaduran shepherd or Galician
clodhopper, in terms of the most profound respect,
informing him that they had just learned that he was
a man of great rank and wealth, closely related to
the celebrated Duke of Alva. The fact that the
prisoner when taken wore a sound pair of shoes
or an untorn cloak ranked him at least as the son
of a Count, or the cousin of some mighty noble. A
barefooted monk, on the strength of an untattered
habit, was classed as a Prince of the Church, and might
be considered fortunate if his benevolent captors were
content to let him sink to the humble position of a
Patriarch or Archbishop. Sosa's personal experiences
are in point: "Of their own authority, *et plenitudine
potestatis*, they made me, a poor priest, a bishop, and then
private secretary to the Pope. Eight hours each day was
I engaged with His Holiness in a room where we two
alone discussed the most weighty public affairs of
Christendom. Next, they made me a Cardinal; then,
Governor of Castelnuovo in Naples; and now I am
confessor and director to the Queen of Spain, and for
this end they suborned Turks and Moors who affirmed
it." [1] Moreover, some few Christians, anxious to curry
favour with their lords, supported these statements
with regard to the excellent divine, whose master
finally confronted the unlucky man with a crowd of
Turks recently returned from Naples, who obstinately

[1] Haedo, ff. 128-129.

averred that they had been Sosa's slaves when he was
Governor of Castelnuovo, and that he had employed
them as cooks and scullions in his vast Italian home.
If a lowly priest of Sosa's estate underwent a trans-
formation so startling, we may be very sure that those
unhappy recommendatory letters of Don John and the
Duque de Sesa were the cause of numberless afflictions
to Cervantes. It was at once assumed that the bearer
of these damnatory documents must be a man of so much
importance that a heavy ransom might easily be obtained for him. This, combined with his physical
incapacity for severe manual labour, caused him to be
placed in the *Baño del Rey*, where the more important
captives were closely confined. No sooner was he
imprisoned than he began to mature schemes of escape.
His first attempt was a complete, and even abject, failure.
He engaged a Moor to conduct him and his companions
—Castañeda, Castilla, Meneses, Navarrete, Osorio, Ríos,
and Salto y de Castilla—to Oran, the nearest point
occupied by the Spaniards. The omens were not
reassuring. Some time previously a young Italian
renegade had reverted to Christianity, had fled towards
Oran, had been recaptured on the banks of the Wad-
Safra, near Mostagan, and was brought back to Algiers
where he was summarily executed.[1] But Cervantes

---

[1] This treatment of reverting renegades appears to have been
quite common. Any relapse from Mahometanism was very severely
punished up to a comparatively recent date. Lane (" Modern
Egyptians," vol. i., pp. 136–137, ed. 1871) once saw a Moslem woman
who had become a Christian (denounced to the Cadi by her own
father) led amid the jeers of the mob through the streets of Cairo to

was not to be daunted by his own experiences, much
less by the experiences of others. The expedition
started; but at the end of the first day's journey the
Moorish guide abandoned them, and nothing remained
for the unfortunate fugitives but to limp back to Algiers,
where Cervantes, as the ringleader of the prisoners,
was manacled and confined more closely than before.[1]
Meanwhile, the father and mother far off in Alcalá had
heard of the capture of their sons, and had got together
every *real* they possessed in payment of the ransom.
But the sum did not reach Dali Mamí's idea of Miguel
de Cervantes' worth : and it was accordingly devoted to
the freeing of Rodrigo, who had not had the misfortune
to carry recommendatory letters from victorious generals
or ducal pro-consuls.

A second attempt to escape was soon afoot. When
in August, 1577, Rodrigo was ransomed, he was
charged by Miguel to arrange for a rescue, by means
of an armed frigate which he might hope to obtain
through the letters of Antonio de Toledo and Francisco
de Valencia (two Knights of St. John imprisoned in
Algiers) to the Viceroys of Valencia, Mallorca, and
Ibiza.[2] Viana, a slave released at the same time with
Rodrigo, went to Mallorca, his native place, on the

the banks of the Nile. She was stripped, strangled, and thrown into
the river, and her fate became the subject of a very popular Caireno
song.

[1] " El dicho Miguel de Cervantes fue muy maltrado de su patron,
y de alli en adelante tenido con mas cadenas y mas guardia," etc.
—Navarrete, p. 321.

[2] Navarrete, p. 322.

same mission. About three miles from Algiers, in the garden of the Alcayde Hassan, a Greek renegade, Miguel, for some months previous to the release of Rodrigo, had, with the help of the Dey's Navarrese gardener, been busily constructing a hiding-place in which fourteen Christians engaged in the plot had secreted themselves. Here their food was brought to them by a repentant renegade known as *El Dorador.* The envoys appear to have lost no time, and on September 28 Viana's expected frigate arrived. Eight days previously Cervantes had escaped from the town and joined his comrades in the cave. Viana's vessel was about to run up on the beach when some passing Moors sighted her and gave the alarm; whereon the commander was forced to stand out to sea again. In the cave, the fifteen lay hopefully waiting the moment of release. Two days passed by, and some of the fugitives began to show signs of illness, brought on by the dampness of their hiding-place. At this point, "the devil, the enemy of man, blinding *El Dorador,*" put it into the renegade's heart, says Haedo, to revert to Islamism; he accordingly walked into Algiers and discovered the whole plot to the Dey Hassan. A troop of Moorish horse and a company of foot-soldiers surrounded the runaways and captured them, together with some of the crew of the frigate, which had returned a second time. Cervantes at once took all the blame upon his own shoulders, declaring that he alone had organised the plan of flight and induced the others to join in it. He was separated from his comrades and led bound into the presence of Hassan, who threatened him with torture and with death; but these menaces were without result. The captive refused to answer any question which might inculpate others, and obstinately adhered to his first statement that he alone had conceived and elaborated the idea, adding that whatever punishment was awarded should fall on him only. For some reason very difficult to conjecture, Hassan spared his prisoner's life. The unlucky gardener was made the victim: he was hung up by one foot, and so suffocated by effusion of blood.[1] The Dey seems to have thought that Cervantes would be safer in his hands than in those of Dali Mamí, from whom he purchased the arch-conspirator for five hundred ducats, no very great sum if, as Hassan declared, the slaves and galleys and even the whole city of Algiers were secure enough as long as the maimed Spaniard was safe in custody. No sooner was Cervantes in the Dey's dungeon than his efforts were renewed. By some means or other he possessed himself of a reed and a sheet of the glazed Venetian paper sold in Algiers, whereon he wrote an urgent letter of entreaty to the Spanish officer in command at Oran, begging that some one might be sent to enable him and three others, prisoners

---

[1] Haedo, ff. 184–185. See also the testimony of Alonso Aragonés, Navarrete, p. 330: "Que la fragata . . . fue dos veces á Argel, y se perdió en la segunda." Doctor Sosa is careful to dwell significantly on the fact that El Dorador died three years later on the anniversary of his treason: "Murió en el mismo dia que descubrió este negocio al rey Azan."—Navarrete, p. 343.

with him in Hassan's dungeon, to escape. This letter
he induced a Moor to carry; but just as the messenger
was about to enter Oran, he was met by some com-
patriots who searched him and discovered the in-
criminating letter. The Moor was seized and brought
before Hassan, who ordered him to be impaled, while
Cervantes was sentenced to receive two thousand blows.
The punishment was for some reason remitted, as we
know from a very characteristic passage in *Don Quixote*
that Cervantes was never struck during his captivity.[1]

But the prisoner was incorrigible in his efforts to
escape. Hassan may well have said : " As often as I
strike a *woted* for him he hangs up another barley
sack."[2]　In September, 1579—the year of famine,
which witnessed also the completion of the Great
Mosque — another scheme was prepared. A certain
licentiate named Girón, a renegade from Granada, who
was known as Abdulrahman among the Algerines,
desired to revert to his old creed and to return to his
mountain home in Spain once more. With him, and

---

[1] Navarrete, p. 330. Alonso Aragonés says : "Mandó echarle de
entre sus esclavos cristianos y darle dos mil palos; pero no se los
dieron por haber mediado empeños." In the story of the Captive,
Cervantes, speaking of Hassan, says that among his prisoners was one
something or other Saavedra to whom he never gave a blow or
ordered a blow to be given : "Jamás le dió palo, ni se lo mandó dar,"
etc. ("Don Quixote," chap. xl.). It is right to add that the Moor died
game, without revealing anything which might make matters worse :
"Murió con mucha constancia sin manifestar cosa alguna."—Navarrete,
p. 324.

[2] John Lewis Burckhardt's " Arabic Proverbs " (London, 1875),
p. 197. A very amusing and instructive collection.

with two Valencian merchants, by name Onofre Exarque and Baltasar de Torres, Cervantes arranged that an armed vessel should be brought to Algiers, by means of which he and some sixty other prisoners should make their escape. The plan was on the eve of achievement when once again the whole design was discovered by a renegade Florentine named Cayban, and a Spanish Dominican monk, Juan Blanco de Paz. A great deal has been written about the impelling motives of the treachery of Juan Blanco de Paz, and, as he always remained a professing Christian, his motives are by no means clear. But motives, unless they are obvious to the meanest intelligences, are usually impenetrable by the keenest minds; and the vast bulk of the discussion on such points is mere verbiage. Certain it is, however, that Blanco de Paz betrayed Cervantes to the authorities; and Onofre Exarque, with a very natural alarm that Cervantes might implicate him by confessions extorted under torture, offered to pay the prisoner's ransom if he would embark at once for Spain. These terms were refused, and Cervantes, fearing in his turn that some of the weaker brethren might be put to the torture, came out of the hiding-place which Diego Castellano had provided for him, and surrendered himself to the tender mercies of the Dey.[1] A rope was fastened round his neck, his hands were tied behind him, and he was dragged before the tyrant: but all Hassan's threats were vain, and nothing could induce

---

[1] Navarrete, pp. 324, 330, 331–333, 336, 338–339; also the evidence of Sosa, p. 345 *et seq.*

him to exceed the statement that he had planned the
escape with four others who were now at large, and
that none of the sixty were aware of what was intended.
Blanco de Paz tried to place the guilt of his treachery
upon the blameless head of Domingo de Becerra, but
fortunately, without avail; and in the fulness of time
he received the wages of sin in the shape of a gold
ducat and a jar of butter.[1]

A far more ambitious design floated from time to
time before the captive's mind—a plot to enable the
twenty thousand Christian slaves to rise, overwhelm
their masters, and seize Algiers for the Spanish crown :
but, like most other ambitious schemes, nothing ever
came of it. The whole story of this captivity reads
like a page from some wild, impossible romance. It
seems strange that if, as we are given to understand,
the *Baños* were closely guarded by janissaries, Cervantes
should not only have escaped twice himself but should
have arranged for the escape of other prisoners, assisted
in hiding them in a cave of his own construction, sent
them food, supplied them with money, despatched
letters to the outside world, and planned a general
rising.[2] Still more inexplicable is the long-suffering

---

[1] See the evidence of Alonso Aragonés (ibid. p. 330): "Á
quien (Blanco de Paz) el rey agasajó con un escudo de oro y una jarra
de manteca." Domingo de Becerra lived to translate the "Galateo"
of Giovanni della Casa, Archbishop of Benevento. According to
Antonio's "Bibliotheca Hispana Nova" (vol. i. p. 328) the Spanish
translation first appeared at Venice in 1585.

[2] Haedo, f. 185. Méndez Silva (f. 60), speaking of Cervantes,
says: "Fue tal su heroico animo, y singular industria, q̃ si le corre-
spõdiera la fortuna, entregara al Monarca Felipe 2. la ciudad de

patience of Hassan.   If Cervantes was such a persistent
organiser of rebellion, the magnanimity of the Venetian
renegade is scarcely in keeping with what we know of
him.   Hassan was, indeed, a perfect monster of depravity and cruelty—a denationalised Venetian living
among a nest of corsairs was not likely to be hampered
by inconvenient scruples.[1]   He was one of those portents,
like Ezzelino da Romano, who seem to revel in blood-
shed and torment from mere wantonness—a man to
whom human life was of no more value than the life
of a fly.   Italy, as every reader of Mr. Symonds' *Age of
the Despots* knows, produced a bounteous crop of such
wretches, and certainly the necessary softening influences were not likely to be found in Algiers.   However,
there can be no doubt about the facts—whether from
the kindred sympathy of one strong spirit for another,
from admiration of the invincible intrepidity of his
prisoner, or from the hope of a large ransom, Cervantes'
life was spared.   We should hesitate to believe all the
details of this extraordinary story on the unsupported

Argel."   Méndez Silva appears not to have known that Cervantes
was the author of " Don Quixote."   Writing in 1648, he never
alludes to the book, and Cervantes is interesting to him solely
because of his descent from Nuño Alfonso.   For the rest, he seems
to have contented himself with following Haedo.

[1] For a sketch of Hassan's character see Haedo (" Epitome de los
Reyes de Argel "), ff. 83–86.   For instances of the most appalling
cruelty among the Turks or Saracens, read the account of Ibrahim-
ibn-Ahmed, in Michele Amari's " Storia dei Musulmani di Sicilia "
(Firenze, 1854–1872), vol. ii. pp. 50–61.   It would be scarcely
possible to reproduce in English the details of this very distinguished
man's atrocities.   The murder of his wives, children, and brothers is
the least of the horrors.

authority of Cervantes, or on the uncorroborated statement of Haedo, who probably derived his information
from the hero of these marvellous adventures; but each
incredible incident is, as we shall see, fully authenticated
by credible independent witnesses.

In the summer of 1579, Cervantes had written a
versified letter of passionate appeal to Mateo Vázquez
de Leca Colona, the Spanish Secretary of State. The
earlier tercets are filled with a somewhat ungraceful
flattery of the great man's superhuman worth—"*Privado
humilde, de ambición desnudo*"—but a little courtier-
like insincerity may well be pardoned to the prisoner
pleading for his life. Then follow the inevitable pæan
on Lepanto, an account of his capture on board the
Sol, and a description of the life in the *baños*, ending
with a strenuous supplication to Philip to send his delivering fleet against the head-quarters of the Algerine
pirates. Nothing came of it; Philip's delivering
fleet sailed to enslave Portugal, and Vázquez probably
threw the appeal on one side and troubled himself
no more about the humble petitioner and his prayer.
The letter disappeared till the spring of 1863, when
it was discovered, together with Lope de Vega's *Los
Benavides*, by D. Luís Buitrago y Peribañez, among
a packet of papers labelled *Diversos de Curiosidad*,
in the archives of the Conde de Altamira.[1] The

---

[1] In Mrs. Oliphant's "Cervantes" (Edinburgh, 1880), *n.* p. 9,
there is a singular statement: "This letter, it is believed, never
reached Philip's eyes at all. A curious story of chicanery, prolonged
to our own days, is told of it. It was sold to the British Museum
with a quantity of other papers—bought in order to secure it—but

final quatrain and the preceding twenty-one tercets have been re-employed by Cervantes in the first act of *El Trato de Argel.*

Far away in academic Alcalá, the two old people did what they could to gather together the amount necessary for their son's redemption. But the task was beyond their powers. The aged father went down to the Court to plead for the captive, if by any chance help might come that way. His declaration is dated March 17, 1578, and few things are more pathetically significant of the distressed state of the family than the unanimous confirmation by the four witnesses, Mateo de Santisteban, Gabriel de Castañeda, Antonio Godínez de Monsalve, and Beltrán del Salto y de Castilla, of the sorrowful statement in the sixth plea that the elder Rodrigo de Cervantes was a very poor man of excellent family, absolutely devoid of means, since he had spent all he possessed in ransoming his elder son.[1]   Doubtless, some careful

was found not to be among them." Mr. James Y. Gibson, in his admirable translation of the "Viaje," takes occasion to repeat this statement (p. 302) or something very like it. Mrs. Oliphant has, no doubt, excellent authority for the story, but she omits to give it; and my friend Mr. G. K. Fortescue, of the British Museum, who is in a position to know the facts, informs me that he is unable to find the slightest record of the transaction, or any confirmation of so unlikely a legend. My independent inquiries in the MS. Department have been equally unsuccessful. I am, indeed, assured by those most likely to know that the entire story is without foundation.

[1] "El dicho Rodrigo de Cervantes es hombre hijodalgo y muy pobre, que no tiene bienes ningunos, porque por haber rescatado á otro hijo, que ansi mesmo le cautivaron la mesma hora que á dicho su hermano, quedo sin bienes algunos."—Navarrete, p. 316 *et seq.*

Government official informed him that a note would
be made of his application, and the guileless, innocent
old man went away in happy ignorance of the fact
that he had been told not to come troubling the
slumbers of Barnacle in his impertinent officious way.
Within a year the father had died, and on the last
day of July, 1579, the widowed mother of Cervantes
and her daughter Andrea (married some years previously
to Nicolas de Ovando) were appealing to the good
offices of the Redemptorists, an admirable order, the
members of which devoted themselves to the task
of freeing the galley-slaves by purchase, or in some
instances by taking the prisoner's place in the dungeon,
or at the oar, trusting him to do his utmost to relieve
them in turn. The two women had collected three
hundred ducats, which Father Juan Gil and Antonio
de la Bella took with them to Algiers. Hassan, as
we have seen, had paid Dali Mamí five hundred
ducats for his slave, and, according to Haedo, he
determined to ask double that amount for ransom.
He flatly refused to accept the paltry three hundred
ducats offered by Father Juan Gil, but finally was induced to abate his demand to some five hundred ducats,
which sum the Redemptorists raised by loan and by
a grant from the general fund of the order. The
term of Hassan's viceroyalty was at an end, and
Cervantes was already on board the galley which was
to bear his owner to the Bosporus, when at the last
moment the ransom money was paid. It was September 19, 1580, when he stepped on land a free

man once more, five years, save seven days, since the
date of his capture on board the *Sol.* Before he
returned to Spain, he had one piece of work to do
in which he displayed something more than his
ordinary caution and foresight. His old enemy, Juan
Blanco de Paz, who either was, or assumed to be, an
officer of the Inquisition, was busily engaged in drawing up a series of false charges against him, filing
informations and endeavouring to suborn witnesses.[1]
Cervantes, in his turn, drew up a list of twenty-five
interrogatories which form a complete history of his
captivity — the flight to Oran, the expected arrival
of Viana's frigate, the betrayal by *El Dorador,* the
letter to the Governor of Oran, the murder of the
messenger, and the treachery of the Dominican monk.
On October 10, 1580, the evidence of eleven of the
chief prisoners, acquainted with the circumstances of
Cervantes' captivity, was taken down by the notary
Pedro de Ribera in the presence of Father Juan Gil,
and the proceedings ended on October 22 with the

---

[1] Diego Castellano's testimony is clear: "Juan Blanco de Paz fue
á rogar al capitan sardo Domingo Lopino, cautivo alli á la sazon *con
muchas* mandas de ruegos y sobornos, y promesas de darle ó hacerle
dar libertad, y diez doblas, que ante todas cosas, le dió para sus
necesidades, y mas le dijo, que no tuviese pena por verse pobre, que el
le proveeria de lo necesario, y que si él sabia quien le emprestase
dineros que los buscase, que el saldria por fiador" (Navarrete, p. 332
et seq.). Sosa says: "Juan Blanco usando todavia de oficio de
comisario de santo oficio, habia tomado muchas informaciones contra
muchas personas, y particularmente contra los que tenia por
enemigos, y como contra el dicho Miguel de Cervantes, con el cual
tenia enemistad" (ibid. p. 347).

evidence of Sosa, whose deposition was taken in prison.[1]

So closes the story of the captivity. The long years of waiting were ended at last; the oft-deferred hopes were realised. Hassan was speeding to Constantinople to render an account of his stewardship, while the manumitted slave, after so many years of expectant longing, of vehement struggle and silent renunciation, was turning his face towards the little western town of his boyhood, the Mecca of his visions, where his widowed mother lived. He had not lacked gall to make oppression bitter; but the sternest fates and the hardest taskmasters were powerless to sour that fine nature or to deaden that buoyant, sympathetic temperament. The dungeon and the imminence of torture, the suspicion of half-hearted friends, and the malignant baseness of the vilest enemy, left him still the same open, generous spirit. To say that when he left his home of servitude he was in every respect the same

[1] The witnesses were (1) Alonso Aragonés, of Córdoba; (2) Diego Castellano, of Toledo; (3) Rodrigo de Chaves, of Badajoz; (4) Hernando de Vega, of Cádiz; (5) Juan de Valcázar, of Málaga; (6) Domingo Lopino, of Sardinia; (7) Fernando de Vega, of Toledo; (8) Cristóbal de Villalón, of Valbuena; (9) Diego de Benavides, of Baeza; (10) Luís de Pedrosa, of Osuna; and (11) Fray Feliciano Enríquez, of Yepes.

Sosa's evidence, as he himself says, was taken separately "por causa di mi continuo y estrecho encerramiento en que mi patron me tiene en cadenas."

Fray Juan Gil and his fellow-worker, Fray Jorge de Olivar, are introduced in the fourth act of the *Trato de Argel*:

" Un fraile trinitario cristianísimo
Amigo de hacer bien y conocido," etc., etc.

man as when he entered it, would be to say that he
was deaf to the voice of wisdom and blind to the
disillusioning teaching of experience.   He had had
borne in on him " the sense that every struggle brings
defeat," and had realised the width and depth of the
vast abyss which yawns between the easy project and
the painful, nebulous, far-off achievement.   Something
of the invincible confidence, the early ardour, the unquestioning trustfulness of youth had passed with the
passing years and melted into the gray, sombre ether
of the past; but nothing misanthropic mingled with
his splendid scorn, his magnificent disdain for the
base and the ignoble; nothing of the cruel, fierce indignation of Swift gleamed from those quiet, searching
eyes, which watched the absurdities of his fellow-men
with a humorous, whimsical, indulgent smile.   In the
squalid prison life his strenuous courage, his iron
constancy and self-sacrificing devotion had drawn every
heart towards him with one exception—that of the
scandalous, shameless friar, Blanco de Paz.   But Blanco
had his reward—his eternity of infamy.   Cervantes
also, as he himself says, did many things which will
be for ever unforgotten.   In his thirty-fourth year he
sailed for Spain, after an exile of nearly eleven years.

Hoc est quod unum est pro laboribus tantis.

APPENDIX TO CHAPTER III.

SUBJOINED is Haedo's narrative of the captivity of Cervantes ("Topographia ó Historia General de Argel," ff. 184–185). With the exception that the long "s" is not reprinted, the passage is reproduced here as it stands in the original. It would have been easy to condense it, to modernise its form, and to correct some obvious typographical and other blunders. But the legitimacy of such a process appeared so doubtful, and the difficulties of deciding how far it might go so considerable, that even the retention of such monstrosities as "nutor" and "rambien" seemed less open to objection. The extract may be taken as a fair example of Haedo's somnolent, slipshod style, and the four forms of "Ceruãtes," "Cerbãtes," "Ceruantes," and "de Ceruantes," testify to the careful manner in which he, in common with most contemporary writers, corrected for the press. One of the strangest things in literary history is that Morgan, in his "History of Algiers" (London, 1727), has incorporated the whole passage without any apparent idea that it refers to the author of "Don Quixote." His remark, already quoted, is (p. 566): "It is Pity, methinks, that Haedo is here so succint in what regards this enterprising Captive." This is quite equal to Méndez Silva's performance.

"En el mismo año mil y quiniĕtos setenta y siete a los primeros dias de Setiembre ciertos Christianos cautiuos, que en Argel entonces se hallauan todos hombres principales, y muchos dellos Caualleros Españoles, y tres Mallorquines, que seriã por todos quinze, concertaron como de Mallorca viniesse vn bergantin, o fregata, y los embarcasse vna noche, y lleuasse a Mallorca, o a España. Este concierto hizieron con vn Christiano Mallorquin, q̃ entonces de Argel yua rescatado; que se dezia Viana, hombre platico en la mar, y costa de Berberia, el qual qual en pocos dias se obligo a venir; partido el Viana de Argel con este intento y proposito, a este tiempo casi todos los quinze Christianos estauan recogidos en vna cueua que estaua hecha, y muy secreta en el jardin del Alcayde Asan renegado Griego, que está hàzia Leuante como tres millas de Argel, y no muy lexos de la mar, porque era lugar muy comodo, y a proposito de su intento, para mejor, y mas seguramente estar escondidos, y

poderse embarcar. Solos dos Christianos lo sabian, vno de los quales
era el jardinero del jardin, que hiziera muchos antes la cueua: el qual
estaua siẽpre en vela mirando si alguno venia: y el otro era vno
(combidado tambiẽ par yr en el bergantin) que naciera, y se criara en
la villa de Melilla, vn lugar q̃ esta en la costa de Berberia, sujeto al
Rey de España, en el Reyno de Tremecen doziẽtas millas mas allende
de Orã hãzia Poniente, y ciẽto antes de llegar a Velez, y al Peñon, el
qual auiendo renegado, siendo moço, despues boluio a ser Christiano,
y aora la segunda vez auia cautiuado, el qual por sobre nombre se
dezia el Dorador: y este particularmente tenia cuydado (de dineros q̃
le dauan) comprar todo lo necessario, para los que en la cueua estauan,
y de lleuarlo al jardin desimulada, y ocultamente. Por otra parte el
Viana Mallorquin, llegado que fue a Mallorca, en pocos dias como
hombre diligente, y de su palabra, luego que llegò (segun yo lo supe
despues de tres Christianos q̃ entonces con el vinieron) començo jũtar
otros compañeros marineros, hombres platicos, y muy en breue, cõ el
fauor del señor Virey de Mallorca (para quiẽ auia lleuado cartas de
aquellos Christianos y Caualleros) en pocos dias puso a punto el bergantin: y como tenia concertado a los vltimos de Setiembre salio de
Mallorca, y tomò su camino para Argel, do llego a los veynte y ocho
del mismo mes. Y conforme a como estaua acordado: y siendo media
noche, se acosto a tierra en aquella parte de la cueua y Christianos
estaua (que el antes que partiesse auia muy bien visto) con intẽcion
de saltar en tierra, y auisar los Christianos que era llegado, para que
viniessen a embarcarse. Pero fue la desuentura, que al mismo punto
y momento q̃ la fragata, o bergantin, ponia la proa en tierra, acertaron
a passar ciertos Moros por alli, que quanto hazia obscuro diuisaron
la barca, y los Christianos a ellos: y començaron luego los Moros
dar vozes, y apelidar a otros, diziendo, Christianos, Christianos, barca,
barca, como los del vaxel vieron y oyeron esto, por no ser des-
cubiertos, fueron forçados hazerse luego a la mar, y boluerse por
aquella vez sin hazer algun efeto. Con todo los Christianos que
estauan en la cueua, aunque passados algunos dias, veyan que tardaua
el bergantin, ni sabian como auia llegado y se tornara: tenia muy
gran confiança, que el Señor Dios los auia de remediar, y que Viana
como hombre de bien, no faltaria de su palabra: y por tanto alli
do estauan en la cueua (que era muy humida y obscura: de la qual
todo el dia no salian, y por tanto ya estauan enfermos algunos

dellos) se consolauan con la esperança de salir con su intento, quando
el demonio enemigo de los hombres, cegando al Dorador (que dizimos
les lleuaua de comer) hizo en el q̃ se boluiesse otra vez Moro, negando
la segunda vez la Fè de nuestro Señor Iesu Christo: y por tanto
pareciondole a el ganaria mucho cõ el Rey, y con los Turcos, y particularmente con los amos y patrones, de los q̃ en la cueua estauan
escondidos el dia de san Geronymo; q̃ son treynta de Setiẽbre,
se fue al Rey Asan renegado Veneciano, diziendole que el desseaua
ser Moro, y que su Alteza lo diesse para ello licencia: dixo mas;
que para hazerle algun seruicio, le descubria como en tal parte,
y en tal cueua estauã quinze Christianos escondidos, que esperauan
vna barca de Mallorca.   Holgose el Rey, y le agradecio mucho esta
nueua que le daua, porque como era en gran manera tirano, hizo
cuenta de tomarlos todos por perdidos para si, contra toda razon,
y costumbre, y ansi no podiendo mas de mora en esto, mandò al
momento q̃ llamassen su guardian Baxi (el que tenia guardia de sus
Christianos esclauos de guardarlos) y le dixo que llamasse otros
Moros y Turcos, y lleuãdo aquel Christiano (que se queria hazer
Moro) por guia que se fuesse al jardin del Alcayde Asan, y que
hallaria alli quinze Christianos ascondidos en vna cueua: y que todos
se los truxesse a buen recaudo: juntamente con el jardinero al punto
hizo el guardian Baxi, lo que el Rey le mandò, y lleuando consigo,
hasta ocho o diez Turcos a cauallo, y otros 24 a pie y los mas con sus
escopetas y alfanjes, y algunas con lanças: fueron con tan buena
guia (como otros Iudas yua delante) al jardin: y prẽdiẽdo luego
al jardinero fuerõse a la cueua, q̃ el falso Iudas les mostro, y haziẽdo
salir della los Christianos los prendierõ luego a todos, y particular-
mẽte maniatarõ a Miguel Ceruãtes vn hidalgo principal de Alcala de
Henares q̃ fuera el autor deste negocio y era por tãto mas culpado, porq̃
ansi lo mãdo el Rey, a quiẽ los presentarõ luego.   Holgose mucho el
Rey, de ver como los auiã traydo: y mãdando por entõces lleuarlos a
su baño, y tener alli en buena guardia (tomandolos, y teniendolos ya
por sus esclauos) retuuo solamẽte en casa, a Miguel Cerbãtes, del qual
por muchas pregũtas q̃ le hizo, y cõ muchas y terribles amenazas, no
pudo jamas saber quiẽ era deste negocio sabedor, y autor porq̃ pre-
sumia el Rey, que el reuerẽdo George Oliuar, de la Orden de la Merced,
Comendador de Valencia (que entonces alli estaua por redentor de la
Corona de Aragon) ordenara esta: y aun se tenia por cierto que el

mismo Dorador Iudas, se lo auia dicho, y persuadido, y por tanto como
codicioso tyrano, con esta ocasion desseaua echar mano del mismo
padre para sacar del buena cantidad de dineros, y como con todas sus
amenazas, nunca otra cosa pudiesse sacar de Miguel Ceruantes, sino
que el, y no otro fuera el autor deste negocio (cargandose como
hombre noble a si solo la culpa) embiole a meter en su baño,
tomandole rambien por esclauo, aunque despues a el, y à otros tres
o quatro huuo de boluer por fuerça, a los patrones cuyos eran. El
Alcayde de Asan luego que en su jardin prēdieron los Christianos, y
truxeron al jardinero con ellos, fue de todo auisado a casa del Rey
requeriale con grande instancia, que hiziesse justicia de todos muy
aspera : y particularmēte que le dexasse a el hazerla a su gusto,
y contento del jardinero : mostrandose cōtra este en estremo furioso,
y ayrado, y la causa era porq̃ el Rey a ymitacion suya castigasse
a los demas Christianos q̃ auiã estado escōdidos en la cueua. Cosa
marauillossa, q̃ algunos dellos estuuierō encerrados sin ver luz, sino
de noche quando de la cueua salian, mas de siete meses, y algunos
cinco, y otros menos, sustentãdolos Miguel de Ceruantes, cō grã
riesgo de su vida : la qual quatro vezes estuuo a pique de perdella,
empalado, o enganchado, o abrasado viuo, por cosas que intēto, par
dar libertad a muchos. Y si a su animo y ndustria, y traças, cor-
respondiera la ventura, oy fuera el dia que Argel fuera de Christianos,
porque no aspirauan a menos sus intentos : Finalmente el jardinero
fue ahorcado por un pie, y murio ahogado de la sangre. Era de
nacion Nauarro, y muy buen Christiano. De las cosas que en aquella
cueua sucedieron en el discurso de los siete meses que estos Christianos
estuuieron en ella, y del cautiuerio, y hazañas de Miguel de Ceruantes
se pudiera hazer vna particular hystoria. Dezia Asan Baxà Rey
de Argel ; que como el tuuiesse guardado al estropeado Español tenia
seguros sus Christianos, baxeles, y aun a toda la ciudad : tanto era lo
que temia las traças de Miguel de Ceruantes, y sino le vendieran
y descubrieran los que en ella le ayudauan, dichoso vuiera su
cautiuerio, con ser de los peores q̃ en Argel auia, y el remedio q̃ tuuo
para assegurarse del, fue cōpralle de su amo por 500 escudos en
q̃ se auia cōsertado, y luego le acerrojo, y le tuuo en la carcel muchos
dias, y despues le doblo la parada, y le pidio mil escudos de oro en q̃
se rescato, auiēdo ayudado en mucho el padre fray Juan Gil, redentor
que entonces era, por la santissima Trinidad en Argel."

CHAPTER IV.

Soft Lesbian airs from lutes like mine
  But faintly murmur forth thy praise. . . .
                              Anon.

Ora toma a espada, agora a penna.
                    CAMOENS, *Son.* 192.

Fu Pan il primo che d' Arcadia venne.
                    MOLZA, *La Ninfa Tiberina.*

THE process of political and social change, except in
ultra-revolutionary epochs, is as a rule so gradual as
to be almost imperceptible to the generation which
undergoes the experience; yet to the keen eyes of
Cervantes it must have been clear that the Spain to
which he had returned was not quite the Spain which
he and Acquaviva had left ten years ago.   The halo of
the glorious days of the Great Emperor—for, to the
Spanish imagination, the figure of Charles assumed, and
still very pardonably assumes, heroic dimensions—which
had radiated over his immature youth with all the
magnificence of an iridescent after-glow, heralding the
night like some seraphic poursuivant, had almost faded
out of memory.   All Spanish life, taking colour from
the sombre, reticent, sinister, central figure of the

monarch, had lost its bright, chameleon hues, had grown
less mobile, less buoyant, less triumphantly joyous, and
had become more and more imbued with that stern
spirit of fanaticism which fell across the brilliant,
careless, pagan rapture of the waning Renaissance like
a funeral pall. The meridian brightness of the golden
age was passing, if it had not already passed away; the
ominous, crepuscular shadows were slowly creeping up,
and the spring-tides were already at the turn. The old
perennial fountains of delight were run dry; the last,
pale, ashy embers of the ancient fires were quenched and
cold: the motor nerves were paralysed with cursed
hebenon, and the body politic, enervated to immobility,
lay as though dead. The first outburst of fierce
enthusiasm and passionate, reckless intoxication was
well-nigh spent; and the glad flames streaming from
the torches round the car of victory were replaced by
the spectral flicker of the tapers round the solemn
catafalque. "De toute cette belle vie flamboyante
il ne reste pas même de la fumée; elle s'est envolée.
De la cendre, rien de plus." It is the note which
differentiates *Hernani* from *Ruy Blas.* "Dans *Hernani,*
le soleil de la maison d'Autriche se lève; dans *Ruy Blas,*
il se couche."

The prospect for Cervantes was not promising.
During his captivity in Algiers his old chief and patron,
Don John, had been appointed to the Viceroyalty of the
Low Countries. Philip's constant aim was to banish
Don John from Spain, and, by setting the young hero
impossible tasks, to keep him so fully occupied as to

prevent any of his vague dreams of dominion assuming more palpable form. The subjugation of the stubborn Flemings served as an appropriate employment.

> On garde les bâtards pour les pays conquis.
> On les fait vice-rois.   C'est à cela qu'ils servent.

Two years before the date of Cervantes' release, Don John had died upon the hill of Bouges, outside Namur, his early visions of empire still floating before him baffled and unfulfilled.   To Cervantes the loss was almost irreparable.   To have suffered additional rigours of imprisonment on account of those damning letters commendatory might have been endurable had promotion followed.   But now, his one influential protector gone, all hope of military preferment had vanished; and yet, unless he obtained some post at Court, there seemed nothing for the ransomed prisoner to do but to shoulder his musket and take his place in the ranks once more.   He probably felt no great vocation for Court life; he was scarcely of the clay of which courtiers are moulded, and, though the possessor of a thousand good qualities, even the partiality of a biographer must admit that he might not have made an ideal Gold-Stick-in-Waiting.   The slight experience he had already had of princes was not precisely alluring; and the base law of gilded servitude which enslaved Tasso, and against which the author of *Pastor Fido* stormed, was not likely to be one whit less galling to Cervantes than it had been in an earlier generation to the brilliant, infamous Aretino.   Aretino, however,

was the terror of monarchs and of courtiers, as we may
judge from the allusion to him in *Orlando Furioso*,
where, probably for the first and last time in his life, we
find him in the company of tolerably decent people :

> Ecco due Alessandri in quel drapello,
> Dagli Orologi l' un, l' altro il Guarino.
> Ecco Mario d' Olvito, ecco il flagello
> De' principi, il divin Pietro Aretino.[1]

But Aretino,[2] besides being the scourge of princes,
was a sort of literary skunk, and could always
avenge the foulest insult by retaliating in kind. It
may be easily imagined that the author of the *Sonetti
Lussoriosi* was not likely to be squeamish. But more
respectable men are not blessed (or cursed) with

---

[1] "Orlando Furioso," Canto Quarantesimosesto, s. 14.

[2] Aretino's pictures of Court life are of such a character that I
must crave the reader's pardon for placing them before him. Selection
in Aretino's case is more than ordinarily difficult; but I will content
myself with two citations. The first is from the first act of the
Cortigiana (Venezia, 1535) : "La principal cosa il Cortigiano vuol
saper bestemmiare, vuole esser giuocatore, invidioso, puttaniere,
heretico, adulatore, maldicente, sconoscente, ignorante, asino vuol
saper frappare, far la nimpha & essere agente e patiente." This
speech of Maestro Andrea to Messer Maco may be coupled with the
utterance of Pietro Picardo in the "Ragionamento nel quale M.
Pietro Aretino figura quatro suoi amici che favellano de le Corti de
Mondo et di Quella del Cielo" (Novara, 1538) : "La Corte, Messeri
miei, è Spedale de le speranze, sepoltura de le vite, baila de gli
odij, razza de l' invidie, mantice de l' ambitioni, mercato de le men-
zogne, serraglio de i sospetti, carcere de le concordie, Scola de le
fraudi, Patria de l' adulatione, Paradiso dei vitij, Inferno de la virtù,
Purgatorio de la bontà, e Limbo de le allegrezze."

Guarini's *Pastor Fido* is only one degree less severe. But there
can be no difference of opinion as to his comparative decency,

similar secretions; and Cervantes, under corresponding circumstances, would have retired from the hallowed precincts with the calm, haughty humility which characterises all those higher spirits who disdain the petty struggles for sovereignty in a Della Cruscan Inferno. Reflection must soon have made it painfully clear to him that, even if it were prudent to recall his ill-omened name to the unforgetting memory of the vindictive Philip, no obtainable position at Court would suit his vehement, outspoken temperament, even were he fortunate enough to have the refusal of one. No other course occurred to him, or seemed possible, save a return to the old-time camp life in the files of Figueroa's Theban legion.

Cervantes, as we have seen in the foregoing chapter,

Bellarmine's view notwithstanding. I quote from the speech of Carino to Uranio (Act V. sc. i.):

> " L' ingannare, il mentir, la frode, il furto,
>   E la rapina di pietà vestita;
>   Crescer col danno e precipizio altrui,
>   E far a sè dell' altrui biasimo onore,
>   Son le virtu di quella gente infida.
>   Non merto, non valor, no riverenza,
>   Nè d' età nè di grado nè di legge;
>   Non freno di vergogna, non rispetto
>   Nè d' amor nè di sangue; non memoria
>   Di ricevuto ben," etc.

I may be permitted to remind the reader of the fact that Aretino's *Cortigiana* is merely a brutal parody of Baltassare Castiglione's *Il Cortigiano*. Boscàn's translation of Castiglione's masterpiece was enthusiastically praised by Garcilaso de la Vega, and probably those few belated readers who are acquainted with *Il Cortigiano* will agree with Johnson in thinking it "the best book that ever was written upon good breeding."

had written from his hopeless prison-cell in Algiers a passionate, despairing appeal for help to Mateo Vázquez de Leca Colona, praying that the Spanish fleet might be sent against the lair of the Barbary corsairs. It is not probable that the supple Secretary of State thought it necessary to trouble his august master with this modest prayer; and assuredly, had the taciturn, brooding monarch been aware of its existence, the high-flying petition of an obscure prisoner would never have turned his persistent, Sphinx-like gaze from his careful, well-pondered designs. His eyes, then as always fixed on far-off goals, were directed not to Algiers but to Portugal. The disastrous rout and death of the young Dom Sebastian upon the fatal field of Al-kasr al-Kebir, in August, 1578, had thrown the whole Lusitanian kingdom into confusion. The crash of the catastrophe resounded throughout Europe, and a century later the last reverberations of its echoes had not altogether died away. History, stern, impartial, and brutally unmindful of our picturesque prejudices, has done something to dissipate the charmed, romantic mist which once enshrouded the central figure of Dom Sebastian; but the tragedies of Peele and Dryden will always keep his memory green in the minds of all students of English literature.[1]

> And even among the thickest of his lords,
> The noble king of Portugal we found,
> Wrapt in his colours coldly on the earth
> And done to death with many a mortal wound.

---

[1] Though the authorship of *The Battle of Alcazar* (1594) is questioned by many competent critics, I have followed Mr. Dyce in

The entire fabric of Portuguese politics was shaken to its last foundations, and not even the most discerning of political meteorologists could pretend to forecast the future. But Philip, always provident, had his own aims, his own views of reasonable probabilities, and was inflexibly determined to be prepared for any fate. A seductive phantom of peninsular sovereignty hovered before him, and his earliest lessons in statecraft had taught him that the consummation of political visions is never hindered by the material support of a powerful armament. The aged Cardinal Henrique had succeeded to the gloomy inheritance of Sebastian's throne, and after a brief and troubled reign had died in January, 1580.

Instantly there were six Richmonds in the field. Amongst other pretenders the succession was disputed by Catherine, Duchess of Braganza; by Philibert Emmanuel, Duke of Savoy; by Ranuccio, Duke of Parma; by Pope Gregory the Thirteenth; by Antonio,

attributing it conjecturally to George Peele. Mr. Saintsbury, the most recent critic of the literary history of the period, assumes Peele to be the author, apparently without any hesitation ("A History of Elizabethan Literature," p. 71).

Don Sebastian (1690) ranks above all Dryden's plays with the possible exception of *Love for Love*. Johnson's declaration that it is "not without sallies of frantic dignity and more noise than meaning, yet, as it makes approaches to the possibilities of real life, and has some sentiments which leave a strong impression, it continued long to attract attention," is among the curious infelicities of criticism. To those who class the scene between Sebastian and Dorax among the most powerful in dramatic literature, Johnson's appreciation must always seem painfully inadequate.

The history of the Portuguese impostors who impersonated Dom Sebastian after Al-kasr al-Kebir is well told in M. Miguel d'Antas' "Les Faux Sebastien" (Paris, 1865).

Prior of Crato, the natural son of Luiz, Duke of Beja; and, lastly, by Philip of Spain. The validity of the Pope's claim is not perhaps immediately obvious to the mind of the constitutional lawyer. But in any case it was brusquely set aside (probably because there was no material force behind it), and the other claimants retired one by one, leaving the disputed prize to be contested by the King of Spain and by Antonio, the somewhat unworthy representative of the national cause. This conjuncture of affairs had long been foreseen by Philip, and the fleet, which Cervantes had modestly begged might be sent to rescue him and his fellow-prisoners in Algiers, was despatched to blockade Lisbon under the command of the celebrated Santa Cruz. There was a moment of hesitation before the Generalissimo of the land forces was appointed. There could be no doubt that the Duke of Alva was the first soldier in Spain, if not in Europe. Whatever opinion may prevail as to his policy in the Netherlands, there can be no question as to his consummate capacity as a commander. But he had never enjoyed the complete confidence of Philip, who, for personal reasons, had leaned rather to the policy of Ruy Gómez, the complaisant husband of the Princess of Éboli; and soon after his return from the Low Countries, where he had incurred unexampled obloquy in his master's cause, an opportunity was easily found for visiting Alva with a vicarious chastisement.[1]

---

[1] The story of Alva's disgrace may be followed in vols. vii., viii., and l. of the "Colección de documentos inéditos para la historia

The story throws so curious a light upon the relations which subsisted between Philip and his trustiest
servants as to make it worth while to repeat it in
some detail. Alva's eldest son, Don Fadrique de
Álvarez, Marqués de Coria, had, as far back as 1566,
become entangled in the meshes of a siren named Doña
Magdalena de Guzmán, a Maid of Honour to the Queen.
The affair was bruited abroad owing to an hysterical
outburst on the part of the lady, and before long it
was whispered to the King. Don Fadrique was alleged
to have promised the Maid of Honour marriage, but it
seems probable that his offence had not stopped short

de España, por los Señores Marqués de Miraflores, D. Miguel Salvá
y D. Pedro Sáinz de Baranda " (Madrid, 1845–1867). For some few
details I am indebted to the " Historia de Don Fernando Alvarez de
Toledo (llamado comunmente El Grande) primero del nombre, Duque
de Alva. Por Don Joseph Vicente de Rustant" (Madrid, 1751). Cp.
also P. C. Hooft's " Nederlandsche Historien met aanteekeningen en
ophelderingen van de Hoogleeraren M. Siegenbeck," etc. (Amsterdam,.
1821–1823), iii. pp. 85–87. It is seldom indeed, as every one who
has used the " Documentos inéditos " can testify, that D. Miguel Salvá
and D. Pedro Sáinz de Baranda are caught tripping. In vol. vii.
p. 464, Doña Magdalena de Guzmán, in an editorial note, is styled
" dama de la Reina Doña Ana." This seems scarcely possible. Her
adventure with D. Fadrique took place not later than 1566–1567,
whereas Anne's marriage with Philip was not solemnised till 1570,
and as late as 1578, Doña Magdalena was still in the Convent of
Santa Fe. An examination of the dates shows that she must have
been Maid of Honour to Isabel of Valois.

For a most able statement of the case on the other side with
regard to the Princess of Éboli, I must refer the reader to the
" Vida de la Princesa de Éboli, por Don Gaspar Muro " (Madrid,.
1877). While I am happy to recognise the consummate skill with
which D. Gaspar Muro's case is presented, I do not find myself
able to agree with his conclusions.

at this point, and, without undue uncharitableness, it may be assumed that matters had reached a further stage of development. If the case were merely one of breach of promise, the punishment was severe. The Lovelace of this young romance was interned in the fortress of Medina del Campo, and was only released on condition of purging his unexampled contempt by providing ten lancers at his own cost and serving with them personally at Oran for three years.[1] The too-fascinating heroine of the adventure was sent to Toledo, and was placed in a state of semi-captivity in the superb Convent of Santa Fe, from the *mirador* of which she had magnificent opportunities of studying the characters who thronged that Plaza de Zocodover which is inseparably associated with the memory of Guzmán de Alfarache. But Doña Magdalena was not another Mateo Alemán,—or perhaps she looked down on the *picaresco* novel. What her offence actually was it would have puzzled Philip, with all his tortuous ingenuity, to say.

A dozen years passed by, and it might have been imagined that Don Fadrique's brilliant services in Flanders would be taken as an expiation of his juvenile

---

[1] The Royal edict releasing Don Fadrique conditionally is dated February 11, 1567 ("Documentos," l. pp. 288-289). Don Fadrique does not appear to have reached Oran, for he was still at Murcia when a second edict, dated May 7, 1568, was issued, cancelling the sentence of the previous year and ordering him to join the army under his father's command in Flanders. This command was obeyed speedily enough, for a letter of Don Fadrique's, dated August 18, 1568, and written from Flanders, apparently to his uncle Don García Álvarez de Toledo, may be found in the "Documentos," l. 292-293.

offence. Even Philip, who seldom forgave and never forgot, appears to have inclined to this view, since he wrote to Alva in Flanders with reference to arranging another marriage for Don Fadrique. But this weak, relenting mood soon ceased, and the monarch, dissatisfied, it may be, with the results of Alva's Viceroyalty, resolved to be rid, once and for ever, of the Duke and all his brood. Revenge, in Gibbon's celebrated phrase, is profitable; gratitude is expensive; and the splendour and reputation of the house of Alva were by no means to the taste of the jealous despot. In such cases, one excuse is as good as another—especially when absolute sovereigns deign to use them—and, in default of anything else, the threadbare story of the old *liaison* was raked up once more. Twelve years after the commission of the fault, Don Fadrique was peremptorily ordered to marry Doña Magdalena de Guzmán. That cloistered damsel appears to have kept up an almost incessant clamour, and the bombardment of the King with incoherent letters from the convent cell seems to have been admirably sustained. In the June of 1578, we find Doña Magdalena pressing Philip to enforce the alleged promise made by Don Fadrique, and complaining bitterly of her prolonged imprisonment. As a preliminary step, the unlucky officer was sent to prison, and was treated with a severity which would have been considered unmeasured in Turkey.

Philip seems to have shown unusual interest in the affair, and his instructions to the Committee

appointed to investigate it are highly characteristic.
No detail is too minute to escape his observation, and
his marginal notes are more than ordinarily copious.
No prosecuting counsel could have scanned a brief
with a keener, a more sympathetic eye. " The cold
neutrality of an impartial judge" was thrown aside,
and all affectation of judicial decorum was neglected.
Doña Magdalena's case became his own, and the one
question with him was how to bend the recalcitrant
lover to the Royal will. The task was not easy.
Philip's first step was to refer the matter to a carefully
packed *junta*, presided over by Antonio Mauricio de
Pazos y Figueroa, the supple Bishop of Ávila. It
soon struck the Commissioners that the culprit was
hopelessly stubborn, and on June 25, 1578, we find
Pazos advising the King to cease threatening, and
to speak Don Fadrique fair. He further advises that
the matter be referred to the Archbishop of Toledo
to adjudicate upon as an ordinary matrimonial suit.[1]
Duplicity seems to reach its high-water mark in this
episcopal letter, which goes on unblushingly to suggest
that, as the investigation of matrimonial cases is
generally prolonged, and as it is desirable that the
defendant should not be liberated, the King should
inform Don Fadrique that he is imprisoned not on
account of Doña Magdalena, but on other grounds

---

[1] " No veo buen medio que se pueda dar interviniendo la autoridad
de V. M., aunque sea por palabras blandas, que no se entienda haber
fuerza ó á lo menos temor y reverencia de Rey y Señor, que es
cuasi tanto como fuerza expresa, en especial tiniendo preso á D.
Fadrique como lo está."—*Documentos,* vii. 472.

which appear just. In this way, adds Pazos, he and his family may be induced not to drag out the case. Even after the lapse of three hundred years, it is not easy to read the Bishop's letter without a sense of shame.[1]

It argues some relaxation of Philip's customary, vigilant prudence that he should have entered into a contest with the Duke of Alva on a point which touched the family pride to the quick. Don Fadrique's position was very much that of Don Salluste de Bazan :

> Oui, pour une amourette
> —Chose à mon age, sotte et folle, j'en convien !—
> Avec une suivante, une fille de rien ! . . .
> Ordre de l'épouser. Je refuse. On m'exile.
> On m'exile ! Et vingt ans d'un labeur difficile,
> Vingt ans d'ambition, de travaux nuit et jour. . . .

Alva's son remained sternly obstinate. The very idea that the heir of the house of Álvarez could ally himself with a Maid of Honour of damaged reputation awakened inextinguishable laughter in the minds of those who knew the unbending pride of the famous general. A family deputation waited on Philip to set before him with all possible plainness the extreme unreasonableness of his ordinance.[2] But the entrance and address of these self-appointed delegates would

---

[1] "Y porque los pleitos matrimoniales suelen ser largos, conviene que D. Fadrique se esté en la prision que tiene hasta el fin deste, dándose V. M. á entender que no es por causa del matrimonio sino de otras que á V. M. le parescen justas, y desta manera procurarian él y sus padres no alongar la causa."—Documentos, vii. 473.

[2] Rustant, vol. ii. pp. 252 *et seq.*

seem to have been characteristically brusque, and the
scared monarch waxed more wroth than ever, and
angrily insisted on being obeyed. Alva and his son
were at least as inflexible as their sovereign, and
they were determined not to comply with what they
regarded as a most insolent command. Don Fadrique
escaped from his prison one dark autumn night, and was
secretly married to his first cousin, Doña María Álvarez
de Toledo, the daughter of Don García Álvarez de
Toledo, Marqués de Villafranca, formerly Viceroy of
Naples. On October 20, 1578, Pazos communicated
the unwelcome intelligence to the King as an un-
doubted fact, quoting the Duke of Alva as his authority.
He further reports that he has been visited by Juan
de Guzmán, the furious brother of the injured heroine,
and by Doña Brianda, Magdalena's sister, who had
previously warned him of the intended secret marriage.
It is impossible to read Pazos' letter without a hearty
contempt for the feeble, timorous tool.

Philip was completely outmanœuvred for the
moment; but the last word was always his, and his last
word was seldom pleasant. The end was not yet. The
packed Commission was set to work, and the old Duke,
who in a written document dated October 2, 1578, had
given the final proof of incorrigible contumacy by
authorising his son to marry Doña María, was, on the
recommendation of the Committee, to be exiled to
Ocaña, to Talamanca, or to Uceda. It was soon discovered that the Duke had some sympathetic friends in
Ocaña, and his generous master accordingly fixed on

Uceda as an appropriate place of banishment.[1] On January 10, 1579, the Royal decree of exile was read to Alva by Martín de Gaztelu. Albornoz, Alva's secretary, and Esteban de Ibarra, a clerk of Don Fadrique's, were both laid by the heels in the Court jail, as accessories after the fact.[2] The plaintive letters of the Bishop of Ávila become more and more ridiculous as the correspondence unfolds itself. The Duke, he complains, is now laid up with the gout, and "as it is impossible to prove to any one that his foot does not hurt him, we do not know what to say in this matter."[3] But even under the despotic rule of Philip a man of Alva's distinction could not be spirited away without remark. Some bold, bad men actually went to the length of getting up petitions for the Duke's release ; but this soon came to the Bishop's knowledge, and, says Pazos, with a really ludicrous fatuity, "I put a stop to this as soon as I knew of it."[4] About this time the health of Dom Henrique, King of Portugal, began to fail rapidly, and it seemed possible

[1] Ocaña was not acceptable because, says Pazos, "creo que allí hay algunas gentes que le son aficionadas, é sino en Toledo que está muy cerca; que todo cesa yendo á Uceda ó á Talamanca" ("Documentos," vii. p. 518).

[2] A letter of Gabriel de Zayas to Don Bernardino de Mendoza, the Spanish Ambassador in London, dated January 14, 1579, announces the imprisonment of these two secondary criminals ("Documentos," viii. p. 499).

[3] The original is so *naïf* as to be worth reproducing: "como no se puede probar á nadie que no le duele un pie no sabemos que decir en esto."

[4] Pazos' letter is dated June 9, 1579: "Yo lo estorbé luego que lo supe" ("Documentos," viii. p. 508). Agustín Álvarez, one of

that Alva's services might soon be needed again. The rigour of Don Fadrique's lot was accordingly relaxed. He was allowed to move to a healthier house, the same guards being retained, and his wife was permitted to stay with him for a month or two.[1] As every day made it more likely that the abilities of the elder prisoner would soon be called for, further developments took place in the magnanimity of the Bishop. In October, Pazos exhorts the King, in a strain that borders closely on blasphemy, to exercise his Royal prerogative of pardon.[2] Philip, one of the most industrious of monarchs—even in a private station he would scarcely have been regarded as an idle man—coldly replies that he has not time to discuss this matter; that several

the organisers of the crime, was severely reprimanded by the Bishop, whose authority to reprimand any one was surely questionable. Philip's marginal note is characteristic: "Fué muy muy bien que lo estorbásedes esto." But any outrage on the house of Álvarez always received similar commendation. "Fué muy bien hecho" is a stock phrase of Philip's.

[1] "Por tiempo limitado de un mes ó dos" ("Documentos," viii. p. 510), is Philip's own phrase.

[2] Pazos writes: "Y en esto los Príncipes tan grandes como V. M. se asemejan ó deben asemejar á Dios que es sumo misericordioso" ("Documentos," viii. p. 512). Philip's comment is worth quoting: "Hay otras particulares que á mi se me ofrecen de mucha consideracion y calidad. Y porque no tengo aun la mano para escrebir mucho con ella, ni aun el tiempo que seria menester, por ser cosas largas y que se habrán describir di mi mano, ó decirse de palabra, lo dejaré por agora para cuando se pueda hacer lo uno ó lo otro, que creo que entonces se entenderá que son de consideracion las cosas que se me ofrecen. . . ." The day for the exposition of these weighty objections never dawned. Philip's hand was always too tired, though he found strength to write on almost every other subject under the sun.

points occur to him which are worthy of consideration; but that his hand is tired and he cannot enter upon the exposition of his ideas now. Accordingly, because Philip's hand was tired, Alva remained a prisoner. The tone of the whole correspondence throws a curious light upon current notions of Royal industry and application to affairs.

The death of Dom Henrique brought matters to a crisis. There was at first a vague idea that Philip himself might command the Army of Portugal; but probably he was not anxious to conduct a campaign in person, and it is certain that the Spanish troops openly expressed their deep dissatisfaction at losing the services of the old chief who had always led them to victory, and whose very name was worth ten thousand men. Pazos in one of his absurd letters tells the King of the prevalent discontent in terms of unusual frankness, and proceeds apologetically to urge the speedy release of Alva;[1] but Philip was not easily to be moved, and snubbed the Bishop severely by replying to his representations that Alva's release depended upon the course of events in Portugal. The swift march of affairs proved too strong for the sullen, resentful King, and it

---

[1] " Bien sabe y ve el consejo el justo desdeño que V. M. tiene del Duque, y con mucho razon está en donde se le ha mandado. . . . Vemos el grande descontento que entre todos los soldados hay de no entender quel Duque haya de ir por cabeza ó lugar tiniente, y con cuan mayores é alegres animos irán sabiendo que V. M. se sirve del " (" Documentos," viii. 518). The sycophantic Pazos has just previously warned Philip against the " riesgo y peligro," the "trabajo y cansancio," and the "malos alojamientos," which kings meet in war—" de los cuales se siguen indisposiciones que causan la muerte."

became evident that Alva's release could no longer be
delayed. Ungracious to the last, Philip ordered that
Albornoz should not be discharged, but should be
admitted to bail on a surety of ten thousand ducats,[1]
while Ibarra, if the Duke specifically demanded his
release, was to be let out on some unspecified bail, on
the express condition that he did not rejoin Don
Fadrique—a superfluous stipulation, one might have
thought, as Don Fadrique was still in custody. Later
still, the shameless Pazos, in a singularly heartless letter,
formulated a scruple.[2] Married people, he says with
inimitable gravity, should not live apart, and Don
Fadrique and Doña María are obviously hopelessly
married. It seems to have occurred to Pazos that
eighteen months was a long period of gestation for a
scruple, for he continues with edifying solemnity that it
was quite proper that Doña María should suffer a little
on account of the misdeeds of her husband and father-
in-law. As a peculiarly cogent argument, Pazos lays it
before Philip that Don Fadrique is so completely wrecked
in health and fortune that he is not likely to congratu-
late himself on the matter.[3] The vindictive King

[1] "Documentos," vol. viii. pp. 523–524. Philip's dislike of
Albornoz breaks out in his remark : " Yo no sé si hace al Duque mas
daño que provecho su compañía, y temo que fue el consejero de la
cedula que el Duque dió á su hijo para que se casase."

[2] " Yo formo escrúpulo de que esten apartados el uno del otro ó
no hagan vida maridable . . . parecio era cosa conveniente dejarle
sentir el yerros de sus suegro y marido."—Documentos, vol. viii. p. 527.

[3] " Documentos," pp. 528, 529. Don Fadrique was to be pardoned " cuanto mas que él está tan bien castigado ó tan gastado
de salud y hacienda que no se irá alabando del negocio."

Some tender souls have tried to follow out the fate of Tilburina's

accepted the proposal of the Commission that Don Fadrique might be sent to Alba, but their recommendation that he should be allowed a circuit of two or four leagues was sternly cut down, and Don Fadrique was limited to one league. So ends a story of truly Royal magnanimity. The King's necessity was overpowering; and thus out of the plenitude of the monarch's bounty, Alva's iniquities were pardoned.

The war-worn veteran was in his seventy-second year, and his health, undermined by fifty years of battle, was by no means strong; but the clash of arms thrilled through his blood like a trumpet-call, and his active, inextinguishable spirit gladly hailed the opportunity of escaping from the listless exile to which he had been condemned by a grateful moralist whose morality was on a level with his gratitude. The snows of seventy winters had not yet quenched the volcanic fires beneath, and Alva at once assumed the command of the mobilised troops. The iron-handed warrior had not forgotten his old cunning during his retirement; and the remorseless vigour which had displayed itself at Mühlberg, and again, at the battle of Jemmingen, had disposed of seven thousand Flemings, with a corresponding loss on his own side of seven individual Spaniards, was soon to

oyster crossed in love. For these I may add some details about Doña Magdalena. Philip's sincerity may be gauged from the conclusion of the story. Doña Magdalena finally applied to be restored to her old position at Court. Philip's brutal reply, conveyed through Pazos, was to the effect that she was too old and that she had better stay where she was. But she found a tardy consolation. On October 4, 1581, she married the Marqués del Valle. She seems, however, always to have been *mal vista* by the courtiers.

be terribly manifest in the Portuguese campaign. On August 25, 1580, Alva's squadrons met those of the bastard Prior at Alcántara. The defeat of the national party was decisive, and the pretensions of Dom Antonio at once melted into thin air. Count Louis of Nassau swimming for his life across the Ems was not more utterly overwhelmed. Alva occupied Lisbon without resistance, while the fleet under Santa Cruz overawed the inhabitants from the sea. The unwarlike citizens submitted with a facile meekness which half justifies Byron's bitter sneer at the Lusian slave, the lowest of the low. Only in the outlying districts a few sputterings of rebellion (for so the manifestations of the national spirit were styled in the canting jargon of the official, and officious, chroniclers of Spain) were heard from time to time.[1] But the mainspring of the resistance was broken into fragments; and from this period we may date the sixty years of Portugal's captivity from which, in the next century, she was to be released by the national leaders, João

---

[1] The authorities which I have mainly followed in sketching the outlines of the campaign are : (1) "Cinco libros de Antonio de Herrera de la Historia de Portugal, y conquista de las Islas de los Açores, en los años de 1582 y 1583" (Madrid, 1591), and (2) "Comentario en breve compendio de disciplina militar, en que se escriue la jornada de las islas de los Açores. Por El Licenciado Christoual Mosquera de Figueroa" (Madrid, 1596).

I have also found much information in that very vivid and lucid work, the "Historia de Portugal nos seculos XVII. e XVIII., por Luiz Augusto Rebello da Silva" (Lisboa, 1860-1871). The first volume contains a striking account of the state of Portugal between the death of Sebastian and the death of Henrique.

Pinto Ribeiro and Pedro Mendonça Furtado, acting under the inspiration of Luiza de Guzman, the heroic wife of the torpid João de Braganza.

In the Portuguese campaign, Cervantes, as may be gathered from his *información* of May 21, 1590, took part; but it is clear that his share in the fighting must have been very slight, as the decisive contest of Alcántara had been fought and won by the man of destiny while Cervantes was still a prisoner in Hassan's dungeon. But the struggle was not confined to Portugal; nor was Alcántara the one great battle of the campaign. Far off in the Northern Atlantic, away in

the golden remote wild west where the sea without shore is,

most of the islands in the little group of the Azores, resisting the solicitations of Pedro de Castilho and João de Bettencourt Vasconcellos, remained faithful to the fugitive Dom Antonio, who, hunted out of Portugal by Alva's harquebussiers, had found refuge in Terceira, where he was solemnly crowned.[1] Terceira became the central stronghold of opposition and, under the able leadership of the local governor, Cypriano de Figueiredo, an undaunted resistance was offered to the Spanish pretensions. It was resolved in council at Lisbon that so formidable a nucleus of resistance could not be disregarded, more especially as the homeward-bound Spanish galleons, returning from the Indies, were a

---

[1] For an account of the rediscovery of this group by Gonzalo Velhal Cabral, see "The Life of Prince Henry of Portugal, surnamed the Navigator. By R. H. Major. London, 1868" (pp. 235-238).

tempting prey to the enemy. An expedition against the Azores was accordingly organised, and the supreme command was entrusted to the Marqués de Santa Cruz, Don John's Chief of the Staff during the Tunisian campaign.

There was no time to be lost. Every day strengthened the ascendency of Dom Antonio, and unpleasant rumours were abroad that the adventurous Drake, now famous throughout Europe after his return on board the *Golden Hind*—the rechristened *Pelican* —from the spoliation of the Spanish colonies, was sailing with a host of buccaneers to make the Azores a base of operations with a view to driving Spanish merchantmen off the sea. Pedro de Váldez was accordingly sent out with a small force to bring the islanders to reason; but his mission was purely diplomatic, and he had neither the means nor the authority to resort to force.[1] Moreover, it was well understood that Lope de Figueroa would soon join him. The diplomatic embassy was a complete failure. Figueiredo declined to receive Váldez, and refused to read his minatory despatches. On St. James's Day, July 25, 1581, Captain Diego de Váldez, burning with a desire to do something brilliant in honour of

---

[1] Herrera, f. 152: "Para aguardar alli las flotas de las Indias Ocidentales, y encaminarlas à España que tocassen en la Tercera, por escusar el peligro que podiã correr; y se le auia dado comission, para de camino persuadir à los naturales que se pusiessen en la obediencia del Rey, ofreciendoles como antes perdon, y qualquiera partido q̃ ellos pidiessen. Pero no lleuaua orden para vsar de la fuerça quando no le quisiessen acetar."

the national patron saint, and anxious to strike a
blow before Figueroa's invincibles arrived, persuaded
his uncle to sanction an attack upon the village of
San Sebastião, some six miles to the east of Angra.
Six hundred men were landed under the joint command of Diego de Váldez and Luís de Bazán. But
the supporters of Dom Antonio held their own.
The formation of the Spanish troops was thrown into
disorder by a vast herd of bulls goaded against them
by the islanders, who, following close upon the cattle,
despatched the broken infantry with their swords.
The Pyrrhic device appears to have been adopted
on the suggestion of a wily monk, not learned in
the bookish theoric, perhaps, but none the less a
worthy member of the Church Militant. Pedro de
Váldez witnessed the catastrophe in impotent despair.
His marine artillery was silenced, as, in the hand-to-
hand conflict between the combatants, it could not
be employed against Figueiredo's troops without equal
danger to the outnumbered Spaniards ashore. So far
as it went, the victory was complete. Diego de Váldez
and Luís de Bazán were killed, and three hundred
and fifty of their men died with them. The Portuguese
success was more absolute than Figueiredo had dared
to hope. The triumph of the Athenians at Cynossema
was not more unlooked-for. Figueiredo's troops got
out of hand and disgraced themselves by mutilating
the Spanish dead and wounded on the field of battle.

> Revenge, at first though sweet,
> Bitter ere long back on itself recoils.

For these excesses Santa Cruz was to take a terrible retribution. On the very day when this encounter took place, Lope de Figueroa sailed from Lisbon, and the tidings of the ludicrous disaster greeted him as soon as he reached the Azores. The disgusted old martinet speedily became convinced that Váldez was an impracticable with whom all concerted action was impossible, and, after a careful reconnaissance of the position, he returned to Lisbon in October.[1]

While Philip continued his preparations, Dom Antonio on his side was not idle. With a thoughtful foresight worthy of all commendation, he had carried away with him from Lisbon the Crown jewels; and, armed with these persuasive arguments, he presented himself at Elizabeth's Court and endeavoured to interest the English sovereign in his cause. His tactics show a shrewd knowledge of Elizabeth's vulnerable point. He was not

> Too poor for a bribe and too proud to importune.

But the Queen's vanity, immeasurable as it was, was never so fatuous as to interfere with her policy. One by one the jewels passed from Dom Antonio's hands to hers; but, though profuse promises were

---

[1] The ruse of employing cattle was brought about "por cosëjo de vn frayle, que eran los principales en todas las cosas," says Herrera bitterly (f. 153. The folio is actually numbered 151, but this is an obvious misprint). A spirited account of the engagement may be found in his Fourth Book, ff. 152–154 : ". . . se juntaron y se vieron estos Capitanes, entre los quales huuo siempre poca conformidad" (Herrera, f. 154).

not wanting, no material assistance was forthcoming, and the disappointed exile passed on to France, where Fortune's finger sounded happier stops. Henry III. and Catherine de Medici were not unwilling to pay off old scores, and the proffer of Brazil, in case of Dom Antonio's success, may have been an added inducement to join his enterprise. A fleet was accordingly equipped, and in June, 1582, the joint armament sailed from Belle Ile under Philippe de Strozzi (the friend of Brantôme, and a descendant of the famous Florentine), with Brissac and Vimioso as lieutenants.[1] Meanwhile, Dom Antonio's confidence in

---

[1] "La Vie, Mort, et Tombeau, de haut et puissant Seigneur, Philippe de Strozzi, etc. Par H. T. S. de Torsay. Paris, 1608." This curious tract by Strozzi's old tutor may be found reprinted in the "Archives curieuses de l'histoire de France (vol. ix. 1ʳᵉ Série)," edited by L. Cimber and F. Danjou. Paris, 1835. Pp. 403–460.

Rebello da Silva speaks of Strozzi's inextinguishable hatred of the Spaniards (iii. pp. 44–45): "Contando apenas trinta e cinco annos, neto d' aquelle austero republicano Strozzi, de Florença, que antes de se atravessar com a propria espada, gravára nas paredes do carcere o sombrio verso:

'Exoriare aliquis, nostris ex ossibus, ultor,'

Filippe bebêra com o leite da infancia inextinguivel odio á soberba hespanhola." Cp. this with Brantôme: "Il estimoit fort la nation espaignolle et surtout les soldatz, et en faisoit gran cas, et louoit fort leurs valleurs et leurs conquestes, et pour ce, prenoit-il plaisir d'avoir affaire à eux. Il y a eu force Espaignolz qui lui ont voulu mal, pensant que ce fust leur ennemy mortel. Ilz se trompoient, car il ne l'estoit point. Il aymoit trop leur valeur, leur façon de faire, et surtout leur gloire et leur superbetté et leur langage; et cent fois m'a dict qu'il eust voulu avoir donné beaucoup, et sçavoir parler espaignol comme moy" ("Œuvres Complètes, etc. Publiées pour la Société de l'Histoire de France par Ludovic Lalanne. Couronnels Français," vi. 87–88).

Figueiredo had been undermined by some of the intriguing parasites who encompass pretenders,[1] and in the spring of 1582 that able officer had been superseded in the Viceroyalty of Terceira by the supple, inefficient, truculent Manuel da Silva, Conde de Torres Vedras. Philip's armada, with Lope de Figueroa's regiment on board, sailed from Lisbon on July 10, 1582; sighted San Miguel on July 21; and, on July 26—Dom Antonio having thoughtfully disembarked at Terceira on the previous day—gave battle to Strozzi.[2] After five hours of furious conflict Dom Antonio's partisans were completely routed, Strozzi and Vimioso being mortally wounded during the engagement.

The great avenging day had come at last. On August 1 Santa Cruz, to the horror of his own officers, caused the prisoners to be executed in the market-place of Villafranca, in the island of San Miguel. The earnest entreaties of his lieutenants were disregarded. To their honour be it said, they paid a needful tribute to humanity by succouring and concealing as many of the condemned as was possible. But the orders of the chief were carried out; the place became a shambles. The officers were beheaded; and the rank and file died beneath the ignoble hands of a German hangman.[3] No

---

[1] Rebello da Silva, iii. p. 42.

[2] Herrera, ff. 170, 178 : "se fue à la Tercera vn dia antes do la batalla."

[3] Herrera scornfully lays stress on the executioner's nationality— "un verdugo Aleman" (f. 177). Before the campaign closed, the defeat at San Sebastião, brought about by an anonymous monk, was

needy Spaniard could be found base enough to under-
take the disgusting office ; but to certain other races
gold is always an inducement. It is impossible to
censure too unsparingly the hideous barbarity of this
ordinance ; but censure to be effective should be discriminating. Almost every writer who has touched
the subject has placed Santa Cruz in the pillory : nor
can it be denied that his conduct merits the severest
reprobation. It would be the very ecstasy of irony
to represent Santa Cruz as an amiable, tender character.
But it must be remembered that he was a mere
executive officer, in no way responsible for mandates
actuated, presumably, by motives of high policy ; and
to every reader of contemporary records it is abun-
dantly evident that the Spanish Admiral was acting
under direct orders from Philip. On Philip the guilt
must fall ; not all great Neptune's ocean will wash
this blood clean from his hand. The companion of
Sir Roger in the *Spectator*, when asked to adjudicate
upon the Saracen's head, thought "that much might
be said on both sides." This cautious opinion is
generally true of most points that are not axiomatic ;
and yet on Philip's side there is little to say. It may,

avenged on the persons of the clergy : "fueron presos otros culpados
clerigos, y frayles, que andauan en abito indecentes, con las barbas
crecidas, que fueron alboratadores publicos," etc. (Mosquera de
Figueroa, f. 91).

Madrid was illuminated in honour of the victory. Cp. Henrique
Cock's "Mantua Carpentana" (v. 251–253):

> "Victis in pelago Gallis mersisque sub undis
> Egregiam incendit portam, cui Carraca nomen."

however, be pleaded that, though no amount of pro-
vocation on the part of the Portuguese auxiliaries could,
according to our present ideas, extenuate the shame
of this atrocious edict, it is lamentably certain that
the mutilation of the Spaniards at San Sebastião would
seem to many mediæval (and, judging from some recent
instances to which a more particular reference is unnecessary, to some modern) minds to justify this resort
to the *lex talionis.*

The saturnalia of carnage ended, Santa Cruz, in
September, 1582, returned to Lisbon. But Dom
Antonio, though beaten to the ground, was not annihilated. On May 17, 1583, a reinforcement of French
troops, under the Commandeur de Chaste, sailed from
Havre to join those shattered battalions of Strozzi
which had, in the previous year, escaped the avenging
sword of Santa Cruz. De Chaste reached Terceira on
June 11, and Santa Cruz soon followed in his wake.
The Spanish fleet left Lisbon on June 23, and on
July 24, under an intensely hot sun, Santa Cruz
hoisted the signal to come to anchor a few miles to
the east of Angra, the capital of Terceira. The fierce
combat of the previous year was not destined to be
repeated. But to a biographer of Cervantes it is
interesting to note that in a brilliant skirmish at
Porto das Moas, about two leagues from Angra,
Rodrigo de Cervantes greatly distinguished himself.
Mosquera de Figueroa, the semi-official eulogist of the
Spanish Admiral, has done his utmost to confer immortality on Rodrigo by finding a modest place for

him in his long, Homeric catalogue of quaternary heroes.[1] Far off in the dismal north, among the *grachten* and swampy *kleiboden* of Holland, Rodrigo, freed from his Algerine captivity by the fraternal magnanimity, had been serving a grateful country without any very appreciable personal result. But his great opportunity had come at last, and it is pleasant to think that, after a dozen years of hard service, the simple soldier had obtained a commensurate reward. It is very gratifying to reflect that, before the end came, he had entered into possession and dazzled the world—as an Ensign. War, according to Macchiavelli's ideas, if we may judge from *Il Principe*, should be the only study of a king.[2] However questionable this worldly-wise advice may appear to the moralist, it would be rash to deny that princes of most ages have found, in following it, the path to an easy, lucrative, and not too perilous career. The scoffing sceptic who questions its personal advantages as regards the simple man-at-arms, may be speedily

[1] " Llegarō breuemēte las barcas a tierra, dōde saltarō los Españoles cō grāde esfuerço entre aɋllas lajas a los dos lados de los fuertes : algunos poniā el pie seguro en vna piedra, para escaparse d̄ la resaca, ɋ era grāde : otros ɋ no podiā esperar esta coyūtura, se abālaçuā, y se sumergiā, de suerte ɋ el agua les cubria hasta la cinta, y cō la resaca ɋdauā luego esentos para salir. Echòse al agua animosamēte cō su vādera, por auer encallado la barca, Frācisco de la Rua alferez de dō Frācisco de Bouadilla, y tras el el capitā Luis de Gueuara, y Rodrigo de Ceruātes, a quiē despues auētajo el Marɋs," etc.—Mosquera de Figueroa, f. 58.

[2] " Deve adunque un Principe non avere altro oggetto, nè altro pensiero, nè prendere cosa alcuna per sua arte, fuori della Guerra," etc.—*Il Principe*, cap. xiv.

silenced by pointing to the dazzling spoil gathered by our fortunate Bezonian, Rodrigo de Cervantes. Even the most carping critic must admit that the material advantages of such a career, though not among its most potent attractions to the adventurous youth of a nation (honour, doubtless, pricks them on), are irresistible to the least sordid mind. "The lower people everywhere desire War. Not so unwisely; there is then a demand for lower people—to be shot!" Teufelsdröckh's remark is more than ever incomprehensible in its "deep, silent, slow-burning, inextinguishable Radicalism."

The campaign of 1583 was soon over. From Porto das Moas the Spanish troops advanced and occupied Angra without resistance. Da Silva fled ignominiously, and De Chaste, though strongly posted at Guadalupe, seeing that success was hopeless, began to treat for a surrender. His first proposal—that the French force should be allowed to retire with banners flying and all the honours of war—was sternly rejected. Santa Cruz' word was simple — unconditional surrender. But on this occasion his staff proved too strong for him, and, on August 3, a compromise was accepted, the French capitulating and leaving their flags and arms in possession of the victors. One blow was followed by another. Manuel da Silva was lurking inland while a plan for his escape was secretly organising. But there is no armour against Fate. A large ransom was offered, and he was soon captured and brought into the Spanish lines. The unfortunate man at first strove to put a bold face upon matters; he was then tortured, and, according to the

Spanish version, "confessed" many remarkable things. It is unnecessary to follow in minute detail the last act of this miserable tragedy. The captive ex-Viceroy was taken from the rack to the scaffold, and execution followed upon execution, some German again acting as the squalid minister of death. With these horrible incidents the campaign closed; the sword and the headsman's axe had vanquished, and the Azores were at peace after three tumultuous years of conflict. Order reigned in Angra when in August, Santa Cruz, leaving behind a garrison of 2,000 troops under the Spanish Military Governor, Juan de Urbina, sailed from the recking slaughter-house for Cádiz, where he disembarked on September 15, 1583.[1]

[1] "Recit de l'expédition, attaque et conquête de l'ile de Tercère et des autres îles Açores . . . et d'autres événements remarquables qui se passèrent en cette conquête. 1583" ("Archives de Voyages. Par H. Ternaux-Compans," i. pp. 423-445). Also "Relation de l'expédition de la Tercère, traduite du manuscrit espagnol inédit. Bibl. royale. MS. de Colbert inédit" (Ternaux-Compans, ii. pp. 302-305). "Relacion de lo sucedido en la Isla de la Tercera, desde veynte y tres de Iulio, hasta veynte y siete del mismo mil y quinientos y ochenta y tres Años" (Alcalá de Henares, 1583). "Voyage de la Tercere fait par M. le Commandeur de Chaste," in the "Relations de divers voyages curieux qui n'ont point esté publiées . . . données au public par les soins de feu M. Melchisedec Thevenot" (Paris, 1696), vol. ii. Pinkerton has reprinted this narrative.

The torture of Silva is admitted on all hands (Ternaux-Compans, ii. p. 305). Mosquera de Figueroa shuffles, and on f. 106 talks of threats—"fue necessario hazerle comminacion"; but on f. 130 he says plainly enough: "resulto de la côfesion y declaraciõ q̃ Manuel da Silva *hizo en el tormēto.*" Herrera is more straightforward (f. 210): "mandò al Auditor General que vssase de los tormentos." Herrera insists on the executioner's nationality once more: "degollado por mano de un verdugo Tudesco" (f. 210).

At this distance of time it is impossible to say what share Cervantes had in this prolonged campaign. That he served against the Portuguese is certain; but whether he took part in every battle, including the reconnaissance-expedition of Lope de Figueroa and the great battle against Strozzi, or whether, as later researches seem to indicate, he was concerned solely in the final developments of the campaign, is by no means clear. Fernández de Navarrete inclines, apparently, to the former, and D. Ramón León Máinez to the latter, opinion. Cervantes, it may be noted, was not the only unrevealed miracle serving under Santa Cruz. In at least one of the expeditions a musket was shouldered by an unknown marvellous boy destined before long to reach the topmost pinnacle of contemporary dramatic fame, and to outshine Cervantes and all his generation in the struggle for popular applause. Lope de Vega, the future *Fénix*, not yet in his sixteenth year, served against the Açorianos at Terceira. Cervantes returned with Santa Cruz and served in Portugal for another twelvemonth.[1] The obscurity which overhangs so much of his history still follows him. We

---

[1] The career of Santa Cruz is so well known that it is needless to recapitulate it. A long, unreadable eulogy may be found at the end of Mosquera de Figueroa's "Comentario," a volume which also includes a commemorative sonnet by Cervantes and a poem by Ercilla.

Lope de Figueroa died as Captain-General of Granada on August 28, 1585 (Navarrete, p. 300). Cp. also Henrique Cock's "Relación del viaje hecho por Felipe II. en 1585 á Zaragoza, Barcelona y Valencia," etc. (Madrid, 1876), pp. 171–172. Calderón introduces him in "Amar despues de la Muerte" and in "El Alcalde de Zalamea."

know that he was sent on some sort of embassy to
Mostagan and to Oran; but whether this took place
immediately after his captivity, or whether it was
deferred until after his return from his campaign in the
Azores, is one of the many unanswered questions which
may be asked. The usual conflict of opinion meets us;
Fernández de Navarrete and D. Ramón León Máinez
are at odds, and D. José María Asensio agrees with the
last named in thinking 1580 the more probable date of
this embassy. But the point is scarcely worth labouring,
especially as the mission seems to have been of the most
trivial character. Somewhere about this time Cervantes
is alleged to have served as tax-gatherer, probably in
Montanches.

It has been generally asserted that, at this period
of Cervantes' life, his natural daughter Isabel de
Saavedra was born; but it is not easy to perceive the
grounds for this dogmatic utterance. The only certainty
in the matter is that he had a natural daughter, who in
1605 declared herself to be twenty years of age.
Fernández de Navarrete, with a mild scepticism unusual

The First Soldier in the first act of the latter play gives a trenchant
sketch of the old warrior's character:

> ". . . es cabo desta gente
> Don Lope de Figueroa,
> Que, si tiene fama y loa
> De animoso y de valiente,
> La tiene tambien de ser
> El hombre mas desalmado,
> Jurador y renegado
> Del mundo, y que sabe hacer
> Justicia del mas amigo,
> Sin fulminar el proceso."

in his writings, thinks that Doña Isabel understated her age—"*es tan comun en las mugeres (especialmente en las solteras) el aparentar menos edad, ó decirla al poco mas ó menos*";—but when she was born, whether she was or was not born in Lisbon, and whether her mother was or was not sprung from some illustrious Portuguese house, are points upon which we are doomed to remain in ignorance. These are all matters of such infinitesimal importance that it might have been imagined that little or no interest would be displayed in their elucidation. Unfortunately there is a type of mind which revels in the discussion of such questions, as every one knows who has laboriously toiled through the innumerable pamphlets which go to prove that the "woman colour'd ill," the "dark lady," "black as hell, as dark as night," is Mistress Mary Fitton or some one else. It is so much easier to indulge in windy speculation as to the personality of the "dark lady" or Mr. W. H., than to have a tolerable acquaintance with the "Sonnets," that probably the explanation lies close at hand. But when all is written and read we are scarcely nearer the truth than we were before. These ingenious treatises find their way to the trunk-maker and the butterman; and most of the attempts to throw light upon the personality of Isabel de Saavedra's mother are fortunately destined to make the same golden pilgrimage. Nothing whatever is known of her; nothing at this day is likely to be discovered about her; and the whole question might be passed over were it not for the *curiosos impertinentes*, the literary ghouls who manifest their interest in high literature by leaving *Don Quixote* unread, and striving to discover the name of Cervantes' mistress.   Luckily this æsthetic, pure-minded devotion is in this instance its own reward.   So far as Cervantes himself is concerned in this matter, his biographer must be content to admit that his subject was no saint, but an impetuous man of genius with quite as full a share of frailty as though he had been a peer.   The moral pathologist may be left to do his worst with a problem which is as soluble as most questions in morbid psychology.   The plain man may be content to leave the uncovering of this incident to the literary Hams of the day, and to turn to Cervantes' *Galatea.*

It was the noontide of that mediæval pastoral romance of which Jacopo Sannazzaro may be considered the creator.   He had discovered in Arcadia a new continent which differed as widely as possible from our gray, work-a-day world—a land of spells and of enchantment where, by the melodious murmur of sapphire waves, in magic caverns, or amid banks of fern and asphodel, under rustling palm or lisping elms, the beauteous-voiced shepherds sang their lays disconsolate or fleeted the time carelessly as they did in the golden world.   Here the songs of Apollo silenced the harsh words of Mercury, and from dawn till night life was spent in grove and glen that echoed perpetually to the charmed sound of lute and canzonet.   It is the land of perpetual midsummer.   The wild rush, the multitudinous whirl of the outer life is far away, faded beyond remembrance. Man is but a hopeless exile from the enchanted streams of Arcady, from the region of ivy thickets, the land of Dionysian apples and Hesperidean blossoms. The Arcadian night is always very still, its intense silence broken only by the whisper of the silver rippling of the magic mere beyond some hyacinth dell, or by the song of the nightingale in some all-fragrant coppice. Then with the dawn the shepherds waken, and the earliest rays smite these happy Memnons of the sunlit vale into pastoral song. So with a background of fairy brakes and glades, in an air divinely sweet with violet and amaranth, with jasmine and narcissus-blooms, the contending foresters live on as in the youth of the world, hymning the praises of their mistresses and, between their madrigals, telling their sad, gracious stories, or, in the intervals, listening to the rhythmic music of those perfumed founts of Sybaris which ring by Castaly. From beyond the moss-covered hillocks there echoes back the refrain of the pæan of the shepherdesses; and the notes of viol and of rebeck resound across the mead, past the blossoming almond-grove, above the long rushing of the filmy waterfalls. Far from the midday heat, Ergasto sings of Amaranta as Daphnis sang of Nais, or Rosaura gives a *cinque-cento* echo of the half-fierce, half-pathetic invocation of Simaetha in the moonlit Theocritean idyll. Down the hillside winds a long procession of superb beauties shepherding their tender

flocks. This perfect phalanx moves to the Dorian
mood of flutes and soft recorders, and at last, when
the sunset dies, seated by the crystal mountain springs,
under scented domes of pleasure and of peace, they
stir the slumberous wood and silent bowers with songs
of contented calm or indolent desire. So with these
blameless Hyperboreans life floats on as in a sylvan
dream. Far away beyond the Pillars of Hercules,
across the thousand leagues of water, where on the
shores of another continent the fierce Atlantic bursts
into its clouds of spume, Columbus had discovered
a new world. But to this new life only the wilder,
more daring spirits of the time had access. To the
Italianised Spaniard Jacopo Sannazzaro belongs the
credit of discovering nearer home a more reposeful
planet where the gentler, more cultured spirits of the
age could roam amid marvels even more incredible
than those which greeted the fierce adventurers who,
by the side of Cortés or Pizarro, cut their paths to
fame over hecatombs of dead. Sannazzaro could take
his legions not only to a new, but to an antique,
world—a world of pleasurable sadness and aromatic
despondency where passion is exhausted in some
plaintive sonnet, or where, from the hallowed limbec
of artificial sentiment, the common grief is distilled in
some mournful lay. Breathing such an atmosphere, it is
perhaps not all affectation when Luigi Tausillo writes:

> Le lagrime e 'l pensier son quegli amici
> Che non mi lascian mai dovunque io vado;
> E quando piovon più gli occhj infelici,
> Allor ne le mie pene più m' aggrado.

But there is a silver reverse to this golden shield.
Nothing could be more alien, more untrue to real life
than these elaborate pictures. Those who wrote and
those who read alike knew that nothing could be
more impossible than these politely-mournful foresters
leading the lives of bereaved demigods, their desires
quenched, their melancholy immortal. Nothing could
be more unreal, nothing more remote from nature
than their highly-wrought courtly simplicity. Compare with the Grandisonian foresters of Sannazzaro
the shepherds of Theocritus. Take Elpino and Sincero,
and place them beside the sunburnt Milon, beside
Menalcas the flute-player. The former pair are in
no sense shepherds, though they might have seemed
so at the Hôtel Rambouillet more than a century
later; they are ambassadors in retirement; polished
diplomatists whiling the hours away with amateur
music; or courtly gentlemen, with scarcely more
liking for green fields than Dr. Johnson, who, having
been unfortunate in their love affairs in town, have
gone into the country for a few weeks to get over
their disappointment. They alternate between fashion-
able immobility and a carefully measured, though
somewhat ostentatious, wistfulness. The free, un-
studied note of natural rapture which rings through
the Theocritean idylls would seem strangely out of
place in the mouths of these accomplished courtiers
all-conscious of the foot-lights and their well-bred
audience. Everything moves with a smoothness which
borders on monotony if not inanity; but the lack of

incident, the deficiency of animation and of motive, would seem never to have palled on contemporary readers. It would have been no taunt to them to say that here "old Saturn's reign of sugar-candy" had come again. The characteristics summed up in that phrase were just those which they admired. This studied avoidance, at least in literature, of all that savoured of the stir of marts, the strife of camps, the overflowing energy of that abundant life which found its outlets in privateering and in exploration, in the subjugation of strange races under strange constellations—this was their idea of a return to nature, and the men of the sixteenth century hailed its literary embodiment with enthusiasm.

The note struck by Sannazzaro at Nocera and Posilippo was echoed back by the whole world. In every land he found a host of followers and disciples who wrote for their device upon their unfurled standards, —*Juventus Mundi*. In Portugal the dying fall was caught up in a perfect cadence by Ribeiro in his *Menina e Moça*, which, like some of the Vergilian eclogues,—such as *Formosum Corydon ardebat Alexim* and *Cuium pecus? an Melibœi*—takes its title from its opening words. In France the *Bergeries de Julliette* of Nicolas de Montreux (published by him under the transparent anagram of Ollenix du Mont-Sacré) and the *Astrée* of Honoré d'Urfé became the rage. The heathen mechanism of d'Urfé seemed to call for an antidote in the shape of a more spiritual school of pastoralism ; and this dubious sedative was administered

by Jean-Pierre Camus in *Le Cleoreste*, in *Hellenin,*
in *Calitrope*, and in many other interminable novels
of the good Bishop of Bellay, to whom Franciscan monks
and pastoral romances seemed the source of all evil.
The more effective weapon of sarcasm was employed
with consummate skill by Charles Sorel in his *Anti-
Roman*, a work published under the pseudonym of Jean
de Lalande. If ridicule could have killed a parasitic
growth pastoralism would have been a dead thing; but,
like most of the lower organisms, it possessed invincible
vitality. Nothing availed to check the growth of a
mode which, passing from one generation to another,
through the hands of Mademoiselle de Scudéry to those
of Florian, at last became an absolute pest. Yet we
can scarcely regret the development of a mania which
by way of compensation indirectly produced *Les
Précieuses Ridicules*. In Holland the *Arcadia* of
Johan van Heemskerk represents the Batavian aspect of
Arcady, while in Germany, where the Court poets outdid
the wildest absurdities of Cathos and Magdelon, the
Schäfferen von der Nimfen Hercinie of Martin Opitz
and the *Adriatische Rosemund* of Philip von Zesen (published by him under the fictitious name of Ritterhold von
Blauen) in their tedious extravagance and shrill falsetto
sentiment touched the nadir of pastoral achievement.[1]

---

[1] "Geschichte der Deutschen Litteratur von Wilhelm Scherer"
(Berlin, 1883), p. 322: "Die Nürnberger Dichter gründeten 1644
ihre Gesellschaft der Pegnitzschäfer oder den gekrönten Blumenorden
an der Pegnitz, dassen hervorragendste mitglieder Harzdörfer, Klaj
und Birken sich mit besonderem Enthusiasmus in das Schäferwesen
warsen," etc.

The seed scattered by Sannazzaro's hand fell upon good ground in England where the influence of the Italian school was already strong. The contributions to Tottel's *Miscellany* of Wyatt and Surrey, the "two chieftaines" of the "company of courtly makers," are among the earliest manifestations of the working of the Tuscan spell; and Surrey's "raptured line," with Geraldine substituted for Laura, reads like a free paraphrase of Petrarch. Of Wyatt it may be fairly said that in the celebrated sonnet,

Unstable dream, according to the place,

he gave the model to all subsequent sonneteers. The author of *The Arte of English Poesie* is within the mark when, referring to Wyatt and Surrey, he says that "hauing trauailed into Italie, and there tasted the sweete and stately measures and stile of the Italian Poesie as nouices newly crept out of the schooles of Dante, Ariosto and Petrarch, they greatly polished our rude and homely maner of vulgar Poesie from that it had been before, and for that cause may justly be sayd the first reformers of our English metre and stile."[1] From the publication of Tottel's *Book of Songes and Sonnetes* (the same, doubtless, which Master Slender preferred to forty shillings) the advance of the new current is uninterrupted, and gathers force and volume as it flows along. Before the close of the century the public interest was sufficiently awakened to call forth trans-

[1] Puttenham, "The Arte of English Poesie" (Arber's reprint), p. 74.

lations of many of the Italian masterpieces. In an
earlier generation the attention of Sir Thomas More had
been occupied by Pico della Mirandola.[1] The travels
of Ser Marco Polo, dedicated by him (in what tongue we
know not) to Messer Rustichello in the Genoese prison,
were read in John Frampton's version.[2] Castiglione's
celebrated book was Englished in *The Courtyer* of
Thomas Hoby.[3] The *Trionfi* and the *De remediis
utriusque fortunæ* of Petrarch were rendered, the first
by Lord Morley, the second by Thomas Twyne.[4]
Guicciardini's *Istoria d'Italia* was translated by Sir
Geoffrey Fenton, and a version of Tasso's *Aminta* was
included by Abraham Faunce in *The Countesse of
Pembrokes Yuychurch.*[5] The licentious *novelle* of

[1] "Here is conteyned the life of Johan Picus Erle of Myrandula a
grete lorde of Italy an excellent connynge man in all sciences and
vertcous of lyunge. With divers epistles and other werkes of ye
sayd Johan Picus full of grete science vertue and wysedome"
(London, 1510).

[2] "The most noble and famous trauels of Marcus Paulus, one of
the nobilitie of the state of Venice. . . , Translated into English"
(London, 1579). The book is dedicated to Edward Dyer, to whom
the translator, John Frampton, "wisheth prosperous health and
felicitie."

[3] "The Courtyer of Count Baldessar Castiglione Castilio diuided
into foure bookes . . . done into English by Thomas Hoby" (London,
1561).

[4] "The tryumphes of Fraunces Petrarcke translated out of Italian
into English by H. Parker knyght Lorde Morley" (London [1565?]).
"Phisicke against Fortune as well prosperous as adverse conteyned
in two Bookes. . . . Written in Latine by Francis Petrarch, a most
famous Poet and Oratour. And now first Englished by Thomas
Twyne" (London, 1579).

[5] "The Historie of Guicciardin. . . . Reduced into English by
G. Fenton" (London, 1599). "The Countesse of Pembrokes Yuy-

Matteo Bandello (a refugee Italian who, after a life of curious experience, was nominated to the sinecure bishopric of Agen) were at the height of their popularity ; and — probably through the French version of Pierre Boaistuau — Arthur Broke, in his metrical paraphrase of the *Tragicall Historye of Romeus and Iulieit,* gave the English reader in 1562 his first opportunity of forming an acquaintance with a story which was to supply the plot of one of Shakspere's masterpieces. In the following years more *novelle* of Bandello, stories from the *Decamerone* and from the collection of Tommaso Guardato, better known as Masuccio Salernitano (whose history of the loves of Mariotto Mignanelli and Giannoza Saraceni contains the germ of the legend of Romeo and Juliet), were given in William Painter's *Palace of Pleasure,* which also included selections from the *Hecatommithi* of Giraldi Cinthio.[1] Whitehorne's version of Macchiavelli's *Arte della Guerra* became popular.[2] Boccaccio found a

church. Conteining the affectionate life and unfortunate death of Phillis and Amyntas " (London, 1591).

[1] " The Palace of Pleasure Beautified, adorned and well furnished, with Pleasaunt Histories and excellent Nouelles, selected out of diuers good and commendable Authors. By William Painter Clarke of the Ordinaunce and Armorie " (London, 1566).

" The second Tome of the Palace of Pleasure, conteyning store of goodly Histories, Tragicall matters, and other Morall argument, very requisite for delighte and profit. Chosen and selected out of diuers good and commendable Authors. By William Painter, Clerke of the Ordinance and Armorie " (London, 1567).

[2] " The Arte of warre, written first in Italiã by N. Macchiavell and set forth in English by Peter Whitehorne, student in Graies Inne " (London, 1560–1562).

translator of more than average merit in George
Turberville ;[1] and the *Suppositi* of Ariosto (an
Italianised amalgam of the *Eunuchus* and *Captivi*)
was brilliantly given by George Gascoigne in his
Supposes, the earliest prose comedy, it is said, in our
language.[2] The invasion of England by a company of
Italian actors serves to mark the tide of progress.[3]

Some subdued echo of the Italian note may be
found in an earlier phase of English letters. Within
certain well-defined limits it is obvious in *Troylus
and Criseyde* and the *Knightes Tale*, in the *Fall of
Princes* and in *The Two Married Women and the*

---

[1] "Tragical Tales and other poems translated by Tvrberville in
time of his troubles out of sundrie Italians" (London, 1587). Reproduced at Edinburgh (for private circulation only) in 1837.

[2] *Supposes: a Comedie written in the Italian tongue by Ariosto,
Englished by George Gascoyne of Grayes Inne Esquire and there presented* (London, 1566). Included in "The Posies of George Gascoigne Esquire" (London, 1575).

[3] Cp. Kyd's "Spanish Tragedy" (Act. v.):
          "The Italian tragedians were so sharp of wit
          That in one hour's meditation
          They would perform anything in action."
And again, Middleton's "Spanish Gipsy" (Act iv. sc. 2):
"*Soto.* We are promised a very merry tragedy, if all hit right of
Cobby Nobby.
Fernando. So, so ; a merry tragedy ! there is a way
          Which the Italians and the Frenchmen use,
          That is, on a word given, or some slight plot,
          The actors will extempore fashion out
          Scenes neat and witty."
Decidedly, Salvini's earliest predecessors made their impression.
In France, in a later generation, the success of the Italian actors seems
to have excited the bitterest professional jealousy. Cp. Grimarest's
"Vie de Molière" (Paris, 1877, Malassi's edition), p. 69.

Widow. But the indebtedness of Chaucer, Lydgate, and Dunbar scarcely extends beyond suggestion and design. In the Elizabethan development the manifold characteristics of the great Italian writers are reproduced with extraordinary fidelity and minuteness. Not only the subtler working of their spirit, but the very form and method of their song is elaborately set forth; and the whole framework of production is interpenetrated with the inspiration of their example. The suppleness, the easy grace and concentrated melody of the foreign models are manifest in the metrical innovations of Wyatt and Surrey: and, in the *Induction* of Sackville, there is for the first time some approach (however slight) to the sombre impressiveness, the intense vigour, the mournful music and sustained dignity of the mighty Florentine.

Throughout the Elizabethan period the Italian note, its "ingenuity" more and more accentuated, proceeds in a continuous *crescendo* which reaches its climax in Lyly's *Euphues*, "that all-to-be-unparalleled volume" which Sir Piercie Shafton, one of Sir Walter Scott's least successful figures, took for his manual. The influence of *Euphues* is noticeably strong in *The Countesse of Pembrokes Arcadia*, the publication of which, in 1590, marked the definite inauguration of the pastoral order in England; for the efforts of Henryson are so indirect and tentative as scarcely to entitle them to be classed as serious examples of the style. The *Shepherd's Calendar* had savoured strongly of the foreign stimulus; but in the *Arcadia* of Sir Philip Sidney the triumph of the Italian influence is manifest, palpable, complete. Sidney delights in "the prettie tales of Wolves and Sheepe," and to him it is always conclusive against a given mode that[1] "neyther Theocritus in Greek, Virgill in Latine, nor Sanazar in Italian, did affect it."[2] But if this brilliant, post-mediæval "inheritor of unfulfilled renown," whose old-time masterpiece now lies discrowned and unhonoured, has been taken as the typical example of Arcadian romance in England, it must not be inferred that he stands alone. The difficulty is to choose among so many; but the *Menaphon* of Greene and the *Rosalynde* and *Margarite of America* of Lodge must be included in any reference. They also are lineal descendants of Sannazzaro, and every line of their pastoral fictions testifies to their intellectual ancestry; the songs of Menaphon are but the echoes of the songs of Uranio, and Doron's

---

[1] Sidney's "Apologie for Poetrie" (Arber's reprint), p. 43: "Is it then the Pastorall Poem which is misliked? (for perchance, where the hedge is lowest, they will soonest leape ouer). Is the poor pype disdained, which sometime out of *Melibeus* mouth, can shewe the misery of people, vnder hards Lords or rauening Souldiours? And again, by *Titirus*, what blessednes is deriued to them that lye lowest from the gooduesse of them that sit highest? Sometimes, vnder the prettie tales of Wolves and Sheepe, can include the whole considerations of wrong dooing and patience. Sometimes shew, that considerations for trifles, can get but a trifling victorie."

[2] Ibid. p. 63. Sidney's quaint curse on his foes is worth quoting: "that while you liue, you liue in loue, and neuer get fauour, for lacking skill of a Sonnet: and when you die, your memory die from the earth, for want of an Epitaph" (ibid. p. 72).

description of Samela to Melicertus is absolutely in
the Italian manner. Shakspere himself condescended
to borrow the name of Ophelia from Sannazzaro and
the name of Mopsa from Sidney; while Arthur Broke's
version of Bandello's story is not more obviously the
basis of *Romeo and Juliet* than is the *Rosalynde* of
Lodge the source of *As You Like It.*

The triumph of the innovators was absolute and
complete; but it would be a mistake to suppose that the
followers of "beastly Skelton" surrendered without a
struggle. The somewhat ungrateful proverb—*Inglese
italianato è un diavolo incarnato* — was never from
their mouths. Ascham overflows with denunciations of
the Englishmen who travelled in Italy and who, "beyng
Mules aud Horses before they went, returned verie
Swyne and Asses home again." In his eyes nothing
could be more pestilent than the "fonde books of late
translated out of Italian into English, sold in euery shop
in London, commended by honest titles the sooner to
corrupt good manners." Sir Thomas Malory was bad
enough; but even he wrought not "the tenth part so
much harm as one of these bookes, made in Italie, and
translated in England." The self-righteousness of the
hide-bound dominie is amusingly displayed in such
utterances as: "I was once in Italie my selfe: but I
thanke God my abode there was but ix. days."[1] The
success of Greene's pastorals aroused the wrath of Gabriel
Harvey, a miserable pedant over whose annihilation by
Nash subsequent ages have made merry. This writer,

---

[1] Ascham's "Scholemaster" (Arber's reprint), pp. 77, 78–79, 83.

who longed for the doubtful honour of being " epitaphed'
the Inventour of the English hexameter," though
willing enough to admit that " Petrarck was a delicate
man," fills the air with his lamentations over the
contemporary decadence with its " strange fancies " and
" monstrous newfanglednesse." But every day the tide
rose higher and higher ; every creek and every channel
filled, and not all the grisly spectres raised by dismal
Dons could stem the invading waves. Under cover
of the general demoralisation even the thrice-accursed
Spaniard was creeping into the land. Mexia, Guevara,
Ávila, and Santillana found translators in Fortescue,
Fenton, Wilkinson, and Googe ; but, for the moment,
the Italian was the enemy. Nothing availed, however,
against the universal madness, which went its way,
touching Browne and Drayton on the road, till at last
pastoralism, growing more and more artificial, became
the haunt of Pope's Dresden shepherdesses ; and finally
Thenot, Colinet, and Hobbinol perished from sheer
degeneracy and inanition in the flaccid hands of
Ambrose Phillips, the prototype of Namby-Pamby. In
the last moment of its life, pastoralism, in the *Shepherd's Week* and in the *Gentle Shepherd*, offered some
sincerity of handling, some reminiscence of the free
Theocritean touch. As Gay himself says, his shepherdesses may be found, not " idly piping on oaten reeds,
out milking the kine, tying up the sheaves, or, if the
hogs are astray, driving them to their styes." [1]   But it

---

[1] The entire Proem to the "Shepherd's Week" is worth reading:
" Albeit, nor ignorant I am, what a rout and rabblement of critical

was too late. Pastoralism was dead beyond revival, and no one could recall it from beyond the grave. The foreign influences had ceased to work; what was food in them had been absorbed, and Fielding's avowed determination in *Tom Jones* to "hash and ragoo" human nature, "with all the high French and Italian seasoning of affectation and vice which courts and cities afford," reads like a belated echo of extinct controversy.

In Spain the same battle was fought; the twin poets, Juan Boscán and Garcilaso de la Vega—*par nobile fratrum*—led the van. Boscán himself has named Andrea Navagiero's as the hand which first led him into the perfect way, and, in the preface to his second book, he gives an amusing account of the objections with which the foreign innovations were received by the Old Guard.[1] Cristóbal de Castillejo in many passages — but especially in his well-known poem, *Contra los que dejan los metros Castellanos y siguen los italianos*— struggled manfully against the flowing tide; nor was

gallimawfry hath been made of late days by certain young men of insipid delicacy, concerning, I wist not what, golden age, and other outrageous conceits, to which they would confine Pastoral. Whereof, I avow, I account nought at all, *knowing no Age so justly to be instiled Golden, as this of our Sovereign Lady ¡Queen Anne.*" "This idle trumpery (only fit for schools and schoolboys) unto that ancient Dorick Shepherd Theocritus, or his mates, was never known; he rightly, throughout his fifth Idyll, maketh his Louts give foul language."

[1] "Otras dezian, que este uerso, no sabian, si era uerso, o si era prosa. Otros arguian diziendo, que esto principalmente hauia de ser para las mugeres," etc.—Las obras de Boscan y algvnas de Garcilaso de la Vega (Salamanca, 1547), f. 28.

other protest wanting.[1]   But all in vain; the current
ran too strongly. The genius of Garcilaso had secured
for the new school an impregnable position: and the
(perhaps unwitting) adoption of the Italian *versi
sciolti* by Boscán in his *Leandro* testifies to an un-
discriminating enthusiasm which did not stop short
of admiring the painfully laboured versification of
Giovanni Giorgio Trissino's *Italia Liberata.*   As in
verse, so in prose; the Italian victory was complete.
The pastoral (like the chivalrous) fit reached Spain by
way of Portugal.   As the Portuguese Vasco de Lobeira
had, in the previous century, introduced *Amadis,* so did
the Portuguese Jorge de Montemayor introduce the
Diana Enamorada.   Within a few years of his death,
Alonso Pérez and Gaspar Gil Polo each produced a
continuation, Gil Polo's version rivalling the original in
popularity, while it perhaps excelled it in intrinsic
merit.[2] The elixir was working.   Jerónimo de Arbo-

---

[1] " Bien se pueden castigar
    a cuenta de Anabaptistas,
    pues por ley particular
    se tornan a baptizar,
    y se llaman Petrarquistas.
    Han renegado la fe
    de las trobas castellanas,
    y tras las Italianas
    se pierden, diziendo que
    son mas ricas y galanas."
Las obras de Christoval de Castillejo (Anvers, 1598), p. 111.

[2] Montemayor's "Diana Enamorada" was first published at
Valencia in 1542.   The writer died at Turin, under somewhat
mysterious circumstances, in 1561.   The continuations of Gil Polo
and Alonso Pérez were both produced in 1564.   We have already

lanche's metrical pastoral, *Las Havidas*, was published at Zaragoza in 1566 : and so frantic was the popular gusto that even Antonio de Lo Frasso's *Fortuna de Amar* — a work of such delirious drivel as to cast serious doubts on the writer's sanity—found a multitude of readers. Luís Gálvez de Montalvo in 1582 took up the cadence in his *Pastor de Fílida*. He protests in several passages against the prevailing modes : but despite his worse, or better, judgment he follows meekly in the foreign paths.

It seems certain that in the winter of 1583 Cervantes had retired from the Army of Portugal and returned to Spain, taking up his residence, after some trifling embassy to Mostagan and Oran, in the little town of Esquivias. Genius is always susceptible, especially in early manhood, and Cervantes became infected with the prevalent mania. In the following year his pastoral romance *La Galatea* probably saw the light. Though the volume almost defies analysis, the task must be attempted, as it seems unlikely that the English reader will turn two pages of the only translation accessible to him. The first book opens with a song on the banks of the Tagus by Elicio, one of the many worshippers at the shrine of the beautiful, passionless Galatea. Then follows another song, after which Elicio is joined by Erastro,

seen how Bishop Jean-Pierre Camus produced Christian pastorals in France. A similar antidote to the prevailing evil in Spain was administered in the " Primera parte de la clara Diana, a lo divino, repartida en siete libros. Compuesto por el muy Reverendo Padre fray Bartholome Ponce " (Çaragoça, 1599).

a friendly (because humble) rival in Galatea's affections.
They interchange confidences, and in alternate verses
are singing, like Daphnis and Menalcas, the charms
of their mistress when Erastro is interrupted by the
entrance of a shepherd in full flight, pursued by another,
who, overtaking the runaway, stabs him to death under
the eyes of the two swains. The murderer conjures
them to leave the corpse unburied, and then betakes
himself to the neighbouring hills. Disregarding his
prayer, Galatea's lovers go homewards, and, later,
Elicio sallies forth to sing in the moonlit groves when
he hears the voice of the assassin—whose name, ejacu-
lated by the last breath of the murdered man, he
knows to be Lisandro—uttering a midnight plaint in
which the names of Leónida and Carino mingle. Elicio
waits till Lisandro's song is over and then presents
himself to the unhappy wight, and asks him to tell
his story. This, accordingly, Lisandro does; and,
beneath the blue, he recounts with pastoral minuteness
the history of his star-crossed love for Leónida, once
the glory of the Guadalquivir. To help him in his
suit, complicated by an old family feud, he had, some
six months earlier, sought the aid of Silvia, the beloved
of Leónida's brother, Crisalvo. Crisalvo, whose reputation was not of the best, in order to ingratiate himself
with Silvia, availed himself of the good offices of her
kinsman, Carino, the villain of the story. Carino,
who had long dissembled an ancient grudge against
Lisandro's brother and against Crisalvo, took the
opportunity of insinuating to the latter that his un-

successful suit was due to the fact that Silvia was already the mistress of Lisandro. Meanwhile, Lisandro's love-affair had prospered exceedingly, and finally it was arranged that, under escort of Carino, Leónida should meet her lover at a neighbouring village and there marry him. Betraying the confidence placed in him, Carino informed Crisalvo that Lisandro's triumph with Silvia was so absolute that, on such and such a night, the pair were to elope. On the appointed day, he induced Libeo (another of his foes) to escort the disguised Leónida to the trysting-place. Crisalvo, whose love for Silvia had turned to hate, secreted himself by the roadside with four of his kinsmen, and, under the impression that the muffled figures before him were those of Leónida and Lisandro, murdered the two wayfarers. Lisandro, who had been anxiously awaiting the arrival of Leónida and Carino, walked along the road, came upon Leónida, gathered from her dying lips her story, and almost instantly killed Crisalvo, who, having learned his blunder, had returned to see for himself whether he was in truth the murderer of his own sister. The last act of the tragedy had culminated that day in the slaughter of Carino. Lisandro's vengeance is complete. Like the singer of the *Hymn to Proserpine,* he has

Lived long enough, having seen one thing, that love hath an end,

and death remains his one desire. However, he is prevailed upon to spend the night in Elicio's dwelling. Next day Erastro appears, and the trio, sallying forth, find Galatea wandering by the streamlet in search of her friend Florisa. Finally, the two shepherdesses go their way, and shortly meet a forlorn damozel named Teolinda, who falls to telling the story of her love-passages with Artidoro, when the interesting recital is interrupted by the sudden entry of Aurelio, Galatea's father. The book closes with a somewhat cynical song from Lenio (who is answered, in verse by Elicio, and in prose by Erastro), with a ballad from Florisa, and with the departure of Lisandro.

In the second book Teolinda completes her story. All her disasters have arisen from her fatal resemblance to her sister Leonarda, who, being taken by Artidoro for Teolinda, gives that too-greatly-daring swain a scornful dismissal. She tells to sympathetic ears how on a tree by Henares' bank, like Rosalind in Arden, she found a poem from her despairing lover in which, with grim significance, he talked of his approaching end. These lugubrious stanzas caused her to quit her native province and wander forth in search of Artidoro : hence her presence here. At this point Damon and Tirsi, on their way to the marriage of their common friend Daranio with Silveria, appear singing alternate stanzas. Hearing Elicio's voice, they find the singer, and Damon introduces Tirsi as the "*Gloria del castellano suelo.*" Later, the singing and sonneteering ended, they meet Silerio, who, with a singular want of reticence, straightway relates to them the adventures of his friend and townsman the Jerezano Timbrio, who, quarrelling with Pransiles, had fled the country, offering his enemy a somewhat vague *rendezvous* at Milan or Naples. Silerio started to join his friend, and putting into a Catalan port, found Timbrio being taken through the streets on his way to the gallows, where he is to be hanged on a false charge of highway robbery. Silerio rescues Timbrio, but himself falls into the hands of justice; and the unfortunate deliverer is in jail under sentence of death when the confusion, caused by a Turkish attack on the port, enables the prisoners to escape. Finally, Silerio, sailing from Barcelona, joins Timbrio at Naples, where he finds his friend enamoured of Nísida. Silerio, always ready to sacrifice himself in friendship's cause, disguises himself as a jester, and, under the name of Astor, obtains entry to Nísida's house, where, singing sonnets in her praise, he ingratiates himself with her parents, secures his footing, and presently finds an opportunity of declaring his friend's passion to the enchantress. Meanwhile he has himself succumbed to her charms, and accidentally discovers the fact to Timbrio, who overhears one of his love-ballads. He is telling how he successfully feigned to Timbrio that his love was not Nísida but her younger sister Blanca, when Daranio's wedding-train enters and the rest of the story is adjourned till the evening.

In the third book Silerio takes up his tale, showing how Nísida, moved by the imminence of Timbrio's duel with Pransiles, avows her love for him, when Mirenio intervenes with a doleful ballad denouncing Silveria, who—according to the jilted singer—is about to wed Daranio from mercenary motives. Silerio, continuing, relates how he undertook, in case of Timbrio's success against Pransiles, to return with a white scarf tied round his arm, and how, in the haste and excitement occasioned by his friend's triumph, he forgot the token. Nísida, seeing him thus returning, fell into a faint so profound that she was taken for dead, and Timbrio fled the country in despair. In Naples, in Jerez, and in Toledo Silerio sought his friend in vain, and finally abandoning the hopeless quest he settled down to a life of melancholy shepherding.

Next day, Mirenio's grief at the faithlessness and venality of Silveria breaks out anew in the form of sixteen stanzas. But no providential catastrophe intervenes to save him; the marriage takes place, and the day closes with an almost interminable series of songs from the lovesick swains Orompo, Marsilio, Crisio, and Orfenio. Damon, too, discourses on artless jealousy, the injured lover's hell, and is only cut short by the entry of Francenio, Lauso, and the elderly Arsindo, who chaunt their lays in the approved manner.

In the fourth book we find Teolinda setting forth once more in quest of Artidoro. As Galatea and Florisa accompany her on the road they meet with some sportsmen, to whom enter two shepherdesses, one of whom, named Rosaura, addresses the principal horseman of the party — one Grisaldo — with extreme violence. Grisaldo's crime is that, deceived by, and perhaps weary of, Rosaura's simulated disdain, he has engaged himself as a *pis aller* to Leopersia. The unlucky man defends himself as well as may be from the attack of the angry damsel, who thereon endeavours to commit suicide ; she is prevented by Grisaldo and by the attendant nymph, who is discovered to be Teolinda's sister Leonarda. Satisfactory explanations are interchanged; and Grisaldo, repenting his weak inconstancy, passes on, forgiven. Rosaura, in the true pastoral manner, tells the bystanders her story, which is to the effect that, wishing to pique Grisaldo, she had flirted with Artandro so flagrantly and so successfully that Grisaldo fell in with his family's desire that he should marry Leopersia. This, however, was more than Rosaura could bear, and accordingly she had set out in quest of the faithless one, with what good result we have seen. Leonarda, following, tells how the synchronous disappearance of Teolinda and Artidoro had forced upon the charitable public the conclusion that the two had eloped. Search was made, and Artidoro's double, Galercio, was wrongfully arrested. After divers adventures Galercio was released; but not before Leonarda was deeply in love with him.

The shepherds meanwhile are not idle. Meeting a company of strangers by the way, Damon, after a brief conversation on the advantages of a pastoral life, sings them one of Lauso's songs, and the misogamist Lenio, like Sydney Smith's Scotch girl, discourses on love in the abstract. Just as he is beginning, Aurelio, Galatea, and her train, appear. Lenio's lecture ends, as usual, with a song, and the scandalised Tirsi replies for the other side. Elicio incidentally gathers that one of Galatea's companions is Nísida, and further learns that Timbrio is present. Mutual explanations are interchanged, and Darinto rides off to find Silerio. The episode of Galercio's love for Gelasia is then introduced, and both Teolinda and Leonarda go into hysterics, one of them taking Gelasia's lover for Artidoro; while the other — correctly enough — believes him to be Galercio.

In the fifth book we find Timbrio, Nísida, and Blanca outside the dwelling of Silerio, listening to his song. In the moonlight Timbrio gives forth a quatrain in reply, and Silerio, recognising his old friend's voice, comes out and learns how Timbrio found Nísida and Blanca on board the vessel in which he himself set sail for Jerez; how, falling in with a fleet of Algerine corsairs commanded by Arnaut Mamí, they were captured; and how the galley which bore them was separated from the rest of the squadron, and, finally, was driven by stress of weather into the same Catalan port where Silerio had rescued Timbrio.

At this point Aurelio arrives with the news that Darinto, whom he has left profoundly dejected on account of his hopeless love for Blanca, is being consoled by Elicio and Erastro. The company set forth to seek him; but Darinto has vanished, and, to the general surprise, Elicio and Erastro are found in the last extremity of despair. The reason is soon apparent. Damon learns from Elicio that Galatea is to be married to a rich Portuguese suitor, and the two swains mingle their sympathetic tears. Turning towards the village, Damon and Elicio pass eight armed maskers who also make for the village by another path. Later, they

find Galatea singing her woes in melodious stanzas to
Florisa, Rosaura, and the rest. As she seems averse
to the match, Elicio is emboldened to offer her his
assistance ; but, as she is about to answer, the eight
maskers reappear, and, overpowering Elicio and Damon,
carry off Rosaura. The ringleader discovers himself to
be Artandro, and avers that Rosaura is affianced to him.
Elicio and Damon return crestfallen to the hamlet,
where they learn that Silerio, resigned to the loss of
Nísida, is betrothed to Blanca. Naturally, every one
sings, and Lauso appears cured of his love by the fair
one's high disdain. This falling away is atoned for by
an announcement on the part of the elderly Arsindo—
who has entered with Maurisa—that the cynical Lenio,
who but yesterday scoffed at love, has found salvation
in the person of Gelasia. Maurisa's tidings are still
more remarkable, for she proclaims that Galercio also is
enamoured of Gelasia, and that Artidoro is married to
Leonarda (who has passed herself off as Teolinda); while
the forlorn Teolinda is only sustained by directing her
regard towards Galercio, who, naturally enough, is
somewhat embarrassed by these attentions. Maurisa,
accompanied by Arsindo, hastens away to inform
Grisaldo of Rosaura's abduction, leaving the rest to
marvel whether it be really with justice that "Young
men think old men fools."

Finally the venerable priest Telesio, entering, bids
the shepherds come on the morrow to the cypress valley
(where Meliso's ashes lie), and assist at the ceremony
which takes place yearly on the anniversary of that

famous shepherd's death. Then the repentant Lenio comes forward; and with his formal recantation of old heresies the section closes.

The last book opens with the memorial rites for Meliso—no light thing, if, as it should seem, the celebration lasted from dawn till sunset. After Tirsi, Lauso, Damon, and Elicio have sung, the figure of Calliope rises from the cypress-pyre, and the goddess chaunts the names of the contemporary Spanish poets worthy to be filed on fame's eternal bede-roll. More singing follows; and an epidemic of recitation is only stamped out by an attempt on the part of Galercio to commit suicide because of his unrequited passion for Gelasia. Teolinda repeats the twice-told tale of Leonarda's treachery, and Galatea, through Maurisa's hands, sends Elicio a letter begging him to rescue her from this unpalatable marriage. The romance closes with a prospective deputation of remonstrance to Aurelio: and, should this moderate remedy fail, with a determination on the part of the conference of shepherds to terrorise the Portuguese suitor into withdrawing his pretensions.

Nothing is easier than to point out the shortcomings, gross and palpable enough, of the *Galatea.* But great as these deficiencies are, they are due at least as much to the nature of the work as to the author. The underlying idea of the school of pastoral romance was radically vicious. The writers, striving to reproduce in an artistic form the lives of their courtly Troglodytes, were engaged on an impossible task. In the *Galatea* the neglect of a natural background is flagrant; probability goes by the board. The customs and manners of the Arcadians are distinctly quaint. Shepherds stay away from their flocks for a fortnight; and the fact that the hungry sheep look up and are not fed gives them little or no concern.[1] They dwell in a land of leisure; yet, as the day is not long enough, they sit up all night to listen to a comrade's experiences. Their conversation is in the too precious mould of Don Adriano de Armado. We might say of every one of them that he was

> A man in all the world's new fashion planted,
> That hath a mint of phrases in his brain;
> One whom the music of his own vain tongue
> Doth ravish like enchanting harmony.

Ben Jonson's criticism that " Lucan, Sidney, Guarini make every man speak as well as themselves, forgetting decorum," might well include all writers of this exotic style.[2] The author himself is at last driven to apologise for the accomplishments of his puppets.[3] Few things

---

[1] "Consoléle yo lo mejor que supe, y dejándole libre del pasado parasismo, vengo acompañando á esta pastora, y á buscarte á ti, Lauso, que fueres servido, volvamos á nuestras cabañas, pues ha ya diez dias que dellos nos partimos, y podrá ser que nuestros ganados sientan el ausencia nuestra, mas que nosotros la suya."—Galatea, lib. v.

[2] "Ben Jonson's Conversations with William Drummond." Printed for the Shakespeare Society (London, 1842).

[3] "Si conocieras, señor, respondió á esta sazon Elicio, cómo la crianza del nombrado Tirsi no ha sido entre los árboles y florestas, como tú imaginas, sino en las reales cortes y conocidas escuelas, no te maravillaras de lo que ha dicho, sino de lo que ha dejado por decir:

are more amazing than the memories of these Arcadians; every one pours forth poems in profusion, and recites long love-letters word for word. Nothing short of a catastrophe gives them pause. The mere machinery of the story runs halt and creaking. The curious similarity of the characters, the continual repetition of the same device, the incredible villainy of Carino, the sudden introduction and equally abrupt elimination of Lisandro, the quiet indifference of these paragons to human life— though not to human suffering—all point to a meagreness of conception and to a certain poverty of execution. The style is too often stilted; exaggeration is the prevailing note; all the shepherds are *discretos*, all the nymphs *hermosas*, and the entire company are " *todos enamorados, aunque de diferentes pasiones oprimidos.*" The insatiable, eager curiosity, the sensibility which melts into floods of tears, the loquacious confidences and petty dialectics of these mild Lotos-eaters, are all likely to waken mirth in the cold-blooded reader. A bastard classicism, a sickly savour of literary coxcombry reigns throughout. When Lenio and Tirsi discourse on love we feel that their eloquent periods, more suited to the Ilissus than the Tagus, might have obtained them votive statues at Delphi from Phædrus the Myrrinhusian; and even when a harmless allusion to the Guadalquivir is

---

y aunque el desamorado Lenio, por su humildad ha confesado que la rusticidad de su vida pocas prendas de ingenio puede prometer, con todo eso te aseguro que los mas floridos años de su edad gastó, no en el ejercicio de guardar las cabras en los montes, sino en las riberas del claro Tormes en loables estudios y discretas conversaciones."— Galatea, lib. iv.

made we are conscious that the writer has not forgotten his Martial :

Bætis olivifera crinem redimite corona,
  Aurea qui nitidis vellera tingis aquis;
Quem Bromius, quem Pallas amat; cui rector aquarum
  Albula navigerum per freta pandit iter.

Hazlitt's complaint of Sidney's *Arcadia* is to the point. "The original sin of alliteration, antithesis, and metaphysical conceit," the "systematic interpolation of the wit, learning, ingenuity, wisdom and everlasting impertinence of the writer," "the continual, uncalled-for interruptions, analysing, dissecting, disjointing, murdering everything, and reading a pragmatical, self-sufficient lecture over the dead body of nature," are always with us in the *Galatea*.[1]

Like most pastoral novelists, Cervantes strove, with questionable success, to lighten the general monotony and to impart a touch of life and movement to the tale by the continual introduction of secondary episodes. In this, as in many other respects, he has but followed his models. Elicio and Erastro open the story in exactly the same manner as Sannazzaro's Ergasto and Selvaggio ; and the funeral rites for Meliso are but a variant on the Feast of Pales in the *Arcadia*. The *Canto de Caliope*, in which the writer sings the praises of one hundred (for the most part, excessively minor) poets, is an obvious imitation of Gil Polo's *Canto de Turia*. To the introduction of contemporary personages under

---

[1] See William Hazlitt's "Lectures on the Dramatic Literature of the Age of Elizabeth" (London, 1821), pp. 265 *et seq.*

feigned names—a literary vice in all ages—the pastoral school was greatly given. Montemayor as Sereno, Ribeiro as Bimnardel, Sidney as Pyrocles, were all precedents for the introduction of Cervantes himself as Elicio. Gálvez de Montalvo is figured by Siralvo, Luís Barahona de Soto by Lauso, Pedro de Láinez as Damon, Francisco de Figueroa as Tirsi, Alonso de Ercilla as Larsileo, and Pedro Liñán de Riaza as Lenio; while Meliso represents the famous Diego Hurtado de Mendoza who had died some ten years previous to the publication of the *Galatea.* The tradition as to the identity of the female characters is less precise. It has been suggested that Galatea may be the Lisbon lady of whom we have already heard too much; it has been hinted also that she may be Doña Magdalena Pacheco de Sotomayor; but there seems no reason to reject the old hypothesis that by Galatea the writer intended to indicate his future wife, Doña Catalina de Palacios Salazar y Vozmediano. In sketching her, Cervantes may have had before him Sannazzaro's presentation of Carmosina Bonifacia as Amaranta, or even Lorenzo de Medici's picture of his Lucrezia Donati.

Weak as the *Galatea* undoubtedly is, it would be unfair to dismiss it as merely food for laughter. I cannot, indeed, agree with an English critic who declares it to be "an admirable pastoral romance." But, when all deductions are made on the ground of artificiality, prolixity, and faulty invention, we are forced to admit the sustained imagination, the Asiatic luxuriance of

phrase, the rich felicity of epithet, the easy grace and
sonorous rhetoric of many passages which, if not always
appropriate to the context, are undeniably good in
themselves. The extravagant episode of Teolinda and
Leonarda, Artidoro and Galercio — suggested, like the
Comedy of Errors, by the *Menœchmi* of Plautus—is
not very happily worked out; but the adventures of
Timbrio, though abounding in fantastic and improbable
incident, are given with great spirit, and the interest in
his experiences, whether related by himself or by Silerio,
is admirably maintained. Now and then we come across
an autobiographical touch, as in the reference to Arnaut
Mamí, and the writer turns as fondly to "*la famosa
Compluto*" and "*la ribera y el soto del manso Henares*"
as does Fielding to "the pleasant banks of sweetly-
winding Stour."[1] Cervantes lived long enough to see
the absurdities of the pastoral. In his masterpiece, Don
Quixote's niece expresses a very reasonable fear that
her uncle, cured of knight-errantry, may go mad as a
shepherd; and the excellent knight, with his burlesque

---

[1] Cp. the spirited ballad in Agustín Durán's "Romancero"
(Madrid, 1829), vol. ii. p. 140:

"Sulcando el salado campo,
Que el Dios Neptuno gobierna,
Y el licor amargo, á donde
Estan las marinas deas,
Va el fuerte Arnaute Mami," etc.

"A esta sazon dijo Teolinda: Si los oídos no me engañan,
hermosas pastoras, yo creo que teneis hoy en vuestras riberas á los
dos nombrados y famosos pastores Tirsi y Damon, naturales de mi
patria; á lo menos Tirsi, que en la famosa Compluto, villa fundada
en las riberas de nuestro Henares, fué nacido," etc.—Galatea, lib. ii.

nomenclature of Quijotiz, Pancino, Sansonino, Niculoso, Curiambro, Teresona, and the rest, gives abundant ground for alarm.   In the *Coloquio de los Perros*, through the mouth of Berganza, Cervantes showers a flood of good-natured ridicule upon the shepherds and shepherdesses who passed their whole lives " *cantando y tañendo con gaitas, zampoñas, rabeles y churumbelas, y con otros instrumentos extraordinarios.*"

Even if we say the worst, and admit that *Galatea* " is in the very manner of those books of gallantry and chivalry which, with the labyrinths of their style and ' the reason of their unreasonableness,' turned the fine intellects of the Knight of La Mancha," we may still regret that Cervantes never found time to finish it.   It has been cynically observed that a merciful Providence invariably interfered to prevent the completion of pastoral novels, and the instances of Montemayor, Ribeiro, and (in a later age) D'Urfé are to the point. It would, however, have been interesting to see the skilled fingers of the veteran rehandling the old theme once more ; perhaps imparting new life to the dry, dead bones, or—more probably—anticipating Sorel, doing for pastoralism what he had done for the literature of chivalry.   It is certain that the story was always by him.   A few days before his death he was still full of it, still hopeful.   His intention to finish it to-morrow was always excellent.   But that to-morrow was not to be.

> There in seclusion and remote from men
>   The wizard hand lies cold,
> Which at its topmost speed let fall the pen
>   And left the tale half-told.

Ah ! who shall lift that wand of magic power
And the lost clew regain ?
The unfinished window in Aladdin's tower
Unfinished must remain.

Nearly two centuries later, a young French ex-
officer of dragoons, named Jean-Pierre Claris de Florian,
answered this question in his own favour, compressed
the six books of the *Galatea* into three, and modestly
added, on his own account, a fourth book, in which all
the personages, pairing off, marry and live happily ever
afterwards. His version, which is characterised by the
quaint grace and fatal fluency which distinguished all
his work, may be commended to those who are debarred
from reading the original. A few years later, in 1798,
an enterprising Spaniard, Cándido María Trigueros, with
characteristic intrepidity, undertook to improve on both
Cervantes and Florian in *Los Enamorados ó Galatea y
sus bodas.* But this disastrous display is among those
which posterity has most willingly let die ; nor is the
justice of the irrevocable decision likely to be questioned
by any one who has glanced through its pages. It is,
indeed, as Horace Walpole said of the *Arcadia,* "a
tedious, lamentable, pedantic, pastoral romance which
the patience of a young virgin in love cannot now wade
through."

The *aprobación* which precedes the *Galatea* was
signed by Lucas Gracián Dantisco (the author, later, of
the *Galateo Español*) on February 1, 1584, and the
book was probably published during the next twelvemonth. Cervantes is supposed to have written it to
gain the favour of Doña Catalina de Palacios Salazar y

Vozmediano. So far, at least, he was successful. On December 12, 1584, she was married to him at her native town of Esquivias. At this time Cervantes was thirty-seven, and Doña Catalina nineteen, years of age.

APPENDIX TO CHAPTER IV.

BIOGRAPHICAL NOTES ON THE POETS MENTIONED IN THE *CANTO DE CALÍOPE.*

I HAVE compiled the following biographical notices of the poets mentioned in the "Canto de Calíope" from a multitude of sources. It would be impossible to overestimate the value of the contributions of D. Cayetano A. de la Barrera to the edition of the "Obras" produced by Hartzenbusch and Rosell. I have used them freely; but I greatly regret that the majority of my notes were already concluded before I was aware of the existence of Barrera's work. Otherwise I might have spared myself no small amount of labour. In the process of revision I have found my predecessor's ample knowledge and research invaluable, and I have not hesitated to avail myself of his results. I believe I have made a separate statement in each case; but I trust that this more general acknowledgment may not be reckoned insufficient. I have not thought it necessary, in a book intended primarily for English readers, to indulge in the same amount of detail as I should have employed in a book which was to be read by Spaniards. Condensation and compression have been largely used; and the process of minute correction has been, so far as the very incomplete state of my knowledge allows, unremitting. I must finally acknowledge the large extent of my obligations to the Spanish translation of Ticknor.

AGUAYO (JUAN).

AGUILAR (DIEGO DE).—A sonnet by this writer—"Garça en en alto Olympo remontada"—prefaces Enrique Garcés' translation of Camoens. He is probably identical with the Diego de Aguiar (*sic*) whose sonnet, "Que perla tendrá el Indo mar, ó el Moro," is prefixed to López Maldonado's "Cancionero."

ALCÁZAR (BALTASAR DE).—Born at Seville about 1540, and served under Santa Cruz. His contributions to Pedro Espinosa's "Flores de poetas ilustres," with other fugitive verses, may be found in vols. xxxii., xxxv., and xlii. of Rivadeneyra's "Biblioteca de Autores Españoles." His works have been edited by D. José Asensio y Toledo (Seville, 1856), and more recently—in 1878—have been reproduced by the Sociedad de Bibliófilos Andaluces. He died in his native city, January 16, 1606.

ALFONSO (GASPAR).

ALVARADO (PEDRO).

ARGENSOLA.—See LEONARDO DE ARGENSOLA.

ARTIEDA (ANDRÉS REY DE).—Born about 1549. His birthplace is doubtful. (See Antonio, "Bibliotheca Hispana Nova," vol. i. p. 83.) He is claimed both by Valencia and Zaragoza; but on this point Lope de Vega, who must have known him well, is distinct enough in his "Laurel de Apolo" (sc. ii.):

> " Y al capitan Artieda
> Aunque Valencia lamentarse pueda,
> Pondrá en sus cuatro Zaragoza el dia
> Que de la numerosa monarquía
> Apolo nombre un senador supremo,
> Que como aquel celeste Polifemo
> Unico dé su luz á los dos polos
> Pues no es de un siglo para los dos Apolos."

Artieda, like Cervantes, received three wounds at Lepanto. Later on he served in the Netherlands under the Duke of Parma. His valour was conspicuous, and a story is told of his having swum across the Ems in midwinter, under the fire of the enemy, with his sword in his teeth. He is perhaps best known by his "Discursos, epistolas y epigramas de Artemidoro" (Çaragoça, 1605). He died at Valencia, November 16, 1613.

AVALOS Y DE RIBERA (JUAN).

BACA Y DE QUIÑONES (HIERONYMO).—A sonnet and *cancion* by this writer are among the prefatory poems to the "Luzero de la tierra sancta, y grandezas de Egypt, y monte Sinay agora nouamente vistas y escriptas por Pedro de Escobar Cabeça de Vaca" (Valladolid, 1587).

BARAHONA DE SOTO (LUÍS).—Born at Lucena about 1535. His

best known work is, of course, "La primera parte de la Angélica" (Granada, 1586). He is represented in Espinosa's collection; and four of his satires, together with the "Fábula de Acteón," may be found in López de Sedano's "Parnaso Español" (vol. ix. pp. 53–123). Lope refers to him in the "Laurel de Apolo" (sc. ii.). According to Barrera he died at Archidona, November 6, 1595. I am somewhat inclined to doubt the accuracy of this assertion, as Barahona de Soto contributed a complimentary sonnet to Mesa's "Restauración de España" (Madrid, 1607). See Rivadeneyra, vols. xxxv. and xlii.

BAZA (DOCTOR).

BECERRA (DOMINGO DE).—Born at Seville about 1535. He was a prisoner with Cervantes in Algiers, and, like him, was released in 1580. He translated Giovanni della Casa's work, "Il Galateo" (Venecia, 1585). The only edition which I have seen is that included in the polyglot version of "Il Galateo" published at Geneva in 1609. The Latin and German versions are by Nathan Chytræus. The name of the French translator is not given. The French translation varies considerably from that published in Paris in 1562 by Jean du Peyrat.

BERRÍO (GONZALO MATEO DE).—Born about 1550 at Granada, where he studied law. He is mentioned by Lope in the "Dorotea," and again in the "Laurel de Apolo" (sc. ii.) :

> "Mas ya quejoso el celo y el decoro
> Del cristalino Dauro,
> Quiere que tenga oposicion el lauro
> Que bastará el doctísimo Berrío
> Jurisconsulto insigne," etc.

Espinel also refers to him in the prologue of "Marcos de Obregón." In 1599 he signed the *aprobación* of Cairasco's "Templo militante," and in Espinosa's collection he is represented by two sonnets.

CÁIRASCO DE FIGUEROA (BARTOLOMÉ).—Born at the Canaries in 1540, took orders, and became Prior of the Cathedral there. According to Ticknor, his colossal "Templo militante, flos santorum, y triumphos de sus virtudes" was published in four parts : the first at Valladolid in 1602, the second at Valladolid in 1603, the third at Madrid in 1609, and the fourth, posthumously, at Lisbon in 1614. Degenerate readers of to-day may well shrink from attacking this immense work; and their curiosity will probably be satisfied with the selections given by López de Sedano (vol. v. pp. 332–363, vol. vii. pp. 191–216). Mesa's "cándido canonigo Cáirasco" would seem to have been a man of very lovable temperament, judging from the manner in which his contemporaries (by no means inclined to favourable estimates of their rivals) speak of him. He contributed a prefatory poem to Carranza's "Libro de las grandezas de la espada," and is the author of an unpublished version of Ariosto's "Gerusalemme." He died in 1610. See Rivadeneyra, vols. xxxv. and xlii.

CALDERA (BENITO DE) is best known as a translator of Camoens. "Los Lusiadas de Camoes traduzidos en octava rima Castellaña por Benito Caldera" appeared at Alcalá de Henares in 1580. There is a prefatory letter commendatory by Láinez, with prefatory sonnets by Láinez, Garay, Luís de Montalvo, and Vergara. In the same year Luís Gómez published another version of Camoens at Salamanca.

CAMPUZANO (FRANCISCO). — A doctor practising at Alcalá de Henares, of which place he seems to have been a native. A poetical epistle by this writer is printed in López Maldonado's "Cancionero" (ff. 120–122); and from a poem of López Maldonado's (f. 125) it is clear that Campuzano was a widower in 1586. A "Cancion al seraphico sant Francisco" by Campuzano may be found in Padilla's "Jardín Espiritual" (ff. 223–226). He contributed a prefatory poem to Gracián Dantisco's "Galateo Español."

CANGAS (FERNANDO DE).—"El culto Cangas" would seem to have been an especial favourite with Mesa, who has dedicated a sonnet to him in the "Rimas" (f. 230). Mesa again refers to him in the "Restauración de España" (lib. x. st. 108).

CANTORAL.—See LOMAS.

CARRANZA (HIERONIMO).—Born at Seville, 1552. The date of his birth is inferred from the title-page of his "Philosophia y destreza de las armas," published, with a copy of dedicatory verses to the Duque de Medina Sidonia, at Sanlúcar de Barrameda in 1582. In 1589 Carranza became Governor of Honduras. The "Libro de las grandezas de la espada, en que se declaran muchos secretos del que compuso el Comendador Geronimo de Carrança" (edited by Luys Pacheco de Narvaez) was published at Madrid in 1600. Bobadil admitted Carranza's authority. See his speech to Master Mathew (*Every Man in his Humour*, Act. i. sc. 4): "By the foot of Pharoah, an 'twere my case now, I should send him a chartel presently. The

bastinado   a most proper and sufficient dependence, warranted by
the great Carranza."

CARVAJAL (GUTIERRE).

CERVANTES SAAVEDRA (GONZALO).—Barrera thinks that the reference may be to the author of a novel entitled "Los Pastores del
Betis."   I am not acquainted with this work.   *

COLOMA (JUAN), Conde de Elda.—Born at Elda in Alicante.
Published at Caller, in 1576, the "Década de la Pasion de Jesu
Christo."   Luís Zapata refers to him in the "Carlo famoso"
(c. xxxviii.) :

> "La honrra don Iuã Coloma, y de una fuẽte
>   Van todos a beuer en competencia."

He became Governor of Sardinia, and in his later years lost his sight.
His son, Alonso Coloma, contributed two prefatory poems to Mosquera de Figueroa's "Elogio" on Santa Cruz (f. 175).

CÓRDOBA (MAESTRO).—His chief title to fame is that he had
Lope de Vega for a pupil.   The scholar has introduced the teacher
in the "Laurel de Apolo" (sc. iv.) :

> " Hoy á las puertas de su templo llama
>   Una justa memoria,
>   Digna de honor y gloria,
>   Antes que pase el alto Guadarrama
>   Que mi maestro Córdoba me ofrece
>   Y las musas latinas me dan voces
>   Pues con tan justa causa la merece.

CUEVA Y SILVA (FRANCISCO DE LA).—Born at Medina del Campo
about 1550.   His reputation as a lawyer was immense.   He is
represented in Espinosa, and contributed a prefatory poem to Escobar
Cabeça de Vaca's "Luzero de la tierra sancta."   Lope de Vega's
"Mal Casada" is dedicated to him, and he is mentioned in the
"Laurel de Apolo" (sc. iii.).   Cp. also Quevedo's sonnet in the
"Parnaso Español" (Melpomene) :

> " Este, en traje de túmulo, museo,
>   Sepulcro, en academia transformado,
>   En donde está en cenizas desatado,
>   Iason, Liango, Bartulo y Orfeo ;
>   Este polvo, que fué de tanto reo
>   Asilo, dulcemente razonado,
>   Cadaver de las leyes consultado,

En quien, si lloro el fin, las glorias leo ;
  Este de Don Francisco de la Cueva
Fué prision que su vuelo nos advierte
Donde piedad y mérito le lleva.
  Todas les leyes, con discurso fuerte
Venció ; y ansí parece cosa nueva,
Que le vinciese, siendo ley, la muerte."

Cueva is reputed to have written a play entitled *El Bello Adonis.*
(Cp. Rojas, "Viaje Entretenido," p. 126.)

CUEVA (JUAN DE LA).—Born in Seville about 1550. His "Conquista de la Bética, Ejemplar poetico," and "Inventores de las Cosas," are well known. Examples of his style are given in López de Sedano (vols. viii. and ix.). The "Coro Febeo de romances historiales " was published at Seville in 1587, and his dramatic works in 1588. The date of his death is uncertain. See Rivadeneyra, vols. x., xvi., and xlii.

DAZA (LICENCIADO).

DÍAZ (FRANCISCO).—Lecturer on Philosophy and Medicine at the University of Alcalá de Henáres. He published a " Compendio de Cirujía " at Madrid in 1575, but I have not met with any of his poems.

DURÁN (DIEGO).—The eighth prefatory poem to López Maldonado's "Cancionero" is by this writer. His lines are so full of grace and polish—*e.g.* in the sonnet :

  " Raro pintor de la encendida llama "—

that one would willingly know more of his work.

ERCILLA (ALONSO DE).—Born at Madrid, August 7, 1533. He began life as Court page to Philip II. After eight years of South American campaigning he returned to Spain in 1562. Seven years later the first part of " La Araucana " appeared ; the second part was issued in 1578, and the third part in 1590. A Dutch version by Byl was published at Rotterdam in 1619. A French translation by Gilibert de Merlhiac was issued in 1824, and another, by Alexandre Nicholas, was published at Paris in 1869. A German version was produced at Nürnberg in 1831 by C. M. Winterling.

The exact date of Ercilla's death is unknown, but it seems safe to assume that it was not later than 1595 ("Laurel de Apolo," sc. iv.).

ESCOBAR (BALTASAR DE).—Born at Seville about 1555. His productions, so far as I know them, are limited to those included in Espinosa's collection. A complimentary letter to Virués on the publication of "El Monserrate" is given in Rivadeneyra's sixty-second volume.

ESPINEL (VICENTE).—Born at Ronda in December, 1550. After a brief career as a soldier he took orders. His chief works are his "Diversas Rimas" (Madrid, 1591), and his "Relaciones del escudero Marcos de Obregón" (Madrid, 1618). The *espinelas* are named after him, and he is said to have added the fifth string to the guitar, neither of which innovations met with Lope de Vega's approval: "perdóneselo Dios á Vicente Espinel que nos trujo esta novedad y las cinco cuerdas de la guitarra con que ya se van olvidando los instrumentos nobles" ("Dorotea," Act i. sc. 8). An English translation of "Marcos de Obregón" was published by Major Algernon Langton (London, 1816), and a German version by Ludwig Tieck was issued at Breslau in 1827.

Espinel died at Madrid, February 4, 1624 ("Laurel de Apolo," sc. i.).

ESPINOSA (SILVESTRE).

ESTRADA (ALONSO DE).

FALCÓN (JAIME JUAN).—Born at Valencia, 1522. His "Quadratura circuli" (Valencia, 1587) and his posthumous "Obras poeticas latinas" (Madrid, 1600) are his chief productions. Some of his Latin epigrams, with metrical translations into Spanish, may be found (pp. 55–63) in a small volume entitled "Poesías selectas de varios autores latinos" (Tarragona, 1684). An earlier reprint of his Latin epigrams appeared at Valencia in 1647. His name occurs in the "Canto de Turia":

> "A tí, que alcanzarás tan larga parte
> Del agua poderosa de Pegaso,
> A quien de Poësia el estandarte
> Darán los moradores de Parnaso,
> Noble Falcón, no quiero aquí alabarte,
> Porque de tí la fama hará tal caso,
> Que ha de tener particular cuidado
> Que desde Indo al Mauro estés nombrado."

Falcón died at Madrid, August 31, 1594.

FERNÁNDEZ DE PINEDA (RODRIGO).

FERNÁNDEZ DE SOTOMAYOR (GONZALO).

FIGUEROA (FRANCISCO DE).—Though it has been stated that this

very eminent writer was a Portuguese, there can be little doubt that
he was born at Alcalá de Henares about the year 1535. After
serving in the Spanish army he lived some years in Italy, where
he became an accomplished scholar. He is little known in England;
but those who are acquainted with his poems will assuredly admit
that the immense reputation which he enjoys in Spain is not
undeserved. The date of his death is uncertain; but it is known
that his "Obras en verso"—which he ordered to be destroyed—were
published posthumously at Lisbon in 1625.

FRÍAS (DAMASIO DE).—This Castilian writer is mentioned by
Espinel in the "Casa de la Memoria" (c. ii.). The only specimens
of his work with which I am acquainted are those printed in López
de Sedano's "Parnaso Español" (vol. ii. pp. 346–352, and vol. vii.
pp. 53–57) and the *canción* in the "Floresta."

GÁLVEZ DE MONTALVO (LUIS).—Born at Guadalajara about 1545.
His novel, "El Pastor de Fílida," was published at Madrid in 1582.
The *aprobación* is signed by Pedro de Láinez. He was drowned at
Palermo in 1591. Rivadaneyra (vol. xxxii.) prints a "Juicio crítico
acerca de Cristóbal de Castillejo."

GARAY (MAESTRO).—Espinel mentions this writer in the "Casa
de la Memoria" (c. ii.); and Lope de Vega in the "Arcadia" styles
him a *divino ingenio*. See also the "Laurel de Apolo" (sc. iv.).
Some specimens of his work are given in Rivadeneyra's forty-second
volume.

GARCERÁN DE BORJA (PEDRO LUÍS).—Born about 1538. He was
Captain-General of Oran, possibly about the time of Cervantes'
captivity. Gil Polo names him in the "Canto de Turia":

> "Quando en el grande Borja, de Montesa
> Maestre tan magnánimo imagino,
> Que en versos y en qualquier excelsa empresa
> Ha de mostrar valor alto y divino," etc.

He was Captain-General of Catalonia when he died, March 20, 1592.

GARCÉS (HENRIQUE).—In 1591 "Los sonetos y canciones del
Poeta Francisco Petrarcha que traduzia Henrique Garces de lengua
Thoscana en Castellano" appeared at Madrid. In the same year,
while the writer was in Lima, "Los Lusiadas de Luys de Camoes,
Traduzidos de Portugues en Castellano por Henrique Garces" also
appeared at Madrid. Pedro de Padilla signed the *aprobación*.

García Romero.

Gil Polo (Gaspar).—Born at Valencia and filled the Greek chair there. While still a very young man his continuation of Montemayor's "Diana Enamorada" appeared (Valencia, 1564). It seems probable that he was yet living in 1615.

Girón y de Rebolledo (Alonso).—Born at Valencia in 1530. He published "La Pasion de Nuestro Señor Jesu Christo segun San Juan" (Valencia, 1563), a work which I have not seen, although it has passed through not less than three editions. The name of this writer may be found in the "Canto de Turia":

> "Tendreis un don Alonso, que el renombre
> De ilustres Rebolledos dilatando
> En todo el universo irá su nombre
> Sobre Marón famoso levantando," etc.

He should, of course, be carefully distinguished from Count Bernardino de Rebolledo, the author of the "Ocios," "La Constancia virtuosa," "Selvas Dánicas," etc. A laudatory sonnet by this writer is prefixed to the "Diana Enamorada" of Gil Polo.

Gómez de Luque (Gonzalo).—Born at Córdoba, and published the "Libro primero de los famosos hechos del principe Don Celidon de Iberia" at Alcalá de Henares in 1583. I have not met with this book, and the only poems by this writer with which I have any acquaintance are (1) a prefatory poem—"Donde de flores variedad no poco"—in López Maldonado's "Cancionero," and (2) some verses reprinted in Pedro de Padilla's "Jardín Espiritual" (f. 231).

Góngora y Argote (Luis de).—Born at Córdoba, June 11, 1561. He was educated at Salamanca, but appears not to have proceeded to his degree. In 1605, while a middle-aged man, Góngora took orders, and was appointed Canon of the Cathedral in his native city. He died at Córdoba, May 23, 1627. Most English readers probably know him best as the "jeune bachelier corduan . . . le plus beau génie que l'Espagne ait jamais produit," mentioned by Fabrice in "Gil Blas" (vii. 13). His poems, edited by Juan López de Vicuña, were first printed at Madrid in 1627. The second edition, edited by Gonzalo de Hozes y Córdoba, was published in 1633.

Gracián Dantisco (Lucas de).—The son of Charles V.'s secretary, he himself became secretary to Philip II. He wrote an imitation of della Casa's book under the title of "Galateo Español, de lo que se debe hazer y guardar en la comun conversacion por ser bien quisto y amado de las gentes" (Barcelona, 1594), to which Gálvez de Montalvo, Francisco de Campuzano, Lope de Vega, and Gaspar de Morales, contributed prefatory poems. Sir William Stirling-Maxwell ("Annals of the Artists of Spain," London, 1848, i. 416) says this writer was "an amateur painter of no mean skill."

GUZMÁN (FRANCISCO DE).—The "Triumphos Morales" and the "Decretos de Sabios" of this writer were both published at Alcalá de Henares in 1565. An edition of the "Triumphos Morales" is said to have been published at Antwerp in 1557, but I have not seen it. He is best known as a *glosador* of Jorge de Manrique's "Coplas."

HERRERA (FERNANDO DE).—Born at Seville about 1534. His admiration for Garcilaso de la Vega led him to produce his "Anotaciones" (Seville, 1580). His poems, published at Seville in 1582, placed him at a bound in the first rank as a lyrical poet. In his own country his reputation is as high as ever. He died at Seville in 1597.

HUETE (PEDRO DE).—A sonnet commendatory by this writer may be found in the "Versos espirituales" of the Dominican monk Pedro de Enzinas (Cuenca, 1597). The title-page bears the name Ezinas (*sic*); but the misprint, like most of those in the Spanish books of that time, is hideously obvious. Huete himself was a Jeromite friar, and was Procurador-General when Enzina's book was published.

IRANZO (LÁZARO LUÍS).—Two sonnets by this writer may be found in Rivadeneyra, vol. iv. pp. 180, 364.

LÁINEZ (PEDRO DE).—The work of this excellent poet, whose name is frequently met with in the *aprobaciones* of the period, is known to us chiefly through Espinosa's collection, the "Flores de poetas ilustres." A poem by Láinez may be found in Padilla's "Jardín Espiritual" (ff. 226–230). His contemporary reputation was undoubtedly high. Cp. the "Laurel de Apolo" (sc. iv.) and also Lope de Vega's "Arcadia":

> "Vaya tambien la fama
> Amante Apolo de la verde rama
> El nombre dilatando
> Por cuanto cielo el sol los polos mide

"De Pedro de Láinez celebrando
  La pura estrella, que á la noche impide
  El paso original, que maldecia
  El que esperaba tras la noche el dia."

LEIVA (ALONSO DE).—I know nothing of this poet's work, but the character of his talent is gathered from Espinel's "Casa de Memoria" ("Diversas Rimas," f. 43):

"El animo gentil, el dulce llanto,
  El blando estilo, con que enternecido
  Don Alonso de Leyua quando canta
  A Venus enamora, á Marte espanta."

Cp. also Mesa's "Restauración de España" (lib. x. s. 92).

LEÓN (LUÍS DE).—Born at Belmonte in 1528. He entered the Augustinian Order and became Professor of Theology at Salamanca in 1561. Twelve years later he was arrested by order of the Inquisition on a charge of having translated the Song of Solomon into the vernacular for a nun. The more general accusation of heresy was afterwards brought against him. After an imprisonment of five years he was acquitted and returned to his professorial chair. His "Perfecta Casada" was published in 1583, and in 1588 he published St. Teresa's writings, of which he had been appointed editor. His health was completely broken by his imprisonment, and the last years of his life were a burden to him. Fortunately for himself he died in 1591. His poetical works remained unpublished till they were given to the world by Quevedo in 1631. Cp. the "Laurel de Apolo" (sc. iv.).

LEONARDO DE ARGENSOLA (BARTOLOMÉ).—Born at Barbastro in 1564, and, like his elder brother, studied at Huesca. In 1609 he published his "Conquista de las Islas Malacas" at Madrid, and in May, 1610, went with the Conde de Lemos to Naples, where he made a very considerable figure during the next six years. His "Anales de Aragón" appeared at Zaragoza in 1630. He died in 1631, and in 1634 were published at Madrid "Las Rimas que se han podido recoger de Lupercio, y del Doctor Bartolomé Leonardo de Argensola."

LEONARDO DE ARGENSOLA (LUPERCIO).—Born at Barbastro in 1562. His life was spent in the service of the crown. He is the author of the tragedies *Isabela*, *Filis*, and *Alejandra*. The first and third of these were published by López de Sedano (vol. vi. pp. 312–524). *Filis* would seem to be irrevocably lost. Though highly praised, the contemporary success of these plays would appear to have been slight; hence, perhaps, the prominent part taken by this writer in the entire suppression of theatrical performances in 1598. He formed part of the suite of the Conde de Lemos, and died at Naples, March 13, 1613. His poems, with those of his brother, were published posthumously at Madrid in 1634, as stated above.

LIÑÁN DE RIAZA (PEDRO) is said to been born at Calatayud. Agustín de Rojas, in the "Viaje Entretenido" (Madrid, 1603), mentions him as a distinguished writer of comedies; Ximénez Patón, using the word *aliñanado*, "que es decir imita á Liñán," gives us some glimpse of Liñán's vogue at the time ("Mercurius Trismegistus," p. 61): and with Lope de Vega he would seem to have been an especial favourite. His comedies have not reached us, but some fine specimens of his work, *e.g.*,

> "Los pámpanos sarmientos
> El estío va trocando,"

may be found in the "Romancero General."

An excellent edition of Liñán's poems was published by the *Diputación Provincial* of Zaragoza in 1876, in the first volume (Sección Literaria) of the "Biblioteca de Escritores Aragoneses." Lope de Vega ("Laurel de Apolo," sc. iv.) introduces him as an *Ingenio raro y dulce, aunque severo.*

LOMAS CANTORAL (HIERONIMO DE).—The "Obras" of this writer were published at Madrid in 1578. The first nine ff. contain a "Tradvcion de Las Piscatorias del Thansillo." The originals, (1) "L' ire del mar, che tempestoso sona," (2) "Qual tempo avrò giammai, che non sia breve," and (3) "Tu che da me lontana, ora gradita," are the Canzoni numbered VII., VIII., and IX. (pp. 109–120) in the "Poesie liriche edite ed inedite di Luigi Tansillo con prefazione e noti di F. Fiorentino" (Napoli, 1882).

LÓPEZ MALDONADO.—Born at Toledo. The dates of his birth and death are alike unknown. His "Cancionero" (Madrid, 1586), which contains some *décimas* by Cervantes, together with a prefatory sonnet by the same hand, found a place of honour in Don Quixote's library. He contributed a sonnet to Padilla's "Jardín Espiritual" (f. 230).

Luján.—It has been suggested to me that the Isidro de Luján— "de Madrid gloria"—referred to in Lope de Vega's "Jerusalén" (lib. xv. and xvii.), may have some direct connection with this personage. I can scarcely imagine anything more unlikely. May not the reference be to Mateo Luján de Sayavedra, the pseudonymous writer of the second part of "Guzmán de Alfarache"?

Maldonado (Hernando).

Martínez de Ribera (Diego).

Medina (Francisco de).—Born at Seville about 1550. Some of his verses may be found in Herrera's "Anotaciones." He died at Seville, March 20, 1615. See Rivadeneyra, xxxii.

Mendoza (Diego de).—It is possible that this may refer to the great proconsul who died in 1575. If so, he is the only dead poet mentioned in the "Canto de Calíope." On the other hand two sonnets—"Pedis, Reyna, un Soneto, ya lo hago," and "Ya commienza el inuierno rigoroso"—are printed in the "Flores de poetas ilustres" (ff. 65 and 79) as late as 1605, by a Diego de Mendoza, who would seem to be an entirely different person.

Mendoza (Francisco de).—Barrera thinks this must refer to the Francisco Lasso de Mendoza who wrote the sixth sonnet prefatory—"Si al claro ilustre son, que con victoria"—to Luis Gálvez de Montalvo's "Pastor de Fílida."

Mesa (Cristóbal de).—Born at Zafra about 1560. The chief works of this voluminous writer are "Las Navas de Tolosa" (Madrid, 1594), "La Restauración de España" (Madrid, 1607), the "Valle de lágrimas" (Madrid, 1607), and "El Patrón de España" (Madrid, 1611). He translated the "Æneid" and the "Georgics," and is the author of the tragedy "Pompeyo" (Madrid, 1615).

Meztanza (Juan de).—This writer is mentioned again in the "Viaje del Parnaso." I have not seen any of his work, nor can I recall any other allusion to him.

Montesdoca (Pedro de).—The only specimen of Montesdoca which I know is prefixed to Espinel's "Diversas Rimas," and as a unique example of his style it may be given here.

> " Produzga en vano el Indico terreno
> Plantas de olor suaue, y peregrino,
> Que si otro tiempo fue precioso, y fino,
> Ya de su estima se conoce ageno :

" Ya nueve planta el mundo tiene lleno
De otro mas soberano olor diuino :
Ya estan rendidas al dichoso Espino
El hardo puro, el Amaranto ameno ;
  Ya famoso Espinel, por vos la planta
De vuestro nombre, esparze mil olores,
Con q̃ el Pindo se alegra, y se enriquece :
  Ya solo vuestro nombre allí se canta,
Ya declarado està, que vuestros flores
Se dĕ por premio al que Laurel merece."

MORALES (ALONSO DE).—Scarcely anything by this writer appears
to have survived (at least in print), though his work would seem to
have been extensive in range if the reference of Agustín de Rojas
in the "Viaje Entretenido" (p. 131) be taken literally.

" De los farsantes que han hecho
  farsas, loas, bayles, letras,
  son Alonso de Morales
  Grajales, Zorita Mesa," etc.

I presume he is the author of the two romances—"Las Princesas
encantadas"—in Durán's collection. See Rivadeneyra, xvi.

MOSQUERA DE FIGUEROA (CRISTÓBAL).—Born at Seville, 1553.
He wrote the preface to Fernando de Herrera's "Relación de la
guerra de Cipre" (Sevilla, 1572), and some of his verse is included
in the same writer's "Anotaciones." His most important work,
however, is his "Comentario en breve compendio de disciplina
militar" (Madrid, 1596), which includes the official eulogy on Santa
Cruz, in whose honour Cervantes contributed a sonnet (f. 177).
His eulogy on Alonso de Ercilla, prefixed to the edition of the
"Araucana" published at Brussels in 1592, is well known. He
died at Écija in 1610.

MURILLO (DIEGO).—Born at Zaragoza about 1555. He entered
the Franciscan Order, and obtained a certain reputation as a preacher.
Some of his religious writings have reached us and, if the "Fun-
dacion milagrosa de la capilla angelica y apostolica de la Madre del
Dios del Pilar" (Barcelona, 1616) may be taken as a fair example of
his style of sacred eloquence, one may freely rejoice at the loss of the
remainder. His poems, published under the title of "Divina, dulce
y provechosa poesia" (Zaragoza, 1616), though, in my judgment,

almost invariably affected, mawkish, and tumid, have been much
admired.

ORENA (BALTASAR).

PACHECO (FRANCISCO).—Born at Jerez de la Frontera in 1535.
He took orders and became Canon of Seville Cathedral. He was
a prolific writer of fugitive Latin verse, in which sort some of his
productions may be seen in the cathedral at Seville. He died in
1599, and should be distinguished from his nephew and namesake,
the author of the "Arte de la pintura."

PADILLA (PEDRO DE).—Born at Linares de Baeza about 1530.
The "Eglogas pastoriles" (Sevilla, 1582), "Romancero" (Madrid,
1583), and "Jardín Espiritual" (Madrid, 1585) represent his best
work. The "Romancero" is of peculiar interest to the Cervantista,
for while Cervantes contributed a prefatory sonnet, his old master,
Juan López de Hoyos, signed the *aprobación*. Padilla's "Romancero" has recently (Madrid, 1880) been splendidly reproduced by
the Sociedad de Bibliófilos Españoles, under the editorship of the
Marqués de la Fuensanta del Valle. In later life Padilla joined
the Carmelite Order. He died at Madrid, August, 1585.

PARIENTE (COSME).

PICADO (ALONSO).

RIBERA (SANCHO DE).—I have not met with any original work
by this writer, nor have I any large recollection of references to his
productions among the authors of his time. There is, however,
a sonnet addressed to him by Henrique Garcés in that writer's
"Sonetos y canciones de Francisco Petrarcha."

> " Sancho, que augmento das con tu ribera,
>   a la que del biscipite Parnaso
>   baxa, por beneficio de Pegaso
>   que si por el, quiça no paresciera,
> Pues con vena corres tan entera
>   que della lleno tienes el Ocaso,
>   supplicote consientas qu' en mi vaso
>   pueda al menos coger vna gotera.
>   Que espero que con ella la dureza,
>   qu' es à mis versos como vn mal de herencia,
>   se conuierta en torrente de dulçura
> Obrando en ellos como leuadura
>   de aquella mal hallada quinta essencia
>   que buelue al cobre en oro con presteza."

Rufo (Juan Gutiérrez).—Born at Córdoba, 1535. He is best known by his "Austriada," published in 1582. The earliest edition which I have seen is that published at Alcalá de Henares in 1586. I am not acquainted with "Los seyscientos apotegmas de Juan Rufo y otras obras en verso" (Toledo, 1596).

Salcedo.—This probably refers to the Juan de Salcedo Villandrando who contributed a prefatory sonnet to Diego d'Avalos y Figueroa's "Miscelánea Austral" (Lima, 1602).

Sánchez (Francisco).—Born at Las Brozas in 1523. This illustrious scholar is best known, perhaps, as "El Brocense." He was Professor of Greek and Rhetoric at Salamanca, and his place among contemporary scholars is deservedly high. The most complete edition, so far as I know, is the "Opera omnia," in four volumes (Geneva, 1766). He edited Garcilaso (Salamanca, 1581), Juan de Mena (Salamanca, 1582), Horace (Salamanca, 1591), Vergil (Salamanca, 1591), Politian's "Silvae" (Salamanca, 1596), Ovid (Salamanca, 1598), and Persius (Salamanca, 1599). A posthumous commentary on Epictetus was published in 1612. His "Paradoxa" appeared at Antwerp in 1582. A "Grammatica Reformata, or a General Examination of the Art of Grammar, as it hath been successively delivered by Franciscus Sanctius in Spain, Gaspar Scioppius in France, Gerardus Joannes Vossius in Lower Germany," was "designed for initiating the Lower Forms in the Free-School of Newark upon Trent," by John Twells, Schoolmaster (London, 1683). "A Practical Grammar of the Latin Tongue," founded on Sánchez, was published in London as late as 1729. (Cp. "Laurel de Apolo," sc. iii.) Sánchez died at Salamanca in January, 1601.

Santisteban y Osorio (Diego de).—Born at León. He became a soldier, and wrote a fourth and fifth part to the "Araucana" (Salamanca, 1597). Another edition—the only one which I know —was published at Barcelona in 1598. "Las guerras de Malta y toma de Malta" appeared at Madrid in 1599.

Sanz de Portillo (Andrés).

Sanz de Zumeta (Juan).—Born at Seville. His sonnet "Al saco de Cádiz" is given by Juan Antonio Pellicer in the "Vida de Cervantes" ("Don Quixote," vol. i. p. lxxxvi., Madrid, 1797).

> "¿De que sirve la gala y gentileza,
>   Las bandas, los penachos matizados,
>   Los forros roxos, verdes y lesnados,
>   Si pide armas el tiempo con presteza?

" Quando lleva robada la riqueza
  De Cádiz el Britano, y profanados
  Dexa templos y altares consagrados :
  Eterna infamia, o España, á tu grandeza :
Quando el amigo llora del amigo
  Los daños, y lloramos las deshonras
  De nuestra lealtad amargamente :
Quando en desprecio nuestro el enemigo
  Con palabras ensalza nuestras honras :
  Y el Dios de los atunes lo consiente."

SARMIENTO Y CARVAJAL (DIEGO DE).—Barrera thinks that the allusion refers to the fourth Conde de Portoalegre, who was ambassador at Lisbon.   He was wounded at Al-kasr al-Kebir, and later became Captain-General of Portugal.   I have never seen any of his verse.

SILVA (JUAN DE).—It may be conjectured that this is the Conde de Portoalegre whose "Introducción" is prefixed to Mendoza's "Guerra de Granada."

SORIA.—I have very little doubt that this writer is identical with the Licenciado Pedro de Soria whose sonnet, "Aqui de un grande ingenio consagrada," is prefixed to the "Obras" of Hieronimo de Lomas Cantoral.

SUÁREZ DE SOSA (FRANCISCO).—Barrera describes him as doctor, philosopher, and poet.

TERRAZAS (FRANCISCO DE).—The author, I presume, of the sonnet, "Soñé que de una peña me arrojaba," in the "Floresta."

TOLEDO (BALTASAR DE).

VALDÉS (ALONSO DE).—The only writing of this author which I can recall is the Prologue (in praise of poetry) to Espinel's "Diversas Rimas," from which it would appear that in 1591 Valdés was secretary to Rodrigo de Mendoza.

VARGAS MANRIQUE (LUÍS DE).—Born at Toledo, and served for some years in the army.   Prefatory sonnets by this writer may be found in the "Galatea" and in the "Cancionero" of López Maldonado.   Barrera accepts the statement (p. 218) of García de Salcedo Coronel (Madrid, 1648) that Góngora's sonnet, "Tu cuyo ilustre entre una y otra almena," is dedicated to Luís de Vargas Manrique. D. Adolfo de Castro (Rivadeneyra, vol. xxxii. p. 430) follows an earlier editor, Gonzalo de Hozes y Córdoba (p. 8) in his assertion that this sonnet is dedicated to the Court Chronicler, Tomás Tamayo de Vargas. See "Laurel de Apolo" (sc. iv.).

> ". . . aquel mancebo ilustre y desdichado
> Don Luís de Vargas, que las ondas fieras
> Del mar Tirreno tienen sepultado."

VEGA (DAMIÁN DE).—This writer is said to have been born at Salamanca. According to Barrera, a sonnet from his pen may be found prefixed to the "Viaje y naufragios del Macedonio" by Juan Bautista de Loyola. I have not seen Loyola's book, and this statement, therefore, is made at second-hand.

VEGA (MARCO ANTONIO DE LA).—Born, it is said, at Alcalá de Henares. I have no acquaintance with his work. Lope de Vega refers to him in the "Laurel de Apolo" (sc. iii.).

> "Aquel ingenio, universal, profundo,
> El docto Marco Antonio de la Vega,
> Ilustre en verso y erudito en prosa."

VEGA CARPIO (LOPE FÉLIX DE).—Born at Madrid, Nov. 25, 1562. He was therefore about twenty-two years of age when the "Galatea" was published, and had already served in at least one of the expeditions against the Azores. It is impossible in a brief note to give any idea of the merit or extent of his productions. An excellent bibliography, the work mostly of that industrious scholar, the late Mr. John Chorley, is appended to Rivadeneyra's fifty-second volume. Lope de Vega died at Madrid, August 27, 1635.

VERGARA (JUAN DE).—This writer, who is referred to by Rojas in the "Viaje Entretenido," contributed a sonnet prefatory—"Tratan entre la tierra, y entre el cielo"—to López Maldonado's "Cancionero."

VILLAROEL (CRISTÓBAL DE).—This writer contributed two sonnets to Espinosa's collection. One of these—"Al árbol de vitoria está fingida"—is reprinted by López de Sedano (v. p. 318). Two sonnets from the same hand are prefixed to Garcés' version of Petrarch.

VIRUÉS (CRISTÓBAL DE).—Born at Valencia about 1550. He fought with Cervantes at Lepanto. His "El Monserrate" (Madrid, 1587–1588) represents the high watermark of his production. His "Obras trágicas y líricas" were published at Madrid in 1609.

VIVALDO (ADÁN).—The only Vivaldo I ever heard of is the personage mentioned in "Don Quixote" (Pt. I. ch. xiii.) who, on his way to Seville, met the knight just previous to the funeral of Chrysostom.

VIVAR (BAUTISTA DE).—This writer is mentioned by Lope de Vega in the "Dorotea" (Act. IV. sc. ii.): "Bautista de Vivar, monstruo de naturaleza en decir versos de improviso con admirable impulso de las musas." I know nothing of his work.

ZÚÑIGA (MATÍAS DE).

CHAPTER V.

"Que faire donc? Je crois définitivement qu'il ne m'est donné que d'écrire."—ÉTIENNE PIVERT DE SÉNANCOUR.

CERVANTES for some time after his marriage, which had been brought about in the face of considerable opposition on the part of his wife's relatives, continued to reside in Esquivias. This little town lies in the province of Toledo, about thirty-three *kilomètres* from Madrid, and, in Don Quixote's epoch, it enjoyed a certain œnological reputation—a circumstance to which Cervantes, who knew a good thing when he tasted it, makes more than one characteristic reference. Some parts of the desolate old place still show traces of its former industry; but the glory has long since departed, and the empty-cellared Esquivias of to-day must be classed among the meanest, the most squalid of small provincial towns.[1] Cervantes'

[1] "Diccionario geográfico-estadístico-histórico de España y sus posesiones de Ultramar por Pascual Madoz" (Madrid, 1846-1850), vii. p. 585.

Ticknor's statement (ii. p. 119) that Cervantes alludes but twice to Esquivias is not quite accurate. Besides the references to Esquivias in the "Cueva de Salamanca" and the Prólogo to "Pérsiles y Sigismunda," mentioned by Ticknor, Cervantes introduces the name of the

sojourn there was not entirely due to unfettered choice.
Business transactions relating to the modest dowry of
his wife kept him in Esquivias for a while, and its
proximity to Madrid made it a less impossible abiding-
place than might be thought. Madrid, which at the
present time is little more than a superficial, second-rate
copy of Paris, without the Parisian concentration or the
Parisian intellectual activity, was in the reign of Philip II.
the focus of all interests, political, social, and literary.
In the latter respect, indeed, Valencia had some claims
to be considered; and men of wide, deep, and varied
learning were to be found both in the monasteries and
in the university towns; but in the end the highly
centralised government of the country drew all the
younger, more ambitious, aspiring intellects to Madrid.
Self-interest and political pressure combined proved
irresistible : the intellectual sceptre passed to the
capital, and the provinces were well-nigh stripped of
their unfledged talents. Cervantes, while his wife's
small *dot* was getting itself arranged, had to look
about for some means of earning his bread and of
supporting the members of his family, who would seem
to have been almost entirely dependent on him. There
was a rapidly growing taste for the stage, and Cervantes,
who certainly never lacked self-confidence, determined

town in " La Elección de los Alcaldes de Daganzo," in " El Coloquio
de los Perros," and in " El Licenciado Vidriera." Perhaps I may
mention that Tirso de Molina also, in " La Villana de la Sagra," makes
Cervantes speak of

> " El soberano licor
> De Esquivias " . . . (Act I. sc. vi.)

to appeal to the public as a dramatist. The Spanish theatre was still in an inchoate, embryonic state, and he may well have imagined in his Quixotic ardour that he was born to reduce it to consistency and form.

The intense struggle with the Moors had for centuries absorbed almost the entire energy and talent of the nation. It is a commonplace to say that the scene reflects the genius of a people, and one might have looked for a great national drama with that prolonged historic battle for its leading theme. But the stage requires leisure and peace as an atmosphere for its full development. The existence of the Elizabethan drama might, indeed, seem to contradict this dogmatic assertion; but—apart from the fact that the Elizabethan dramatists were not, as a rule, men of action—some of the most superb, triumphant products of what is roughly styled the Elizabethan era were the first-fruits of the reign of James. In Spain the conditions necessary to slow crystallisation were entirely absent. Song had no time wherein to dress its wing for a sustained flight, and the national conflict of ages remains mirrored to us only in the fleet, strong lyrics of the *Romanceros.* The popular amusements in Spain, as elsewhere, found their earliest outlets in the grossest and most vulgar forms. Jousts and bull-fights—the former among the upper classes, the latter with the crowd — were among the most æsthetic forms of entertainment.[1] Egg-throwing and

---

[1] "Tratado historico sobre el origen y progresos de la Comedia y del histrionismo en España. . . . Por D. Casiano Pellicer" (Madrid, 1804), i. p. 2.

tumblers, marionettes and hoop-jumping, blackguard songs, giants, dwarfs, monstrosities, menageries, and exhibitions of naked women were highly popular.[1] A pig let loose among a crowd of blind men (who, armed with swords, hacked each other to pieces in the vain attempt to slay the brute) afforded æonian enjoyment to the general.[2] The dramatic flame, if it flickered into life, was but feebly fanned by the breath of the *jongleurs.* This state of things—the nadir of diversion—was the earlier stage of development; but the dramatic skiff had touched bottom. Granada was captured in 1492, and immediately a promise of better things followed. In 1499 the celebrated *Celestina* appeared. This tragi-comedy,—in its final form the joint work of Cota and of Rojas—though it may never have been acted, is above all things dramatic in spirit and inspiration, if not in form. Its success was unprecedented: it went the round of the civilised world: Latin, French, German, Italian, and Dutch translations were brought out, and in 1631 a tardy version by James Mabbe finally saw the light in England under the slightly forbidding title of *The Spanish Bawd.*[3] By one of those curious

[1] "Tratado historico sobre el origen y progresos de la Comedia y del histrionismo en Espana. . . . Por D. Casiano Pellicer " (Madrid, 1804), i. pp. 2, 5, 8.

[2] ". . . á lo último entre otros regocijos sacaron al medio de la plaza un puerco y á unos ciegos armados para matarlo, siendo con-dicion que habia de ser de quien lo matase ; y errando por lo comun el golpe, le solian acertar contra si mismos, hiriéndose malamente, y excitando así la risa publica de los espectadores." Quoted by Pellicer (p. 5) from a MS., apparently by N. Antonio, in the Biblioteca Real. The same incident is given by the learned Mariana.

[3] " Pornoboscodidascalus Latinus. . . . Lingua Hispanica ab in-

prostitutions of patriotism to which mankind seem
subject, high claims have been put forward on behalf of
the *Celestina*. Men, with every appearance of gravity,
have been found to declare that the *Celestina* is a work
inspired with a high moral purpose; and Cervantes
himself, in a copy of burlesque verses prefixed to *Don
Quixote*, calls it, half in earnest, a divine book.[1] But
this eccentric judgment cannot be sustained, and critics
of a later generation are agreed with the verdict
incidentally given in *El Rufián Cobarde*. Bartolomé
de Torres Naharro published his *Propaladia* at Naples
in 1517, but none of his comedies would appear to have
attained any popular vogue. Living almost entirely in

certo avctore instar ludi conscriptus Celestinæ titulo. . . . Caspar
Barthivs. . . . Latio transscribebat " (Francofurti, 1624).

"Celestine en laqvelle est Traicte des deceptions des seruiteurs
enuers leurs Maistres, et des Macquerelles enuers les Amoureux "
(Paris, 1542).

" Ain Hipsche Tragedia võ zwaien liebhabendū mentschen ainen
Ritter Calixstus uñ ainer Edlñ junckfrawen Melibia genāt " (Augspurg,
1520). The translator was Wirsung.

"Celestina . . . nouamente tradocta de lingua castigliana in
italiano idioma " (Venetia, 1519).

" Celestina, Een tragicomedie van Calisto ende Melibea " (t'Hant-
werpen, 1574).

[1] Cp. the prefatory lines "Del Donoso, poeta entreverado, á
Sancho Panza y Rocinante."

> " Soy Sancho Panza escude—
> Del manchego Don Quijo—
> Puse piés en polvoro—
> Por vivir á lo discre—
>   Que el Tácito Villadic—
> Toda su razón de esta—
> Cifró en una retira—
> Segun siente Celesti—
> Libro en mi opinión divi— " etc.

M

Italy, he wrote for Italian audiences, or at least for
audiences of which Italians formed the majority; and it is
in the highest degree doubtful if any of his plays ever
saw the Spanish stage. The *Tenellaria* may deserve
some mention from the fact that it is written in seven
languages : but save as a literary curiosity its interest is
of the slightest.[1] In any case, the influence of Cota,
Rojas, and Castillejo (whose grossly indecent *Costanza*

[1] A citation from this curious work may serve as an example. I
quote from the volume edited by D. Manuel Cañete in the valuable
series entitled " Libros de Antaño."

" *Fabio.*	Ecco là il portogalese
	Che gli era anchor in presencia.
Portugués.	Nau sei nada.
	Ia lle dera hua pancada,
	Que voto a o corpo de Deus ;
	Mais teverenme da spada
	Aqueles porcas judeus.
Tudesco.	Ego non,
	Per Deum. . . .
Matía.	¿ Qué ? Solamente Sevilla
	Puede sacar una hueste.
Portugués.	Eu vos fundo,
	Eu os concedo o segundo
	Que Sevella he muito boa. . . .
Miguel.	No crideu,
	Que quant vos altres dieu
	Que vull parlar ab paciencia
	Es no res. . . .
Vizcaíno.	Digo, hao,
	Yo criado estás en nao,
	Vizcaíno eres por cierto
	Mas iuro á Dios que Bilbao
	La tieno mucho buen puerto.
Petijan.	Nani rien.
	Vus ete vus sabi bien
	Notre studi de París." (Pp. 367, 368, 369.)

is thought, fortunately, to have perished), if it existed
at all, was but transitory.[1] The real father of the
Spanish theatre is, by general admission, Lope de Rueda,
a goldsmith of Seville. The late M. Louis de Viel-
Castel has thought it necessary to deny to Lope "*ce titre
éclatant*"; but the unanimous voice of experts is, on
this point, against the accomplished Academician, who
seems inclined, on what I venture to think insufficient
information, to base Lope's title to fame on the
material improvements introduced by him in the
apparatus of the theatre.[2] It is not probable that
Spain was in advance of the rest of Europe in this
respect, and some reform was urgently needed if the
pictures drawn of the early theatre have any connection
with fact. It requires an effort of the imagination to
realise a stage with Paradise at one end of it, raised by
a few steps from above the rest of the rude plank
plateau, where the devil went in and out of a barrel,
and an inverted wine-cask represented the Mount of
Temptation. In Juan de Enzina's time, in Spain as
elsewhere, a red-headed Judas, concealing a crow and
the entrails of some beast under his coat, allowed his
disgusting burdens to pass away from him before he

[1] Luiz Velázquez, however, in his "Origines de la Poesia Castel-
lana " (Málaga, 1754), says that the *Costanza* exists in the Library of
the Escorial. I am not acquainted with the original work of Velázquez, which I know only in the translation by Johan Andreas Dieze,
entitled " Geschichte der Spanischen Dichtkunst " (Göttingen, 1769).
—". . . die Costanza, die in einer Handschrift in der Bibliothek des
Escurials liegt " (p. 321).

[2] "Essai sur le théâtre espagnol, par M. Louis de Viel-Castel "
(Paris, 1882), i. pp. 9, 11.

slid down an obliquely inclined rope to hell in company
with Satan, in full view of the spectators.[1]   In Lope de
Rueda's zenith, the stage, consisting of six planks
supported by four benches laid out square-wise, was
cut off from the audience by an old blanket, hung on
two ropes, behind which a few unaccompanied singers
sang between the acts.   The entire apparatus of a
theatre, says Cervantes, was contained in a bag, and
there is the less difficulty in accepting the statement
when it is known that the stage trappings consisted of
four or five cloaks, staves, wigs, and beards.   During
Lope's career all the characters (excluding, presumably,
the female parts which were played by boys) appeared
with beards.[2]

Among other obstacles which lay across the path of
the aspiring dramatist was the coldness, if not the
disapprobation, of the Church.   The conflict was of long
standing.   The affected passions, the feigned loves,
angers, sighs and tears, the necessary disguises and
counterfeits of the stage were denounced in the sternest
terms as early as the first century by Tertullian.   Can
it be, he asks bitterly, that the same hands which are
lifted up to the Almighty are degraded to the applause
of a mere player?   He recalls with fierce exultation

---

[1] Cp. "Miracle Plays and Sacred Dramas, a Historical Survey,
by Dr. Karl Hase.   Translated from the German [Das geistliche
Schauspiel] by A. W. Jackson, and edited by the Rev. W. W.
Jackson" (London, 1880).   The original was published at Leipzig in
1858.

[2] Prólogo to the "Ocho comedias, y ocho entremeses nuevos."
(Madrid, 1615).

more than one instance of spectators being struck down
with a mortal illness on the very day of their visit to
these vile stews, where obscene buffoons strutted their
little hour away ; and in a terrible passage of invective
gloats, with savage anticipatory delight, over the wild,
despairing shrieks of mummers rising up from the red
pit of hell.[1] Now and then there was a lull in the
prolonged battle. The comedians, anxious to come to
terms and meet their enemy half-way, were bold enough
to elect as their patron saint Genesius, a pagan actor,
who, originally baptised on the Roman stage in mockery
of the Christian rite, became a convert and was
martyred under Diocletian.[2] The Church had in her

---

[1] "Non amat falsam auctor veritatis : adulterium est apud illum
omne quod fingitur. Proinde vocem, sexus, ætates mentientem,
amores, iras, gemitus, lacrymas asseverantem non probabit, qui omnem
hypocrisin damnat " (Par. xxiii.).

. . . "illas manus quas ad Deum extuleris, postmodum laudando
histrionem fatigare ? " (Par. xxv.)

"Constat et alii linteum in somnis ostensum ejus diei nocte que
tragœdum audierat, cum exprobatione nominatim tragœdi, nec ultra
quintum diem eam mulierem in sæculo fuisse " (Par. xxvi.).

"Tunc magis tragœdi audiendi, magis scilicet vocales in sua
propria calamitate : tunc histriones cognoscendi solutiores multo per
ignem : tunc spectandus auriga, in flamma rota totus ruber " (Par.
xxx.).

I quote from the " De Spectaculis " as printed in the edition of
Tertullian included in Caillau's " Patres Apostolici " (Paris, 1842).

Cp. Tertullian's denunciation of the theatre, " quod est privatum
consistorium impudicitiæ, ubi nihil probatur, quam quod alibi non
probatur " (Par. xvii.), with St. Augustine's expression, " caveæ
turpitudinum . . . fora vel mœnia, in quibus dæmonia colebantur "
(" De consensu evangelistarum," i. 33).

[2] Hase, pp. 2-3. It is right to say that great doubt exists
as to the actual date of the martyrdom of Genesius. It is variously

own person a painful experience of the invincible passion of the public for any kind of dramatic spectacle. Actresses of infamous repute had crept into the palaces and the affections of great prelates in a manner so flagrant as to call down the indignant fulminations of the Provincial Council of Toledo.[1] In many lands, but especially in France, to the anger and scandal of all decent persons, the Feast of Fools had become an established celebration, and the faithful saw, with indignant horror, the very sanctuary of the great cathedrals polluted by a shameless ceremonial, during which an ass — a thrice-hallowed beast — bearing a vestment on its back and a mitre on its head, was led to the high altar by some members of the clergy, while a disgusting travesty of the religious rites was performed and the orgiastic chorus of ecclesiastical and lay buffoons broke out into some such hideous canticle as—

> Amen dicas, Asine,
> Jam satur ex gramine,
> Amen, amen itera,
> Aspernare vetera,
> Hé, sire Asne, hé!

Then the priest intoned his *Deus in adjutorium,* and the general congregation raised a blackguard refrain of hee-haws, followed by the vilest and most undisguised indecencies. The grotesque formularies of Isis, with a tame bear dressed in women's clothes, an ape decked with the Phrygian cap, and an ass bestridden by a

stated to have occurred in 285, 286, and 303. A similar legend with regard to Gelasinus of Heliopolis is attributed to the year 297.

[1] Pellicer, pp. 9–10.

decrepit dotard, in parody of the fable of Bellerophon and Pegasus—these grotesque improprieties, which had scandalised easy-going pagans, were now outdone in the desecrated temples of Christian worship.[1]

The Church may well have thought that, as nothing could sink beneath this blasphemous burlesque of sacred things, introduced into the holy places by her chosen sons, terms might be made with the unspeakable enemy. The Moralities and Mystery-plays—which are represented in Spain by Juan de Enzina's eclogues, and in England by the Chester Plays—were performed in churches with the ecclesiastical approval.[2] As recently as 1542 they were thus given in England; and it seems certain that in Spain the truce had lasted sufficiently long to allow of Lope de Rueda's pastorals being represented in the chief cathedrals of the land. But the contest was not yet over. More than two generations later the celebrated Jesuit Mariana, in a well-known tractate, contended against the patent hypocrisy by which the comedians sheltered themselves beneath the threadbare cloak of the pious confraternities who gave representations with a view to collecting funds for the poor. The vanity of the shameless

[1] Cp. Du Tilliot's learned "Mémoires pour servir à l'histoire de la Fête des Fous" (Lausanne et Genève, 1741)—a work of curious erudition which is scarcely likely to be superseded. See also the well-known passage in Apuleius ("Metamorphoseon," lib. xi.).

[2] Enzina is most accessible in Juan Nicolás Böhl von Faber's "Teatro Español anterior á Lope de Vega" (Hamburgo, 1832), pp. 3–38. The Chester Plays may be followed in Mr. Thomas Wright's edition, printed for the Shakespeare Society (London, 1843).

amateur still lurks behind the same flimsy curtain. The fact may serve as a measure of progress. To the learned, holy priest it was a frightful thought that there existed on the planet well-intentioned but misguided men, who could imagine that the canonised saints of God were honoured by the performance of mundane plays, and who further conceived, in their blind infatuation, that actors could be admitted to the sacraments of the Church.[1] That unworthy members of the clergy could be found to assist at these licentious exhibitions filled the saintly writer with horror and consternation. Almost a century later the controversy raged as hotly as ever. The illustrious Bossuet could find no gentler phrase than "this scandalous dissertation" for the moderate, Laodicean treatise in which the Theatine father Caffaro had put forward a half-hearted defence of the stage. To the mind of the mighty bishop the poor stroller's was still an *infame métier*, nor could he refer to the death of Molière without a shudder for the post-mortem destiny of the great comedian, to whom he applies the quotation: "Woe unto you that laugh now! for ye shall mourn and weep."[2] Jeremy Collier's

---

[1] "Joannis Marianae e Societatis Jesu Tractatus VII." (Coloniae Agrippinae, 1609). The "De Spectaculis" is the third treatise. The titles of App. viii. and ix. are suggestive in Mariana's Spanish version of his work ; "Que las mujeres no deben salir á las comedias á representar:" "Que los farsantes están privados de los sacramentos." It would perhaps be undesirable to quote from Mariana's text in a work intended for general circulation. He simply hated and loathed the degraded beings whom he scornfully styled *hombres cómicos*.

[2] Cp. Bossuet's "Maximes et Réflexions sur la Comédie." "La posterité saura peut-être la fin de ce poète comédien, qui, en jouant

fulmination against dramatists for "Their Swearing, Profaneness and Lewd Application of Scripture; Their Abuse of the Clergy; Their making Their Top Characters Libertines, and giving them Success in their Debauchery" is scarcely more violent than their denunciation by Bossuet, who, like Mariana, is especially horrified at the vicarious participation of the clergy in these infamous doings.[1]

> The enemy faints not, nor faileth,
> And as things have been they remain.

In Boston, the most recent home of generous culture and enlightened liberty, as late as 1792 an American comedian was arrested on the heinous charge of having acted in the *School for Scandal*.[2]

Still, as we have seen, both sides would agree from time to time to call a truce; and during one of these

son *Malade imaginaire* ou son Médecin par force, reçut la dernière atteinte de la maladie dont il mourut peu d'heures après, et passa des plaisanteries du théâtre, parmi lesquelles il rendit presque le dernier soupir, au tribunal de celui qui dit : *Malheur à vous qui riez ! car vous pleurerez.*" Bossuet had a short way with actors. His policy is summed up in five trenchant words : "Fermer à jamais le théâtre." I quote from the "Œuvres" of Bossuet, printed in the "Panthéon Littéraire" (xi. pp. 458–480).

[1] "A Short View of the Immorality and Profaneness of the English Stage. By Jeremy Collier" (London, 1698), p. 2.

[2] "History of the People of the United States from the Revolution to the Civil War. By John Bach McMaster" (New York, 1883), i. p. 94. The culprit's name was Harper. I take this opportunity of acknowledging my admiration for Mr. McMaster's book, which seems to me unrivalled in its kind. Indeed, the only American historian who deserves to be named in the same breath with him is Mr. Parkman, and it has been to me a source of amused surprise that these two remarkable writers are so little read in England.

favourable interludes it must have been that Cervantes
and a keen-eyed boy, famous in after life as Antonio
Pérez, saw Lope de Rueda in some cathedral, or,
perhaps, in the most convenient public square.[1]   We
know next to nothing of Lope's *versos pastoriles*, so
highly commended by Cervantes; and it must be admitted that his set pieces, *Eufemia*, *Armelina*, *Los
Engaños*, and *Medora*, are not very allicient examples
of high comedy.   Of these, the *Eufemia*, the motive of
which may be described as an amalgam of the story of
Susanna and Imogen, is distinctly the most successful
attempt ; and the final scene, in which the heroine, in
the presence of Valiano, exposes the villainy of Paulo, is
given with a vivacity and precision previously unknown
to the Spanish stage.   The *Coloquio de Timbrio* and the
Coloquio de Camila are written in a more ambitious
style, but the laboured effort at elevated diction contrasts ludicrously with the undignified train of thought
followed by the speakers.   The most representative, as
well as the most fruitful, of Lope's productions remain
to us in such of his *pasos* as *Las Aceitunas*, *El Con-
vidado*, and *El Rufián Cobarde*.   Of these, the first
(and distinctly the best) deals amusingly with a violent
quarrel between Toruvio and his wife Águeda over the
price to be charged for olives as yet unplanted ; the
second treats, with much freshness and spirit, the
threadbare story of a man inviting another to dine with
him, well knowing that there is no dinner for either

---

[1] Cp. the " Epistolario Español por D. Eugenio Ochoa," p. 548
(Rivadeneyra's " Biblioteca," xiii.).

himself or his guest; and in the third there is a ludicrous picture of the character of Sigüenza, the incarnation of the swaggering, cowardly bully of the age. This type—a favourite one with Lope, who has handled it also in the character of Gargullo in the *Medora*—is obviously modelled after a study of Pyrgopolinices in the *Miles Gloriosus* or Therapontigonus Platagidorus in the *Curulio*. Lope de Ruela may or may not have read Theocritus, as his admirers declare;[1] it is as certain as anything can be that, by some means or other, he had obtained a very workmanlike, serviceable knowledge of Plautus. Lope is best seen, as we have said, in his *pasos*; the story is clearly and definitely displayed, and the whole is written in a simple, natural key. Nowhere in the *pasos* do we find any absurdity to equal that in the *Armelina*, where Neptune and Medusa intervene to settle the differences of a parcel of Andalusian blacksmiths and serving-wenches. The *pasos* (save in the matter of length) and the comedies may be likened to such productions as *Gammer Gurton's Needle*. There is in Lope the same boisterous humour, the same coarse wit, seasoned (though to a less degree) with the same coarse jokes which we meet with in Still. The triumphant effect of Lope's plays on their audiences was doubtless due to his excellence as an actor—an excel-

---

[1] Cp. the preface dedicatory to Gregorio López Madera which is prefixed to the "Trezena parte de las Comedias de Lope de Vega Carpio" (Barcelona, 1620). "El uso de España no admite las rusticas Bucolicas de Teocrito, antiguamete imitadas del famoso Poeta Lope de Rueda." The most convenient reference to most readers will, doubtless, be Rivadeneyra, xli. p. 157.

lence probably unsurpassed on the Spanish stage.
Sénancour's pregnant observation is to the point : "*Pour
les pièces dont le genre est le comique du second ordre, il
peut suffice que l'acteur principal ait un vrai talent.*"[1]
According to all available evidence, Lope de Rueda was
himself a consummate embodiment of all the conditions
necessary for success, according to the gospel of *Obermann.*

His immediate successor was the Toledan Naharro.
Nothing from Naharro's pen—so far as I know—has
come down to us. He, and not Lope de Rueda, deserves
M. Louis de Viel-Castel's eulogy, for he is known to
posterity, not merely as an admirable comedian, but
also as the father of stage-management in Spain. He it
was, as Cervantes tells us, who brought the musicians
before the curtain, abolished the senseless custom which
had grown up of every actor playing in a beard, and he
it is who deserves whatever immortality is due to the
inventor of side-scenes, stage thunder, and mimic battles.[2]
We have seen the appreciation with which the Italian
comedians were received in England. In Spain a similar
Schwärmerei was called forth by Ganasa, whose consummate art was a revelation to the Spanish public. This
celebrated Italian invaded Spain with his troupe in
1574.[3] His success was immediate and complete. He

---

[1] "Obermann par De Sénancour. Avec une préface de Sainte-
Beuve" (Paris, 1833), i. pp. 208–209.

[2] Prólogo al Lector ("Comedias").

I must confess that I find much difficulty in following, or
adjusting, the involved chronology of Pellicer. Ganasa, according to
that useful writer (i. p. 53), arrived in Spain in 1574. He seems to

forced a faint, reluctant smile from the thin lips of Philip, and thirty years later his performances were still the delight of a younger generation of playgoers.[1] He would seem to have played almost the entire range of theatrical characters with immense effect, and the fact that he excelled especially as a mime is not likely to be held against him by those who remember that Garrick, no lenient judge, classed the mime Sachi among the three best comic actors of the world in his day.[2]

Things were at this pass when Cervantes came forward with that invincible buoyancy which never left him. He was ready for anything: "tragedy, comedy, history, pastoral, pastoral-comical, historical-pastoral, tragical-historical, tragical-comical-historical-pastoral, scene individable or poem unlimited"—the managers had but to ask, and he was prepared to supply them with masterpieces for ever. His old favourites, Lope de Rueda and Naharro, had done admirably well; but he was born, he thought, to show a more excellent way.

Curiously enough, so contagious, so irresistible was his sublime self-confidence that he actually persuaded

have been still playing in 1579 (i. p. 72). Are we then to understand that Ganasa's first tour extended over five years? Yet it seems
difficult to attach any other meaning to Pellicer's phrase: "Sin
duda seria este" [*i.e.* el año 1603] "el tiempo de su segunda venida"
(i. p. 73).

[1] "Dicese que Felipe II. en medio de su seriedad gustaba de las
comedias mímicas de Alberto Ganasa."—Pellicer, i. p. 74.

[2] See M. Kelly's "Reminiscences" (London, 1826), i. p. 49.
Sachi was, apparently, a Venetian. The others of this interesting
trio were Cassaciello, at Naples, and Préville, at the Comédie
Française.

managers into a belief in him. Most of his dramatic
work is lost to us, and we must form our judgment
chiefly on the *Numancia* and on the volume of plays
published in 1615.[1] But we know on his own testimony that he produced some twenty or thirty comedies
—the delightful vagueness of the statement is
eminently characteristic—which, if not highly distinguished, at least escaped being hissed off the stage. We
can only judge by what we know, and the specimens
which have survived for us were hardly likely to set
the world ablaze. Fanatical adorers of Cervantes have
been found to worship his dramatic genius, but it
requires the eye of faith to see any very high form of
dramatic talent in the examples which have come down
to us. These judicious friends who have seen in his
plays an occult wealth of wisdom and a constant richness of psychological reference are of the same kidney as
those too ingenious Teutonic commentators, who have

[1] Among the lost plays are *La Batalla Naval, La Jerusalen, La
Amaranta ó La del Mayo, El Bosque Amoroso, La Unica y la Bizarra
Arsinda,* and *La Confusa* (cp. the " Adjunta al Parnaso)." We may
probably assume with safety that another play, entitled *La Gran
Turquesca,* is identical with *La Gran Sultana,* printed in the volume
published in 1615. *La Confusa* would seem to have been the author's
favourite among his plays :

> " Say por quien *la Confusa* nada fea
> Pareció en los teatros admirable,
> Si esto á su fama es gusto se le crea " (Viaje, c. iv.).

Cp. also the "Adjunta al Parnaso": "Mas la que yo mas estimo, y
de la que mas me precio, fué y es, de una llamada *La Confusa,* la
cual, con paz sea dicho de cuantas comedias de capa y espada hasta hoy
se han representado, bien puede tener lugar señalado por buena entre
las mejores."

made themselves ridiculous by the curious moral lectures, the quaint evangels which they have discovered in Shakspere.

The *Numancia* probably saw the stage in 1585–6, but it remained unprinted till 1784, when it was published by Antonio de Sancha in a volume containing also the *Viaje del Parnaso* and the *Trato de Argel*. Sancha never deigned to inform the curious public where the *Numancia* was discovered, nor how he came by it; but the putative parentage ascribed to it is borne out fully enough by internal evidence. It has had the good fortune to receive the suffrages of critics the most eminent and diverse. Men as far apart in constitution as Sismondi and Schlegel have united in admiring it. Ticknor and Lemcke have crowned it with their judicial approbation; and—by no means the least of its happy experiences—it has been translated excellently well by the late Mr. Gibson.[1] If scholastic authority could silence criticism, if literary dogmatism could stereotype opinion, then the *Numancia* might be

---

[1] Cp. "La Littérature du midi de l'Europe" (Paris, 1813), iii. 370–391, 401–406, and August Wilhelm von Schlegel's "Vorlesungen über dramatische Kunst und Litteratur" ("Werke," Leipzig, 1846), vi. 379–380. Sismondi's judgment is worth quoting: "La tragédie ne fait pas répandre de larmes, mais le frisson de l'horreur et de l'effroi devient presque un supplice pour le spectateur. C'est un premier symptôme du changement que Philippe II. et les *autos da f*" avaient opéré dans la nation castillane." . . .

Cp. also the "Handbuch der Spanischen Litteratur von Ludwig Lemcke" (Leipzig, 1855–1856), iii. 113 *et seq.*; Ticknor, ii. pp. 125–131.

"Numantia. Translated from the Spanish with introduction and notes by James Y. Gibson" (London, 1885).

left undisturbed on the pedestal where enthusiastic
optimism has placed it ; and, indeed, it may be readily
granted that it is Cervantes' most successful dramatic
effort.   Mr. Gibson, with a generous ardour which does
honour to his heart, but which only tends to darken
wisdom, has compared the *Numancia* to the *Seven
against Thebes* and the *Persians*.   It seems scarcely
possible that any one can regard the Æschylean drama
as dramatic in the modern sense.   Nobility, vigour,
imaginative power, lyrical abundance — it has them
all—it has everything, save only the dramatic instinct.
Something of these qualities, diluted and enfeebled,
flows through the sonorous metres of the *Numancia*.
It is essentially undramatic : but it possesses something
of the severe splendour, the virility, the mournful 'Aναγκη
of the great Athenian.   The theme is susceptible
enough of heroic treatment, since it deals with that
immortal defence against Scipio which the necessities of
space and the frigidity of the historian usually dismiss
in a few peremptory lines.   The despairing valour, the
frantic heroism of the children of Thunder, their indomitable patriotism are, in Cervantes' play, deftly
mingled with the pathetic love story of Lyra and
Morandro and the self-sacrificing friendship of Leoncio.
A glorious historic incident, reflected through the lenses
of centuries, might well awake a glow of eloquent
patriotism ; but beyond eloquence, brilliant and fervid,
the play scarcely goes.   Yet its fine, intoxicating
quality may be measured when we read the judgment
of the frigid Ticknor on the invocation of the corpse

by Marquino: "There is nothing of so much dignity in the incantations of Marlowe's *Faustus* . . . nor does even Shakespeare demand from us a sympathy so strange with the mortal head reluctantly rising to answer Macbeth's guilty question."[1] *Il y a des reproches qui louent et des louanges qui médisent.* One could not say more if one were dealing with a masterpiece; and, with all reverence for Cervantes' genius, the *Numancia* is far from being a masterpiece. It is faulty in conception, hesitating in movement, uncertain in execution. The abstractions occupy too vast a space: and the choric utterances of War, Sickness, and Hunger (not to speak of Spain, Duero, Orvïon, Tera, and Minuesa) are a weariness and an affliction. Still it has, within limits, the true lyrical rapture, the genuine expressive note of hopeless passion and disdainful pain. No other play in the wide sweep of Spanish literature is so penetrated with what Schlegel styles the *energische Pathos*, the superb motive of unflinching patriotism, the candid vision of heroic contest. The rhetoric, if exuberant, is sincere; if too resounding, it is, at least, earnest and direct. More than two hundred years later, while the cannon of Mortier, Junot, and Lannes thundered round the citadel held by the valiant Palafox, the besieged citizens of Zaragoza hailed with patriotic enthusiasm another, and perhaps a final, representation of the *Numancia*.[2]

[1] Ticknor, ii. p. 128.

[2] It may be worth while to mention a parallel case in this connection. Martínez de la Rosa's tragedy "La Viuda de Padilla,"

With the exception of *El Trato de Argel*, no other play of this period has survived.   But we are not without means of judging that Cervantes' success as a dramatist was less triumphant than he had once hoped. So much might be inferred from his sudden retirement from the scene.   Some thirty years later, the then celebrated author of *Don Quixote* published a volume of unacted plays which he had previously hawked the round of all the managers and booksellers of Madrid.[1] No one would look at them.   Managers, publishers, and actors were unanimously agreed that nothing dramatically good could come from that pen.   It can scarcely be conceived that the writer's reputation as a playwright had ever stood very high, nor does an examination of his sorry volume lead to any reversal of the contemporary verdict.

In *El Gallardo Español*, the scene of which is laid in Oran, Fernando de Saavedra is challenged to single combat by the Moor Alimuzel, at the instigation of his mistress Arlaja, whose interest in Saavedra rests entirely on his fame.   The Spanish commander refusing the necessary permission, Saavedra escapes to the enemy's lines, where, passing himself off as a Mahometan con-

imitated from, or rather influenced by, Alfieri, was produced at Cádiz in 1812 during the bombardment of the city by the French.   "Obras completas de D. Francisco Martínez de la Rosa" (Paris, 1844–1845), ii. pp. 29–30.

[1] The statement in the text may require some modification.   There can be very little doubt that the volume of plays published in 1615 included pieces written at great intervals, some of which had been accepted and others rejected by the managers.   (Cp. the *Adjunta al Parnaso*.)   Still, the title-page of the book gives one pause.

vert, he meets the captive Margarita, with whom he had previously had some love passages. In a general assault on Oran, Saavedra suddenly turns, beats off the infidel, declares himself a Christian, and is forgiven by his chief. The marriages of Saavedra and Margarita on the one side, and of Alimuzel and Arlaja on the other, are the appropriate conclusion. There is a certain insolent verve in this play which has its attraction. *La Casa de los Celos* is the most unmitigated rubbish. It would be hopeless to attempt to analyse a play in which are set forth the rivalries of Reinaldos and Roldán for Angélica—a play in which Venus, Fear, Charles the Great, Despair, Merlin, Jealousy, Curiosity, and Cupid are introduced. Enough, surely, to know that Angélica is finally left in the care of an unnamed Grand Duke of Bavaria, while Charles and his twin amorous paladins go forth on a crusade against the Moors. In *Los Baños de Argel* (which is a variant of *El Trato de Argel*) we are asked to follow the loves of the captives Fernando de Andrada and Constanza. Caurali, governor of Algiers, becomes enamoured of Constanza, and his wife Alima seeks consolation from Fernando. Finally, Zara, a converted Moorish girl, helps Fernando, Constanza, and the other Christian prisoners to escape, and, herself flying to Spain, the play closes with the usual quadrilateral marriage—Fernando and Constanza, with Zara and a certain Don Lope, figuring as the principals.

El Rufián Dichoso sets forth the eventful legend of Cristóbal de Lugo, who, after a stormy youth in Spain, becomes a saintly Dominican friar in Mexico, takes on himself the sins of Doña Ana de Trevino, is struck with leprosy, and dies prior of his monastery.   In *La Gran Sultana* we have the true story of a beautiful captive, who becomes the wife of the Grand Turk on the express condition that she is allowed to retain her faith.   This case, and that of *El Rufián Dichoso*, would seem more suitable for dissection by the hagiologist and moral theologian than for dramatic treatment.   The real interest of *La Gran Sultana*, such as it is, centres upon what should be the subsidiary love affair of Clara and Lamberto, while a slight relief to the barbaric monotony of the play is afforded by the buffooneries of Madrigal.   The *Laberinto de Amor* is written in a more ambitious style, a more involved manner, a manner which savours strongly of Lope's influence.   Rosamira, daughter of the Duke of Novara, is betrothed to Manfredo, Duke of Rosena.   Dagoberto, son of the Duke of Urbino, in the presence of Rosena's ambassador forbids the banns on the (perhaps irrelevant) ground that Rosamira is already dishonoured by an intrigue with an unnamed lover. The lady, confronted with her accuser, listens to the charge in silence, and, refusing to reply, is imprisoned. Anastasio, son of the Duke of Orlán, disguised as a peasant, rebukes Dagoberto for his slander.   Julia and Porcia then appear on the scene (as shepherds named Camilo and Rutilio), and discover themselves as, respectively, the sisters of Anastasio and Dagoberto. Manfredo has just heard of Rosamira's calamity, when a herald from Dorlán's Court appears with a challenge from his lord, who charges the luckless Manfredo with the abduction of Julia and Porcia. In the meanwhile, Rosamira's innocence or guilt, it has been decided, shall be submitted to the infallible arbitrament of arms. Anastasio, Rosamira's champion, induces Porcia to enter the cell of the imprisoned beauty with a message. Porcia accordingly, in the masquerade of a countrywoman, enters the cell and changes clothes with Rosamira. In the lists, a messenger from Dagoberto appears, admitting that the charges against Rosamira are false—the best proof of which, as Urbino's son drily says, is that he is about to marry her himself. Manfredo and Julia, Porcia and Anastasio, pair off, and the play ends in the approved manner.

A farcical motive is manifest throughout *La Entretenida*. Antonio confides to his sister Marcela his love for a namesake of hers, who resembles her in every way. While she ponders over what she fears may be an incipient incestuous passion, Cardenio, instructed by her flunkey Múñoz, successfully palms himself off as her betrothed American cousin, Silvestre de Almendárez. The embarrassments which follow the imposture are neatly worked out by the appearance of the true suitor : and the comedy ends with the exposure of Cardenio, the refusal of the Papal dispensation to Marcela and Almendárez, and the repulsion of the maid Cristina by both Quiñones and Ocaña. In *Pedro de Urdemalas* we have the hero as factotum to the leather-headed Alcalde Crispo. Leaving the Alcalde in the lurch, Pedro joins a company of gipsies, falls in love with Belica, and, next day, takes part in a performance "commanded" by the

King and Queen. The attention of the King to Belica arouses the jealousy of his consort, and finally the handsome gipsy is discovered to be the daughter of the Queen's brother. In the natural course of things, Belica remains at Court, while Pedro, not wholly disconsolate, remains with his strollers.

In the *Entremeses* the bright, mirthful side of the writer's character is uppermost. In the set dramas we only see the marked limitations of a gift hampered by the restraining conditions of production. In the *Entremeses* are discernible some indications of a talent, not ample indeed, but pleasing, affable, clear. This is only to say, in other words, that a man may fail hideously as a writer of high comedy, and may yet produce a very tolerable farce. To analyse these agreeable trifles is impossible. Their greatest attraction for us lies in the side lights which they cast upon the writer's idiosyncrasy. Thus it is not without interest to find him, in *El Juez de les Divorcios*, poking fun at the poets who produced sonnets with as great a facility as that with which the spider spins his web; or at the wives who modestly assumed that their untempted, and therefore unspotted, chastity compensated for an entire lack of every other virtue under heaven; or, in *El Rufián Viudo*, to read his good-humoured banter of those (of course, fictitious) ladies who fondly imagine that a too-wise minimism, as regards their age, deceives a credulous generation; or, again, to note that the exquisite gustatory sense of Juan Berrocal in *La Elección de los Alcaldes de Daganzo* is put forward as a recommendation for office; or, in the *Guarda Ciudadosa* to light on the quizzing shoemaker, who remarks that a glosa with the ghastly refrain of " *Chinelas de mis entrañas*" must be Lope de Vega's, as are all such good things; or, in *El Retablo de las Maravillas*, to listen to Benito Repollo solemnly expounding a deep philosophy which associates wisdom with great beards; or, in *La Cueva de Salamanca*, to watch the writer dealing his retributory blow at his old enemies the sacristans; or, in *El Viejo Celoso*, to meet with a somewhat unwonted girding at monks; or, in *Los Habladores*, to observe how Roldan anticipates the frantic bombast of Holofernes. Every one who has stayed in Seville will give a sympathetic approval to a passage in *La Cárcel de Sevilla*, which by implication condemns the pestilence that walketh in darkness in that loveliest of Spanish cities; and those (no doubt benighted) persons who fail to see the poetry of the *Christian Year* will be amused with Pero Díaz's definition of sacred poetasters in *El Hospital de los Podridos*: " Estos que hacen villancicos la noche de Navidad, que dicen mil disparates, con mezcla de herejía."

The interest of the *Entremeses*, then, is personal. They show us the careless author, fond of a joke, his ease, a bottle of Esquivias wine : less fond of crapulous sacristans, village bores, and *pimbêches*. But, if the interest of the *Entremeses* is personal, the interest of the more formal plays is equally, though in a different sense, personal throughout. We have seen in the

Prólogo of the plays of 1615 the stress which Cervantes
lays upon the material improvements of the stage.   We
can imagine the altitude of the *sublime punto* which
they had attained when we read the curious stage
directions given in the *Numancia*.[1]   One of Cervantes'
most acute delusions was that he was the first great
reformer who cut down the five acts of a play to three.
I confess that I cannot attach as much importance to
this trivial change as the late Mr. John Chorley.[2]   But
probably every one would be willing to admit that the
innovation, though by no means without its own disadvantages, was rational enough.   Other claims have
been advanced—those of Artieda and Virués, for
example—but it is certain that the credit of its
introduction (be it great or small) is due to Francisco
de Avendaño, who produced the *Florisea* in this form
as far back as 1551, when Cervantes was still a child.[3]
Probably nothing would have annoyed Cervantes more

---

[1] *E.g.* : "A este punto han de entrar los más soldados que
pudieran y Gayo Mario, *armados á la antigua, sin arcabuces*"
(Jornada I.).   "Con el aqua de la redoma clara baña el hierro de la
lanza, y luego hiere en la tabla, y debajo ó sueltense cohetes, ó hagase
el rumor el barril de piedras " (Jornada II.).

For the later arrangements in the auditorium, cp. "Relación de
las cosas sucedidas en la Córte de España desde 1599 hasta 1614.
Obra escrita por Don Luis Cabrera de Córdoba, Criado y Cronista del
rey Don Felipe II." (Madrid, 1857), p. 298.

[2] (*Fraser's Magazine*, July, 1859, p. 53).   "Notes on the National
Drama in Spain," a most suggestive essay, to which my obligations
are considerable.

[3] "Catálogo bibliográfico y biográfico del teatro antiguo español
desde sus orígenes hasta mediados del siglo XVIII. por D. Cayetano
Alberto de la Barrera y Leirado " (Madrid, 1860), p. 19.

than to find that he had been anticipated in what he clearly thought to be a most beneficent reform.

In the plays, we find the writer recording his impressions of those stolen revels of which, years ago, he had been the agonarch in Algiers. We see him faintly disguised under the translucent allonym of Saavedra in *El Gallardo Español*, or, again, figuring beneath the same diaphanous mask in *El Trato de Argel*.[1] His old tyrants, Arnaut Mamí and Hassan, are met with in *El Trato de Argel* and *Los Baños de Argel*. In *La Casa de los Celos* we see the passing influence of a modish literary craze. Rinaldo's speech, penetrated with *préciosité*, is made up of

> Taffeta phrases, silken terms precise,
>   Three piled hyperboles, spruce affectation,
> Figures pedantical,

after the manner of the straitest sect of the Gongorists —a manner which charmed the Spanish courtiers as much as it delighted Rosaline's lover in the King of Navarre's park, and which proved a source of mingled pleasure and bewilderment to the mighty Lope de Vega.

It must be admitted, however, that no one would ever turn the leaves of a single act of these plays had not the writer been Cervantes. Mr. Chorley is scarcely too severe when he says that " worse attempts, indeed,

---

[1] As an example of Cervantes' carelessness about trifles, it may be noted that he had forgotten the name of this piece when he wrote the " Viaje del Parnaso," where he styles it *Los tratos de Argel* (Adjunta).

no man of transcendent genius has ever made." It is
only as the tertiary work of a transcendent genius that
they continue in all ages to find curious readers. Yet,
save in the cases of some fanatical biographers, no one
can be found to say a good word for them—the *Numancia*
always excepted. His own countrymen have been the
foremost to revolt; and the loyal Lampillas has been
driven desperately to assert that the publishers sup-
pressed Cervantes' comedies, and substituted forged
rubbish instead. It would be difficult to point to a
stronger instance of the credulity of hero-worship.[1]

When Cervantes' plays appeared, the drama in Spain,
as the distinguished writer above quoted has said, was
scarcely accounted as literature. Plays were not serious
things, in any sense; they were but the playthings of
an hour, elegant trifles, mere *cosas de entretenimiento*.
And so Cervantes himself would seem to have regarded
them. They were to him so many vehicles for the
utterance of his personal feelings, his likings, his resent-
ments, his individual impressions of men and things:

---

[1] Cp. Thomás de Erauso y Zavaleta's "Discurso Critico sobre . . .
las Comedias de España" (Madrid, 1750), p. 9: "El estilo de
Cervantes, es cierto, que desdice mucho del presente: no se pueden
leer sus comedias sin molestia del oido, y aun del entendimiento."
Cp. also the "Saggio Storico-Apologetico della Letteratura Spagnuola
. . . del Signor Abate D. Saverio Lampillas" (Genova, 1778–81),
iv. pp. 181–182: "Io dunque a vista di queste riflessioni direi, che
nella publicazione di quelle otto commedie ebbe il Cervantes l' istessa
disgrazia, che in tante altre ebbero il Lope di Vega, il Montalvan, il
Calderon, ed altri, come altrove diremo; cioè, che la malizia degli
Stampatori sotto il nome, e prologo di Cervantes, pubblicò quelle
stravaganti commedie conformi al corrotto gusto del volgo, sopprimendo
le genuine del Cervantes, o trasformandole del tutto."

and, as such, every stroke in them is of pleasing interest. This is not to say that he was not proud of his dramatic work ; no man admired it half as much as he did. No music was sweeter to his ears than the hoarse applause of the *mosqueteros* of the pit. No man was more sublimely confident of the sincerity of his own mission ; no man more certain that he deserved success. Years afterwards, when he had found his true way, when the fame of the author of *Don Quixote* was gone abroad in every land, he still turned his wistful eyes to the memory of the days when he had hoped to win immortality upon the stage. Nor does he ever seem to have imagined that the cause of failure lay in himself. Even his hopeful spirit was a little staggered by the knowledge that his plays could get no hearing. That was a fact which no amount of self-delusion could blink ; and Cervantes accounted for it by assuming, not that his plays were poor, but that he had fallen on evil days.

This somewhat self-complacent explanation, though incomplete, is not without more reasonable ground than appears at first sight. No one can read the *Numancia* without thinking that Cervantes was capable of much better dramatic work than he actually produced, and without wondering why that better work was never forthcoming. The truth is that he had not arrived at a happy moment for himself. His own dramatic taste lay in the direction of the approved classical models. He was all for precedent, all for treading as closely as might be in the steps of the old-time masters, and in the *Numancia* he has presented the embodiment of his

dramatic ideals.   But the popular taste ran in a very
different channel.   The national spirit had risen, was
rising, very high.   Spain, if it purchased unity at the
price of freedom, was at least and at last united.   Leon
and Castile, Andalusia and Aragon, were integral parts
of one strong kingdom.   The final stronghold of the
infidel invader had been recovered.   The last faint
flicker of civic independence was stamped out at Zaragoza.   Portugal was now added as the last stone to the
imperial edifice, and, while the peninsula for the first
time was swayed by one sceptre, the proud banner of
the victorious Spaniards floated on the two extremes of
a new world.   Spain was the mistress of the earth.

> To her no more the bastion'd fort
> Shot out its swarthy tongue of fire ;
> From bay to bay, from port to port,
> Her coming was the world's desire.

Such at least was the Spanish legend.   The names of
Cortés and Pizarro, of Charles V. and the Great
Captain, of Alva and Don John, were in all men's
mouths from the Arctic Circle to Cape Comorin, from
the frozen Caspian to the still, long billows of the vast
Pacific.   These men, whatever their faults may have
been,—and their faults were not small—were great
among the greatest ; at least, the Spaniard thought so,
and he further thought that, in placing Spain upon the
topmost pinnacle of glory, they builded better than they
knew.

Their achievements, resounding through the world,
fanned the embers of the national pride into an intense

white flame.   Their success intensified, it even cari-
catured the lineaments of the national characteristics.
In a word, it brought to birth the *Españolismo* of
Spain. Matamores, Spaventos, and Copper Captains,
their heads fired both with glory and vainglory,
swarmed everywhere, ruling everything; and their
truculent enthusiasm set the nation ablaze.   The iron
lungs of these grim prætorians echoed loudly in the
covered *patios*; and, if they refrained from hissing the
plays of an old comrade, that was the limit of their
complaisance.   It was not enough for them that some
heroic old-world note should sound.   Their drama, as
they conceived (and, as I think, rightly conceived),
should be something that embodied magnificently the
motives of chivalric honour, careless gallantry, bright
intrigue, and the other mainsprings of the national
life.   Had not they themselves daily supplied the
dramatist with plots more ingeniously labyrinthine than
the cunningest artificer could dream? Were *capa y
espada* never to be seen upon the boards? Were they
and their great deeds alone to be unhonoured and
unsung? While Cervantes still stood at the parting of
the ways, hesitating between his private inclination and
the public taste, the question was solved by another
hand.   Lope de Vega was born to be the prophet of
the new school.   His ductile gifts lent themselves to
any turn of the wheel.   If his public wished for
Españolismo, for a drama racy of the soil, Lope lent his
great talents, his unrivalled facility to gratifying its
desire.   His copiousness carried all before it.   After

two or three performances no piece could be repeated.[1]
Lope was always ready with another play to take its
place. The less fertile writers were driven ignominiously from the field. But if Lope triumphed over
every rival, those rivals also had their revenge. The
cataract of facility which had submerged them was
destined to overcome their victor. Improvisation was
the ban of all their tribe, and Lope, the greatest
improvisatore of them all, was vanquished by the
exuberance of his own genius. No longer master of his
easy, melodious numbers, Lope too often degenerated
into the slave of words. He sank to be a mere fountain
of expression, a shallow spring of "situations," an
ingenious mechanician, an accomplished drudge, a
superior Hardy. He produced at least twenty million
verses—a mass of material before which even the
literary courage of the omnivorous Fox faltered,[2] of
which more than nineteen million lines are as completely forgotten and ignored as anything can be. Lope
the mighty, Lope the *Fénix* of the world, has paid the
penalty of his wilful, unscrupulous, mad ambition. But
if impartiality compels us to censure his shortcomings
with freedom, justice will extort the admission of his
virtues. That Lope made an enormous stride in the

---

[1] "Con el número asombroso de Drámas que Lope dió á los
corrales de tal modo se acostumbró el publico á la novedad, que
despues de las primeras representaciones no se repetian, aún pasado
algun tiempo."—La Poética ó Reglas de la poesía en General, y de sus
principales especies, por Don Ignacio de Luzán (Madrid, 1789), ii. p. 26.

[2] "The Early History of Charles James Fox," by George Otto
Trevelyan (London, 1880), p. 305.

right direction is beyond all doubt. He stamped the drama with the impress of the national life; he is in some sense the intellectual father of the adorable Calderón, and for this last gift alone—if it stood alone —he would deserve the eternal gratitude of posterity.

Against this resistless, all-conquering tide Cervantes fought in vain. He also was in his way an improvisatore; but he was slow, silent, dumb, by the side of the redundant Lope. His plays, if they had ever pleased, ceased to attract the public. Managers looked shyly at him; playwrights ceased to count him as a rival; playgoers turned their backs on him. His day was over; he belonged to the old school; he believed in the old methods. Popularity went by him. He had always longed for it : but he had never stooped to any common arts to obtain it. He never stood more in need of it than now. He had a wife, a daughter, sisters dependent on him. The years were fleeting by him. Playwriting at the best (save in the case of the phenomenal Lope) was ill-paid, and as his responsibilities became most acute, fate closed the gates of the theatre upon him.

> Men shut their doors against a setting sun.

His wife, indeed, had a modest dowry, which the care of the pious biographer has shown to consist of four or five vineyards, an orchard, a few cocks and hens, and a little furniture.

> An hundred pounds of marriage-money, doubtless,
> Is ever thirty pounds stirling, or somewhat less ;
> So that her thousand pounds, if she be thrifty,
> Is much near about two hundred and fifty.
> Howbeit, wooers and widows are never poor.

Yet even Matthew Merrygreek would have admitted that this particular wooer was miserably poor. There was nothing for it but to resign the proud aspirations which had once filled his sanguine soul and seek his scanty bread elsewhere.

But though the resolution was inevitable, Cervantes never quite abandoned hope. In 1592, years after he had removed to Seville, he signed a contract with one Rodrigo Osorio undertaking to write six comedies at fifty ducats each—the money not to be paid unless each play was "one of the best ever represented in Spain."[1] It is not probable that the writer ever fingered a maravedi of the money. Moreover, as the century came to a close, the position of the struggling dramatist became more and more difficult. The old quarrel with the Church broke out anew. In 1586–87 the question of the sinfulness of plays was gravely referred to the theologians: and even the Augustinian monk Fray Alonso de Mendoza, the *princeps laxistarum* of his day, could only venture to put forth a cautious, tentative approval.[2] Eleven years later Philip's daughter Catalina died; and, during the mock-solemn period of Court mourning, the representation of all plays was temporarily suspended. The clerical courtiers—among them Lupercio Leonardo de Argensola, whose *Isabela*

---

[1] " Nuevos documentos para ilustrar la vida de Miguel de Cervantes Saavedra con algunas observaciones . . . por D. José María Asensio y Toledo " (Sevilla, 1864), pp. 26–29.

[2] It may be worth while to give Mendoza's exact words: " el representar las Comedias, como aora se representan en España . . . de ningun modo es pecado mortal " (Pellicer, i. p. 120).

and *Alejandra* would seem to have been most deservedly damned—took this opportunity to put an end
to the theatre altogether.[1]   Four months before the
death of Philip II. a Royal rescript was issued, sup-
pressing the Spanish theatre at a blow.   At one fell
swoop all the playhouses were simultaneously closed.
Even though Cervantes had not already gone, it was
time for him to be gone now.

---

[1] The decree was issued May 2, 1598. There would seem to have
been reason for it if it were true to say of the comedians, " Que salian
á representar desnudos, y que sin ninguna reverencia ni temor del cielo
ni de la tierra, ni respeto del auditorio, imitaban estrupos y acciones
desvergonzadas." (Pellicer, i. p. 147).   But it would be impossible
to exaggerate the contempt and hatred felt at this time by most
Spaniards of position for players and almost all connected with the
boards; "esos infames y disolutos," "gente perdidísima," "estos
indecentes," "rufianes sucios y deshonestos," are moderate specimens
of the invective poured forth on the mummers of the time.   Dramatists were of course exempted from the public disdain which concentrated itself on the actors.   The same feeling, though diminished,
continues in Spain to this day, and, in a lesser degree, in France.
Cp. M. Jules Lemaître's "Impressions de Théâtre" (Première Série,
pp. 307–318): . . . "je me trouve un peu gêné pour louer les
comédiens."   M. Jules Lemaître's *pudeur* (so he says) stands in his
way.   Irony apart, it does stand in the way of most Spaniards, who
have always in their minds what Bossuet calls "la prostitution de
corps purifiés par le baptême."   Thus they inconsistently love the
theatre and despise the actors.

CHAPTER VI.

DIE WANDERJAHRE : THE FIRST PART OF
DON QUIXOTE.

In tenui labor, at tenuis non gloria.
Georgics, iv. 6.

None are so surely caught, when they are catch'd,
As wit turn'd fool.
Love's Labour's Lost, Act V., sc. ii.

WHEN Cervantes left Esquivias in 1587, Lope's star had not yet risen on the Madrileño stage. That miraculous boy, having tried his wings on the boards during his exile at Valencia, was about this time alternating between brief paroxysms of sorrow, on account of the death of his first wife, Isabel de Urbina, and prolonged agonies of despair because of his rejection by his pseudonymous Filis. But Lope was not the man to break his heart about a woman and, after addressing a number of fruitless ballads to his mistress' eyebrow (he was always copious), came back to the regions of common sense once more, and enlisted in the squadrons of the Great Armada. At this period it should seem that he looked rather to London than to Madrid for immortality.

The great desire of needy Spaniards in all ages has

been to obtain some post in the Administration—a
curious ambition which, however, is shared by other
peoples under both democratic and absolutist systems.
Beggars cannot be choosers ; and Cervantes, who shared
to the full the average ideas of his countrymen, probably
thought himself fortunate in obtaining some humble
post under Diego de Valdivia, in the Audiencia Real at
Seville in 1587. Grotesque as the notion is, it is
scarcely likely that the sympathetic nations which gene-
rously provided for Burns as a gauger, for Hawthorne as a
consul, and for M. Coppée as a petty clerk, will appreciate
the incongruity of Cervantes serving a grateful country
as a process-server and tax-gatherer. He himself had
no time, and probably little inclination, to philosophise
over the general unfitness of things mundane; and he was
no doubt glad enough to keep the wolf from the door by
any honest means. His capacity for sanguine self-
delusion was so inordinate that he may have persuaded
himself that he was once more on the high road to
fortune when in June, 1588, he was promoted to the
post of deputy-purveyor to the Armada, with Antonio
de Guevara as his chief.[1] He was by temperament the
least exact, the least formal, the least methodical man
in the world. Naturally he was appointed to discharge
functions where exactitude, formality, and method were
indispensable. Conscious of his own unfitness for the

[1] Cp. Navarrete, pp. 411 *et seq.*, and Asensio y Toledo, pp. 1–2
and 43. Cervantes' letter, as given by Asensio y Toledo, is dated
February 24, 1588. León Máinez (pp. 101–102) maintains that
there must be a mistake with regard to this date. I confess I fail to
see any force in the argument which he offers.

administrative and executive duties which fell to him, he seems to have exerted himself strenuously to satisfy the official ideas of regularity and decorum. The new functionary, thirsting for distinction, entered on his work with characteristic vigour. It was not long before his pious zeal got him into trouble. His methods were probably more military than civil. His energy so far outran his discretion as to bring down on his unhappy head a sentence of excommunication with regard to some high-handed proceedings in the town of Écija.[1] His guarantors, Juan de Nava Cabeza de Vaca and Luís Marmolejo, must have already begun to feel some uneasiness. In the meantime, the energetic official scoured the country on all sides, collecting oil, grain, and (it may be feared) *duelos y quebrantos.* But even the preparations for the Invincible Armada came to an end at last; and, in default of any other resource, Cervantes, in May, 1590, on the strength of his past services, addressed a petition to the King (his courage was always prominent), humbly praying that he might be appointed (1) Accountant-General of the new kingdom of Granada; or (2) Governor of Seconusco in Guatemala; or (3) Paymaster of the galleys at Cartagena; or (4) Corregidor in the city of La Paz—all of which posts were then vacant. This modest supplication was not unnaturally disregarded, and remained in the dusty, discreet, official

---

[1] The letter of February 24, 1588, is clear on this point . . . "les pedir y suplicar me manden asolber remotamente o a reinsidencia de la sensura y escomunion que contra mi por aber yo tomado y enbargado el trigo de las fabricas de la dicha ciudad de Écija," etc.

pigeon-hole till Juan Agustín Ceán Bermúdez unearthed it in 1808.[1] In 1591–2 the petitioner was serving under Pedro de Isunza, collecting wheat, *garbanzos*, and other commissariat necessaries. Perhaps things were looking up—perhaps they were more than ever desperate—when Cervantes signed his Quixotic contract with Rodrigo Osorio in 1592. In August, 1594, he was in Madrid on business connected with his office, and later on in the year he was at Baza, having been appointed tax-gatherer in the province of Granada.[2]

Now and again his thoughts turned back from tax-gathering to *belles lettres*. As in, 1583 he had contributed a sonnet to Padilla's *Romancero*, as he had done the same kind office to the *Austriada* of Juan Gutiérrez Rufo (1584) and the *Cancionero* of López Maldonado (1586), so in his contributions to the *Filosofía cortesana moralizada* of Alonso de Barros and the *Dragontea* of Lope de Vega[3] he once more showed his conjoint good nature and love of literature. In 1595 three prizes were offered by the Dominicans of Zaragoza

----

[1] Navarrete, pp. 312–313. The official note on this application is : "Busque por acá en que se le haga merced."

[2] Ibid. pp. 415, 418, *et seq.*

[3] Ticknor (ii. p. 203) states very positively that the "Dragontea" was not published till 1604, when, as he says, it was issued with the "Hermosura de Angélica." Both statements are incorrect. The "Dragontea" was published separately at Valencia in 1598, and the "Hermosura de Angélica" was issued in Madrid in 1602. It is right to say that, with regard to the latter work, Ticknor's statement is given with a reservation suggested by Salvá (ii. p. 201). And, on the whole, it is impossible not to admire the sagacity with which Ticknor has made his way across the trackless deserts which environ the bibliography of Lope.

for the three best *glosas* on a *redondilla* in honour
of St. Hyacinth, recently canonised by Clement VIII.
It may be doubted whether the three silver spoons
which Cervantes carried off from this literary joust as
the first prize freed him from all pecuniary troubles.
In 1596 Cádiz was sacked by the English under the
aspiring, arduous, brilliant Essex. The pillage over, the
spoil-laden invaders retired, and the sluggish Duke of
Medina Sidonia triumphantly entered the evacuated
city at the head of the Spanish troops—a cheap feat of
valour celebrated by Cervantes in his disdainful sonnet :

> Vimos en julio otro semana santa
> Atestada de ciertas cofradías
> Que los soldados llaman compañías,
> De quien el vulgo, y no el inglés, se espanta.[1]

But his literary labours were necessarily brief. He
had, indeed, very serious preoccupations of his own. His
official obligations were no joke. In (or before) 1595 he
had entrusted 7,400 *reales* of official moneys to one
Simón Freire de Lima, of Seville, to pay into the
treasury at Madrid. Freire de Lima, like other fidu-
ciaries before and since, became bankrupt and absconded.
The victimised Cervantes returned to Seville to give an
account of himself, and to recover as much as possible
from the estate of the defaulter. Some two-thirds of
the debt were thus summarily discharged : but, as the
remainder was still unpaid in 1597, a writ was issued

---

[1] Juan Sanz de Zumeta, mentioned in the "Canto de Calíope,"
wrote a sonnet on the same subject. See pp. 153–154 of this volume.

against Cervantes, who was seized and imprisoned from September till December.[1]

The history of the next five or six years is more than ever obscure. On September 13, 1598, Philip II. died. His funeral rites were magnificently celebrated through the length and breadth of Spain. In Seville the ceremonial was of unwonted splendour; and the catafalque of Juan de Oviedo was reckoned among the wonders of the age. But the solemnity of the occasion was marred by a vulgar brawl between the Inquisition and the civil power with regard to the right of the lay President to cover his seat with a piece of black cloth. The tribunal of the Inquisition (in 1598) had a short method with recalcitrants. The civil power was excommunicated, whereon the priest at once retired to finish his mass in the sacristy, the preacher ran hastily out of the pulpit, while the civil officials and the inquisitionary familiars kept up a hideous wrangle till four in the afternoon, to the scandal of all decent people.[2] This edifying scene took place on November 26. Finally the matter was referred to arbitration; the obsequies were adjourned till the end of December;

---

[1] The *Real Provisión* with regard to Freire de Lima, is given in Navarrete (pp. 435–436). For the imprisonment of 1597, cp. Navarrete (pp. 437–439).

[2] "Segunda parte de la Historia y Grandezas de la Gran Ciudad de Sevilla por El Licenciado Don Pablo de Espinosa de los Monteros" (Sevilla, 1630). This writer is full of unconscious humour: *e.g.* Juan de Oviedo draws his sketch of the *túmulo*, "y acabada la presento en el Cabildo de que todos quedaron muy agradados, pareciendo cosa muy superior" (f. 112). And again, "Sera impossible describir

and in the meanwhile country bumpkins, round-eyed,
gaping, poured in by the shoal, and, seated in the superb
silleria of Nufro Sánchez, passed their patronising,
provincial judgments on the handiwork of Vasco
Pereyra, Salcedo, Pacheco, and Delgado.[1] The opportunity was irresistible to the satirist, and Cervantes, in
his irregular sonnet,—

> Voto á Dios, que me espanta esta grandeza
> Y que diera un doblon por describilla ;
> Porque ¿ á quién no sorprende y maravilla
> Esta máquina insigne, esta riqueza ?—

gives us a much clearer idea of the occasion than can be
derived from the tremendous *Historia y Grandezas de la
Gran Ciudad de Sevilla* of Espinosa, who would seem
to have taken for his model the twenty-fifth, twenty-
sixth, and twenty-seventh chapters of Exodus.

Soon after this sonnet was written Cervantes made
his way into La Mancha where the eager, arduous man
of genius picked up a scanty, squalid living as tithe-
proctor to the Priory of St. John. In an interesting
series of articles, entitled *Cervantes en Valladolid*,
published by that admirable scholar, D. Pascual de
Gayangos, in the *Revista de España*, it is suggested
that Cervantes had applied for some such office as early

---

ni pintar la grandeza, primor y bizarreria que tuvo " (ibid.). After
which statement he gives a most minute description (ff. 112–115).
Canon Luciano de Negrón said the mass; Fray Juan Bernal was in the
pulpit. " Y el Regente se sentó solo en banco cubierto cõ un paño
negro " (f. 171). This official's name was Pedro López de Alday.

[1] Cp. " Annals of the Artists of Spain, by William Stirling "
(London, 1848), vol. i. p. 403.

as 1584.[1] It is with profound self-distrust that I venture to dissent from the theory of an expert so eminent. His height is six cubits and a span; his helmet, his coat of mail, his greaves, his target of brass are terrible; his spear is like a weaver's beam; yet I, even I, with five smooth stones out of a brook, must hazard an encounter with a foe so formidable. The authority upon which D. Pascual de Gayangos relies is a MS. letter from the Licenciado Sanctoyo de Molina to Mateo Vázquez—a letter from which he quotes the following passage: "Para Segura de la Sierra vienen propuestos (por el Consejo) Rubín de Celis, Cervantes y Canto. El Rubín no conviene de ninguna manera; el Cervantes es muy benemérito, y sirvió ya el partido de Montanches muy bien: á Canto no le conozco." On this basis rests D. Pascual's contention that in, or previous to, 1584 Cervantes had already been officially employed in Estremadura.

The contention is new, and I am quite willing to admit that, to use a celebrated phrase, it is "important, if true." I shall endeavour as briefly as possible to show cause why the new hypothesis should be rejected. Any one reading the citation of D. Pascual de Gayangos would naturally imagine that the phrase cited by him occurred in the text of the letter. Will it be believed that the words quoted do not exist in the text? The actual passage, so far as I can decipher it, runs as follows:

A Segura de Sierra va rubin de celis: yo no le conozco: es de los de respetos y fabores y no ay q̃ hazer caso del y si no fuera por

---

[1] "Revista de España" (vol. xcvii. p. 49 *et seq.*, and vol. xcix. p. 5 *et seq.*).

fabor no fuera ay puesto ni en otro officio. El lic^{do} ccuantes (?) va en 2° lugar y en razõ y justicia abia de ir en el primero porῆ este estaua en Montanches quãd su mag^t vino de Portugal y paso por alli cerca y V. oiria dezir en aquella tierra mucho bien y ῆ no a tenido tal juez y asi sin duda mereze mejor el off^o ῆ esotros. El canto tanpoco le conozco ni se si es bueno ni malo : y asi no tengo que dezir sino ῆ si su mag^t no se lo da le hara mucho agravio porῆ dio la mejor residencia que yo e visto y tiene todas las buenas partes ῆ se requierẽ y porῆ entiendo que es consciencia quitarselo digo esto.[1]

The words quoted by D. Pascual de Gayangos do not, then, occur in text. They do, however, in a slightly different form, occur in an endorsement, in another hand, and of much later date, on the back of Molina's letter. D. Pascual de Gayangos, it would seem, has merely altered the *précis* of the endorser from the third to the first person. It is by no means certain that the *Ceuantes* of the text should be read Cervantes ; and in any case there is not the slightest ground for thinking that the passage refers in any way to the author of *Don Quixote.* There is no reason to suppose that Cervantes ever studied law, or that he had the slightest acquaintance with its principles. Had it been so, he would assuredly have let us know it. It is absolutely certain that he never calls himself a Licenciado, nor is he ever so styled by any one who knew him ; on the contrary, some wits of the baser sort made merry over the unclerkly man on the ground that he had never taken his degree.[2] Nor is it credible that the newly ransomed

---

[1] The letter is from the Licenciado Sanctoyo de Molina to Vázquez. It is dated April 1, 1584, and may be found in the British Museum Library, Add. 28,364, f. 209.

[2] I give this on the authority of Navarrete, who quotes from Tamayo de Vargas the phrase *ingenio lego* (p. 32).

slave had ever previous to 1584 held the position of judge at any court. Whatever Cervantes learned in Algiers, we may take it for certain that his studies did not lie in the direction of jurisprudence. It is beyond belief that in the Spain of the sixteenth century any magistrate of even the most inferior tribunal should within two years have sunk so low as to go a-begging for the humble, not to say odious, office of process-server. I must confess that I find myself, then, unable to accept D. Pascual de Gayangos' suggestion, which I venture to think would never have been made had he examined more attentively the document from which he professes to quote. From a controversial point so distasteful, I turn with pleasure to Cervantes in La Mancha.

Here, probably at Argamasilla de Alba, according to a too likely legend, the much-enduring man was sent to jail. He had been imprisoned before, and was destined to be imprisoned again ; but there was nothing exceptional in the experience. Imprisonment was unhappily an incident common enough in the lives of Spanish writers. In the earliest dawn of Spanish literature, the celebrated Macías *El Enamorado* had been imprisoned at Arjonilla before the javelin winged by marital jealousy silenced that passionate voice for ever.[1] The penultimate days of the illustrious Diego Hurtado de Mendoza were passed in exile and disgrace. The great

---

[1] Very little precise information with regard to Macías *El Enamorado* can be gathered. I must avow myself much disappointed with the account in "Die alten Liederbücher der Portugiesen oder Beiträge zur Geschichte der portugiesischen Poesie etc. herausgegeben von Dr. Christian F. Bellermann" (Berlin, 1840), pp. 24-26.

Garcilaso himself was pent up in one of the Danubian islets. The saintly Luís de León was kept in custody by the Inquisition for five years.[1] Mateo Alemán, the author of that masterpiece of *picaresco* writing, *Guzmán de Alfarache*, was laid by the heels, for irregularities in his official accounts not unlike those attributed to Cervantes. Lope de Vega was imprisoned for satirising one Jerónimo de Velázquez; and the learned Jesuit Mariana expiated some portions of his *Tractatus VII.* in like manner. In a later generation Quevedo, the most pungent of Spanish wits, was imprisoned time upon time. In his younger days he had the misfortune to kill in a duel a noble who had struck and otherwise insulted a woman in the church of San Martín in Madrid. Perhaps if he had killed a mere gentleman Quevedo might have brazened it out; but society has always drawn an equivocal (and certainly not unnecessary) distinction between a gentleman and a man of rank. He fled to Naples, where he had obtained the highest distinction as a diplomatist, when a turn of the wheel in political affairs threw him into prison for two years. Later, in the *Chitón de las Tarabillas*, careless, or perhaps ignorant, of Mariana's castigation for his *De Mutatione Monetae*, Quevedo attacked the debasement of the coinage. Taken in conjunction with the publication of his *Memorial por el patronato de*

---

[1] The life contributed by D. Eustaquio Fernández de Navarrete to vol. xvi. of the "Documentos Inéditos" contains much valuable information with regard to Garcilaso. The painful story of the inquisitionary examination of Luís de León is given in vol. x. of the same series.

Santiago, his offence was grave, and was atoned for by another period of imprisonment. Monstrous as this appears, it can scarcely be doubted that if Walpole, Grafton, and the corrupt Whiteshed could have had their own way in the matter of Wood's halfpence, Swift —with more reason—would have similarly expiated the publication of *The Drapier's Letters*. In Quevedo's sixtieth year a copy of caustic verses beginning—

> Católica, sacra, y real majestad
> Que Dios en la tierra os hizo deidad :
> Un anciano pobre, sencillo y honrado,
> Humilde os invoca y os habla postrado—

was found under the King's serviette. Rightly or wrongly, Quevedo was suspected of being the author. By order of Olivares, the infirm, gray-haired poet was arrested without a particle of evidence, dragged from his bed at midnight, and whisked off to the monastery of San Marcos de León, where he was confined till the downfall of the Minister four years later.[1]

It is obvious, then, that imprisonment was no new, strange thing to the unhappy quill-drivers of Spain. It befell those who lived before Cervantes as it befell those who came after him ; nor could even the bitter malignity of literary and political faction base upon an incident so commonplace any allegation against their (or his) honour. It is always safe to assume of every eminent Spanish writer of the period that he has been in prison. The

---

[1] With regard to Quevedo I have followed the sketch of his life given by D. Aureliano Fernández-Guerra y Orbe. See Rivadeneyra, xxiii. (Madrid, 1852).

only disputed point which can arise is as to the actual scene of the imprisonment. Of absolute evidence that Cervantes was imprisoned at Argamasilla de Alba there is no jot. Navarrete, on the authority of Fray Antonio Sánchez Liaño, quotes a line and a half from an alleged letter of Cervantes, written from the prison house in Argamasilla de Alba, to his uncle Juan Bernabé de Saavedra, of Alcázar de San Juan, begging for assistance. The exact words are: "Luengos dias y menguadas noches me fatigan en esta cárcel, ó mejor diré caverna."[1] There is no proof that this reputed letter was written from Argamasilla de Alba, and it is important to observe that the original is unknown. Sánchez Liaño himself does not profess to have seen it, though he states that he once had a copy of it. He does not state where, or by whom, the copy was taken; he does not explain how he became possessed of it: and it is, to say the least, unfortunate that even the copy, with the suspicious, if not fatal, tendency of Spanish documents, should have disappeared during Sánchez Liaño's lifetime. It seems strange, too, that he should never have made a second copy of a paper so important. Such, however, seems to have been the case, and for the correctness of the passage cited above we have to trust to Sánchez Liaño's memory.

The story of Cervantes' imprisonment at Argamasilla de Alba rests chiefly on tradition, and all sorts of ingenious theories have been invented—as though any were needed!—to explain it.[2] One legend is that it was due to his unpopularity as a tax-collector; another,

---

[1] Navarrete, pp. 450–453.   [2] Ibid. p. 95.

that it was because of the pollution of the Guadiana,
to the injury of the neighbouring farmers, by a manu-
factory in which Cervantes was interested; a third
version accounts for the disaster by attributing to Cervantes the utterance of some satirical remarks on—if
not to—an Argamasillan lady, whose influential friends
gave their retort this unpleasant form. There is not
much probability in the two latter theories. Cervantes
was never lucky enough to be connected with manu-
factories—unless, it may be, in some such humble
position as that of night-watchman, a position which
would protect him from notice. As to the last story,
it should be observed, firstly, that nothing that we
know of Cervantes leads us to think it at all likely
that he was the sort of man to insult a woman; and,
secondly, it should be said that, if the Argamasillans
of his time at all resembled those of to-day, an insult
to a lady would have been avenged by her relatives
in a manner much more peremptory and final than by
mere imprisonment. The lady, according to the local
mythus, is said to have been the niece of a certain
Rodrigo de Pacheco, who at one time or another had
been something of a lunatic. The tradition still lingers
in Argamasilla de Alba that the likeness of this interesting couple are worked into a votive picture of
the Virgin which overhangs an altar in the parish
church. Whether or no Argamasilla de Alba was the
scene of Cervantes' imprisonment, whether *Don Quixote*
was or was not conceived there, and whatever the reason
of that imprisonment may have been, there can be no

doubt that Cervantes knew the topography of the district minutely. Argamasilla de Alba is almost certainly Don Quixote's town. Indeed, the natives still claim him as their townsman. But, apart from this, the references to Puerto Lapice, the Field of Montiel, and the course of the Guadiana—to give but a few examples —place it beyond reasonable doubt that Argamasilla de Alba, and no other, was that place in La Mancha, " the name of which," as the author of *Don Quixote* drily said, "I have no desire to recall." [1]

The local legend, which still points to the cellar of the *Casa de Medrano* as the scene of the imprisonment, was believed by Hartzenbusch to an extent sufficient at least to induce him to print two editions of *Don Quixote* in the dismal hole.

This period of imprisonment has generally been dated 1599–1601. D. Ramón León Máinez, however, states that a document has been brought to light in the Municipal Archives of Seville which goes to show that Cervantes resided in that city between 1600–1603.[2] But the document has not been offered for examination, and without minute scrutiny it is impossible to accept it as genuine. In 1601 Philip III. and the Court left Madrid for Valladolid.[3] Judging from Góngora's sonnets—

---

[1] "En un lugar de la Mancha, de cuyo nombre no quiero recordarme."—Don Quixote, Pt. I. c. i.

[2] León Máinez, p. 107.

[3] Cp. Cabrera de Córdoba's " Relación de las cosas sucedidas en la Corte de España desde 1599 hasta 1614 " (Madrid, 1857), pp. 93, 95.

Valladolid, de lágrimas sois valle
Y no quiero deciros quien las llora,

and

¿Vos sois Valladolid? Vois sois el valle
De olor? Oh fragrantísima ironía,—

there was at least one very vocal person by whom the courtly flitting was disapproved, and the ultimate return to Madrid would seem to show that the Cordovan poet by no means stood alone.[1]

In 1603, Cervantes, who had apparently sunk in a Serbonian bog of poverty, reappeared on this brilliant scene to have his paltry, dog's-eared, muddled account-books audited once more. It is scarcely doubtful that he came, too, with the hope of picking up a few crumbs from the official table; or, at least, with a view to begging help towards the publishing of a MS. which he brought with him. The Duque de Lerma, the first Minister of the day, was very much of Pitt's opinion, that literature could take care of itself; and, in any case, Cervantes was not to Lerma what he is to us— one of the world's heroes. He was only a crippled, threadbare suppliant—one of the ten thousand needy

---

[1] Sonnets 78 and 81 in Rivadeneyra (vol. xxxiii.). Quevedo also seems to have hated Valladolid. See Rivadeneyra, vol. lxix. p. 198.

"No fuera tanto tu mal,
Valladolid opulenta,
Si ya te deja el rey,
Te dejáran los poetas. . . .
No quiero alabar tus calles
Pues son, hablando de veras,
Unas tuertas y otras bizcas,
Y todo de lodo ciegas."

P

place-hunters who infested the Ministerial anterooms. It is just possible that if Lerma had realised that the roll of paper under the shabby applicant's arm was the original of *Don Quixote*, even his ducal sense of appreciation might have been quickened; but, as it was, literature, left to take care of itself, was speedily shown the door. The poverty-stricken, shabby petitioner, not unaccustomed to rebuffs, gathering his papers together, walked contentedly away, and betook himself to any humble copying or common hack-work which came to his hand.

While the patron still lingered dubiously on the vague horizon of hope, Cervantes had had a too painful experience of the proverbial concomitants of patronage. Toil, envy, want, the jail and the squalid son of genius were old, almost inseparable, companions. It was high time for the patron to appear, and at last the necessary man was found in the person of the Duque de Béjar.[1] An entirely unsupported but agreeable legend tells us that the Duke, though at first by no means anxious to accept

---

[1] The Duque de Béjar was obsequiously worshipped by many men of letters of the time. Cp. a sonnet of Lope's in his "Rimas" (Lisboa, 1605), f. 33, s. cxxxi. :

"Con nuevo timbre, y nuevos Coroneles
  Vuestro nombre, con letras de diamante
  Pondra su fama en su dorado Alcazar."

Six years later Cristóbal de Mesa in his "Rimas" (Madrid, 1611), f. 95, addresses the Duke as " el Mecenas de nuestro edad, y el Augusto de nuestro siglo "; and again—

"La espada en una, el libro en otra mano,
  Sacro Apolo Español, y Marte fiero " (f. 97).

the dedication, finally consented that the author should read some specimen chapters to a roomful of critical listeners in the Duke's house, and that the delighted appreciation of the audience decided him in the writer's favour. It would be difficult to say what *Don Quixote* is not: it certainly is, among many other things, a merciless parody of the whole school of chivalrous romance. As *Don Florisel de Niquea*, one of the most ludicrous examples of the type, had been dedicated to a former Duque de Béjar by Feliciano de Silva, some preliminary hesitation was not unnatural in a man who may be said to have had an hereditary interest in extravagant absurdity. The current legend further asserts that the hostile bias of the Duke was strengthened by the confessor of the family. Every one knows the passage in *Don Quixote* which pillories " a grave ecclesiastic, one of those who regulate noblemen's houses ; one of those who, not being nobly born themselves, never succeed in teaching noble conduct to those who are so born ; one of those who seek to level the nobility of the great to the pettiness of their own minds ; one of those who, striving to teach economy, impart meanness to those under them." If the accusation against the Duque de Béjar's chaplain be just, Cervantes' fierce lunge was not without cause.[1]

It may be taken as certain that the public reading in the Duke's house by no means stood alone. More than six months before the publication of *Don Quixote*, we find the Dominican Andrés Pérez mentioning the

---

[1] "Don Quixote," Pt. II. cap. xxxi.

immortal Manchegan madman in a copy of truncated *sextillas* in the *Pícara Justina* :[1]

> Soy la Reyn de Picardi
> Mas que la Rud conoci,
> Mas famo que doña Oli,
> Que Don Quixo y Lazari,
> Que alfarache y Celesti,
> Sino me conoces cue,
> 　　Yoy so due
> 　　Que todas las aguas be.

The *Privilegio* of the *Pícara Justina* is dated August 22, 1604. *Don Quixote* did not appear until December, 1604, or January, 1605.

Lope de Vega was now almost in the zenith of his fame. His *Arcadia*, his *Dragontea*, his *Fiestas de Denia*, his *Hermosura de Angélica*, and the first volume of his *Comedias*, were before the world. He had also published his *Peregrino en su patria*, a work interesting in itself, and, bibliographically speaking, invaluable on account of the prefatory list of two hundred and nineteen plays already produced by the writer. He had tried almost every school of writing. He had succeeded greatly in most kinds and had failed in none. He was the foremost man of letters in Spain and

---

[1] "Libro de Entretenimiento de la Pícara Justina, etc. Compuesto por el Licenciado Francisco de Ubeda, natural de Toledo" (Medina del Campo, 1605), lib. ii. pt. iii. f. 180. Rivadeneyra has reprinted this work (Madrid, 1854). The reference, which I give for those to whom the original is inaccessible, is vol. xxxiii. p. 143.

This period of Cervantes' life is delightfully told in "La locura contagiosa," by Hartzenbusch. "Cuentos y fábulas" (Madrid, 1861), pp. 1-15.

could afford to be generous. But he had heard of a certain romance by Cervantes which, as it had not been condemned out of hand, stirred the anger of the magnanimous poet. In a letter given by Schack we find the triumphant writer expressing his opinion of the unpublished book in the following terms : " I speak not of poets. Many are in blossom for the coming year, but none of them is as bad as Cervantes—none of them so foolish as to praise *Don Quixote*."[1] It is not worth while to inquire whether this opinion were sincere or not. It is not more difficult to imagine the cause of Lope's querulous communings than to guess the origin of Richardson's scandalised references to *Tom Jones.* Lope, like Richardson, had the advantage of not having read the book which he criticised ; and Richardson, like Lope, knew a rival when he saw one.

And so, the trial at the Duke's over, the book got itself published at last. The *Privilegio* was signed on September 26, and the *Tassa* on December 20, 1604. In the early part of 1605, Juan de la Cuesta, of Madrid, issued *Don Quixote* in a clumsy, ill-printed quarto volume of 316 folios. Its success was immediate. Slow

---

[1] "Nachträge zur Geschichte der dramatischen Literatur und Kunst in Spanien von Adolph Friedrich von Schack" (Frankfurt-am-Main, 1854), p. 33.

"De Poetas no digo. Muchos en cierne por el año que viene, pero ninguno hay tan malo como Cervantes ni tan necio que alabe á Don Quixote . . .

'A satira me voy mi paso a paso,'

cosa para mi mas odiosa, que mis comedias a Cervantes." This is dated from Toledo, August 4, 1604. Lope's quotation is from Garcilaso's second Elegy—á *Boscán.*

as the sale of books was in the south-west of Europe at that time, within seven months the volume had run through four editions, and a private bookseller in Lisbon found it worth while to print an edition for Portugal. No work ever became more suddenly or more permanently the vogue. This is not the place in which a formal criticism of *Don Quixote* need be attempted, but the unexampled popularity of the new romance showed that a fresh vein had been struck. The day of the old, dreary, interminable, labyrinthine, impossible, crack-brained romances of chivalry was over. *Don Quixote* only tolled their knell. The day of the romance of manners, with its acute introspection, its keen analysis of motive, its problems of morbid psychology, had not yet dawned. But there was perhaps a more excellent way. There was still room for a large utterance on the great commonplaces of existence—on love and death—

> Fratelli, a un tempo stesso, Amore e Morte
> Ingenerò la sorte.

There was still room for a declaration, an exposition, of the true and false ; of the painful, necessary contrast of the ideal with the actual ; of the pathetic difference between aspiration and accomplishment ; of the stormy ocean which divides the vision from the retrospect ; of the immeasurable interval which separates the magnificent blue of poetry from the subdued drab of prose. Don Quixote is the cavalier always blind to obvious fact, always soaring into the breathless empyrean ; Sancho, the humble squire, the grotesque Quaker who, reducing his master's delusions to their lowest terms,

keeps as much as possible to the turnpike road. The
one treads on the crooked path of the stars; the other,
while he is saved by pondering on the path of his feet,
is too often led astray, in defiance of his senses, by
the contagious enthusiasm of his companion. Prose
and poetry struggle for the mastery; delusion and
what we ironically call common sense contend for possession. The balance sways this way and then returns.
Yet if Sancho be in some sort the confessor, Don Quixote
is never the penitent. A hell of witchcraft lies in the
subtle *finesse* of this ironical, kindly, contemptuous
scrutiny of life. Never before had satire taken to
herself a form so enticing. Never before had illusion
reached a point so high. Yet even in laughter the
heart is sorrowful and the end of mirth is heaviness.

To say that the work has its limitations is to say
that the author was mortal. But whatever its shortcomings may be, the eager public which pored over
it in the spring and summer of 1605 were in no mood
for importunate fault-finding. Some part of their pleasure
was found, no doubt, in the sly allusions to contemporaries—a piquant characteristic which charmed at
least one generation of readers as much as its smiling
wisdom, its fine observation and deep philosophy delight
their posterity. The book was in every hand, and a
gleam of success at last shot across the penurious,
sordid life of the author. It was high time. Born for
immortality, Cervantes' genius blossomed late. When
he was correcting his proofs for Cuesta, he was in his
fifty-eighth year.

CHAPTER VII.

AT THE CAPITAL : THE *NOVELAS.*

Sir Walter, though he spoke no foreign language with facility, read Spanish as well as Italian. He expressed the most unbounded admiration for Cervantes, and said that the "novelas" of that author had first inspired him with the ambition of excelling in fiction, and that, until disabled by illness, he had been a constant reader of them.—LOCKHART, *Memoirs of Sir Walter Scott,* ch. lxxxiii.

Pareceme, señores, que despues que murio nuestro Español Bocacio (quiero dezir Miguel de Ceruantes). . . .—TIRSO DE MOLINA, *Cigarrales de Toledo,* pp. 193–194.

DURING the months which immediately followed the publication of *Don Quixote,* Cervantes seemed to live on the crest of the wave. After a rigorous life of hardship, poverty, and disappointment, he had fought his way into something like notice and even fame. He probably had a little money at this time and, though it would seem that he spent some of it in very undesirable ways, it may be hoped that the women of the family no longer needed to take in sewing from the Marqués de Villafranca.[1] It is even thought by

---

[1] I gather this episode from D. Pascual de Gayangos' article in the "Revista de España" (xcvii. p. 498). There is something amazingly wrong in D. Pascual's reference to the "Papeles del consejo de los Ordenes y consultos Originales de su Presidente entre los

some that his prosperity was so abounding that he attained the ghastly distinction of becoming a Court historiographer.

Valladolid was the scene of much public rejoicing in the spring of 1605. The future Philip IV. was born on Good Friday, April 8. On May 26, Lord Nottingham, the envoy charged with the ratification of the treaty of peace between Great Britain and Spain, arrived with his suite. The christening of the heir-apparent and the arrival of the ambassador were celebrated with a double splendour which scandalised the unbending Pharisees of the capital. There is in existence an anonymous record of these festivities entitled *Relación de lo sucedido en la ciudad de Valladolid desde el punto del felicísimo nacimiento del Príncipe Don Felipe*, etc.—a supposititious or pseudipigraphal work attributed to Cervantes by some excellent judges.[1] For my own part, I fail to detect the

---

años de 1572 y 1585," which in the Library of the British Museum are numbered 28,364. The actual title of the MS. is "Memorias de Valladolid"; the press-mark is Add. MS. 20,812. The actual passage (f. 209), so far as I can decipher it, is: "Lope Garcia de La Torre coneceis vos, y deixa sua molher muy dama e fermosa 200 o 300 até de manhã e elle vai se deitar, e quando a dama responde, calla y dexadme, no quereis Lope Garcya? Ceruantes, dá me aquella palmatoria, veremos si le hago callar, como jugava de lo vuestro, renid, mientras juego lo mio, callad." For the connection with Villafranca, see Navarrete, p. 455.

[1] The precise title of this pamphlet is "Relacion de lo sucedido en la ciudad de Valladolid, desde el punto del felicisimo nacimiento del Principe Don Felipe Dominico Victor, Ntro Señor, hasta que se acabaron las demostraciones de alegria que por el se hizieron" (Valladolid, 1605). The "Tassa" is dated October 19, 1605.

hand of the master in this bald, commonplace story of
the Court newsman.   Yet it seems clear that contemporary speculation fixed upon Cervantes as the writer.
Góngora refers to it in his usual malevolent style, and
fifteen years later the rumour had lost nothing of its
vitality.[1]   But the authenticity of the pamphlet still
remains to some slight extent in doubt.

Cervantes had played many parts.   He had been
an ecclesiastic's chamberlain, a soldier, a captive, a
slave, an ambassador, a writer of pastoral romance,
a process-server, a jail-bird, an immortal novelist
amongst other things.   The power "which erring
men call chance" had a still stranger experience in
store.   It only remained for him to be arrested on
suspicion of murder to complete the tale, and completed it accordingly was.   There lived about the Court
at this time—probably in the agreeable character of
general hanger-on—a certain gentleman of Pamplona
named Gaspar de Ezpeleta, who had recently been

---

[1] Góngora's sonnet (Juan Antonio Pellicer, p. cxv.) is unmistakable in its assertion ; the last two lines—

"Mandáronse escribir estas hazañas
A Don Quixote, á Sancho y su jumento"—

are decisive.   Barrera ("Obras," vol. i. p. cxlvi.) quotes from an
anonymous writer of 1620 : "Miro la memoria que la antigüedad
hace de los gastos.   Y de otros infinitos se pudiera traer ejemplos
y de nuestro tiempo, lea á Miguel de Servantes, en la Relacion,"
etc.   Góngora's part in this matter is extremely characteristic.   These
shows were so absurd that it was only fit that Cervantes should com-
memorate them.   On the other hand, they were so magnificent as to
lend to Lerma a splendour which Góngora enshrined in verse
(Rivadeneyra, xxxii. p. 437).

thrown from his horse at some joust or bull-fight in a manner so public and opprobrious as to invite the banter of Góngora, who felt called upon to celebrate the misfortune of the unlucky knight in a copy of stinging *décimas*.[1]　On the night of June 27, 1605, after supping with the Marqués de Falcés, the Captain of the Royal Archers of the Guard, D. Gaspar left his friend's house and, after the sauntering manner of the Court gallant, strolled along till, nearly an hour later, he came to a wooden footbridge—perhaps the same mentioned by the disgusted Cordovan—crossing the scanty stream of the Esgueva, at no great distance from the well-known Prado de Magdalena.[2]　Here he

---

[1]　　Cantemos á la gineta
　　　Y lloremos á la brida
　　　La vergonzosa caida
　　　De D. Gaspar de Ezpeleta
　　　O si yo fuera poeta !
　　　Que gastara de papel
　　　Y qué nota hiciera de el
　　　Dixera alomenos yo
　　　Que el majadero cayó
　　　Porque cayesen en el.
　　　　　　　Juan Antonio Pellicer, p. cxvii.

[2] Cp. Góngora's denunciation (Rivadeneyra, xxxii. p. 437)—
　　　"¡ Oh malquisto con Esgueva quedo
　　　Con su agua turbia y con su verde puente ! "—
with Quevedo's (ibid. lxix. p. 199)—
　　　" Pero el mísero Esguevilla
　　　Se corre, y tiene vergüenza
　　　De que conviertan las coplas
　　　Sus corrientes en correncias." . . .

" El sucio Esgueva," Góngora calls it in another passage (ibid. xxxii. p. 527).

paused to listen to some music, and was about to
pass onwards when, out of the dark, there sallied a
mysterious, undiscoverable cavalier, who peremptorily
ordered him to be off. Words passed ; each drew his
sword on the other ; both were touched, and Ezpeleta
finally lay prostrate with two dangerous wounds, one
in the right thigh and the other in the abdomen. The
assailant made away in the dark, while the wounded
man shouted for aid. Close by, Cervantes and his
family lived in a modest house, occupied also (amongst
other persons) by the widow and family of the chronicler
Esteban de Garibay y Zumálloa.[1] The cry for help
reached Luís de Garibay, who hurried downstairs, and,
at the door, found Ezpeleta bathed in blood, his drip-
ping sword in one hand and his shield in the other,
staggering into the little portico of the house. The
lad rushed upstairs and called his fellow-lodger Cervantes from his bed. Ultimately the pair carried the
dying man up to Doña Luisa de Garibay's room, placed
him on a mattress, and sent for the nearest barber-
surgeon, Sebastián Macías. It appears that there was
a protrusion of the peritoneum through the abdominal
wall, and that the superficial femoral artery was injured,

---

[1] I have never had the courage to attack the "Illustraciones
genealogicas de los catholicos reyes de las Españas, y de los christia-
nissimos de Francia, y de los Emperadores de Constantinopla, hasta el
Catholico Rey nuestro Señor Don Philipe el II. y sus serenissimos
hijos . . . compuestas por Estevan de Garibay, Chronista del
Catholico Rey." I should doubt whether many even of the robust
generation of readers which flourished in Madrid in 1596 read from
cover to cover of this formidable folio.

perhaps even severed. The well-meaning Sangrado, seeing that the patient was in the final stage of exhaustion, determined to bleed him. As might have been expected, Ezpeleta died on the morning of June 29. He exculpated his unknown antagonist from all suspicion of foul play, and named, as his executor, the Captain of the Royal Archers. It perhaps did not occur to him to blame Macías.

Urged, probably, by some such consequential person as Falcés, the Alcalde Cristóbal de Villaroel began an official inquiry into the case. It is something of a godsend for those who strive to write Cervantes' life that this was so. Cervantes lived at 11, Calle del Rastro, in a house belonging to one Juan de Navas. With Cervantes lived his wife, his natural daughter, Isabel de Saavedra, his sister Andrea de Ovando and her daughter Constanza (aged twenty-eight), a certain Magdalena de Sotomayor, describing herself as his sister, and María de Cevallos, a servant from Barcena de Toranzo, in Santander, who had been with them since Whitsuntide. The personality of Magdalena de Sotomayor has been a source of some perplexity to Cervantes' biographers. If her statement be taken literally, it involves one of two hypotheses: either that she was an illegitimate daughter of old Rodrigo de Cervantes, or—which seems still more incredible—that Cervantes' mother, Doña Leonor, had married again soon after the death of her husband, probably about 1579. With regard to the first hypothesis, there is no proof, and no *prima facie* reason for believing, that old

Cervantes was unfaithful to his wife. I am overflowing with sympathy for the straits of a biographer; yet I protest against this stigma being fastened on the memory of the estimable old gentleman without the clearest demonstration. The second hypothesis is more easily disproved. When Doña Leonor was married in 1542 (or thereabouts), we may safely assume that she was not less than twenty years of age. Unless the miracle of the plains of Mamre were repeated, the birth of a child in her fifty-eighth year seems highly improbable. To crown everything, we have Magdalena's solemn declaration that in 1605 she was over forty years of age. In other words, she was born at least thirteen years before Doña Leonor became a widow. In the face of such a statement it is surprising that the theory of Doña Leonor's second marriage ever came into existence. A more rational explanation accounts for Magdalena by assuming that she was the wife, or perhaps the widow, of Cervantes' elder brother, Rodrigo. She might still fairly enough describe herself as the sister of Miguel.[1]

On the other side of the house lived Garibay's widow, Luisa de Montoya, with her daughter Luisa, and a son in orders variously styled Esteban or Luís.[2] Amongst the other lodgers were the widow of Pedro Láinez, Juana Gaytán, and her niece Catalina de

---

[1] It has even been wildly conjectured that Magdalena was the mother of Cervantes' natural daughter, Isabel. But no proof is offered in support of this rash surmise.

[2] Cervantes calls the young man Luís; the other deponents call him Esteban (Juan Antonio Pellicer, p. cxxi. *et seq.*).

Aguilar (twenty years old) ; Maria de Argomeda y
Ayala (thirty-five years old), widow of Alonso Enríquez,
with her sister Luisa de Ayala (twenty-two years old) ;
Mariana de Ramírez, a widow, who lived with her
mother and her little children ; Rodrigo Montero (a
toady of Lerma's) with his wife Jerónima de Sotomayor and Isabel de Ayuda (a pious widow, who seems
to have been a member of some religious confraternity).
Entering the shabby house to-day, one can but marvel
how this regiment of people contrived to contract themselves within such scanty space. "Nothing," says Mr.
Mill, speaking of his visit to Bentham at Ford Abbey,
"nothing contributes more to nourish elevation of
sentiments in a people than the large and free character
of their habitations."[1] Assuredly, the restricted outlook
of Isabel de Ayuda seems to have produced a corresponding moral debasement. This revolting woman,
who describes herself as a *beata*, seems to have played
the congenial part of eavesdropper and spy towards
every other person in the house. There was now a
favourable opportunity of appearing as an informer.
The occasion was too perfect to be neglected, and the
admirable person accordingly hastened to make a statement to the authorities in which she declared (1) that
she had observed Mariana de Ramírez (apparently in
the presence of her mother and her children) talking
to, and behaving with, Diego de Miranda in a very
"suspicious" manner ; (2) that persons of note, such
as D. Hernando de Toledo, Señor de Higares, and the

---

[1] "Autobiography of John Stuart Mill" (London, 1875), p. 55.

Portuguese Simón Méndez, came to see the Cervantes family, and that, the offence being so rank and flagrant, she had "thought it her duty" to remonstrate with Méndez for his scandalous misconduct; (3) that the widows Juana Gaytán and María de Argomeda, and the spinsters Luisa de Ayala and Catalina de Aguilar, openly received visits by day and night from gay sparks like the Duque de Pastrana, the Conde de Concentayna, and D. Hernando de Toledo. Finally, this beautiful exemplar "had heard say" that Ezpeleta's death had been indirectly due to some woman. Had she been aware that among Ezpeleta's few belongings a copy of Villalobos had been found, she would doubtless have pointed with pious exultation to that fourth chapter of the *Sentencias* entitled *De la gran perdición y total destrucción del amante vicioso.* But her depravity was not altogether isolated. Jerónima de Sotomayor, wife of Lerma's tool, thought it due to her self-respect to mention the pregnant fact that Ezpeleta had been in the habit of entering the rooms of Juana Gaytán and María de Argomeda.

Reading the depositions nearly three centuries after the event, it is not easy to feel angry with Jerónima de Sotomayor. Moral indignation would be wasted on her. She was the wife of a Court flunkey, and, *ex vi termini*, a tiresome idiot. But, after the first movement of intellectual and spiritual repugnance is over, it is difficult to avoid smiling at the simple venom, the hearty palpable malice of Isabel de Ayuda. Her affectation of virtue has a charm which diurnal repetition never exhausts. But more than one of us must feel inclined to probe her motive in interesting herself in Miranda's demeanour towards Mariana Ramírez; to wonder why she "thought it her duty" to censure poor Méndez; and to inquire how it could possibly affect her that Juana Gaytán or Luisa de Aguilar received visits from the Duque de Pastrana and his companions either at dawn or sunset. What was at the bottom of it? Was it a holy, if misplaced, zeal for virtue? or was it not rather the more degraded feeling of pique that none of these visitors—Miranda, Pastrana, and the rest—ever thought it necessary to visit her in her vestal abode? It is impossible to avoid observing that all the women so disparagingly referred to were younger than the tale-bearer. Probably every reader will draw his own conclusions from this trifling, but significant, indication.

Ludicrous as the story of this disappointed creature was, it had its effect. Cervantes and the women involved by these vague, if heinous, accusations were summarily placed in prison. Among outsiders, Diego de Miranda and Simón Méndez were at once arrested. In jail the prisoners were examined. Their testimony was as direct as it was conclusive. Isabel de Saavedra avowed that Hernando de Toledo had visited her father twice, and she understood that the two men had known each other in Seville. Of Méndez she was only aware that he was a friend of her father's who called on business. Constanza de Ovando had met Hernando de Toledo but once. Méndez she had seen from time to time, and had understood that the Portuguese contractor called on business. Doña Andrea believed that this business was connected with Toledo, and added that people came to see her brother because he wrote and transacted affairs. In answer to a question, put with more than magisterial indelicacy, she declared that she knew nothing of any attentions, undesirable or otherwise, paid by Méndez to her niece Isabel. Juana Gaytán had known Ezpeleta for fourteen years as a friend of her late husband. Seeing her in mourning at Mass, and learning on inquiry that her husband was dead, Ezpeleta had called upon her three months previously to offer his condolence. The visit of Pastrana was explained by the fact that two posthumous books of Pedro Láinez were dedicated to the Duke, who had come, with his friend the Conde de Concentayna, to thank her.

These explanations were at once too simple and too complete for even the mind of the local Dogberry. The upshot was that Cervantes was let out on bail; the women were released on the same terms, though forbidden to quit the house; Diego de Miranda was ordered to leave the Court within a fortnight, and Méndez was kept in custody for further inquiries. Finally the siege was raised with regard to the women (and, presumably, with regard to the luckless Méndez), and nothing further was ever discovered with regard to Ezpeleta's assailant. It may be taken for granted that the interesting trio—Doña Isabel de Ayuda, the Court flunkey and his wife—sought other rooms when their fellow-lodgers came out of jail. Otherwise, it seems probable that they may have realised in full measure the significance of that terrible word, retribution.[1]

Not long after this occurrence, the Madrileños sent a representation to the King, asserting that their city was going to rack and ruin because of the removal of the Court to Valladolid. The new capital was undoubtedly inconvenient in more ways than one; there had been considerable discontent among the courtiers and the literary folk who had grown accustomed to Madrid; and, doubtless, there was no exaggeration in the statement that house property in the city on the Manzanares had greatly decreased in value. The Madrileños had made out a fair case; and the prospect of handling the 250,000 ducats proffered, with curious effrontery, by the deputation on condition that their city were once more chosen as the official centre, proved too much for Philip. On January 20, 1606, the change was made. Cervantes had no special reason for loving the Valisoletanos, no special attachment to the city, and

---

[1] With regard to the Ezpeleta incident and its *sequelœ*, I have followed Juan Antonio Pellicer. The story is told in a more detailed manner by M. A. de Latour in his "Valence et Valladolid" (Paris, 1877). A drama with this motive, entitled "La Hija de Cervantes," by Fernández-Guerra y Orbe, was given at Granada on February 20, 1840 (Morán, p. 123). I am not acquainted with it myself.

The Señor de Higares, whose name is the thirty-first given in the list of maskers in the "Relación," seems to have been a practical joker of the worst type. Cp. Cabrera de Córdoba, p. 19. Pastrana is introduced in the "Viaje del Parnaso" (viii.):

> "Desde allí, y no sé cómo, fui traido
> Adonde ví al gran Duque de Pastrana
> Mil parabienes dar de bien venido," etc.

he probably left it soon after the removal of the Court. Where he wandered and what he did during the years 1606–1607 is not precisely known ; but, from an anonymous letter to Don Diego de Astudillo Carrillo, unearthed in the Biblioteca Colombina by the well-known D. Aureliano Fernández-Guerra y Orbe, and first published (though only in part) in 1852 by Hartzenbusch in his edition of Alarcón, it seems probable that he passed some time in Seville.[1] The letter, which both Fernández - Guerra and Hartzenbusch are agreed in ascribing to Cervantes, describes a burlesque tourney in which, among other writers, the author of *Las Paredes Oyen* and *La Verdad Sospechosa* took part, in July, 1606, at San Juan de Alfarache. The authorship is not, indeed, definitely established, but the epithets of El Caballero de Buen Gusto, of Don Golondronio Gatatumbo, and Don Floripando Talludo, Príncipe de Chunga, seem to come from the cunning hand which coined the felicitous nomenclature of *Don Quixote*.

But at last, soon or late, Cervantes returned to Madrid. In 1608, the year in which César Oudin, according to Navarrete, published in Paris a French translation of *El Curioso Impertinente*,[2] he was once more called upon to give an account of those outstanding debts to the Treasury which he, the excellent, neglectful, unbusiness-like man, had doubtless long

---

[1] Fernández-Guerra y Orbe's transcript (since given in pamphlet form) first appeared in *La Concordia* (Morán, p. 126). Cp. also the "Obras," ii. pp. 255–301.

[2] I have not seen this translation, nor has M. A. Morel-Fatio. Its existence is very doubtful. For once, Navarrete may be mistaken.

since forgotten. The memory of Francisco Suárez Gasco was longer; but in some fortunate way the debt was either discharged or mercifully forgiven. In this same year the defaulting genius had perhaps, in his perfunctory style, corrected the proof-sheets of a new edition of *Don Quixote.* In April, 1609, he became a member of one of the many religious confraternities in which the social magnates and the literary men of the day were commonly enrolled. His wife and his sister Andrea were received as tertiaries of St. Francis in the month of June. Andrea had always formed an intimate part of his life. In spite of accumulated cares—and it should seem that the cares of a thrice-married woman were not slight—Miguel was never from her heart. She had helped, with her small means and her large-hearted indomitable perseverance, to rescue him from the Algerine captivity; and, after her final widowhood, she seems to have lived with him continually. In her modest way she exerted herself towards the support of their common household. Of all his family, she seems most closely to have resembled him, and it is no small loss that we are acquainted solely with the tantalising outlines of her sweet, self-effacing, feminine character, with their soft, shadowy suggestiveness of charm. It must have been no common grief to the aging man when, on October 9, 1609, she died,—probably in the Calle de la Magdalena, where it is known that Cervantes was living in the preceding June. In June, 1610, he and his family moved into the Calle de León. If he had not been fortunate in his applications for employ-

ment at Court, he had at least been happy in finding
two powerful patrons in Bernardo de Sandoval y Rojas,
Cardinal Archbishop of Toledo, and the Conde de
Lemos; the former the uncle, the latter the nephew and
son-in-law of Lerma. Lemos was the good genius of the
old man's last days. Eight years earlier he had been
mentioned as a probable Viceroy of Naples. Long
marked out for promotion, his time had now come, and
in May, 1610, he left Madrid to take up the appoint-
ment. He had, with a judicious taste for letters, a
wholesome delight in the companionship of accomplished
men, and the two Argensolas were among his suite. It
seems probable that Cervantes hoped to be included
herein; but, possibly owing to some intrigue on the part
of the Argensolas, his name did not appear in the list of
nominations. It was beyond doubt a disappointment,
for the sweet-tempered old man alludes to it pathetically
and reproachfully in the *Viaje del Parnaso*. This
omission has been explained away on the ground of his
age; but he was probably not less competent than
Lupercio Leonardo de Argensola, who died before him.
How did Cervantes support his family during these
hard years? If we may fear that the support was not
great, we may equally hope that there was none of the
supererogatory folly which had misled him in Valladolid.
For a moment Lemos had seemed to offer a chance
of ease and even comfort; but that mirage soon faded
into ether when Cervantes saw the author of *La Fénix
de Salamanca* preferred before him. But if disappointment could crush a man, he would long since have been

annihilated, and, if he were not chosen to be a diplomatist or minister, he could always go back to his books
and papers. In any case, it made no difference to his
grateful friendship for Lemos. In 1611 it is thought
that he joined a literary society named the *Academia
Salvaje*, while in 1612 he was probably giving the
finishing touches to his *Novelas Ejemplares*, of which
the *Tassa* is dated August 12, 1613. The volume
included but twelve stories, though Cervantes, in his
preface, speaks of publishing thirteen. It may be that
at the last moment *La Tia Fingida* was cancelled,
owing to some scruple on the part of the licensers.

Perhaps he had found his models in the *Novelle* of
Cinthio or Il Lasca. In the wide realm of Spanish
literature there was certainly space for some such
adaptation. The first story is that of *La Gitanilla*.
Here we are introduced to Preciosa, a gipsy girl with
a face, in Longfellow's phrase,

<blockquote>As beautiful as a saint's in Paradise,</blockquote>

a model of virtue and accomplishment—but with a
sharp savour of cynicism—who, in the Calle de Toledo,
in Madrid, sings romances handed to her by a platonic,
nameless admirer, whom we afterwards know as Sancho.
We have a casual glimpse of the penury in which such
respectable people as Doña Clara lived. Then Juan de
Cárcamo appears and out of hand proposes to marry
Preciosa, who imposes on the youth a two years' pro-
bation, which involves his dwelling among her people.
After some natural hesitation, these hard and unex-

pected terms are accepted, and under the name of Andrés Caballero, the young man enlists beneath the gipsy flag. In the fulness of time another stripling, appearing on the scene, is bitten by a gipsy's dog, and Preciosa's putative grandmother cures him with a hair of the dog that bit him. He discovers himself to Andrés as Sancho, explaining that he has fled from Madrid to escape the consequences of a murderous street brawl; and finally he also remains with the gipsies. The course of their wanderings brings them to an inn at a town in Murcia, where the daughter of the house, Juana Carducha, proposes to marry Andrés. Piqued at her lack of success, she secretes some trinkets among his belongings and accuses him of theft. In a scuffle which follows, Andrés kills a Copper Captain related to the Alcalde, and is carried off to jail. Preciosa, imploring the corregidor, Fernando de Acevedo, to spare her lover's life, is discovered to be the daughter of the excellent official, and in due time the story ends with the conventional marriage.

El Amante Liberal recalls forcibly some of the writer's experiences in Algiers. The scene of the novel is laid in Cyprus, where, after a rhetorical apostrophe to the ruins of Nicosia, Ricardo, a Christian captive from Trapani, confides to Mahamut, a repentant renegade, the story of his unhappy courtship of Leonisa and his jealousy of Cornelio, and explains how a crowd of corsairs swept down on Trapani, carrying off Leonisa and himself. Scarcely has he declared that he believes Leonisa to be drowned, when she is discovered to be a prisoner in Cyprus, beloved by two Pashas and the Cadi.

She remains in the custody of the Cadi, whose spouse, Halima, employs her to carry to Ricardo messages which suggest Potiphar's wife. Ricardo, who changes his name to Mario, becomes in like manner the confidant of the Cadi, and some curious scenes take place between the two messengers. Finally, the enamoured old man starts for Constantinople with Leonisa, Halima, Ricardo, and Mahamut, on the pretext of presenting the Christian slave girl to the Sultan. Hassan and Ali Pashas fit out two brigantines to attack the Cadi. A triangular fight follows, in which the Turks dispose of one another, and the Christians make off with the Cadi's spoil. On reaching Trapani they are met by the chief citizens, in whose presence Ricardo offers to endow Leonisa with all his wealth, and to bestow her upon Cornelio. This extraordinary outburst of generosity is rewarded in an appropriate manner, and *El Amante Liberal* is left in possession of his mistress.

In *Rinconete y Cortadillo* we have the pure *pica-resco* novel in little. The two principals meet in an inn, and, exchanging confidences, discover themselves as rogues of the first water. Entering into partnership, they start for Seville, where, after victimising sacristans and pickpocketing at large in the Plaza de San Salvador, they fall in with Gauchuelo, who introduces them to the illustrious Monipodio, the keeper of an academy and refuge for thieves. The description of Monipodio's abode —the coarse engraving of Our Lady on the wall, the two rapiers, the three-legged stool, the broken-lipped pitchers—is in the finest style of the master. Monipodio, with his retinue of corrupt assistants—alguazils, lawyers, jailers, thieves, judges, pimps, wittols, and strumpets—is of the grand school of comedy. Old Pipota, who makes herself three parts drunk before she goes to light her taper at Madonna's shrine; Ganchuelo, who would rather be a pious thief than a heretic, who says his rosary at least once a week, who never steals on Friday, and whose conscientious scruples forbid him to speak to any woman named Mary on Saturday—both these figures are admirable types of the mingling of blasphemous piety with brigandage, while Gananciosa and Escalanta represent a still more unrestricted abyss of blackguardism. Of Repolido and his battered mistress Cariharta, we are only favoured with a glimpse; but the latter, with her *tigre de Ocaña*, her *notomía*, her *Judas Macarelo*, is no unworthy predecessor of Mrs. Malaprop.

The next story in the series—*La Española Inglesa* —is concerned with the adventures of Isabel, who is carried off from the sack of Cádiz to London by Clotaldo, whose son Ricardo falls in love with her. The tale, in which Arnaut Mamí is incidentally mentioned, is not worth analysing in detail. Enough that, after unexampled trials, the young people are at last made happy. The writer's felicitous knack of nomenclature has for once deserted him, for such names as Lansac, Tansi, and Guillarte can scarcely be accepted as typically English. The amiability of his character is shown in his kindly treatment of his hereditary enemies; but, on the whole, it must be said that the air of plausibility and verisimilitude is absent throughout.

Of *El Licenciado Vidriera* it is difficult to render any good idea in English. The sententious wisdom and apposite proverbs of Radajo—a scholarly Sancho, whose poisoning results in a *plusquam* Quixotic delusion which leads him to think that he is made of glass —defy all translation. The original is said to have been Caspar Barthius, and perhaps the legend is worth mentioning.[1] The Spanish sketch—in which not the least happy touch may be found in the well-known scene where the demented hero deprecates the throwing of stones on the ground that he is not Monte Testaccio— is full of that vivacity and brilliancy which are the peculiar appanage of the writer.

The story of *La Fuerza de la Sangre* is an amplification of the line,

> As wolves love lambs so lovers love their loves.

The brutal outrage with which the novel opens is presumably atoned for, according to the ideas of the time, by the tardy reconciliation of Rodolfo and Leocadia seven years later. The ravishment of Leocadia is handled with an admirable largeness and power which redeem a strong undercurrent of brutality and repulsiveness.

---

[1] This is the orthodox version. But Cellini's castellan would have served equally well as the original, if Cervantes had ever chanced to hear of him. Cp. the "Vita di Benvenuto Cellini" (Firenze, 1829), ii. p. 25: ". . . una volta gli parve essere un ranocchio, e saltava come il ranocchio; un' altra volta parve esser morto. . . . Questa volta si cominciò a imaginare d' essere un pipistrello," etc.

In *El Celoso Extremeño* we have another version of the old story that

> Crabbed age and youth
> Cannot live together.

Threadbare as the theme may be, Carrizales, Leonora, Luís, and the subordinate characters are drawn with no common power and fidelity, while the general gloom in which the tale ends is of the most exemplary and edifying description.

We have a variant of *La Gitanilla* in *La Ilustre Fregona*. Young Diego de Carriazo and Tomás de Avendaño, and, in a less degree, Costanza, are all drawn from life, as are the two wenches Arguëllo and the young Gallega. It is in accordance with the existing ideas of the fitness of things that Costanza, a sort of heavenly scullion, should prove to be the natural sister of Carriazo, and that, leaving behind her the Toledan *venta*, she should marry Avendaño. The life of the pot-house, the world of the inn-servants, and the conversation of the muleteers is given with a sustained spirit and vivacity which places *La Ilustre Fregona* in the front rank of the *Novelas*.

On the other hand, I class *Las dos Doncellas* as the poorest of the series. The complex story of Marco Antonio, Teodosia, Leocadia, and Rafael is handled in a singularly lifeless style and with a reckless disregard of the limits of the possible. The writer's artistic instinct is dormant and irresponsive. The casual meeting of brother and sister and the artificial solution of the difficulties of the situation are beyond all credulity; nor are there any of the happy touches characteristic of the author to compensate for the monotonous extravagance of the central idea.

Spain and Spaniards play an unimportant part in *La Señora Cornelia*, the scene of which is laid in Bologna and Ferrara. Antonio de Isunza and Juan de Gamboa are introduced merely to smooth the course of the true love of Cornelia Bentibolli (to keep the curious spelling of the original) and the Duke of Ferrara. Cornelia's brother Lorenzo is responsible for most of the intricacies which, after due prolongation, are worked out in a manner rather less than more satisfactory.

El Casamiento Engañoso is in a richly comic vein, and here Cervantes' powers are seen almost at their best. Some of its humours are perhaps but little suited to our hypocritical age. Yet there is the sparkle of true merriment in Campuzano's account of the reciprocal deceptions practised by himself and Estefanía de Caicedo, who has firk'd a pretty living for many a year past in ways that will scarcely bear mention. It is another version of the biter bit: and the return of Clementa Bueso awakens the Alférez from a dream still sweeter than that of Christophero Sly. What wonder if the enlightened hero should wish

> it were most high treason,
> Most infinite high, for any man to marry!

Beyond all doubt the best day's work ever done by Campuzano was his transcription of the marvellous

Coloquio de los Perros. Here the Master stands, un-
approached and unapproachable, on his own ground,
and every stroke of the scalpel is given with a merciless
dexterity beyond rivalry. Berganza, indeed, does most
of the talking, the existence of Cipión being justified
by his putting leading questions, and by keeping his
companion to the point. Berganza indulges in an impartial retrospect of a varied life passed among shepherds, merchants, students, alguazils in league with
Monipodio, soldiers, gipsies, and, worst of all, a poet—
the writer, as we are told, of a " comedy such that,
though I am an ass where poetry is concerned, I
thought that Satan himself had written it to ruin
and annihilate this same poet." This superior dog,
who had certainly contemplated life from no restricted
standpoint, discourses with gravity on the foibles of
his various employers, each more unendurable than the
other; and it seems probable that his faithful report of
the projector's conversation in the hospital may have
afforded Ben Jonson, who had read everything, some
suggestions for the character of Meercraft in *The Devil
is an Ass.*

This completes the catalogue of *Novelas Ejemplares*
as originally published by the author, but in recent
editions *La Tia Fingida* finds a place; and though the
authorship of the work may not be definitely demon-
strated, there can be scarcely a doubt as to its authenticity in the minds of competent judges. The truncated
adventures of Don Félix with Doña Esperanza de Torralva
and the curious ethical lessons of Doña Claudia de Astu-

dillo y Quiñones were apparently too much for the age, at once easy-going and strait-laced, in which they were written. To ordinary eyes, there is but a microscopic difference between the atmosphere of *La Tia Fingida* and the general tone of *El Casamiento Engañoso.*

It is not necessary to-day to discuss the validity of the writer's boast that a profitable lesson may be drawn from each story. In any case, he was too accomplished an artist, at his best, to intrude any platitudinous moral on his reader. The tales were derived not so much from literary sources as from a fine, minute observation of life. Yet their literary merit is undoubtedly high. They are all characterised by the same simple, straightforward, uninvolved treatment, and what they lose in analytic ingenuity and complexity they gain in energy and directness. To a later generation, the artificial adjustment of the circumstances, in *La Gitanilla* as in *La Española Inglesa*, may seem inartistic because incredible; but, in a less sophisticated time, when extraordinary incidents filled the air with echoes, every-day miracles received an unquestioning acceptance. The present interest of the *Novelas*, as in the case of Quevedo's *El Alguazil Alguazilado*, lies in the side-lights thrown on the crepuscular phases of existence in the dark corners of a highly centralised society. The life of the Triana and of the courtiers lay side by side as reciprocally unconscious as life and death, and it is to the acute interpretation of Cervantes, amongst others, that we owe our introduction to the quaint contrasts of the time. The singular genius who wrote *The Zincali*, than whom no more competent critic could be found, has admitted in express terms that Cervantes has drawn some striking features of the gipsy character "with wonderful vigour and terseness," though, as Borrow acutely adds, " no sooner does he cause his gipsies to speak, in the course of his narrative, than we perceive that, like the hero and heroine, they too are 'no gipsies,' but Busné in disguise."[1]   How far Cervantes was free to write what he chose is doubtful ; but it may be safely assumed that the main outlines are drawn faithfully from nature, and that such imputations as that of incest (which it is difficult to think that Cervantes believed) were inserted by way of propitiation of the ruling powers.   With no sparing hand, we are given pictures of that profound corruption, that universal prostitution of justice which was eating into the national existence like a corroding ulcer.

> The smuggler's horse, the brigand and the shepherd,
> The march across the moor, the halt at noon,
> The red fire of the evening camp,

the dense ignorance of the people, their astounding amalgam of superstition and irreligion, their highway robberies, their floggings, their corrupt pacts with public officers, their belief in witches, their murders, their expiatory pilgrimages to Madonna's shrine—all these are set forth with extreme definition and firmness in an

---

[1] "The Zincali" (London, 1841), i. p. 84.

extraordinary kaleidoscopic medley, which, whatever its
faults may be, is rarely uninteresting or tedious. When all
deductions are made, we have a vivid picture of the age.

Only the frame of the *Novelas* need be sought in
Bandello or Cinthio or Il Lasca ; for the interstices are
not filled in with that repulsive compound of blood and
lust which forms the groundwork of so many of the
tales of the Italian Renaissance, the last example of
which may be said to have lingered on across the Alps,
in a more concentrated form, to the days of the author
of the putrescent *Justine.* Cervantes, too, has his
occasional lapses from good taste as in his treatment
of the motive of *La Fuerza de la Sangre.* Like most
of his fellow-countrymen, he has a fatal command of
sonorous and commanding eloquence—an eloquence,
gorgeous, epideictic, Rhodian, in which he indulges
with distressing copiousness. His faculty of selection
and discrimination is not always vigilant, and his
demands upon the credulity of the reader are too often
immoderate. But these are the almost inevitable faults
of the literary pioneer ; and in Spain, in these regions
at least, Cervantes was such a pioneer. The ease and
grace of style, the rich humour and Rabelaisian savour
of such work as the *Coloquio*, are more than enough to
blot out a wilderness of minute flaws.

However great their shortcomings may be, writers
of succeeding ages, writers of his own land and of other
nations, have not been chary in seeking their dramatic
themes and freshening their inspiration in these *Novelas*
of *nuestro español Bocacio*, as the brilliant creator of

R

Don Juan Tenorio styled the writer in his *Cigarrales de Toledo*. *La Gitanilla* has surpassed its fellows in popularity. It has been imitated in Spain by Solís and in England by Middleton, who occasionally translates immediately from his original. In 1816 an actor on the Weimar stage, named Pius Alexander Wolff, brought out a version which four years later inspired the lyric genius of Carl Maria Weber to the production of his *Preciosa*. Hugo's Esmeralda in *Notre Dame de Paris*, with her *quelque chose de pur et de sonore, d'aérien, d'ailé*, and Longfellow's Preciosa,—the only character in *The Spanish Student* which shows the least spark of vitality,—both derive their intellectual descent more or less directly from the gipsy heroine of Cervantes. Guérin de Bouscal's tragi-comedy *L'Amant libéral*, published in Paris in 1637, shows its ancestry in 'its name. One of the themes of Middleton's *Spanish Gipsy*, which that virile genius develops with an extraordinary force of passion and horror, is taken from *La Fuerza de la Sangre*. The same story is included in the *anecdote* of Florian entitled *Léocadie*—a model of graceful style and flowing narrative. The lien between *La Ilustre Fregona* and Fletcher's *Fair Maid of the Inn* is close and immediate. Moratín's earliest play, *El Viejo y la Niña*, is an offshoot of *El Celoso Extremeño*. Fletcher, again, in *Love's Pilgrimage* has closely followed *Las dos Doncellas*, and his Marco Antonio, whom Alphonso denounces as

> Young Signior smooth-face; he that takes up wenches
> With smiles and sweet behaviours, songs and sonnets,

has stepped forth straight from the pages of the Spanish novel. This story has also had the doubtful honour of being dramatised for the French stage in 1639 by Jean de Rotrou, under the title of *Les Deux Pucelles*. Once more, Fletcher, who in *The Chances* has followed *La Señora Cornelia*, in *Rule a Wife and have a Wife* has drawn upon *El Casamiento Engañoso*.

It is no small tribute to Cervantes' richness of invention, to the triumphant, inexhaustible fertility of his resource, his incalculable wealth of design, his redundant amplitude of ideas, that one of the mighty twin-brethren of the golden period of the English drama should have found in him a source of inspiration, so strong, so deep, so continuous and abiding, towards magnificent achievement. Across the wide, estranging gulfs of time, and despite all differences of race and language, the author of the *Novelas Ejemplares* and the lesser of our superb Dioscuri clasp hands. There were giants in the earth in those days. *Eripitur persona, manet res.*

CHAPTER VIII.

Was hilft es, viel von Stimmung reden?
Dem Zaudernden erscheint sie nie.
Gebt ihr euch einmal für Poeten,
So commandirt die Poesie.
FAUST, *Vorspiel auf dem Theater.*

No sooner were the *Novelas Ejemplares* before the public than the indefatigable veteran was at work again. The Perugian Cesare Caporali, *Il Stemperato,* had died some twelve or thirteen years earlier, leaving behind him his *Viaggio di Parnaso,* a burlesque poem in *terza rima,* modelled after Berni, the pattern of all the secondary artists of his generation. The Italian poem of 1582 had come into the hands of Cervantes, and had suggested to him a *Viaje del Parnaso* which should be of a peculiarly local, Spanish type. The *Coro Febeo de Romances Historiales* had probably afforded a similar *trouvaille* to his receptive mind. Caporali's leading idea is retained, but the treatment of the theme is in many respects the writer's own.

It had always been the day-dream of Cervantes to be considered, in his own phrase,

> Poeta ilustre ó al menos manifico.

The unexampled success of *Don Quixote*, and the very considerable vogue of the *Novelas*, had apparently brought his name into notice with the widow of Alonso Martín and the other publishers of Madrid, sufficiently at least to induce them to consider with favour his proposal of a poetic satire. *On ne saura jamais combien les marchands de la pensée et de l'écriture des autres, sont bêtes.* The *Tassa* of the poem is dated September 17, 1614, and probably the book reached the public a few weeks later.

In the initial lines, the obligations of the writer to his Perugian predecessor are gracefully acknowledged in a passage which contains a half-reminiscence of Rocinante. The description of Caporali's mule—

> Corta de vista, aunque de cola larga,
> Estrecha en los ijares, y en el cuero
> Mas dura que lo son los de una adarga—

seems taken from an imagination in which the memory of Don Quixote's immortal steed played no common part. There is, then, a confession, half-earnest, half-jesting, but wholly pathetic, of that misplaced desire which for so long a time led the writer to conceive that poetry, pure and simple, was his vocation.

> . . . siempre trabajo y me desvelo
> Por parecer que tengo de poeta
> La gracia, que no quiso darme el cielo. . . .

There are reflections on the proverbial poverty of poets, and an ironical farewell to Madrid, the centre and focus of all human greatness. Then we have a bantering reference to the theatres, the doors of which, closed upon the author of *Don Quixote*, are open to the commonest pretenders.

> Adiós, teatros públicos, honrados
> Por la ignorancia que ensalzada veo
> En cien mil disparates recitados.

And finally there is the inevitable introduction of Don John and his *heróica hazaña*. Beyond Carthage, the wandering bard falls in with Mercury, who hails him *Adán de los poetas*, compliments him on being one of Apollo's elect, and tells him that the enthusiasm with which his works are received move the envy of the base. The poet boards the galley of the fleet-footed god, describing in an "ingenious" passage a barque wherein the port-holes are formed of *glosas*, after the famous model,

> La bella mal maridada
> De las lindas que yo ví,
> Véote tan triste enojada
> La verdad dila tú á mi.

The bank of oars is made up of fleet *Romances*; the poop is beaten out of sonnets good and bad; the stroke oars consist of synchronous tercets; the gangway of a doleful elegy, with its linked sweetness only too long drawn out; the murmuring parrals of swift *redondillas*, and the rigging of light *seguidillas*. In this fantastic galleon, Apollo summons from every part of Spain the bards who hold his name in fealty—Yangüeses, Vizcaínos, and Coritos, all.

Then the long roll-call, a tedious repetition of the *Canto de Calíope*, begins. It is for the most part dreary reading. The few distinguished names are borne down by the disastrous avalanche of illustrious nobodies. Who to-day reads the immortal works of Francisco de Calatayud, Félix Arias, or Antonio de Monroy? Who knows or cares whether they ever published a line? Here and there we meet with a happy touch. The venomous Góngora is pleasantly bantered under the style of *aquel agradable, aquel bienquisto*, and Cabrera de Córdoba, the useful Dryasdust of the day, is ironically classed with Tacitus. The faults of Espinel (and they were by no means small) are passed by with indulgence, and a grateful friendship for the actor Morales is recorded in the phrase,

asilo
Adonde se repara mi ventura.

The obsequious tone in which Cervantes speaks of the works of such grandees as the Conde de Salinas, the Príncipe de Esquilache, the Condes de Salbaña and Villamediana—some of them writers undoubtedly of real merit, but by no means of the first order—testifies to the general consideration enjoyed, the reverential awe inspired, by noblemen in days when it was almost worth while to be a professional aristocrat. The kindly, natural side of the writer's genius is manifested in the gorgeous eulogy of a fifth phœnix, the Marqués de

Alcañices, whose one distinction was that he had contributed a most detestable prefatory sonnet to the *Novelas.* The unhappy physical affliction of Quevedo is alluded to in terms which, if they are not (as they are not) in the best possible taste, are at least such terms as no one but a personal friend, not doubtful of the reception of a *risqué* jest, would have been likely to use. In this instance at least the geniality of the intention snaps the thin thread of humour. The eulogy on Lope de Vega, though ample, has a certain quiet, subdued undertone of judicial reservation, impartiality, and measure, reflecting faintly and distortedly the unrestrained license and extravagance in which the superb playwright indulged in speaking of his rival. Cervantes, on his side, is ungrudging and even generous in judgment; but he is not enthusiastic. His reticence, so exceedingly uncharacteristic of him, suggests that some kind friend had repeated to him Lope's remark that no one was such a fool as to praise *Don Quixote.* Fortunately for his character, his pique did not deprave his sense of justice. To what he considered the lukewarmness, if not the treachery, of the Argensolas, an allusion is made in the third book. Mercury proposes that his passenger should go ashore with a message to the two brothers—a proposition which is received with the dry remark that some one more pleasing to the great twin brethren should do the errand. And then we have a severe handling of the *Diez Libros de Fortuna,* and their Sardinian author, Lo Frasso, who, had he lived three score years earlier, might have

attained a spurious immortality. The unhappy Lo
Frasso! A man born too soon, too much in advance
of his age, may be allowed the consolation of thinking
that posterity will redress the injustice of his contemporaries. Only on the unfortunate born too late are
the gates of mercy permanently closed.

The most interesting—and to biographers the most
important—passage in the *Viaje* may be found in the
earlier part of the fourth book, with its reminiscences,
its personal recollections, its invaluable garrulity, its
bede-roll of such past glories as the *Galatea*, the
Comedias—

que en su tiempo
Tuvieron de lo grave y de lo afable—

Don Quixote, the *Novelas*, some stray sonnets and
infinite *Romances*, and its promise of a great *Pérsiles*
to come. We are given an insight into the poverty
of the writer when Timbreo bids him wrap his cloak
around him.

Bien parece, señor, que no se advierte,
Le respondí, que yo no tengo capa.

The remainder of the canto meanders on in a stream
of reckless, cloying eulogy, which includes even such
minnows as *el bravo irlandés Don Juan Bateo*. In
the fifth book we arrive at the half-hearted, the almost
gentle massacre of the worthless writers of the day.
But it is assuredly not worth while to follow in
detail the castigation of good-for-nothing innocents like
Arbolanche, the author of *Las Havidas*, upon whom the
writer falls with some acrimony. The conflict of the

poets is not very happily managed, though it may possibly have suggested the *Battle of the Books* to Swift. The *coup de foudre*, by which Venus saves the bad poets from the wrath of Neptune by turning them into pumpkins, is obviously an unconscious plagiarism from the 'Αποκολοκύντωσις, and there are several passages which show that Juan de la Cueva's *Coro Febeo* had not been published in vain.

The work would scarcely be Cervantes' if, beside Don John, we were not introduced once more to that prime favourite, Lope de Rueda, who is mentioned with all the enthusiasm characteristic of the writer when speaking of the great ones of his youth. The Duque de Pastrana (the noble whose visits had so disturbed the sensitive conscience of Isabel de Ayuda, the informer in the Ezpeleta affair) is spoken of in terms which would be absurdly exaggerated if applied to Sir Philip Sidney, and a magnificent compliment is paid to Juan de Tassis, the future lover of the wife of Philip IV. Of Tassis Conde de Villamediana, the author of some poems of tolerable merit, Cervantes says that accident had made him a noble, but that letters had crowned him king.

Few works have ever excited greater diversities of critical opinion than this same *Viaje del Parnaso.* Ticknor, unsympathetic but judicious, cold but intelligent, delivers judgment in one brief sentence. "The poem of Cervantes has little merit." M. Guardia declares that in the *Viaje* we find "un critique de la grande école, d'une sagacité rare, d'un goût exquis, incomparable dans l'art si difficile d'enseigner la vérité en riant, et de rendre la sagesse aimable." The late Mr. Gibson, whose death has been sincerely deplored by every lover of Spanish letters, and whose translation of the *Viaje* is as admirable as a command of facile natural verse and an excellent knowledge of the original can make it, thought that, in the quality of self-revelation, the *Viaje* was not unworthy of comparison with Shakspere's *Sonnets*. Bouterwek's opinion is well known : "Next to *Don Quixote* it is the most exquisite production of its extraordinary author." "The poem is interspersed throughout with singularly witty and beautiful ideas, and only a few passages can be charged with feebleness or languor. It has never been equalled, far less surpassed, by any similar work, and it had no prototype."

Mr. Gibson was, undoubtedly, an admirably sympathetic critic ; but he too often suffered from the excess of his quality. So, also, M. Guardia has a generous, loyal enthusiasm for the great writer, whose verses he has rendered in pellucid prose—an exultant appreciation which one who cannot share it may still admire and envy. Yet, after all, the office of every judge is to weigh in fine scales, to balance this way and that, to add and to subtract, to measure, to examine, to dissect, to arrive at his just conclusion after a careful, even a minute, investigation to which hero-worship, and feverish sympathy, and enthusiasm are mortal enemies. To efface himself, to forget his absurd little personal piques, his ludicrous likes and dislikes, to forego his individual tastes, is the critic's paramount

duty.   Unhappily, the too generous enthusiasm of such
zealots as Mr. Gibson and M. Guardia for the man has
discoloured their vision of the author, has outrun their
discretion, distorted their picture, warped their judgment.

The impartial critic must frankly confess that
Cervantes was absolutely in the right in declaring
that heaven had denied him the gift of song.   Euterpe
and Thalia were not among the Muses—there were
still Muses in those days—who smiled upon his cradle.
He assuredly was not one of those

> Olympian bards who sung
> Divine ideas below,
> Which always find us young,
> And always keep us so.

Indignatio facit versum; but the wrath should be
more or less impersonal if the author is to succeed in
poetic satire.   Now in Cervantes there was nothing
of the demoniac, impersonal bitterness of Swift.   Swift,
like Cervantes, attacked people whom he disliked
sincerely enough; but in his writings we hear the
accent of a contempt more general than individual.
And so in the one case we find the expression of
more or less superficial annoyance, and, in the other,
profound, undying, insatiable indignation and hatred.
Place the most acrimonious passage of the *Viaje* beside
an average citation from the *Battle of the Books*.
Collate such mild extracts as—

> Un poeta llamado Don Quincoces
> Andaba semivivo en las saladas
> Ondas, dando gemidos y no voces,—

and the terrible description of Dryden in a helmet "nine times too large for the head, which appeared situate far in the hinder part, even like the lady in the lobster, or like a mouse under a canopy of state, or like a modern beau within the penthouse of a modern periwig," where one blow succeeds another with all the crushing effectiveness of Thor's hammer. We are forced to declare that, though Swift is certainly on the wrong side, and Cervantes, perhaps, on the right side of the controversy, Swift is the satirist of the type of the world, while Cervantes is merely the satirist of the individual. Cervantes is too personal. Now personality, like its co-relative mannerism, is one of the most delightful qualities in literature and art; but, to be effective, it needs restraint. Diderot has justly said: "Pour que l'artiste me fasse pleurer, il faut qu'il ne pleure pas." But this artistic subordination is wanting in Cervantes. His generosity runs away with him. Even to an enemy, even to the lowest hack of all, to the vilest poet at the foot of the sacred mount, he gives no swashing blow. He sets forth with the intention of gibbeting this poet and the other; but his heart fails him. On his friends, on any scribbler not absolutely detestable, and on many who are beneath disdain, he pours his eternal cataract of cloying praise. He does not like Arbolanche and Lo Frasso, and, though he liked writers whose work was quite as worthless, it would be strange if he had thought highly of either. But, though they offer matter enough, his attacks are comparatively lifeless. His satiric verse has no truth, no reality, no movement, no savour but that of careless, good-natured contempt. The lack of bitterness so admirable in the man is disastrous to the satirist. The fine characteristic of the individual ruins his artistic work.

The truth is that Cervantes had completely mistaken the extent of his own powers. He had, unluckily for himself, in his boyhood seen that glorious vision of Poetry, which he describes in the *Viaje* in phrases more sonorous than impressive. It is a hard saying that

> Such sights as youthful poets dream
> On summer eve by haunted stream,

are ever hurtful to the visionaries. But in Cervantes' case they were fatal. He had successfully crushed out one literary pest in *Don Quixote*. He probably disliked the poetasters of his generation as heartily as he disliked the crack-brained romances of chivalry. He thought himself destined in the *Viaje* to repeat the success that had accompanied his masterpiece. He would do for the bad poets what he had done for the bad prose writers ; and perhaps the will was not wanting. But the power is gone. The magician's wand is transferred from the left hand to the right. Cervantes writing verse is working with materials strange to him. Cervantes as a poet is Samson with his hair cut. And even to note his admiration for the nameless homunculi of his generation is pitiable. Is it possible that he admired these men and their work ? It is a deplorable sight to see the giant on his knees before a grotesque assemblage of dwarfs.   There are, indeed, some happy passages in the work—some felicitous strokes of magniloquent rhetoric, graceful banter, and delicate irony.   But these oases are rare and far apart, and on the whole the work must be pronounced a failure.   Bouterwek, in his indiscreet and extravagant eulogy, admits it.   His phrase is : " It yet remains a matter of doubt whether Cervantes intended to praise or ridicule the individuals whom he points out as being particularly worthy of the favour of Apollo."   No doubt.   But could any one pass a more damning judgment on a satire than to say that one knows not whether the writer means to praise or to ridicule ?   Surely such satire must be singularly ineffective.   And yet Mr. Gibson quotes the judgment of Bouterwek with undisguised satisfaction !

Fortunately the *Adjunta al Parnaso*, the too brief appendix of the *Viaje*, is almost in the finest manner of the master.   Coming out of the monastery of Atocha, Cervantes meets with Pancracio de Roncesvalles, who, being an apparently well-to-do person, scares the writer with the brazen observation that he, Pancracio, is also a poet and a dramatist whose works have been more or less deservedly hooted off the stage.   The writer endeavours to console Pancracio by saying that comedies, like pretty women, have their good and bad days—an observation which he repeats a little later in reference to some comedies of his own which no actors or managers can be induced to play.   Pan-

cracio then hands a paper to Cervantes, who receives
it with the remark that, though the proverb has it
that money spent on alms, on doctors, and on letters,
is money well spent, he once in Valladolid paid a
real on a note which contained an abusive sonnet
on *Don Quixote*—a circumstance which has made him
chary of taking in unpaid letters—and, perceiving that
the present epistle will cost him seventeen *maravedis*,
he proposes that Pancracio should take it back again,
since no letter in the world could ever be worth half a
real to the receiver. However, the document in question
is from the Delphian Apollo, who tells Cervantes that
Parnassus is full of poets grumbling about the omission
of their names from the *Viaje*; and, with greetings to
Espinel and Quevedo, the god adjoins a humorous
catalogue or code of rules and axioms with regard to
poets—such as that if a poet says he be poor, the
declaration be accepted on his simple statement; that if
a poet should say he has dined, he be disbelieved and
pressed to eat; that every poet be of a mild disposition
and stand not on points, though he may have holes
in his stockings; that mothers may lawfully use the
names of certain poets as bogies to their children, and
that every poet, though not the author of a heroic
poem or a first-rate play, be styled *El Divino.*

Bouterwek's judgment on the *Adjunta* is worth
quoting for its unique infelicity: "It is only to be
regretted that Cervantes has added to the poem a comic
supplement in prose in which he indulges a little too
freely in self-praise." The curious faculty which can

find delight in the fustian eloquence of the *Viaje*, in
Cervantes at his worst, and can see nothing in a work
in the happiest manner of the writer! After all, the deficiencies of the *Viaje* may be pardoned in exchange for the
large manner, the fine humour of the *Adjunta*. Here
the great man treads untrammelled by the difficulties,
the conditions of verse. In verse he is always hampered
by those technicalities of form for which his feeling is
rudimentary and amid which his genius never has fair
play. When his vehicle is prose, his touch is as delicate, his tact as fine, his humour as exquisite as ever.
Nor is it unnatural that at this moment his vein should
be of the finest. Apollo's letter is dated July 22, 1614.
Two days earlier Cervantes had written the letter which
Sancho sent to his wife Teresa. One is reminded by
Bouterwek's criticism of Bahrám, "that great Hunter"—

> The Wild Ass
> Stamps o'er his head but cannot break his sleep.

CHAPTER IX.

DON QUIXOTE.

O torri, o celle,
O donne, o cavalieri,
O giardini, o palagi ! a voi pensando
In mille vane amenità si perde
La mente mia. . . .

Paraissez, Navarrois, Maures et Castillans,
Et tout ce que l'Espagne a nourri de vaillants ;
Unissez-vous ensemble, et faites une armée,
Pour combattre une main de la sorte animée.

Le Cid, Act V. sc. i.

THE last years of Cervantes' life were fruitful in artistic work. In his house in the Calle del Duque de Alba he corrected the proof-sheets of those *Comedias y Entremeses* to which an extended reference has been made in an earlier chapter. They were neglected by contemporaries ; they have been deservedly condemned by the maturer judgment of posterity as failures the most disastrous. One play indeed—and that not a play included in the luckless volume of 1615—has found an admirer illustrious among the admirers of Cervantes.

The scarcity of such zealous devotees for Cervantes' dramatic work is sufficient excuse for a *verbatim* quotation from Shelley : "I have read the *Numancia*, and after wading through the singular stupidity of the first act, began to be greatly delighted and at length interested in a very high degree, by the power of the writer in awakening pity and admiration, in which I hardly know by whom he is excelled. There is little, I allow, to be called *poetry* in this play; but the command of language, and the harmony of versification, is so great as to deceive one into an idea that it is poetry."[1] *O si sic omnia!*

Shelley's is no doubt a mighty name, and he admired with a generosity which would have appealed to Vauvenargues. Unlike *El Rufián Dichoso*, which is indeed

> One of those comedies in which you see,
> As Lope says, the history of the world
> Brought down from Genesis to the Day of Judgment,

the *Numancia* is redeemed by its solemnity, its sincerity, its majestic pomp. It is in any case infinitely superior both in design and execution to the formal plays and *sainetes* of which the volume of 1615 is composed. On these the judgment of M. Emile Chasles may, with little qualification, be taken as final : "A entendre ces abstractions bavardes, à voir cette recherche étourdie et ce faux goût, on se croirait à

---

[1] In a letter written from Pisa, April 19, 1821. "The Prose works of Percy Bysshe Shelley, edited by Harry Buxton Forman" (London, 1880), iv. p. 200.

mille lieues du bon sens viril qui éclatera dans *Don Quichotte.*" [1]

Posterity, like the friendly critic mentioned in the preface to the volume of the *Comedias*, has decided that Cervantes' verse is good for nothing. But he was a man with many irons in the fire. For thirty years he had been buffeted about by chance and fortune, picking up a scanty living as he could ; shifting from one spot to another ; doing common hack-work ; writing his *Novelas* and his *Viaje*, with a retrospicient eye on the jail ; now and again contributing short poems, as he was pleased to call them, to the ecclesiastico - literary tournaments then so much in vogue ; and finally, working by fits and starts on the second part of *Don Quixote* in such intervals of time as he could snatch from the treadmill of bread-winning. The last words of the first part, a quotation (or, more characteristically, a misquotation) from Ariosto—

> Forse altri canterà con miglior plettro—[2]

left it doubtful whether the writer seriously intended to complete the work himself. Assuredly he mentions the

---

[1] "Miguel de Cervantes : sa vie, son temps, son œuvre politique et littéraire" (Paris, 1866), p. 232.

Longfellow had a passage in the "Arte nuevo de hacer comedias" in his mind.

> " Porque considerando que la cólera
> De un español sentado no se templa
> Si no le representan en dos horas
> Hasta el final juicio desde el Génesis," etc.

> (Rivadeneyra, xxxviii. p. 231).

[2] "Orlando Furioso," xxx. 16. Cervantes, who never verified a quotation, gives it thus : *Forsi altro cantera con miglior plectio.*

forthcoming appearance of *Don Quixote* in the preface to the *Novelas*, but in the same passage he mentions the *Semanas del Jardin* which was never to see the light. A modest writer, however, would never, under any circumstances, have undertaken the task of continuing *Don Quixote*. A scrupulous writer, not to say a respectable man, would never have undertaken the task without the author's consent. Cervantes, working leisurely at the second part and putting into it as much care as his nature would allow, had apparently reached the fifty-ninth chapter when he learned with angry consternation that a spurious continuation of *Don Quixote* had been published at Tarragona, by an allonymous writer calling himself Alonso Fernández de Avellaneda.

It was by no means a new thing in the history of Spanish letters that a work begun by one hand should be ended by another. The *Diana* of Montemayor had been thus continued in 1564 both by Alonso Pérez and Gil Polo; while in 1605 (the year in which the first part of *Don Quixote* was published) Mateo Alemán's *Guzmán de Alfarache* was similarly treated by Juan Marti, under the pseudonym of Mateo Luján de Sayavedra. It may be freely admitted, then, that Avellaneda had more than one bad precedent. But the most shameless of these self-nominated assistants had generally thought it necessary to allude to the original writer in terms of civility, or, at least, to abstain from coarse invective and indecent obloquy. Avellaneda, however, improving on previous examples, overflows with insolence and venom at every pore. He takes the opportunity of sneering at Cervantes' bragging preface, proclaims him a surly grumbler like most other jail-birds, and, with unholy exultation, declares that the tongue of the world-worn veteran wags more freely than his hand—the hand which had been injured at Lepanto.[1] Góngora had, with characteristic amiability, compared Cervantes to the gray, battered castle of San Cervantes; and Avellaneda, whose originality was certainly not his strongest point, hastened to adopt the image of effete senility as his own.[2]

It has been thought that behind the mask of Avellaneda might be discerned the personality of the Inquisitor-General, Luís de Aliaga, of the miserable Dominican Blanco de Paz of Algiers, of Andrés Pérez, the author of the pornographic *Picara Justina*, of Bartolomé Leonardo de Argensola, of Alarcón and, according to the late Mr. Rawdon Browne, the personality of Gaspar Schöppe. This last, the most fantastic conjecture of all, is on a par with the singular theory of the same writer that the original of Sancho Panza was Pedro Franqueza,

---

[1] "Segundo Tomo del Ingenioso Hidalgo Don Quixote de la Mancha, que contiene su tercera salida: y es la quinta parte de sus auenturas. Compuesto por el Licenciado Alonso Fernandez de Auellaneda, natural de la Villa de Tordesillas" (Tarragona, 1614).

"... digo mano, pues cõfiesa de si ŋ tiene sola vna ... tiene mas lengua quo manos. ... Y pues Miguel de Ceruantes es ya de viejo como el Castillo de san Ceruantes, y por los años tã mal contentadizo, ŋ todo y todos le enfadan, y por ello está tan falto de amigos ... pero disculpã los hierros de su primera parte en esta materia el auerse escrito entre los de vna carcel, y assi no pudo dexar de salir tiznada dellos, ni salir menos ŋ quexosa, mormuradora, impaciẽte, y colerica, qual lo está los encarcelados," etc.—Prólogo.

[2] For Góngora's "Romance" see Rivadeneyra, xxxii. p. 513.

once a servant of Lerma's and, later, Secretary of State. Schöppe has enough to answer for without loading him with the burden of Avellaneda's sins. This quaint, distorted idea, unsupported by any shred of evidence, may be disposed of by a comparison of dates. On Mr. Rawdon Browne's showing, Schöppe arrived in Madrid in March, 1614. Assuming that he set to work next day on the congenial task of defamation, it is incredible that he could have written an octavo volume of 282 folios and have had it in a state sufficiently advanced to allow of the censor issuing his official license by April 18. No one who has any appreciation of the possibilities of Spanish official despatch would credit a story so absurd.[1]

The mask of the Tarragonese is not easily pierced; but it can hardly be doubted that, as D. Ramón León Máinez has pointed out, if the hand is the hand of Avellaneda, the voice is the voice of Lope de Vega, still smarting under two or three thrusts in the first part of *Don Quixote*. The ironical apology for the absence of prefatory sonnets by dukes, marquises, counts, and folk of that kidney; the obvious banter of Lope's weakness for classical quotation in the reference to Plato and Aristotle; the satirical allusion to the great man's heraldic emblems, and, worst of all, the fatal forty-eighth chapter, in which a most fertile wit is formally censured

---

[1] See Mr. Rawdon Browne's articles in the *Athenæum* of April 12 (pp. 471–473), April 19 (pp. 503–505) and May 3 (pp. 564–566), for the year 1873. A more ingenious collection of perverse speculation it would be difficult to find.

for playing down to the level of his audiences—all these
gave unpardonable offence to the Behemoth of the stage.
The grossest adulation had hitherto been to him as the
breath of his nostrils. The most gentle criticism was
looked on as the rankest blasphemy.[1] Avellaneda makes
no attempt to disguise his championship of Lope. In his
preface he speaks with bitter resentment of Cervantes'
impertinence in talking slightingly of an honoured
writer who for many years had honestly and fruitfully
amused the Spanish people with marvellous comedies
out of all number, with the variety of style which the
public seeks and the sound principles which are expected
from a minister of the Holy Office. The reference to
Lope is distinct and unmistakable, and it may safely be
assumed that his malignant genius informs every line of
Avellaneda's venomous preface. For malignant Lope
undoubtedly was; his sacred orders never made him
more than a man. Eleven years earlier he had
denounced *Don Quixote* in private letters, and doubtless
among his own clique of parasites. That denunciation
had proved futile. The jealous Titan for ten long years

---

[1] Quevedo fluttered the Volscians in the "Historia de la vida del
Buscón" (lib. i. cap. ix.): " 'Pues oiga vuesa merced un pedacito de un
librillo que tengo hecho á las once mil vírgenes, adonde á cada una
he compuesto cincuenta octavas, cosa rica. . . . Otras más altas he
hecho yo (dijo) por una mujer á quien amo ; y ve aquí novecientos y un
soneto y doce redondillas (que parece que contaba escudos por mara-
vedís) hechos á las piernas de mi dama.' Yo le dijo que si se las
había visto él; y respondióme que no había hecho tal por las órdenes
que tenía; pero que iba en profecía los conceptos." See also the
sonnet, "Lope dicen que vino—No es posible," in the "Adición á
las Musas" (Rivadeneyra, lxix. p. 492).

had nursed his noble rage, until at last, as he realised that the reputation of *Don Quixote* grew and grew continually, his bitterness of soul became unendurable. Some vengeance must be taken, and so it came about that Avellaneda, behind his opaque domino and mask, represented Lope and his train. To Lope the bare thought of rivalry was insufferable. Till *Don Quixote* appeared no rival had ever dared to come within the shadow of his throne, and its lasting success was torment to his soul. It was too plain that the world had gone stark-mad, captivated by the book of the poverty-stricken, maimed wanderer who, after a life of squalid failure, had had the assurance to produce a masterpiece. It was no longer possible to kill *Don Quixote* by the cheap sneer that no one was such an ass as to praise it. Lope had played that card, and no longer cherished any such delusion. It was too obvious that that trick had failed ; the whole world—"mostly fools"—was in the conspiracy of appreciation. But it was still possible to injure ; still possible to defame ; still possible to rob the old man of a few doubloons ; still possible to deride him, to wound his pride, to forestall his market by writing a continuation of the accursed volume which had dared to thrust itself between Lope and the public—

Which, if not victory, is yet revenge.

Impotent to crush the writer or to annihilate his book, it was the wish of Lope to do him as much harm as possible ; and if a bushel or two of insult could be superadded, all that was so much to the good.

Avellaneda's work is, indeed, by no means without merit. Under pain of temerariousness, as the theologians say, one may venture to dissent from the judgment of Sainte-Beuve, who declared the spurious *Don Quixote* to be slow and heavy.[1] It is, in fact, a work of considerable interest and entertainment and, were Cervantes not in possession of the field, it would still find readers. No doubt there are faults of taste and execution in it; forgetfulness, as, for example, in the suppression of Sancho's immortal ass; want of judgment, as in the killing off of Don Quixote's niece; a failure in the power of selection, as in the manipulation of the stories of *El Rico Desesperado* and *Los Felices Amantes* (borrowed from Heisterbach, Passavanti, and other sources); all these are rife. These last two interpolated episodes, though clever enough, are excessively crapulous; and it remains a standing wonder that an Inquisitionary officer should have written or inspired them, and that a clerical censor should have passed them. But the entertaining quality of the book is undeniable. Le Sage championed it with indiscriminating enthusiasm. Writing in 1704, he says that there are points of resemblance between Avellaneda's continuation and that of Cervantes, but that, as Cervantes wrote his second part long after Avellaneda, it is easy to judge which was the copyist. As for Avellaneda's Sancho, it must be admitted, says the brilliant Frenchman, that he is excellent, and even more original than the creation of Cervantes.[2]

---

[1] "Nouveaux Lundis" (Paris, 1885), viii. p. 28.

[2] "Nouvelles Avantures de l'Admirable Don Quichotte" (Paris,

Le Sage's expanded version was read everywhere, and, as appears from a passage in the *Essay on Criticism*, came at last into the hands of Alexander Pope.[1]

M. Germond de Lavigne, in a later age, has repeated the perfidious declaration of Le Sage against the originality of Cervantes. But, accomplished special pleader as he is, M. Germond de Lavigne has forgotten that the case is to be argued, not at Nisi Prius but at the bar of history. It is as certain as anything can be that Cervantes had reached his fifty-ninth chapter before he heard of Avellaneda's version. The false *Don Quixote* was published in 1614, the true in 1615 ; and the resemblances between the two may be accounted for by Cervantes' unwary habit of reading to others what he had written long before it was ready for the press. No doubt it would have been wiser to abjure these fatal *primeurs*; no doubt it would have been more discreet

---

1704). See Preface : " Il faut donc remarquer que s'il se trouve des choses qui ont quelque ressemblance dans ces deux secondes Parties, Cervantes n'ayant composé la sienne que long-tems après celle d'Avellaneda, il est aisé de juger lequel a esté le Copiste. . . . Pour son Sancho, il faut demeurer d'accord qu'il est excellent, et plus original même que celui de Cervantes."

[1] " Once on a time La Mancha's knight, they say,
A certain bard encount'ring on the way,
Discoursed in terms as just, with looks as sage,
As e'er could Dennis, of the Grecian stage ;
Concluding all were desperate sots and fools,
Who durst depart from Aristotle's rules."

Essay on Criticism, v. 267 *et seq.*

There is nothing in Avellaneda about Aristotle's rules. The passage to which Pope refers may be found in Le Sage's version, i. p. 377.

had Cervantes, instead of filling the earth with his indignant lamentations, calmly ignored Avellaneda's larceny, just as it would be better were we all angels or, as Cardinal Newman ironically says, all pigs. But with such beings as ourselves, in such a world as the present, it would be indeed surprising if honest folk showed no indignation against sharpers, whether clerical or lay.

The jeremiads of Cervantes were, however, super-fluous. His enemy's book, considerable as it is, simply ceases to exist when placed alongside the true *Don Quixote*. His angry protests against the appearance of the spurious version, though sufficiently justified from the personal point of view, are so much *charivari* to later generations, since Avellaneda's very name is scarcely known to them, and from his phantom head Cervantes' furious blows recoil ineffectually.

The first part of *Don Quixote* was published in 1605, the second part in November, 1615. It is not difficult to trace the passage of years in the difference of tone which characterises the two parts. Yet no book has more signally contradicted Sansón Carrasco's sweep-ing statement that no second part was ever worth any-thing. The unity of design is maintained throughout, and, save perhaps in the character of Sancho, the con-ception shows a simplicity and firm consistency beyond admiration.

On *Don Quixote* Cervantes' reputation depends. His feeble plays are killed, his admirable novels obscured, by the lustre of his masterpiece. One feels in-clined to reverse the question, and ask how it happened that the fiasco of the *Comedias* did not react on *Don Quixote.* Yet who knows Prévost save as the author of *Manon Lescaut*, Bernardin de Saint-Pierre save as the author of *Paul et Virginie*, Gustave Flaubert save as the author of *Madame Bovary*? The *Galatea* and the *Comedias* are not more neglected than *Cléveland* and the *Doyen de Killérine*, than the *Voyage à l'Ile de France* and the *Chaumière Indienne*, than the *Tentation de St. Antoine* and *Bouvard et Pécuchet.*

By a curious coincidence, *Hamlet* and *Don Quixote* appeared in the same year. M. Ivan Turgenev, in a most discriminating and suggestive paper, has drawn attention to the points of contrast between these two opposed, cosmopolitan types of dreamers.[1] *Don Quixote* stands for faith, belief in the eternal, in the immutability of truth. Miracles, marvels, prodigies are not to him acousmata; they are the stuff of daily experience. Hamlet is the very genius of introspection, of doubt, of discouragement. He perceives things as they are; sees them from even too many points of view; is discouraged at the aspect of himself and all; distrusts, doubts, hesitates, balances, dissects, falters; has the scholar's contempt for the general, the analyst's acid appreciation of the irony of life. Don Quixote, on the other hand, has an imagination too puissant for the laws of logic or the evidence of his senses. For him the filthiest bread is of the finest grain; the stockfish is a

[1] M. Ivan Turgenev's article, to which I am much indebted, may be found in the *Bibliothèque Universelle et Revue Suisse* for July, 1879.

trout; the kitchen wenches are the noblest of dames; the landlord is a knightly warder, the inn an ancestral castle; the hog-gelder tootling on his reed is a herald sounding a challenge in the lists. If the Manchegan knight slashes at the wall and declares thereafter that he has slain four giants tall as towers; if he drinks from a pitcher a draught of cold water and swears it is a potion brought him by the sage Esquife, he is not lying — his imagination runs away with him. Yet even Don Quixote has his lucid moments and can see when he is being made a fool of; as when the trader, anxious for his life, says that if Dulcinea's portrait showed her to be blind of one eye and suppurating sulphur and vermilion from the other, he and his companions would cheerfully, in praise of her matchless beauty, swear to anything that they were asked. But the next moment the spell falls on him once more. He charges a phalanx of knights in all their panoply, and finds that he has slain some score of sheep; he captures Mambrino's helmet, all of the purest gold, and finds that, to the rest of the world, it is an ordinary barber's bowl of base metal; he attacks a mere handful of giants, and is thwacked and buffeted by the arms of windmills. What then? He is never daunted; his faith is too complete, his confidence too sublime; magic has changed them into what they seem. His imagination pierces into prehistoric times. He can even visualise his legendary heroes; the faces and forms of the fictitious knights are palpable to him; he has been there, away, beyond, into the mythic lands; he has seen the mighty men, known them, loved them, honoured them. He has a vein of reminiscence, as it were. Orlando, he thinks, was bow-legged; Rinaldos, ruddy; and Amadis—there is no doubt about Amadis—was tall and black-bearded. So the dreams to him are facts; the facts are dreams. Even while his bones ache from the windmill-blades he holds it proved that the enchanter Friston, or another, rules it so. An officer of the brotherhood cracks Don Quixote's skull; but the victim's faith moults no feather. Ignoring the obvious fact, he calmly talks of "the wound the phantom gave me." Don Quixote has his ideal, his faith, and he is well content to accept it uncomplainingly; for it, no sacrifice can be excessive. Hamlet is perpetually examining the basis, the intellectual fabric of belief. He is content to think himself a coward, content to say:

> Why, what an ass am I !

—yet even of that Hamlet is not quite sure.

He is the cultured, delicate, fastidious aristocrat. The *canaille*, with its loathsome vulgarity, has long weighed upon him. He is urged to say: "this three years I have taken note of it; the age is grown so picked that the toe of the peasant comes so near the heel of the courtier, he galls his kibe." He thinks it right to think the worst. Of his very mother he is forced to say that she posts

> With such dexterity to incestuous sheets.

Then the point of view shifts, and he suspects the devil, who, all in potency, abuses him to damn him.

Even when on the track of truth he is haunted by the dread of hallucination. The groundlings, the unskilful, the barren spectators—these are the objects of his loathing. Don Quixote, old, poor, and weak, makes it his duty to compassionate the wretched, to succour the miserable whom he does not know, whom he has scarcely seen. If a few jail-birds get loose in the process, these are the inevitable incidents of reform. Don Quixote is the incarnation of optimism. Hamlet concentrates in himself the genius of pessimism. To vary the simile : Don Quixote is a mediæval Mark Tapley *in excelsis;* Hamlet finds all things for the worst in this worst of all possible worlds. The village maiden, Aldonza Lorenzo, is transformed by Don Quixote into the peerless Dulcinea del Toboso—the sublime of the ideal. Ophelia, the courtly flower, is degraded by Hamlet into the most abject depths of baseness—a breeder of sinners. And yet Don Quixote has the compensation of his credulity, while Hamlet is racked by the torment of his scepticism. The one has merely his lacerated head, the other his bursting heart. The idealist undergoes a purely physical pain ; the materialist suffers a psychological agony.

Turn to Sancho. His character is a miracle of wit. In Coleridge's phrase, "he reverences his master at the very time he is cheating him." [1] He is the average man who applies the frigid antidote of common sense to his chief's feverish delusions. He is prose, his lord is poetry ; he is commonplace, the knight is romantic.

[1] Coleridge's Works (New York, 1884), vi. p. 411.

He has an intense appreciation of a solid fact. To him sheep are sheep; windmills are windmills; basins are basins. Nothing can persuade him that they are knights, or giants, or helmets. Illusions are not for him. He sees his family as they are. He will not hear of his wife being a queen. He knows her: " she is not worth two maravedis as a queen; countess will fit her better, and that only with the help of God." Yet when his own interest is concerned, he is credulous enough. The knight-errant is wrong about many things; but he may be reckoned on for an island. Sancho's selfishness appears at the outset. He not only is anxious about the immediate delivery of the governorship; he revels in complaint, however small may be his ache—unless, as he says, there be a rule against squire-errants complaining. When his cavalier encounters the Biscayan, he hopes that victory may light upon his chieftain's arms so that the island may be entered on at once. If the singing makes him drowsy, he hypocritically suggests to his leader that the minstrels are tired and long for sleep. He is often enough brutal and vulgar: he would have said with justice that Don Quixote had manners for both. He is loquacious to such an extent that, rather than be silent, he will abandon the hope of governing all the islands in the world, and will even go home to his wife and children, to whom he can chatter as much as he pleases. There is a vein of cunning in his simplicity. If his candour, joined to his sense of absurdity, leads him to tell the curate and the barber that his master is mad, it stops short of revealing the fact that he himself has been

T

soundly blanketed. He has humour ; Don Quixote has good humour. But Sancho improves with the development of the book. His selfishness, his vulgarity, his love of gossip, his hypocrisy, his avarice are diminished till they assume the highly respectable forms of worldly wisdom, outspokenness, cordiality, tact, and providence. He too becomes infected with something of the self-sacrificing enthusiasm of the mad Manchegan knight. He stands for the accessibility of common minds to lofty ideals, for the influence of refinement, for the power of association and environment. Thus the corrupt glutton of the earlier chapters is so purified by association with a superior type that, after having ruled Barataria with credit to his master and himself, he leaves his governorship, not only clean-handed, but as poor as when he entered on it ; and when all his dreams are melted into thin air, and Don Quixote, renouncing all his visions, abjuring his delusions, lies dying upon his hard pallet, the squire, who began by laughing at him and cheating him, bursts into tears at parting from the master he has loved so well. If he starts out with Don Quixote for the love of lucre, he at last remains unselfishly to admire where he had scoffed, and to accept the essential dignity and elevation of a character which he can reverence if he cannot understand.

Sancho has his transitory troubles ; yet he was assuredly not unhappy in this world. He rubs his bruises and forgets them as speedily as may be ; his peptics are too well ordered to let him mope his life away. Don Quixote, dwelling in a diviner air, is never

touched by wounds or pains. While his alienation
lasted he would have said with Torrismond:

> There is a pleasure, sure,
> In being mad, which none but madmen know! [1]

His buffetings, his discomfitures and his humiliations are
his glory and not his shame—works of the powers of
darkness over whom the victory of the children of
light is doubly sure. His sustained faith, his purity
of purpose, his championship of the weak against the
strong, his unmurmuring acceptance of defeat—certain
that the explanation lies, not in the weakness of his
cause, but in his own unworthiness—not only redeem
him from the hand of ridicule, but make him one
of the noblest and most admirable of the mind's
creations.

> Nor have I pitied him ; but rather felt
> Reverence was due to a being thus employed ;
> And thought that, in the blind and awful lair
> Of such a madness, reason did lie couched. [2]

It is unnecessary to discuss the thousand and one
theories of those who maintain that Don Quixote is
a burlesque upon Charles V. or the Duke of Medina
Sidonia; that Pedro Franqueza is lampooned as Sancho;
that the figure of Dulcinea masks " the most dexterous
attack ever made against the worship of the Virgin."[3]
These arachnoid ingenuities are brushed away by the
blunt assertion of the writer, whose primary object, as

---

[1] *The Spanish Friar*, Act II. sc. i.

[2] *The Prelude*, Book V.

[3] Landor fathers the theories with regard to Charles V. and the

he avows, "attempts nothing more than the annihilation of the authority and influence which books of chivalry have over the world and the public." "This has been my one aim," he says ten years later. If any book, written with a purpose, was effectual, *Don Quixote* was that book. After its appearance in 1605 no chivalrous romance was written, and, with few exceptions, those hitherto in greatest vogue remained unread by the public and unprinted by the new generation of publishers. In this sense, but in this sense only, Byron was justified in saying that

> Cervantes smiled Spain's chivalry away.[1]

As the work progresses, it ceases to be mere parody. As in the case of *Les Précieuses Ridicules*, the design

Virgin in the "Imaginary Conversation between Peter Leopold and President du Paty." Works (London, 1876), iii. p. 59.

"*President.*—The most dexterous attack ever made against the worship of the Virgin . . . is that of Cervantes. . . .

"*Leopold.*—I do not remember in what part of his writings he alludes to the worship of the Virgin irreverently or jocosely.

"*President.*—Throughout Don Quixote, Dulcinea was the peerless, the immaculate; and death was denounced against all who hesitated to admit the assertion of her perfections."

Mr. Rawdon Browne (*The Athenæum*, April 12, 1873) puts forward the theory which identifies Pedro Franqueza and Sancho. Defoe makes a similar statement with regard to the Duke of Medina Sidonia and Don Quixote. "The famous History of *Don Quixot*, a Work which thousands read with Pleasure, to one that knows the meaning of it, was an emblematical History of, and a just Satyr upon the Duke *de Medina Sidonia*; a Person very remarkable at that Time in Spain."—Serious Reflections during the Life and Surprising Adventures of Robinson Crusoe: with his vision of the Angelic World (London, 1720), p. iii. of Robinson Crusoe's Preface.

[1] Byron's line in *Beppo*—"Wax to receive, and marble to retain" —is a translation of a phrase of Andrés' in *La Gitanilla*.

becomes wider, till it includes at last the whole Human Comedy. It outgrows the original intention and, begun with a merely moral end and a limited immediate aim, it developes into the most cosmopolitan of books, the literary property of mankind.

Criticasters are pleased to declare that there are lacunæ in the writer's genius, that he paints *en grisaille*, that he lacks delicacy and finesse. Cervantes has not indeed the vast sweep, the wide vision, the power, the universality of Shakspere; but he is second only to the great Master. His vision, if not wide, is deep; his observation, if narrow, is profound; his grasp intense, if restricted. He knew life as he had seen it in the curing grounds of Málaga, the Isles of Riarán, the Precinct of Seville, the smaller market of Segovia, the Olivera of Valencia, the Rondilla of Granada, the strand of Lúcar, the Colt of Córdoba, the taverns of Toledo. If he knew but a section of existence, he knew that thoroughly, and, for the rest, he divined as only genius can. In *Don Quixote* we see the idiosyncrasy of the man, interpenetrated as it was with that lofty, sustained enthusiasm, that romance, that dash of oriental exaggeration, that dignity of senti- ment, that inexhaustible good humour, that tenacious vigour in the prosecution of an object which Carlyle and M. Victor Cherbuliez are agreed in thinking characteristic of the Spanish race.[1] So incomparable

[1] Cp. Professor Dowden's version of Carlyle's sixth lecture (delivered in 1838) in his "Transcripts and Studies" (London, 1888), p. 22, with M. Victor Cherbuliez's "L'Espagne politique" (Paris, 1874) pp. 14–15.

is the verve with which the portrait has been rendered,
that Don Quixote may be said to have supplanted the
Cid Campeador as the popular hero and the national type.

The success of *Don Quixote* was as prompt as it
has proved lasting.[1] Every one everywhere has read
it, but by no race has it been more enthusiastically
received than by the English. Even in the dark days
when Cervantes was forgotten or belittled by his own
people—for, if Cervantes was, as he says, but a step-
father to Don Quixote, Spain was long but a stepmother
to Cervantes — England had naturalised and adopted
his masterpiece.[2] Its popularity in the original, or in
Shelton's version, was as usual turned to account by

---

[1] Every one knows the story of Philip III. seeing a student in
fits of laughter over a book, and of his declaration : "Either the man
is mad, or he is reading 'Don Quixote.'" Sir William Stirling-
Maxwell, who had a weakness for kings, says of Philip : "His high
admiration of 'Don Quixote' . . . shows that he was not insensible
to the beauties of literature" (Artists in Spain, i. p. 408).

I am far from denying the truth of this pleasant legend; but I am
bound to say that my endeavour to trace its genesis has not been
encouraging. Juan Antonio Pellicer tells the story (p. xcix.) on the
authority of Mayans, who, as he declares, quotes Baltasar Porreño in
support of it. I have compared the editions of Mayans for 1738,
1744, and 1777. I find that he gives the story in his fifty-sixth
paragraph. But he does not quote from Porreño : he gives no
authority whatever. I have read Porreño's book, and fail to find any
reference of the kind. The anecdote may have lingered on traditionally
until Mayans' day ; but my own clear impression is that it is purely
apocryphal, and has no existence outside of Mayans' imagination.

[2] For a bitter attack on Cervantes' masterpiece see Thomás de
Erauso y Zavaleta's "Discurso Critico sobre el origen, calidad y
estado presente de las Comedias de España" (Madrid, 1750), *e.g.* :
"Aquel parto ruidoso de la traviessa fantasia de Cervantes, tuvo,
y tiene universal aprécio, que durará mientras haya hombres. Esto

Fletcher in the *Knight of the Burning Pestle*. Ben
Jonson, in *An Execration upon Vulcan*, speaks of

> The learnèd library of Don Quixote,

assuming that every reader would follow the allusion.
Drayton, in the *Nymphidia*, testifies to the vogue.

> Men talk of the adventures strange
> Of Don Quixoit and of their change
> Through which he armèd oft did range,
> Of Sancho Panza's travel.

The author of *Hudibras* read *Don Quixote* as carefully
as Casaubon read the *Characteres* of Theophrastus.
Whatever compliment may be implied by the grosser
forms of imitation is paid by the obscene travesty of
D'Urfey, and by Smollett in *Sir Launcelot Greaves*,
the very name of which suggests *Don Quixote.*[1]
Temple, fresh from his fearful flagellation by Bentley,
found solace in the book which, as satire, he thought

no es fortuna, ni honròso titulo de la Nacion, como creen muchos
. . . porque, bien mirado, mas es borròn, que lustre su Obra, en que
hallan los Estrangeros, testimoniado el concepto, que hacen, de
que somos ridiculamente vanos, tiesos, fanfarrònes, y preciados,
con aprehension errada, de una tan alta, y seria cavallerosidad, que nos
hace risibles. . . . Ya saben los Estrangeros, que aquel escrito no
tiene plausible, ni adequado merito para la estimacion que logra . . .
es seco, àspero, escabròso, pobre, soñado. . . . Esta fuè la magna
Obra del aplaudido Español Cervantes : esta fuè la Gloria, que de èl
recibiò su Patria, y la constante Hidalguìa, que la ilustra," etc.
(pp. 175–176).

[1] The *quijote*, I need scarcely say, is the piece of armour which
protects the thigh. The English equivalent is cuish rather than
greaves, which correspond to *grebas*. Cp. the articles and illustrations
in M. Viollet-le-Duc's "Dictionnaire Raisonné du Mobilier Français,"
v. pp. 306–314 and pp. 482–490.

"to be the best and highest strain that ever has been,
or will be, reached by that vein."[1]   Even Harley
admired it, as his jest at Rowe's expense shows; and
as for Rowe himself, if his Spanish studies did not
lead to the Madrid Embassy, they are only too
probably responsible for the *Fair Penitent*, with its
threadbare, worn tag about the "haughty gallant,
gay Lothario.[2]   Steele appointed "the accomplish'd
Spaniard" patron of the Set of Sighers in the University
of Oxford.[3]   Pope, though he quoted heretically from
Le Sage's version of Avellaneda, was also a fervent
admirer of the genuine *Don Quixote*.[4]   Defoe, in the
preface to *Robinson Crusoe*—and, perhaps, in the more
or less authentic *Memoirs of an English Officer*, by
Captain George Carleton—took up the wondrous tale.[5]
Bowle devoted his life to the study of the original,
and, despite the sneers of Baretti, did more for its
elucidation than any Spaniard before Clemencín.[6]

[1] See the paper which treats "Of Poetry."—Works (London,
1814), iii. p. 436.

[2] The story of Harley and Rowe comes from Johnson, who
perhaps worked it up from a passage in Spence's "Anecdotes"
(London, 1858), p. 134.   The line,

"Is this that haughty gallant, gay Lothario?"

occurs in Act V. sc. i. of "The Fair Penitent."

[3] See "The Spectator" (No. 30) for Wednesday, April 4, 1711.

[4] See the opening lines of "The Dunciad," and the "Moral
Essays," Epistle iv. vv. 159–160.

[5] A certain Don Félix Pacheco, who objected to paradoxes, is
quoted in Carleton's "Memoirs" as saying that "Don Quixote" was
"the best and worst Romance that ever was wrote" (London, 1728),
p. 241.

[6] Bowle's edition was published at Salisbury in 1781.   Five
years later Baretti's foolish "Tolondron" was published in London.

Joseph Andrews is avowedly "written in imitation of the manner of Cervantes"—a writer in whom Fielding delighted and whom, at another time and in another place, he imitated with indifferent success.[1] Johnson confessed that *Don Quixote* was inferior only to the Iliad.[2] The admiration of the arid Godwin knew no bounds. In a later day, and in successive generations, Lamb, Macaulay, and Mr. Ruskin have hailed the masterpiece of the immortal Spaniard in terms of ungrudging appreciation.

Le Bourgeois Gentilhomme shows the influence of Cervantes on Molière, who once played the part of Sancho on an ass ludicrously inobservant of his exits and his entrances.[3] The illustrious author of the *Esprit des Lois* placed in the mouth of Rica a measured eulogy ingeniously contrived so as to offend all Spaniards till the end of time: "Le seul de leurs livres qui soit bon est celui qui a fait voir la ridicule de tous les autres."[4] Possibly, if Usbek's opinion

---

[1] Fielding's "Don Quixote in England" was produced at the New Theatre in the Haymarket in 1773.

[2] "Anecdotes of the late Samuel Johnson, LL.D., during the last twenty years of his life. By Hester Lynch Piozzi" (London, 1786), p. 281.

[3] The scene between Jourdain and his wife (Act. III.) is obviously suggested by the conversation between Sancho and his spouse. Molière's experiences with the ass are amusingly told in the "Vie de Mr. de Molière, par I. L. La Gallois, Sieur de Grimarest" (Paris, 1705), which I only know in the reprint of 1877 by Malassi (pp. 75–77). "Enfin, destitué de tout secours, et désespérant de pouvoir vaincre l'opiniâtreté de son Ane, il prit le parti de se retenir aux ailes du Théâtre, et de laisser glisser l'animal entre ses jambes pour aller faire telle scène qu'il jugeroit à propos."

[4] "Lettres Persanes," 78.

had been recorded it might have saved Montesquieu's reputation as a literary critic. Saint-Evremond, the coldest, most fastidious, delicate, detached, critical genius of his time, speaks with rapture of "Don Quichotte que je puis lire toute ma vie, sans en être degoûté un seul moment."[1] Jean-Jacques, in the second preface to the *Nouvelle Héloïse*, pays a transcendent, if reluctant, tribute to the author when he says: "Les longues folies n'amusent guère; il faut écrire comme Cervantes pour faire lire six volumes de visions."[2] Marivaux, in *Pharsamond, ou le Don Quichotte François*, declares that "l'auteur . . . dans cet ouvrage s'est proposé d'imiter l'ingénieux Michel de Cervantes."[3] Voltaire scarcely mentions Cervantes at all. Perhaps Carlyle, moved to honest indignation at the deliberate omission, may have wished to give a swashing blow of retributory vengeance when he said: "If any one wish to know the difference between humour and wit, the laughter of the fool, which the wise man, by a similitude founded on deep earnestness, calls the crackling of thorns under a pot, let him read Cervantes on the one hand, and on the other Voltaire, the greatest laugher the world ever knew."[4] But if Cervantes has ever been the creditor of France,

---

[1] "Œuvres de Monsieur de Saint-Evremond [De quelques livres espagnols, italiens et françois]" (Paris, 1753), iii. pp. 236–237.

[2] Paris edition, 1830, i. p. 18.

[3] See the edition published at La Haye in 1739.

[4] See Professor Dowden's "Transcripts and Studies" (London, 1888), p. 21. Carlyle scarcely made due allowance for the fact that Spain was of small interest to the whole school of *philosophes*.

the debt has been nobly discharged by the enlightened appreciation and devotion of such men as Sainte-Beuve, Victor Hugo, Mérimée, and Viardot.

Germany has been, as usual, less happy in expressing an admiration which has been cherished by her greatest sons. Her critical genius, though perhaps less defective than it appeared to Mr. Lowell, is verbose but inarticulate, redundant but incoherent. Still Goethe and Heine have given a large, noble utterance to the sincerity of their adoration, and the *Don Silvio de Rosalvo* of Wieland finds its inspiration in the work of the great Spaniard. From Italy, Russia, and Denmark come Meli and Turgenev and Herr Georg Brandes to lay their wreaths of laurel on the hero's unknown grave. But the list is already too long. The earth is full of his glory, and the verdict of mankind upon his masterpiece may be summed up in the words of the translator of 'Umar Khaiyām—"the most delightful of all books,"—or in Macaulay's trenchant phrase, "the best novel in the world." [1]

Writers of the age of reason had little sympathy for writers of the age of belief. Diderot, if I mistake not, shared the general indifference. Beyond a casual mention of Cervantes and an allusion to Sancho in " La Promenade du Sceptique," I can recall no reference in his many volumes.

[1] See a letter of Edward Fitzgerald's to W. F. Pollock (October 28, 1867), "Letters and Literary Remains" (London, 1889). " I have had Don Quixote, Boccaccio, and my dear Sophocles (once more) for company on board: the first of these so delightful, that I got to love the very Dictionary in which I had to look out the words: yes, and often the same words over and over again. The Book really seemed to me the most delightful of all Books: Boccaccio, delightful too, but millions of miles behind; in fact, a whole Planet away "

(i. p. 310). And again to W. F. Pollock (Jan. 22, 1871): ". . . I have read nothing to care about except Don Quixote and Calderon. The first is well worth learning Spanish for. . . . But Don Quixote is *the* Book, as you know ; to be fully read, I believe, in no language but its own, though delightful in any " (i. pp. 327–328).

Macaulay, in a letter to his sister Hannah (Oct. 14, 1833), says: " I am going through Don Quixote again, and admire it more than ever. It is certainly the best novel in the world, beyond all comparison " (i. p. 339). On September 16, 1834, Macaulay embarked at Madras for Calcutta, and amused himself with learning Portuguese. " I read the Lusiad, and am now reading it a second time. I own that I am disappointed with Camoens. . . . I never read any famous foreign book, which did not, in the first perusal, fall short of my expectations ; except Dante's poem and Don Quixote, which were prodigiously superior to what I had imagined. Yet in these cases I had not pitched my expectations low " (i. p. 389). I quote from the 1878 edition of " Lord Macaulay's Life and Letters."

CHAPTER X.

Vous qui m'aiderez dans mon agonie
  Ne me dites rien ;
Faites que j'entende un peu d'harmonie,
  Et je mourrai bien.
        RENÉ SULLY PRUDHOMME, *L'Agonie.*

Lofty designs must close in like effects :
  Loftily lying,
Leave him—still loftier than the world suspects,
  Living and dying.
        ROBERT BROWNING, *A Grammarian's Funeral.*

CERVANTES was now close on seventy years of age, and, at a time of life when the career of most men is ended, was still as buoyant, as full of resources, projects, plans, and hopes, as in the Algerine captivity forty years before. His portfolios in the little room in the Calle de León were heavy with sketches of one kind or another—*Bernardo*, the *Semanas del Jardin*, and *Los Trabajos de Pérsiles y Sigismunda*, all masterpieces, all born for immortality. The two former are gone with last year's snows ; but the *Pérsiles*, which had been promised for over two years, and to the composition and correction of which the last days of the writer were devoted, has survived for us. It may be worth while to examine the labyrinthine argument of a work which the sanguine author foretold would be one of the best—or worst—books in the world.[1]

Periandro is set adrift on a raft by his barbarian captor Corsicurbo, and is finally rescued by a vessel under the command of Arnaldo, heir of the King of Denmark, who is in search of his soul's idol, the most beautified Auristela. It is in the nature of things that Periandro should converse with a lady in the next cabin, and that his neighbour should prove to be Taurisa, Auristela's maid, from whom he learns that her mistress (in whom he also has an interest) has been carried off by corsairs. Periandro gives himself out as a brother of Auristela's, and, at his own suggestion, is landed by Arnaldo on a neighbouring islet; disguised as a woman, he is sold into slavery, still with a view to seeking the interesting captive. In the fulness of time he discovers Auristela, equally disguised as a man. A conflict of barbarians follows, and in the tumult he escapes with the lady; both are sheltered by Antonio and Ricla, who recite a prolix story which extends over two chapters. Sailing to another island, they meet Rutilio, who, in his turn, gives his autobiography, and then makes way for the Portuguese, Manuel de Sosa Coutiño, who, repeating the doleful legend of his love for Leonora

---

[1] See the dedication to Lemos of the second part of "Don Quixote," October 31, 1615. . . . "y con esto me despido, ofreciendo á vuestra Excelencia *Los Trabajos de Pérsiles y Sigismunda*, libro á quien daré fin dentro de cuatro meses, *Deo volente*; el cual ha de ser, ó el más malo, ó el mejor que en nuestra lergua se haya compuesto: quiero decir, de los de entretenimiento; y digo que me arrepiento de haber dicho el más malo, porque segun la opinión de mis amigos, ha de llegar al extremo de bondad posible."

(who became a nun), is so moved by the echoes of
his own melancholy that he incontinently falls down
dead. Then Transila appears, and getting under way
once more, all put into Golandia, whither they are
followed by an English vessel, with Mauricio and
Ladislao, father and lover of Transila, aboard. No
sooner is the usual story interchanged than Arnaldo
arrives, and straightway proposes for Auristela to
Periandro, who puts off the inconvenient suitor by
saying that the matter must be deferred until he and
his sister have made a pilgrimage to Rome, whereon
Arnaldo inconsiderately declares that he will make the
journey with them. Mauricio, as becomes his years, is
something of an astrologer, and foretells that the voyage
will be an unlucky one ; and so it proves, for the ship is
shortly afterwards scuttled by two lustful prætorians,
who had determined to carry off Auristela and Transila.
In taking to the boats, Periandro, Arnaldo, and Ladislao
are parted from Mauricio, Auristela, and Transila. The
latter reach a snow-clad isle, upon which Taurisa and
her two worshippers land from a corsair ship. The
lovers kill one another, Taurisa dies, the corpses are
decently interred, and the surviving trio board the
pirate, the honest captain of which—a man with many
points of resemblance to Lambro—awakens the hideous
passion of jealousy in Auristela's breast by recounting
the *bonnes fortunes* of Periandro in the kingdom of
Policarpo. Soon afterwards Auristela and her companions are wrecked on an island of which Policarpo
is over-lord. It is to be expected that the king's elder

daughter, Sinforosa, should love Periandro, and that
Arnaldo's suspicions of Periandro should be quickened
by Clodio, a manumitted captive. To crown the story,
Policarpo becomes enamoured of Auristela, to whom
Sinforosa also speaks her love for Periandro; and Clodio
and Rutilio conceive a passion for Auristela and Poli-
carpa, the king's youngest daughter. The sage woman,
Cenotia, likewise falls in love with Ricla's son, the
younger Antonio, who grows ill of her potions. Meanwhile Periandro gives the interminable story of his
adventures. Cenotia lifts the spells from Antonio, and
warns Policarpo against permitting the strangers to
leave the island. The advice is bettered later on by
Policarpo, who has the city fired at different points,
having arranged to carry off Auristela and young
Antonio in the confusion. The plot fails; Policarpo is
deposed, Cenotia hanged, and the travellers escape to
the Isle of Hermits, where Periandro goes on with his
endless story till he is interrupted by Renato and
Eusebia, two luckless lovers who dwell therein. Renato
has no sooner made his inevitable confidences to the
company than his brother Sinibaldo arrives from France
with the agreeable tidings that Lisboniro has died,
confessing the grievous wrong done by him to Renato
and Eusebia, who are to be restored to honour in their
native land. With them go Mauricio, Transila, Ladislao,
and Arnaldo, who has just heard of the natural dissatisfaction of the Danes at his long absence. Auristela,
Periandro, and the rest sail for Spain. Landing in
Lisbon, they make their way through Portugal over

Spain as pilgrims, meeting with strange adventures on the road, beginning with the singular episode of Rosanio and Feliciana de la Voz which concludes in a satisfactory manner at Guadalupe. Soon afterwards they fall in with the Pole, Ortel Banedre, who tells them how, after slaying one Duarte in a street encounter in Lisbon, he was nobly sheltered from justice by the dead man's mother, Doña Guiomar de Sosa. Ortel Banedre had evidently read Cinthio years ago and was drawing on his reminiscences. On reaching Quintanar de la Orden, Antonio the elder finds his parents still living and abides there with his wife, leaving his children to continue their journey to Rome with Auristela and Periandro. Near Valencia they have a narrow escape from being given into captivity by an old Moor, whose daughter, however, warns them opportunely. Over the frontier the pilgrims make their way into the Provençal country, where they meet with Deleasir, Belarminia, and Feliz Flora, all in a sense *bonnes amies* of the Duc de Nemours. Struggling with a madman, Periandro and Antonio are seriously hurt, and, after an encounter with Ortel Banedre's wife, are scarcely on the road before they come upon Ruperta, whose husband has been slain by a Scot with the singular name of Claudino Rubicon. The lady is bitter against the Rubicons, and the vendetta is naturally terminated by her marriage with Croriano, the son of the murderer. At Lucca they find Isabel Castrucho, who feigns to be possessed of the devil, so that she may marry Andrea Marula and escape a match already arranged for her by her uncle. Andrea, duly instructed, utters the *vade retro* with miraculous effect and promptly exorcises the non-existent demon. Approaching Rome, they meet Arnaldo and the Duc de Nemours, both apparently dying from wounds inflicted by the one on the other in a duel fought on the question of Auristela's portrait. They succeed in carrying the wounded pair into Rome, where, while their recovery proceeds, Auristela (who seems all this time to have been little better than a pagan) is instructed in the faith *ab ovo*, from the fall of Lucifer downwards.   Periandro is induced by the Jew dog Zabulon to visit Hipólita, who re-enacts the part of Potiphar's wife, and revengefully accuses Periandro of theft, but withdraws the charge before serious harm comes of it.   Arnaldo tells his unavoidable story, and Auristela, shaking her head over the proceedings of Hipólita, falls ill by the magic arts of Zabulon's wife, instigated by the charming courtesan.

> Now, this very instant
> Health takes its last leave of her : meagre paleness,
> Like winter, nips the roses and the lilies,
> The spring that youth and love adorn'd her face with.

The Duc de Nemours retires, and Auristela, recovering her health and beauty, proposes to Periandro that he and she should continue the quasi-fraternal, quasi-platonic relation which they have hitherto observed. Periandro vanishes in despair, and, taking the high road to Naples, sits down near a stream by which he hears the tones of his native Norwegian once again.

> Tonen, den hvisked nævnte sig,
>   og nævnte sig ;
> men bedst som han lytted, den löb sin Vej,
>   den löb sin Vej.

Listening, he finds that the speaker is his old tutor
Seráfido, who is busily explaining that Periandro is in
truth Pérsiles, the younger son of Eustoquia, Queen of
Thule, and that Auristela is none other than Sigismunda,
the elder daughter of Eusebia, Queen of Frislanda.
Maximino, Eustoquia's elder son, is enamoured of
Sigismunda, and is even now upon her track. Periandro,
whom we may now call by his true name of Pérsiles,
hurries off to Rome to warn Sigismunda that Maximino
is at hand, about to claim her as his wife. Arrived
once more in the Eternal City, Pérsiles is recognised by
Seráfido, is stabbed laterally through the body, and falls
as though dead. Maximino appears, and, in a dying
speech, makes over his claim on Sigismunda to Pérsiles,
while the faithful Arnaldo is consoled by Sigismunda's
younger sister, Eusebia.

Given in this bald style, *Pérsiles y Sigismunda*
will scarcely be thought attractive; it is surprising to
learn that, even when decked by the rich fancy of
Cervantes, any reader should have ever found it so.[1]
Cervantes knew nothing of the frozen north, nor does
his imagination supply the deficiency. When he talks
of Frislanda, the spot seems vague and unknown to

---

[1] Sismondi, always indulgent to men of genius, finds but little to
praise in "Pérsiles." He lauds the fertility of invention, but adds:
"il me semble que rien ne fatigue plutôt que l'extraordinaire, et que
rien ne ressemble plus à soi-même que ce qui ne ressemble à rien.
Cervantes, dans ce roman, est tombé dans la plupart des défauts qu'il
avait si plaisamment relevés dans Don Quichotte." In a previous
passage he says: "En général c'est une bizarre boucherie que ce
roman."—De la Littérature du Midi de l'Europe, par J. C. Sismonde
de Sismondi (Paris, 1813), iii. pp. 423, 420.

the reader as that dim Isle of Hermits where Periandro
competed with Scheherazade.   Nothing could be more
absurd, more grotesque than his attempts to impart
a touch of local colour to his northern scenes.   He
talks of what he did not know, of what he had never
seen, of what, clearly, his imagination could not realise ;
and the result in the earlier part of the book is truly
disastrous.   Yet with all its many deficiencies, had
Pérsiles been published without the writer's name, the
authorship might easily have been inferred.   The reckless
profusion with which one story is cast upon another,
the extravagance of incident, the carelessness of construction, the inconsistencies of plot, the cut at the
Inquisitors, the countless digressions, the praise of wine
and women, the playful banter of the tattered poet—
these and a hundred other little touches are all
characteristic of Cervantes and his haphazard method.
The faults of the book are all the faults of a young
writer ; not such as we expect to find in the work of a
sick man of seventy.   The abundance, the prodigality,
the vernal exuberance of the writer are wonderful.   So
far from suffering diminution, his fertility of resource
and invention has increased.   The rhetoric is stiff with
ornament, with rich embroidery.   Nowhere is there a
trace of the reserve, the restraint of the mature artist ;
nowhere anything of the exhaustion, the sobriety, the
lethargy, the languor of old age.   From the uncon-
nectedness of the work it is easy to guess that the story
was written a line to-day, a page to-morrow, dashed off
at any moment when the humour took the author.

Yet no other book by Cervantes shows more signs of care and elaboration of mere style.

He had crushed one school of writing in *Don Quixote*, and, in his hours of reverie, he had dreamed that he would show that there was still room for the true novel of imagination and romantic incident; he would leave a model of what to do as well as what to avoid. But when every allowance has been made, with every desire to do no less than justice, it must be admitted that *Pérsiles* is a failure. Yet it met with contemporary success. It was rapidly reprinted and translated. Fletcher, always on the look-out for fresh material, has used it in *The Custom of the Country*; and a singular use he made of it. *Pérsiles*, whatever its deficiencies may be, is free from the prevailing taint of seventeenth-century coarseness. Dryden, in the Preface to his *Fables*, defends himself and his generation against the attack of Collier by citing Fletcher's drama: "There is more bawdry in one play of Fletcher's called *The Custom of the Country* than in all ours together. Yet this has often been acted on the stage, in my remembrance."[1] Ticknor is scarcely too severe when he declares that *The Custom of the Country* is "one of the most indecent plays in the language."[2] Rutilio, in the novel a harmless, unnecessary character, becomes in the play one of the most scandalous personages in the drama, like Horner in *The Country Wife*. That was Fletcher's way, as

[1] "The Works of John Dryden" (London, 1808), xi. p. 239.
[2] Ticknor, ii. p. 159 *n*.

it was Wycherley's—his reading of a book which, in other respects, he has followed so closely that he has not even taken the trouble to change the names from the original. Clodio, Arnoldo, Rutilio, Darte, son of Doña Guiomar de Sosa, Zabulon, Zenocia, and Hippolyta are boldly annexed from Cervantes ; and their characters are assuredly not bettered in the passage. But Fletcher shows his supreme instinct, his artistic power of selection in confining himself to the one incident of Duarte and avoiding the trackless labyrinth of events which characterises *Pérsiles*.

It has been thought that Cervantes, in writing his romance, followed the *Œthiopica* of Heliodorus, and it is impossible to deny the existence of a certain resemblance between Sigismunda and Chariclea, even though it be less striking than the resemblance between Chariclea and Tasso's Clorinda.[1] Cervantes' knowledge of Greek was probably of the slightest; but, as far back as 1554, an anonymous Spanish translation of the masterpiece of the Bishop of Tricca had been published at Antwerp, and from this, or from the later version of Mena, Cervantes may have derived some suggestion of the moving accidents through which Pérsiles, like the Thessalian Theagenes, has to pass.

Cervantes was in his seventieth year when he gave the finishing strokes to the volume of which he was

---

[1] A passage in the prologue to the " Novelas ejemplares " certainly points in this direction : " Tras ellas, si la vida no me deja, te ofrezco los *Trabajos de Pérsiles*, libro que se atreve á competir con Heliodoro," etc.

so proud. Age was creeping on him, but no sign of lassitude or infirmity is discoverable in the passages of incomparable vigour with which the book abounds. He was never destined to see it in print. The prologue and the dedication are full of interest, for they are the last words of the great man which have come down to us. In the prologue he tells us, with his own inimitable humour, how, returning from his wife's native town of Esquivias, he was overtaken by a student, astride of an ass, who hailed the famous veteran with enraptured enthusiasm. We can imagine the courtly grace with which the old man, conscious of immense possibilities and resplendent gifts wasted amid the uncongenial surroundings of a harassed life, received the compliments and fervour of his young admirer. The grateful dedication to Lemos is full of a tender pathos which, even after the lapse of more than three centuries, is still infinitely touching. It is written from the death-bed of the dying man, the day after his receiving Extreme Unction.

> Puesto ya el pié en el estribo,
> Con las ansias de la muerte,
> Gran señor, esta te escribo.

So he cites, for the last time, from some swinging *coplas* popular by the current of Henares in his old-time youth. There is none of the cheap depreciation of existence, none of the sombre reluctance of the worldling, none of the glad note of departure or the bitter repudiation of the pessimist. Dropsy holds him in her relentless grasp, but, worn out by neglect, by hardship,

by suffering and pain, he faces death calmly, cou-
rageously, cheerfully, with the same confident valour
which he had shown on the field of battle. He holds
to life, the only life he knows, while life remains to
him ; but, when Atropos bares her shears and lays her
icy finger on the thread, he has a heart for either fate.
He will not hasten, neither will he tarry.[1] Without
one whisper of lament, one murmur of regret, one
syllable of unmanly repining, he looks death in the face
with the large-eyed wisdom, the quiet concentration,
the serene fatalism, the contemplative vision, the
amused politeness, the placid smiling acceptance of the
inevitable which Spain has inherited from the Moors.
To the end his mind is active, busy, teeming with new
conceptions and combinations for the future ; but his
last glance is retrospective, and in the final agony, in
the valley of shadows, the word " Galatea " falters on his
tremulous lips as " Léonore " falters on the dying lips of
Thomas Newcome.

---

[1] " Ayer me dieron la Extremauncion, y hoy escribo esta : el
tiempo es breve, las ansias crecen, las esperanzas menguan, y con todo
esto llevo la vida sobre el deseo que tengo de vivir, y quisiera yo
ponerle coto, hasta besar los piés á vuestra Excelencia, que podria ser
fuese tanto el contento de ver á vuestra Excelencia bueno en España,
que me volviese á dar la vida, pero si está decretado que la haya de
perder, cúmplase la voluntad de los cielos, y por lo menos sepa vuestra
Excelencia este mi deseo, y sepa que tuvo en mí un tan aficionado
criado de servirle, que quiso pasar aun más allá de la muerte, mos-
trando su intención."—Dedicatoria of Pérsiles.

Lemos was still at Naples when the dedication was written. He
himself died on October 19, 1622. See " El Conde de Lemos,
protector de Cervantes. Estudio histórico por D. José María Asensio
y Toledo " (Madrid, 1880).

On April 19, 1616, the dedication to Lemos was begun and ended, and, for the last time, the quivering hand of the writer wrote down the phrase : " *Criado de vuesa Excelencia, Miguel de Cervantes.*" Far away, where Avon glides towards the western sea, the mighty Shakspere was sickening unto death. In Huntingdon, the great Protector of the future, still a raw country lad, was turning his face towards Sidney Sussex. But before Shakspere's final hour came, the tragi-comedy of Cervantes' life was over. "*Adiós, gracias; adiós, donaires; adiós, regocijados amigos que yo me voy muriendo, y deseando veros presto contentos en la otra vida.*" He died, as he had said he should, on Sunday, April 23, 1616. Ten days later, in a land where the calendar was still unreformed, Shakspere died also (nominally) on April 23. In their death they were not divided. Cervantes was buried in the convent of the Trinitarian nuns in the Calle del Humilladero, and, on the translation of the Order to the Calle de Cantaranas in 1633, his body may have been removed thereto with the exhumed remains of the religious. But his actual burial-place is unknown. Slighted in his life, he was forgotten after death. No stone, no memorial marks the last abode of so much genius and so much valour; no epitaph denotes the final resting-place or consecrates the eternal sleep of the greatest of all Spaniards. But, as he was beyond the censure of his countrymen, so is he above their praise. The reverent gratitude and benediction of succeeding generations hover round that unknown grave, and rest for ever on that noble, that honoured, that august head.   *Ueber allen Wipfeln ist Ruh.*

They were not many whom he left behind. His natural daughter, Isabel, the offspring of the Portuguese love-romance, is said to have entered the Trinitarian convent before her father was laid to rest therein. For him, then, Isabel was dead. Rodrigo, Andrea, Luisa, his brother and his sisters—doubtless they were all gone before him. His wife, Catalina, survived to publish the *Pérsiles*, and outlived the pious task by some ten years.[1]

As a writer Cervantes has been, perhaps, sufficiently considered. Some examination of his personality may be permitted to complete the picture. In the prologue to the *Novelas* he has given us his own likeness,

---

[1] The evidence that Isabel de Saavedra and, as some say, her mother were members of the Trinitarian convent in 1614 is very slight (Navarrete, p. 254). As a conjecture it may pass. An article in the "Revista de Archivos, Bibliotecas y Museos" (Madrid, 1874), attributed to D. José M. Sbarbi, gives a document which purports to be Isabel's marriage contract, dated August 28, 1608. The lady is described as the widow of Diego Sanz, and the name of her second husband is given as Luís de Molino of Cuenca. There are two or three reasons against accepting the theory that she was the daughter of the Miguel de Cervantes with whom we are concerned.

First, we are asked to believe that between 1605 and 1608 Isabel de Saavedra had been married and had become a widow. Where is the proof of the first marriage?

Second, the marriage contract cited is signed by both contracting parties. But we learn from the Valladolid process that Isabel de Saavedra was unable to write.

Third, the bride is described as the legitimate daughter of Cervantes: his daughter was, as we know, a natural child.

Of Rodrigo we hear for the last time on June 6, 1590, when he

probably with as much fidelity as it was rendered by that famous Juan de Jáuregui to whom, as he proudly tells us, he once sat.[1]   We see the veteran in his sixty-sixth year, with his Roman countenance, his chestnut hair, his smooth, unclouded forehead, smiling eyes (probably blue), aquiline, well-shaped nose, silver beard —once golden, twenty years since—large moustache, small mouth, stature about the mean, neither tall nor short, fresh-coloured face, fair complexion, stooped in the shoulders and slow of foot.   This, drawn by his own hand, is, as the artist tells us, the portrait of the author of the *Galatea*, of *Don Quixote de la Mancha*, and of him who did the *Viaje del Parnaso* in imitation of Cesare Caporali, the Perugian, and other works which stray about dispersedly, perhaps without the name of their creator.

On almost all topics Cervantes was a man of his own age.   His opinions, his prejudices, his tendencies, his virtues and his vices, are all essentially those of his own cycle.   Take, for example, his view with regard to

was serving in Flanders (Navarrete, p. 313).   Andrea, as we have seen, died on October 9, 1609.   Luisa is thought to have entered the Carmelite convent in Alcalá de Henares as far back as 1565, in her twentieth year.   Catalina de Palacios Salazar, Cervantes' wife, died in the Calle de los Desamparados in Madrid, on October 31, 1626, and was buried in the Trinitarian convent (Navarrete, p. 254, etc.).

[1] Juan de Jáuregui, Knight of Calatrava and Master of the Horse, the translator of Tasso and the adapter of Lucan, is highly esteemed by Ticknor (iii. pp. 39–41), and by Sir William Stirling-Maxwell in his "Annals of the Artists in Spain" (London, 1848), ii. pp. 537–538.   He appears to have engraved the plates for Luis de Alcázar's Apocalyptic treatise, and was in some sort an inferior Rossetti.

the Moors. Their expulsion from Spain, involving as it did an unexampled breach of public faith, seemed to him an excellent achievement, a holy work. His prejudice against Jews was at least as strong; and the language which he permitted himself to use with regard to his Algerine captors would bring a blush to the cheek of a dragoon, would have made a whole mess-room turn pale. No one expects from a prisoner an impartial estimate of his jailers, especially when the question is complicated by prejudices, political and religious. Immoderate invective might pass as natural enough; but scarcely any outrage can excuse the gross brutality, and even the extreme indecency, of the sacristan in *Los Baños de Argel.*[1] The writer, however, was well satisfied to be able to discharge two debts at one stroke —his hatred of his captors and his contempt for ecclesiastical parasites, both abiding passions with him. But the license of language in the seventeenth century was so unbounded that we need not be surprised that the gross vituperation of these passages should have been passed by the official censor of literature, who, himself a minister of unimpeachable orthodoxy, confined his attention, as a rule, to such sentiments as seemed directed

---

[1] See, for example, *Los Baños de Argel*, Act II. :
        "; Oh hijo de una puta,
        Nieto de un gran cornudo,
        Sobrino de un bellaco !" etc.

Cp. also an extraordinary allusion in *La Gran Sultana*, beginning :
        " Pues tres faltas tengo ya
        De la ordinaria dolencia," etc.

against the religion of the State.[1] It is to be regretted that the most splendid precept of Christianity should have been, even in those ages of faith, a dead letter.

Attempts have been made, vainly enough, to show that Cervantes was a very liberal-minded man in religious matters; and hero-worshippers, with a singularly latitudinarian idea of hero-worship, have gone further in their endeavours to honour his memory by declaring that in reality he was not a Catholic. The question is neither uninteresting nor unimportant, for the contention involves the hypothesis that Cervantes was among the basest of living men. It is certain that he himself would have been even more astounded than indignant at his orthodoxy being questioned. So far as external conformity went, a man who was never weary of celebrating his share in the last crusade, a man who was the favourite of a Cardinal, who was a member of at least one religious confraternity, who wrote canticles in praise of newly canonised saints, who received Extreme Unction on his death-bed—such a man might fairly be held to have satisfied the severest canon. That his opinions corresponded to his actions can scarcely be doubted. Sensible men may, perhaps, in Shaftesbury's phrase, keep their religious opinions to themselves ; but, dangerous as it may be to infer a man's belief from his conduct, he who voluntarily risks his life

---

[1] The phrase placed in the mouth of the Duchess in the thirty-sixth chapter of the second part of "Don Quixote"—"que las obras que se hacen tibia y flojamente no tienen mérito ni valen nada"— was condemned in the Index of 1667 (Ticknor, iii. p. 509 *n.*).

for a cause may be thought, in a general way, to believe
in it.   And such a man Cervantes certainly was.
Bitterness and cruelty formed no part of his nature;
but he must have seen many a despairing wretch
burned at the stake without any of that ardent sentiment of horror and pity which has wrung from the
most saintly of geniuses the exclamation : "I think the
sight of a Spanish *auto-de-fe* would have been the death
of me." [1]   The point alleged is that during a long life he
actively professed principles and opinions which he
knew to be false, which he hated and despised.   It
would be most painful to think that he was insincere in
professing to believe in a faith for the propagation of
which he was prepared to sanction, to demand, and to
applaud the execution of the severest civil penalties.
No doubt many a sharp cut at unworthy ministers—as
for example at confraternities in *El Retablo de las
Maravillas*, at monks in *El Viejo Celoso*, and at
sacristans in *La Cueva de Salamanca* and elsewhere—
may be found in his writings.   *Dueñas* and sacristans
are equally the objects of his hatred; the first, for
reasons which it might be indiscreet to penetrate; the
second, because he seems to have regarded them as a
set of drunken, crapulous buffoons.   But to deduce on
grounds so slender that he was hostile to the church to
which ostensibly he belonged would be much as if a
charge of atheism were brought against the merciless
creators of Charles Honeyman and Chadband.

---

[1] "Apologia pro vitâ suâ: being a History of his Religious
Opinions.   By John Henry Newman, D.D." (London, 1873), p. 47.

It would be absurd to argue that Cervantes was, at every period of his life, an exceptionally devout man. There are incidents in his career which prevent his being numbered in that elect company, and he would have been the first to disclaim any pretensions of the kind. But, though far removed from the ideal of the churchwarden, that he sincerely believed in the divine mission of the ancient and venerable church of which he was a member may be taken as certain. His indiscreet admirers have apparently failed to see that any other hypothesis would involve his memory in the deepest discredit. He was no chopper of straws; he probably knew little of the subtleties of the schools; he almost certainly speculated not at all on creeds and dogmas and formulæ. There is no trace of any such habit in his writings; but, like most of his countrymen, he had a painfully definite idea of the ultimate consequences of what his church calls sin. He was no fanatic; neither among *Skoptsy* or *Khlysty* should we expect to find his name. Perhaps without any particular religious unction, he said his prayers and obeyed the observances of his creed like others about him, as much from association as from any other motive. But there is a wide difference between silent acquiescence and stealthy rejection.

Yet his instincts were not all conservative; he also had his glimpses of liberalism. According to the tradition of his fellow-countrymen, his hatred of England should have been deep, stern, unrelenting, like the hatred of England for Spain; but he would almost

seem to have felt some dim presentiment that in
England his genius would receive a welcome more
generous, as immediate, and not less enthusiastic than
in his own land; and, in speaking of the English
and even of Elizabeth, whom his friends must have
considered the incarnation of all evil, his language
is admirably free from any taint of religious rancour
or political malignity. For England he had the
kindliest, the most generous expresssions. And this
required no common courage. To most of his acquain-
tances his vein of friendly neutrality must have
rendered him, if not suspect, at least suspect of being
suspect.

What were the attainments of Cervantes? Such
education as he had was slipshod, casual, incomplete,
and desultory. The excellent López de Hoyos had perhaps given a little finish to the smattering of information which he had picked up at Alcalá or elsewhere.
In Italy, as a young man he had acquired a serviceable
knowledge of the language, and of course he could follow Portuguese. Ariosto, Boiardo, Boccaccio, Cinthio,
Camoens, and Petrarch he read with delight, and he
never loses an opportunity of quoting, more or less
incorrectly, from his favourite poets.[1] But it would be

---

[1] Sir Richard Burton in his "Life of Camoens" (London, 1881),
pp. 66-67, says: "Luis de Camoens and Miguel de Cervantes were
contemporaries, and they must often have heard of one another.
Yet, curious to say, Camoens never mentions Cervantes, while
Cervantes alludes to Camoens in only one passage, where he calls

ludicrous to compare his learning with the erudition
of Rabelais, to whose Chevalier de Entamures Don
Quixote has some resemblance, and to whose genius
and personality the genius and personality of Cervantes
are cognate. Both were overflowing with humour;
both wrote poor verse; both were free from bitterness;
both were vagabonds; both had a lusty love of life;
both had heard the chimes at midnight; both hated
the police and the lesser clergy; both had natural
children; both indulge in *turpiloquium*.[1] Cervantes,
like Rabelais, was a *gourmet* so far as his very slight
opportunities permitted him to be. When in *La
Fuerza de la Sangre* he speaks in broken Italian of
li buoni polastri, picioni, presuto et salcicie; when in
El Rufián dichoso he revels in the good fare; when
in *El Trato de Argel* he dwells upon

> Cuzcuz, pan blanco á comer,
> Gallinas en abundancia,
> Y aun habrá vino de Francia,
> Si vino quieres beber,

we feel how heartily he would have echoed the pious

The Lusiads *El tesoro del Luso* (the Lusian's treasure)." The
reference to Camoens in "Don Quixote" (ii. c. 58) appears to have
escaped the writer.

Camoens died on June 10, 1579 or 1580—there is some doubt as
to the year. At that time Cervantes was a prisoner in Algiers. He
had been a private soldier; he had never written anything except the
lines for López de Hoyos; his name was unknown beyond the circle
of his personal friends and his comrades in the regiment. It seems
incredible that Camoens should have heard of him, and, under the
circumstances, it would have been exceedingly curious had his then
obscure name been mentioned by the great Portuguese poet.

[1] Rabelais' son Théodule appears to have died in his third year.

x

exclamation of Panurge: " Mais ne souper point ?
Cancre.   C'est erreur.   C'est scandale en nature."
Cervantes is never more himself than when dilating
on the wines of Esquivias : one feels that he would
have been an admirable third with Hal and Falstaff
at the Boar's-head Tavern.   It is touching to think of
his undergoing the nameless horrors of the Spanish
cuisine.[1]

But the rationalistic spirit of the Frenchman is alien
to him as is the ideal perfection of the Abbey of
Thelema.   He might have inquired with the Curé of
Meudon : *Pourquoy les moines sont refuis du monde,
et pourquoy les ungs ont le nez plus grand que les
aultres.*   The latter part of the thesis is quite in the
manner of Cervantes ; but the revolutionary spirit, the
anarchical ideal involved in the Theleman motto, *Fais
ce que voudras,* would have startled his simple mind as
much as Rabelais' dying exclamation—*La farce est*

---

[1] Compare the plaint of Gaguin to Ferrebout in the " Thesaurus
novus Anecdotorum " (Paris, 1727), i. col. 1838–1839)—" At velim
ego, velim equidem, Francisce, dignosceres hujus regionis apparatis-
sima suscipiendis viatoribus hospitia. . . . Illic præter nudos parietes
& fictilia vascula pauca, conspicies nihil," etc.—with Dumas' lament
in his " Impressions de Voyage " (Paris, 1847–1848) . . . " en
Espagne, le repas est une espèce de devoir que l'on accomplit pour
sa conservation personelle, et jamais un plaisir " (iv. pp. 63–64).   See
also i. pp. 115 and 160.

Every cause finds a champion at last, and fifteen generations later
than Gaguin a traveller was found to take up the cudgels for Spanish
cookery.   " Hitherto I certainly like the Spanish cookery, taking one
place with another, far more than the German or Italian."   See
John Leycester Adolphus' " Letters from Spain " (London, 1858),
p. 131.   This unique testimony deserves to be placed on record.

jouée. Cervantes had a respect for the actual, a reverence for the existing state of things from which Rabelais was completely free. Both are rare types; both are illustrious masters of wisdom; but, if Rabelais' mind had the freer play, his vision pierced somewhat less deeply, and perhaps less tolerantly, into the very marrow of things.

Cervantes may possibly have heard and known something of Rabelais : whether he had any knowledge of Jean de Meung, Villon, Marot, Ronsard, Scaliger, Casaubon, and Montaigne may well be doubted. Much less did he know of his contemporaries Sidney, Spenser, Marlow, Raleigh, Bacon, and Shakspere. He cannot have known them in the originals, and, even had translations existed, his horror of translations was strong and abiding.[1] It is singular to reflect how diminished would have been the area of his fame had the circulation of his masterpiece been confined to readers of Spanish alone. How little he knew of England and the English, despite all his kind feeling, is seen in his nomenclature, though certainly Lansac, Tansi, and Claudino Rubicon, as English names, pale into insignificance beside the Lord Tim-Tom-Jack, Barkilphedro, and Phelem-ghe-Madone of *L'homme qui*

---

[1] It is only fair to Cervantes to point out that he lays stress rather on translations of poetry : " que le quitó mucho de su natural valor, y lo mismo harán todos aquellos que los libros de verso quisieren volver en otra lengua, que por mucho cuidado que pongan y habilidad que muestren, jamás llegarán al punto que ellos tienen en su primer nacimiento " (" Don Quixote, I. vi). He is speaking of Jerónimo Jiménez de Urrea, the translator of the " Orlando Furioso."

rit; nor does he ever produce anything half so grotesque as the verses by which Wergeland sought to impart local colour to *Den Engelske Lods.*[1] From this catastrophe his very ignorance saved him. His methods of work are easily discernible in his writings. Casual, careless, slapdash, haphazard, never in a hurry to begin, he is almost always hasty in writing, desultory in revision, anxious to leave off. But the correction of his countless slips has afforded harmless occupation to those conscientious commentators who point out with owl-like solemnity that Cervantes, in confusing dawn and sunset, or in calling Sancho's wife by two or three different names, is as reckless as Shakspere, who talks of pistols in *Pericles,* who makes Giulio Romano

---

[1] M. A. Morel Fatio, in his most able "Études sur l'Espagne" (Première Série, Paris, 1888), has pointed out similar absurd blunders by Hugo in Spanish nomenclature (pp. 221–222).

See especially "Den Engelske Lods. Et Digt aft Henrik Werge-land" (Kristiania, 1845). Some of the blunders are purely typographical, as on p. 33.

> "Francis so!   Rigth so, my boy!
> Luward up!   Omboard holloy!"

But such passages as

> "Hastings, Pilot, Numero three" (p. 34);

or as

> "Ho, Johnny ho!   How do you do?
> Sing, Sailor, oh!
> Well, Toddy is the sorrows foe!
> Sing Sailor oh" (p. 48);

or, again, as

> "Hun er smukkere end sagt er
> (Kaldes jo af Folket" Loves
> Flower, fairy Queen of Cowes?)" (p. 72),

are beyond explanation. Prosper Mérimée, after his recovery from the romantic fever, would have delighted in them.

contemporary with the Delphic oracle in the *Winter's Tale*, who mentions both Henry IV. and America as coexistent to all men's knowledge in the *Comedy of Errors*, who lets Hector quote from Aristotle in *Troilus*, and who is carelessly guilty of a hundred and one other anachronisms. In both cases the commentator has received equal attention.

It is always important in the analysis of a man's character to appreciate his point of view, to know his opinions, with regard to women. What then were the opinions of Cervantes? Was his married life happy? On what terms did he and his wife live? What utterance, if any, does he deliver on that most difficult, most tragic, of problems—the intercourse, the relation between men and women? It may well be feared that his opinions about women were those of his contemporaries. In this, as in so many other matters, genius as he was, bound down by the conventionalities of his race, he seldom rose above his environment. Of those contemporaries, Lope was the most expressive, and from him the average sentiment is easily gathered. Lope, echoing the opinion of his age, lays it down that physical beauty is the unique charm of woman, the one thing worth considering. Is she beautiful? Then,

> To the rescue of her honour,
> My heart!

It is indeed a delicate task, from which even the curiosity and courage of the hardiest biographer may

shrink, to decide when the first bloom of loveliness
fades, when the first pallor of decadence begins. It
may, however, be safe to assert that in the latitude of
Madrid the hour comes rather sooner than later. What
was the fate of Doña Catalina when that fatal period
arrived? What part did she play, and what Cervantes?
Perhaps we may say truly enough of him: "Lui, se
penchait en souriant, cueillait ce qui s'offrait, envelop-
pant de douceur et d'affabilité légère cet incorrigible
mépris de la femme qui est au fond de tout méridional."
It is impossible to avoid noticing the sinister fact that,
except in the *Galatea*, and perhaps in one or two
of the plays, Cervantes, the most personal of writers,
says nothing, or next to nothing, of his wife.[1]   Little
phrases, such as that in *Don Quixote*, where he says
that marriage is a noose which, once round your neck,
becomes a Gordian knot, are scattered through his
writings with an abundance which suggests that his own
experiment had been unsuccessful.[2]   D. Pascual de

[1] How far the education of Spanish women fitted them to
become in any sense companions of their husbands may be gathered
from the bullying speech of Don Pedro Enríquez in Calderón's "No
hay burlas con el amor" (Act II. sc. ix.):

> " Aquí el estudio acabó,
> Aquí dio fin la poesía.
> Libro en casa no ha de haber
> De latin, que yo le alcance.
> Unas *Horas* en romance
> Le bastan á una mujer.
> Bordar, labrar y coser
> Sepa sola: deje al hombre
> El estudio." . . .

[2] "Don Quixote," II. xix.

Gayangos has shown that it is only too probable that the marital conduct of Cervantes left much to desire, and the birth of his natural daughter just before, or just after, his marriage is, so far as it goes, most damaging to him.

Nothing could be more unjust than to present Cervantes as a libertine, a hoary haunter of such resorts as M. Guy de Maupassant has immortalised in his wonderful story *La Maison Tellier*. There was in his disposition a vein of sanity and strength which forbids an assumption so outrageous. But the little we know of his career, together with the more ample testimony of his writings, tends to show that his wife was no important factor in his existence, that he neglected her, and that, fond as he was of other women, on an essential point he shared the average opinion of the average Spaniard of his time.[1] A modern moralist, whose generalisations are suggestive, if unsound, has declared that women, "though

---

[1] If Cervantes was fond of women's society (as it seems he was) this characteristic differentiates him strongly from Rabelais. Cp. the Nouveau Prologue du livre iv.: "On dit que Gargamelle mourust de joye. . . . Je n'en say rien de ma part; *et bien peu me soucie ny d'elle ny d'autre.*" It is impossible to imagine Cervantes writing the italicised passage. Rabelais probably agreed with the opinion expressed by Jean de Meung in the "Roman de la Rose":

> " Toutes estes, serés, ou futes,
> De fait ou de volenté . . .
> Et qui bien vous encercheroit,
> Toutes . . . vous trouveroit.
> Car qui que puist le faire estraindre,
> Volenté ne puet nus contraindre.
> Tel avantage ont toutes fames
> Qu'el sunt de lor volenté dames."

(l. 9489–9496).

less prone than men to intemperance and brutality, are in general more addicted to the petty forms of vanity, jealousy, spitefulness, and ambition."[1] The latter part of this debatable proposition would have received unquestioning acquiescence from most Spaniards of the seventeenth century.

Such a view of women's character, combined with the immense importance which was attached to physical perfection, caused the modern sentiment of love to be almost unknown. Personal beauty stimulated the sensual appetite, and, as beauty waned, the phantom of an affection, based on the grosser passion, waned with it. Even to-day he would be a courageous man who undertook to define precisely the gradation which separates the first outpost of love from the final boundary of desire.[2] No doubt in some isolated instances the extinction of the old fervour left behind the germs of a more tender and refined sentiment; but those cases were even more the exception than they are now.

So that if, in the conjugal relation, Cervantes was not eminently distinguished or exemplary, he was no worse, as he certainly was no better, than his neighbours. We may say of his married life what La Rochefoucauld says of marriage generally : *Il est de bons mariages; il n'en est pas de délicieux.* He troubled himself but little

---

[1] "History of European Morals, by W. E. H. Lecky" (London, 1886), ii. p. 360.

[2] At the time of writing this passage, I had not yet read Count Léon Tolstoï's "La Sonate à Kreutzer."

about the philosophy of marriage, and contented himself mostly with being in love with Doña Catalina's pretty face. But it has been cynically said that a man is only in love with what he does not understand or what he only half knows; and the discovery that Doña Catalina was a mortal was probably too much for Cervantes. There was nothing to bind him (I do not speak of the sacramental view of marriage which he, of course, held) more closely to a wife who bore him no children; and the moral atmosphere of those theatrical *coulisses* in which he had lived so long was not conducive to domestic happiness. On the other hand, Doña Catalina may, without any fault of her own, have been a disappointment to her illustrious husband, as he, on his side, must necessarily have been a disappointment to her. His probably was the nature of so many artists—uncertain of their own desires, sensuous, fickle, longing for what they are pleased to call sympathy and what is in fact flattery, calling for resourceful tact and hourly angelic ministration in the smallest as in the greatest things of life all day and every day. Is it possible for any human being to accomplish a mission so arduous, so incessant, so exhausting? If Doña Catalina failed, she failed because from the outset, in the nature of things, her task was desperately impossible.

Yet Cervantes, if he were not a model husband, was not the man to flinch from material duties. Though not one of those rare natures which detest idleness, he was always a strenuous, industrious worker. The burden of supporting wife, daughter, sister, and sister-in-law fell to him, and it never occurred to his healthy mind to shirk the squalid work of serving writs, or collecting tithes, or any other odious occupation allotted to him. The proud, famous, sensitive man of genius turned to the first task which came to hand with even more than the energy, earnestness, and promptitude of men of lesser mould, without a single fastidious movement of hesitation or reluctance. If he were not allowed to work with his head, he could at least work with that hand which Lepanto had spared ; nor did he ever indulge in any sickly whining against the hardness of fate. Ambition assuredly was not wanting, for we know that the impoverished gentleman even dreamed (he lived in Spain) of becoming Governor-General of some vast province over sea. He did indeed view with bewilderment the worldly success of men who were absurdly his inferiors. But it must be admitted that Cervantes was probably deficient in that useful, if despicable, quality of supple complaisance, which is so inestimable a factor in cases of personal advancement. *Les délicats sont malheureux,* as La Fontaine says ; and, lacking the odious accomplishment of intrusion, Cervantes, born without the faculty of ingratiation, was easily passed by others who, certainly, were not wanting in cool assurance. He struggled on alone in silent, proud humility.

It might have been thought that the writer's circumstances would have improved after the publication of *Don Quixote* in 1605. But, from one cause or another, that appears not to have been the case.

Perhaps he wasted his substance outside his home; perhaps he made poor terms with his publishers; perhaps he was fleeced by pirated editions and by the insidious volley of Avellaneda. However that may be (and each of the hypotheses is equally plausible), there is no disputing the fact that he was poor—miserably, squalidly, hideously poor. He would have realised to the full the bitterness of Madame de Tencin's saying : " L'homme qui fait des souliers est sûr de son salaire ; l'homme qui fait un livre ou une tragédie, n'est jamais sûr de rien."[1] Whatever ease he knew in his last years was due to the munificence, the bounty of Lemos and Bernardo de Sandoval y Rojas, Cardinal Archbishop of Toledo. Márquez Torres, Sandoval's secretary, in the *aprobación* to the second part of *Don Quixote*, has told us how, when the suite of the French ambassador pelted him with minute inquiries as to the age, profession, rank, and position of Cervantes, he was forced to say that the illustrious man was a soldier, a gentleman, old and poor. But the questions are at least a testimony to the wide-spread contemporary reputation of the author.

Probably his last days were sad enough. The young sprigs of the Court, whose exhibitions of valour were limited to a little harmless pinking in the suburbs, were but languidly amused when they came across an aged man who told them of the umbered faces he had seen in battles fought before they were breeched. But huddled round the *brasero* in his chill, icy room, with

[1] See Marmontel's " Memoires d'un père," etc. (Paris, An XIII.), i. p. 349.

some of his former comrades, one can still see the old man
eloquent, and listen to the stammer dying on his lips,
as he tells his hearers of Aluch Ali's advance, of Don
John's emblazoned standard fluttering in the Levantine
air, of the battle afar off, the thunder of the captains,
and the shouting, with many a picturesque sketch of
heroic deeds done aboard the *Marquesa—quorum pars
parva fuit.*[1]　As the years ebbed by, the opportunities grew rarer every day. The old friends, the
Spartan veterans, his brothers-in-arms, his contemporaries, were gone or vanishing. Padilla, Artieda, Ercilla,
Láinez, Leiva, López Maldonado, with many another
jovial companion, many another Theban legionary, were
dead and gone.[2]　Espinel, feeble, querulous, malicious,
still survived, almost a centenarian. Of the Argensolas,
Lupercio died in 1613, while Bartolomé remained in
Naples with Lemos. Lope, in the full tide of popular
favour, had no kind word for any serious rival, much
less for the rival whom he feared most. Perhaps one
ought to be thankful that Lope's vindictiveness ceased
with the publication of Avellaneda's obscene travesty.
Had Cervantes survived and prospered he might, like
Quevedo, have been dragged before a Tribunal of Just
Vengeance, and have been denounced as a Master of

---

[1] That Cervantes stammered may be inferred from the Prólogo
to the "Novelas Ejemplares": "Que aunque tartamudo, no lo será
para decir verdades, que dichas por señas suelen ser entendidas."

[2] The exact dates of the death of these writers is not in every
case ascertainable; but several were certainly dead years earlier, and
it seems safe to say that all were dead before the publication of
the "Novelas."

Errors, Doctor of Shamelessness, Licentiate of Buffoonery, Bachelor of Filth, Professor of Vice, and Archdevil of Mankind.[1] Góngora, bitter, venomous, jealous, morose, stretched out no friendly hand. Perhaps Morales and Quevedo, alone among the younger school, may be counted among the restricted company of Cervantes' friends. It is singular that they should have been so few. It might have been thought that, genius apart, a man so kindly, so upright, so open, so generous, so benignant, one who felt so keenly the

> delight in little things,
> The buoyant youth surviving in the man,

would have been encircled by troops of friends. Possibly his conversation may have been more mordant than the genial humour of his books. It has been well observed that, strong and keen as a man's wit may be, it is never half as strong as the memory of fools, nor half as keen as their resentment. Old and solitary,

---

[1] "El tribunal de la Justa Vengança, erigido contra los Escritos de D. Francisco de Quevedo, Maestro de Errores, Doctor en Desverguenças, Licenciado en Bufonerias, Bachiller en Suciedades, Cathedratico de Vizios, y Proto-Diablo entre los Hombres. Por el Licenciado Arnaldo Franco-Furt" (Valencia, 1635). It seems probable that this abusive work is by Juan Pérez de Montalván, Lope's panegyrist.

It is instructive to compare the sullen silence or cold indifference of Lope with the enthusiastic admiration of Calderón for Cervantes. Lope (I give the statement on the authority of Ticknor, ii. p. 139) mentions Cervantes but five times in his twenty million lines. Calderón was a boy of sixteen studying at Salamanca when Cervantes died. But he was a native of Madrid, and must often have seen the great man. All his references to Cervantes are in the kindest, most

amid a brilliant, new generation, those last years of
Cervantes' life are pregnant with sombre, sinister
suggestion.

> His golden locks time hath to silver turned;
> O time too swift ! O swiftness never ceasing !
> His youth 'gainst time and age hath ever spurned,
> But spurned in vain, youth waneth by increasing.
>
> His helmet now shall make a hive for bees,
> And lovers' songs be turned to holy psalms;
> A man-at-arms must now serve on his knees
> And feed on prayers which are old age's alms.

But his rich humour cheered him on. His incomparable
irony, his vast sense of the opulence of existence, his
amused appreciation of the many-sided aspect of things,
lit up his squalid life with radiance. In his bare cell, left
to his own reflexions on a mournful, diverting, adorable,
odious world, the noble veteran was assured of his own
immortality. The papilionaceous courtiers, the worldly-
wise of his own contemporaries, not knowing the keen
eye which pierced through their petty absurdities,
smiled at the honourable inflexibility, the courtly,
patient amenity, the gracious, reticent urbanity, the
noble poverty of the simple, gray-haired prætorian,
without ever suspecting that the object of their cheap
sneers, halting painfully onwards, shivering and cloakless

---

appreciative spirit. Cp. *e.g.* the allusions in "La Banda y la Flor"
(Act I. sc. i.), "Los empeños de un acaso" (Act I. sc. vii.), "El maestro
de danzar" (Act I. sc. i.), "El Alcalde de Zalamea" (Act I. sc. iii.),
and "Casa con dos puertas mala es de guardar" (Act I. sc. v.). Tirso
de Molina's references are always friendly too. Cp. "El Castigo de
Penseque" (Act I. sc. x.) and "Marta la piadosa" (Act I. sc. v.).

in the glacial winter air, was after all one of the finest gentlemen in the whole world. But those who knew him better would have agreed with posterity that it was impossible to rise without edification from the study of a life and character which, with all their many blemishes and infirmities, are so rich in genius and pathos, so chequered by stern vicissitude, so sanctified by disillusioning trial, so fulfilled of strenuous battle, of lofty aims, of sustained purpose, of valiant, plenary, persistent, and superb endeavour. *¡ He dicho !*

BIBLIOGRAPHY

OF

THE WORKS OF

MIGUEL DE CERVANTES SAAVEDRA.

1585–1892.

BY

JAS. FITZMAURICE-KELLY.

MIGUEL DE CERVANTES SAAVEDRA

IN

CHRONOLOGICAL ORDER OF PUBLICATION.

Primera parte de la Galatea, dividida en seys libros . Alcalá, 1585.
El Ingenioso Hidalgo Don Quixote de la Mancha . Madrid, 1605.
Novelas exemplares. . . . . . . Madrid, 1613.
Viage del Parnaso . . . . Madrid, 1614.
Ocho Comedias y ocho Entremeses . . . . Madrid, 1615.
Segunda Parte del Ingenioso Cavallero Don Quixote
de la Mancha . . . . Madrid, 1615.

POSTHUMOUS.

Los Trabaios de Persiles y Sigismunda, historia
setentrional . . . . Madrid, 1617.
{ La Numancia . . . . Madrid, 1784.
{ El Trato de Argel . . . . . . Madrid, 1784.

WORKS.

Obras completas de Cervantes. (Vida de Miguel de Cervantes Saavedra por Don Buenaventura Carlos Aribau. Nuevas investigaciones acerca de la vida y obras de Cervantes por Don Cayetano Alberto de la Barrera. Notas á las nuevas investigaciones, etc.) Ilustradas por los Señores J. E. Hartzenbusch y Don Cayetano Rosell. 12 tomos. Madrid, Argamasilla de Alba, 1863–1864. 8vo.

Obras. 16 tomos. Madrid, 1803–1805. 8vo.

Obras escogidas. Nueva edición clásica, arreglada, corregida ó ilustrada con notas por D. Agustín García de Arrieta. (Vida de M. de Cervantes Saavedra. Por D. Martín Fernández de Navarrete. Análisis, ó juicio crítico del Quijote. Por D. Agustín García de Arrieta.) 10 tomos. Paris, 1827. 32mo.

Vol. i., *Vida*; vols. ii.–vi., *D. Quijote*; vols. vii.–ix., *Novelas*; vol. x., *Teatro.*

Obras escogidas. 11 tomos. Madrid, 1829. 8vo.

Obras. Madrid, 1846. 8vo.

This most useful, but incomplete, collection forms the first volume of the *Biblioteca de autores españoles . . . ordenada é ilustrada por D. Buenaventura Carlos Aribau.* It has been frequently reprinted. The second and third edition were issued in 1849 and 1864 respectively. The latest issue is dated 1878.

COLLECTIONS OF SEPARATE WORKS.

[La Galatea, dividida en seis libros : compuesta por Miguel de Cervantes Saavedra. Va añadido El Viaje del Parnaso del mismo autor. Con licencia. A costa de Francisco Manuel de Mena, Mercader de libros. Se hallará en su casa Calle de Toledo, junto a la Porteria de la Concepcion Geronima. 1614. 4to.]

NOTE.—A copy with the foregoing title-page may be found in the library of the British Museum. I have no hesitation in pronouncing it a forgery. The words, *En Madrid por Juan de Zuñiga, Año 1736,* have been clumsily erased, and the date 1614 has been inserted, by some amateur among swindling bibliophiles. I should have thought it impossible to deceive even the meanest intelligence by a forgery so obvious. It is now noted as spurious in the Catalogue of the British Museum Library.

———— Madrid, 1736. 4to.

———— Madrid, 1772. 4to.

Viage al Parnasso compuesto por Miguel de Cervantes Saavedra. Publicanse ahora de nuevo una tragedia y una comedia ineditas del mismo Cervantes : aquella intitulada *La Numancia* : esta *El Trato de Argel.* Madrid, 1784. 8vo.

Obras de Miguel de Cervantes Saavedra. Nueva edición con la

vida del autor por Don Martín Fernández de Navarrete. 4 tomos. Paris, 1841. 8vo.

NOTE.—This forms part of the *Colección de los mejores autores españoles.*

Varias obras inéditas de Cervantes, sacadas de códices de la Biblioteca colombina, con nuevas ilustraciones sobre la vida del autor y el Quijote, por D. Adolfo de Castro. Madrid, 1874. 8vo.

COLLECTIONS OF SEPARATE WORKS: ENGLISH.

The Voyage of Parnassus; Numantia, a Tragedy; the Commerce of Algiers. By Cervantes. Translated from the Spanish by Gordon Willoughby James Gyll. London, 1870. 8vo.

COLLECTIONS OF SEPARATE WORKS: FRENCH.

Œuvres diverses. 8 vols. Amsterdam et Leipsic, 1768. 12mo.

Œuvres complètes . . . . traduites de l'espagnol par H. Bouchon-Dubournial. 6 vols. Paris, 1820–1823. 8vo.

NOTE.—This edition includes only *Don Quixote* and *Pérsiles.*

COLLECTIONS OF SEPARATE WORKS: GERMAN.

Sämmtliche Werke. Aus der Ursprache übersetzt von L. G. Förster. 12 vols. Quedlinburg und Leipzig, 1825–1826. 12mo.

Werke von Cervantes. Aus dem Spanischen übersetzt von Hieronymus Müller und R. O. Spazier. 16 vols. Zwickau, 1825–1829. 16mo.

Romane und Novellen aus dem Spanischen des Cervantes [von F. M. Duttenhoffer]. Mit Illustrationen von Johannot und andern Kunstlern. 10 vols. Pforzheim, 1839–1840. 16mo.

Vols. i.-vi., *Don Quixote*; vols. vii.-x., *Die Novellen.*

Cervantes sämmtliche Romane und Novellen. Aus dem Spanischen von A. Keller und Friedrich Notter. 12 vols. Stuttgart, 1839–1842. 16mo.

Vols. i.-v., *Don Quixote*; vols. vi.-vii., *Die Galathea*; vols. viii.-ix., *Die Novellen.*

POEMS.

Canto de Calíope, Letrilla, Canciones y Sestina : por Miguel de Cervantes Saavedra. (*Parnaso español. Colección de poesías escogidas de los más célebres poetas castellanos.* Por D. Juan Joseph López de Sedano. Tomo viii. pp. 287–328, ix. p. 193.) Madrid, 1774–1778. 8vo.

Poesías inéditas de Cervantes. Cervantes esclavo y cantor del Santísimo Sacramento. MS. de la Bib. Floreciano de la Real Academia de la Historia y artículo del Sr. D. Fernández-Guerra y Orbe. (*De la Revista Agustiniana.*) Valladolid, 1882. 8vo.

GALATEA.

Primera parte de la Galatea, dividida en seys libros. Cõpuesta por Miguel de Cervantes. Dirigida al Illustrissimo señor Ascanio Colona, Abad de sancta Sofia. Con privilegio. Impressa en Alcala por Iuan Gracian. Año de 1585. 8vo. 375 ff.

The *Aprovacion* is dated February 1, 1584 ; the *Privilegio* is dated February 22, 1584 ; the *Fee de Erratas* and the *Tassa* are respectively dated February 28, 1585, and March 13, 1585.

The first edition of the *Galatea* is a rarity of the first magnitude. An edition published at Lisbon in 1590 is said to exist. I have not, however, been successful in tracing it.

―――― Paris, 1611. 8vo.

―――― Valladolid, 1617. 8vo.

Ruís mentions an edition published at Baeza in 1617. I have not seen it.

Los seys libros de la Galatea. Barcelona, 1618. 8vo.

La discreta Galatea. Lisboa, 1618. 8vo.

Los seis libros de la Galatea. Madrid, 1736. 8vo.

―――― Madrid, 1772. 4to.

―――― 2 tomos. Madrid, 1784. 8vo.

―――― 3 tomos. Madrid, 1805. 8vo.

―――― 2 tomos. Madrid, 1823. 8vo.

―――― Paris, 1835. 4to.

― ‥ ‑ Paris, 1841. 4to.

―――‑ Madrid, 1866. 4to.

―――― [Edición diamante.] Madrid, 1883. 12mo.

Los Enamorados ó Galatea y sus bodas : historia pastoral comenzada por Miguel de Cervantes Saavedra. Abreviada despues, y continuada, y ultimamente concluida por Don Cándido María Trigueros. 4 tomos. Madrid, 1798. 8vo.

La Galatea de Miguel de Cervantes Saavedra, imitada, compendiada y concluida por Florian. Traducido por D. Casiano Pellicer. Madrid, 1814. 12mo.

———— Barcelona, 1830. 8vo.

———— Paris, 1840. 8vo.

GALATEA : ENGLISH.

Galatea, a pastoral romance, imitated from Cervantes by M. de Florian. Translated by an Officer. Dublin, 1791. 8vo.

Galatea : a pastoral romance. From the French of Monsieur Florian. By Miss Harriet Highley. London, 1804. 8vo.

Galatea from the French of Florian by W. Marshall Craig. London, 1813. 12mo.

Galatea. A pastoral romance, literally translated from the Spanish by Gordon Willoughby James Gyll. London, 1867. 8vo.

GALATEA : FRENCH.

Galatée, roman pastoral ; imité de Cervantes par M. de Florian, Capitaine de Dragons, et Gentilhomme de S.A.S. Mgr le Duc de Penthievre. Paris, 1783. 12mo.

———— 4e Edit. Paris, 1785. 12mo.

———— Paris, 1793. 12mo.

This *pastiche* is of course to be found in the *Œuvres de Florian*, frequently reprinted.

GALATEA : GERMAN.

Galathea. Ein Schäferroman nach Cervantes. Aus dem Französichen von Mylius. Berlin, 1787. 8vo.

———— Griechisch und deutsch. Wien, 1824. 12mo.

———— Nach dem Spanischen von F. Sigismund. Zwickau, 1830. 8vo.

———— von A. Keller und F. Notter. Stuttgart, 1840. Sämmtliche Werke.

———— von F. M. Duttenhoffer. Pforzheim, 1840.

GALATEA : ITALIAN.

La Galatea, romanzo pastoral; già tirato dallo spagnuolo di Michele Cervantes dal Signore di Florian e dal francese tradotto in Italiano [by Luigi Secreti]. Basilea, 1788. 8vo.

The earliest edition which I have actually seen is that of 1799 ; but the dedicatory letter of Secreti and Florian's reply place the date of the first edition almost beyond dispute.

ANONYMOUS.

Relacion | de lo svcedi | do en la Civdad | de Valladolid, desde | el punto del felicisimo nacimiento del | Principe Don Felipe Dominico Victor | nuestro Señor : hasta que se acabaron las | demostraciones de alegria que | por él se hizieron. | Al Conde de Miranda. | Año 1605. | Con Licencia. | En Valladolid, Por Iuan Godinez de Millis, | Vendese en casa de Antonio Coello en la libreria. | 46 ff. 4to.

NOTE.—This trifling pamphlet is not avowedly written by Cervantes ; but almost all experts admit its authenticity.

ANONYMOUS : ITALIAN.

Relatione di qvanto è svccesso nella città di Vagliadolid. Dopò il felicissimo nascimento del Principe di Spagna Don Filippo Dominico Vittorio. . . . Tradotta di lingua Castigliana da Cesare Parona. Milano, 1608. 4to.

THE FIRST PART OF *DON QUIXOTE.*

Il Ingenioso || Hidalgo Don Qvi || xote de la Mancha, || Compuesto por Miguel de Ceruantes || Saauedra. Dirigido al Dvqve de Beiar, || Marques de Gibraleon, Conde de Benalcaçar, y Baña- || res, Vizconde de la Puebla de Alcozer, Señor de || las villas de Capilla, Curiel, y || Burguillos. Año, 1605. Con Privilegio, || En Madrid, Por Iuan de la Cuesta. || Vendese en casa de Francisco de Robles, librero del Rey ñro señor. 4to. Ff. 316.

The *Privilegio* is dated September 26, 1604, the *Testimonio de las Erratas,* December 1, 1604, and the *Tassa,* December 20, 1604. The text consists of 316 ff., of which the last four are unnumbered. It is preceded by 12 ff. of prefatory matter and is followed by the *Tabla* on 4 ff. all numbered.

———— Año 1605. 4to. Ff. 316.

NOTE.—There are two ludicrous misprints on the title-page—
Barcelona instead of Benalcaçar, and Burgillos instead of Burguillos.
" Con priuilegio de Castilla, Aragon, y Portugal" is printed instead of
" Con Privilegio." The *Privilegio* for Portugal is dated February 9,
1605. In this edition the 316 ff. are all numbered.

———— Em Lisboa. Impresso com lisença da Santo Officio por
Iorge Rodriguez. Anno de 1605. 4to. Ff. 210.

The dedication is omitted from the title-page. The *Aprobacion* is
dated February 26, 1605, the *licença* March 1, 1605. This edition
is printed in double columns.

———— Con licencia de la S. Inquisicion. En Lisboa : Impresso
por Pedro Crasbeeck. Año M. DCV. 8vo. Ff. 448.

The dedication is omitted from the title-page. The licenses are
dated March 27 and March 29, 1605.

———— Impreso con licencia, en Valencia, en casa de Pedro
Patricio Mey, 1605. A costa de Iusepe Ferrer mercader de libros,
delante la Diputacion. 8vo. Pp. 768.

The *Aprobacion* is dated July 18, 1605. Salvá mentions another
impression of this edition of Mey's later in 1605. I have failed to
discover it.

———— En Brvsselas, Por Roger Velpivs, Impressor de sus
Altezas, en l'Aguila de oro, cerca de Palacio, Año 1607. 8vo. Pp. 595.

The *Privilegio* is dated March 7, 1607.

———— Año 1608. Con priuilegio de Castilla, Aragon, y
Portugal. En Madrid, Por Iuan de la Cuesta. Vendese en casa
de Francisco de Robles, librero del Rey ñro señor. 4to. Ff. 277.

Burguillos is misprinted Burgillos on the title-page, as in the
second edition. The *licencia* is dated June 25, 1608. Cervantes is
said to have corrected this edition, which, in consequence, is highly
valued. The statement rests on the authority of Brunet, Navarrete,
and Ticknor, and is entirely a matter of conjecture ; in my opinion
this surmise is worth very little. Some commentators have called this
the second edition. Chronologically, at all events, it is the seventh.

———— En Milan. Por el Heredero de Pedromartir Locarni y
Iuan Bautista Bidello. Año 1610. Con licencia de Superiores, y
Preuilegio. 8vo. Pp. 722.

The dedicatory letter, *" All' Illmo Senor el Sig. Conde Vitaliano
Vizconde,"* is dated July 24, 1610.

———— En Brvcelas, Por Roger Velpius y Huberto Antonio,

Impressores de sus Altezas, en l'Aguila de oro, cerca de Palacio. Año 1611. 8vo. Pp. 586.

The *Privilegio* of March 7, 1607, is reprinted at the end of the *Tabla.*

———— Año 1617. Impresso con licencia, en Barcelona, en casa de Bautista Sorita, en la Libreria. A costa de Miguel Gracian Librero. 8vo. Pp. 736.

The licencia is dated June 4, 1617.

———— Por Huberto Antonio. Brvcelas. Año 1617. 8vo.

THE SECOND PART OF *DON QUIXOTE.*

Segvnda Parte || del Ingenioso || Cavallero Don || Qvixote de la || Mancha. || Por Miguel de Ceruantes Saauedra, autor de su primera parte. || Dirigida a don Pedro Fernandez de Castro, Conde de Le- || mos, de Andrade, y de Villalua, Marques de Sarria, Gentil- || hombre de la Camara de su Magestad, Comendador de la || Encomienda de Peñafiel, y la Zarça de la Orden de Al- || cantara, Virrey, Gouernador, y Capitan General del Reyno de Napoles, y Presidente del su- || premo Consejo de Italia. Año 1615. Con Privilegio, || En Madrid, Por Iuan de la Cuesta. || Vendese en casa de Francisco de Robles, librero del Rey N. S. 4to. Ff. 280.

In the second part *Cavallero* has been substituted for *Hidalgo* on the title-page. The *Aprouacion* of Marquez Torres is dated February 27, 1615; that of Valdiuielso March 17, 1615; and that of Cetina, November 5, 1615. The *Privilegio* is dated March 30, 1615; the *Tassa* and *Fee de Erratas*, October 21, 1615; and the Dedicatory Epistle is dated October 31, 1615.

———— En Valencia, En casa de Pedro Patricio Mey, junto a San Martin. 1616. A costa de Roque Sonzonio Mercader de Libros. 8vo. Pp. 766.

The *Aprouacion* is dated January 27, 1616. The *licencia* is dated May 27, 1616.

———— En Brvselas, Por Huberto Antonio. 1616. 8vo.

The *Permiso* is dated Feb. 4, 1616.

———— En Lisboa, por Iorge Rodriguez, con todas las licencias necesarias. Año 1617. 4to.

The *Aprobaciones* are dated August 12, August 22nd, August

25, and September 10, 1616. The *Tassa* is dated January 17, 1617.

———— En Barcelona, en casa de Sebastian Mathevad. Año 1617. 8vo.

Salvá declares this to be the first complete edition of the two conjoint parts. It may be so; but I have not succeeded in discovering it. Salvá is not altogether trustworthy in bibliographical *minutiæ.* Every statement made by him should be very carefully verified before acceptation.

DON QUIXOTE—THE ENTIRE WORK.

Primera y segunda parte del ingenioso hidalgo, etc. 2 tomos. Madrid, 1637. 4to.

This is the first complete edition according to D. Martín Fernández de Navarrete. There was formerly, and perhaps still is, a copy in the Birmingham Free Library.

———— 2 tomos. Madrid, 1647. 4to.

———— 2 tomos. Madrid, 1655. 4to.

Parte primera y segunda del ingenioso Don Quixote de la Mancha. Madrid, 1662. 4to.

Vida y hechos del Ingenioso Cavallero Don Quixote de la Mancha. Nueva edicion, corregida y ilustrada con differentes estampas. 2 tomos. Bruselas, 1662. 4to.

NOTE.—This is, so far as I know, the first illustrated edition of *Don Quixote*: the title has been changed from *El ingenioso Hidalgo*, etc., and *El ingenioso Cavallero*, to *Vida y hechos del*, etc.

———— Madrid, 1662–1668. 4to.

NOTE.—There is a bibliographical difficulty here : the second part is dated 1662 ; the first part is dated 1668.

Vida y hechos, etc. 2 tomos. Bruselas, 1671. 8vo.

———— Nueva edición, corregida y ilustrada con treinta y dos estampas. 2 tomos. Amberes, 1672–1673. 8vo.

———— Nueva edición, corregida y ilustrada con treinta y cuatro laminas muy donosas, etc. Madrid, 1674. 4to.

———— Nueva edición, etc. 2 tomos. Amberes, 1697. 4to.

———— 2 tomos. Londres, 1701. 4to.

———— 2 tomos. . Barcelona, 1704. 4to.

Vida y hechos, etc. 2 tomos. Londres, 1706. 4to.

———— Dedicada al Ilmo. Sr. D. Diego de la Serna y Cantoral, comendador de la orden de Calatrava, etc. 2 tomos. Madrid, 1706. 4to.

———— Nueva edición, corregida, y ilustrada con treinta y cinco Laminas muy donosas, y apropriadas à la materia. 2 tomos. Madrid, 1714. 4to.

———— Nueva edición, etc. 2 tomos. Amberes, 1719. 8vo.

———— 2 tomos. Madrid, 1723. 4to.

———— 2 tomos. Madrid, 1730. 4to.

———— Con la dedicatoria al mismo D. Quixote, escrita por su cronista, descubierta y traducida con imponderable desvelo y trabajo. 2 tomos. Madrid, 1730. 4to.

———— Nueva edición corregida, ilustrada, etc. 2 tomos. Madrid, 1735. 4to.

———— 2 tomos. Leon de Francia [Lyon], 1736. 8vo.

———— (Advertencias de D. Juan Oldfield sobre las estampas : Vida de Miguel de Cervantes Saavedra : Autor Don Gregorio Mayáns i Siscar). 4 tomos. Londres, 1737–1738. 4to.

———— 2 tomos. Haia, 1739.

———— 2 tomos. Madrid, 1741. 4to.

———— Con muy bellas Estampas, gravadas sobre los Dibujos de Coypel, etc. 4 tomos. Haia. 1744. 8vo.

———— . . . con el resto de las Obras Poeticas de las Academicos de la Argamasilla, halladas por el mas cèlebre Adivinador de nuestros tiempos. 2 tomos. Madrid, 1750. 4to.

———— 2 tomos. Madrid, 1750. 4to.

———— Ilustrada con quarenta y quatro Laminas muy apropriadas à la materia, y es la impression mas añadida que ay. 2 tomos. Madrid, 1751. 4to.

———— 4 tomos. Barcelona, 1755. 8vo.

———— 4 tomos. Amsterdam y Lipsia, 1755. 12mo.

———— 4 tomos. Tarragona, 1757. 8vo.

———— 4 tomos. Barcelona, 1762. 8vo.

———— (Vida de Miguel de Cervantes Saavedra. Su autor Don Gregorio Mayans i Siscar). 2 tomos. Madrid, 1764–1765. 4to.

———— 4 tomos. Madrid, 1765. 8vo.

———— 4 tomos. Madrid, 1771. 8vo.

———— Nueva edición corregida é ilustrada con varias Laminas

finas, y la vida del Autor [by D. Gregorio Mayans i Siscar]. 4 tomos. Madrid, 1777. 8vo.

Vida y hechos, etc. 4 tomos. Madrid, 1777. 8vo.

———— El ingenioso hidalgo Don Quixote de la Mancha. . . . Nueva edición corregida por la Real Academia Española. Vida de Cervantes y análisis del Quixote. 4 tomos. Madrid, 1780. 4to.

Note.—The Life of Cervantes, in this, the first edition issued by the Spanish Academy, is written by Vicente de los Ríos.

Historia del famoso cavallero Don Quixote de la Mancha . . . con anotaciones, indices y varias lecciones : por el Reverendo D. Juan Bowle. 6 tomos. Londres, 1781. 4to.

El ingenioso hidalgo Don Quixote de la Mancha . . . Nueva edición corregida por la Real Academia Española. 4 tomos. Madrid, 1782. 8vo.

———— 4 tomos. Madrid, 1782. 8vo.

El ingenioso hidalgo Don Quixote de la Mancha. Tercera edición, corregida por la Real Academia Española. 6 tomos. Madrid, 1787. 8vo.

———— 6 tomos. Madrid, 1797–1798. 16mo.

———— Nueva edición, corregida denuevo ; con nuevas notas, con nuevas estampas, con nuevo análisis y con la vida de el autor nuevamente aumentada por D. Juan Antonio Pellicer. 5 tomos. Madrid, 1797–1798.

The Grenville Library contains one of six magnificent copies printed on vellum.

———— Con nuevas notas, nuevas viñetas, por D. Juan Antonio Pellicer. 9 tomos. Madrid, 1798–1800. 12mo.

———— 7 tomos. Leipzig, 1800–1807. 16mo.

———— 16 tomos. Madrid, 1803–1805. 8vo.

Vida y hechos del ingenioso, etc. Madrid, 1804. 8vo.

El ingenioso hidalgo Don Quixote de la Mancha. 4 tomos. Burdeos, 1804. 8vo.

———— Con vida del autor y notas por L. Ideler. 6 tomos. Berlin, 1804. 8vo.

Historia del ingenioso hidalgo, etc. 6 tomos. Barcelona, 1808–1814. 12mo.

Vida y hechos del ingenioso hidalgo, etc. 4 tomos. Madrid, 1808. 8vo.

El ingenioso hidalgo Don Quixote de la Mancha . . . por el Rdo. D. Felipe Fernández, A. M. 4 tomos. London, 1808. 18mo.

———— 4 tomos. Leon, 1810. 8vo.

———— 7 tomos. Paris, 1814. 12mo.

———— Nueva edición corregida por el Rdo. Don Felipe Fernández, A.M. 4 tomos. London, 1814. 8vo.

———— 4 tomos. Burdeos, 1815. 12mo.

———— 6 tomos. Leipsique, 1818. 8vo.

———— Cuarta edición corregida por la Real Academia Española. (Con vida por Navarrete.) 4 tomos. Madrid, 1819. 8vo.

———— 4 tomos. Paris, 1825. 18mo.

———— 6 tomos. Paris, 1825. 12mo.

———— 2 tomos. Madrid, 1826. 8vo.

———— 6 tomos. Paris, 1826. 32mo.

NOTE.—This edition forms vols. ii.-vi. of the *Obras Escogidas* edited by Agustín García de Arrieta.

———— 4 tomos. Madrid, 1826. 8vo.

———— Edición en miniatura enteramente conforme á la ultima corregida y publicada por la Real Academia Española. [Edited by Joaquín María de Ferrer.] Paris, 1827. 12mo.

———— Ilustrado con notas, etc. 6 tomos. Paris, 1827. 8vo.

NOTE.—I have never seen this edition.

———— 2 tomos. Berlin, 1831. 8vo.

With a vocabulary by J. B. W. Benecke.

———— 4 tomos. Madrid, 1831. 16mo.

———— 2 tomos. Zaragoza, 1831. 8vo.

———— Nueva edición conforme en todo á la última de la Real Academia Española. 4 tomos. Barcelona, 1832-1834. 8vo.

NOTE.—*La ultima de la Real Academia Española* is, of course, the edition of 1819.

———— 6 tomos. Barcelona, 1832-1835. 8vo.

———— 4 tomos. Madrid, 1832. 12mo.

———— 2 tomos. Paris, 1832. 16mo.

A reprint of Joaquín María Ferrer's edition of 1827, with slight typographical changes.

———— Comentado por Don Diego Clemencín. 6 tomos. Madrid, 1833-1839. 4to.

NOTE.—This edition is of great importance and value.

El ingenioso hidalgo, etc. Con el elogio de Cervantes por D. José Mor de Fuentes. Paris, 1835. 8vo.

Vol. i. of the *Colección de los mejores autores españoles.*

——— Con el elogio de Cervantes por D. José Mor de Fuentes. Leipzig, 1836. 8vo.

——— 2 tomos. Zaragoza, 1837. 8vo.

——— 2 tomos. Boston, 1837. 4to.

——— 4 tomos. Paris, 1838. 12mo.

——— Paris, 1838. 8vo.

——— Barcelona, 1839. 8vo.

——— Edición adornada con 800 laminas repartidas por el contexto. 2 tomos. Barcelona, 1839. 4to. Segunda edición, 1840.

——— Con la vida de Cervantes por D. M. F. de Navarrete. Paris, 1840. 8vo.

——— Paris, 1840.

Historia de la vida del ingenioso, etc. Ultima edición, conforme al original primitivo. 4 tomos. Madrid, 1840. 8vo.

El ingenioso hidalgo, etc. 5 tomos. Barcelona, 1840. Fol.

——— 6 tomos. Barcelona, 1840. 16mo.

Vida y hechos del ingenioso hidalgo, etc. 3 tomos. Barcelona, 1841. 8vo.

El ingenioso hidalgo, etc. Nueva edición clásica, ilustrada con notas históricas, gramaticales y críticas, por la Academia Española, sus individuos de número, Pellicer, Arrieta y Clemencín. Enmendada y corregida por Francisco Sales. Tercera edición. 2 tomos. Boston, 1842. 8vo.

——— Adornada de 125 estampas litográficas, etc. 2 tomos. Méjico, 1842. 8vo.

——— Madrid, 1844. Fol.

——— 4 tomos. Madrid, 1844. 8vo.

——— Nueva edición corregida y aumentada por D. Eugenio de Ochoa. Paris, 1844. 8vo.

——— Nueva edición conforme á la corregida y anotado por D. Eugenio de Ochoa. 6 tomos. Barcelona, 1845. 16mo.

——— 2 tomos. Madrid, 1845. 8vo.

——— Paris, 1845. 8vo.

Vida y hechos del ingenioso hidalgo, etc. 3 tomos. Barcelona, 1845–1846. 8vo.

El ingenioso hidalgo, etc. Madrid, 1846.

—— Paris, 1847. 18mo.

—— Madrid, 1847. 4to.

—— 2 tomos. Barcelona, 1848. 4to.

—— Paris, 1848. 4to.

—— Ilustrada con notas históricas, gramaticales y críticas. Segun las de la Academia Española . . . aumentada con El Buscapié anotado por Adolfo de Castro. [Observaciones del Señor Juan Eugenio Hartzenbusch.] Madrid, 1850. 8vo.

—— 2 tomos. Paris, 1850. 8vo.

—— Madrid, 1851. Fol.

—— Madrid, 1851. 8vo.

—— Anotado por Eugenio de Ochoa. Nueva York, 1853. 12mo.

—— Nueva edición ilustrada con notas de Pellicer, y adornada con láminas finas, bajo la dirección de D. Francisco Bonosio Piferrer. 4 tomos. Madrid, 1853–1854. 4to.

—— 2 tomos. Sevilla, 1854–1855. 4to.

—— Paris, 1855. 8vo.

—— 2 tomos. Sevilla, 1855. 8vo.

—— 2 tomos. Madrid, 1855–1856. 4to.

—— 2 tomos. Barcelona, 1857. 8vo.

—— Anotado por Eugenio de Ochoa. Nueva York, 1857. 8vo.

—— 2 tomos. Barcelona, 1859. Fol.

—— Segun el texto corregido y aumentado por el Sr. Ochoa. Nueva edición americana, accompañada de un ensayo histórico sobre la vida y escritas de Cervantes. Por Jorge Ticknor. Nueva York, 1860. 8vo.

—— Paris, 1859. 8vo.

—— Nueva edición, corregida y anotada por D. Eugenio de Ochoa. Bensanzon, 1860. 8vo.

—— 2 tomos. Leipzig, 1860. 8vo.

—— Paris, 1861. 4to.

—— 2 tomos. Madrid, 1862. 8vo.

—— 3 tomos. Madrid, 1862–1863. Fol.

—— Edición corregida con especial estudio por Don J. E. Hartzenbusch. 4 tomos. Argamasilla de Alba, 1863. 12mo.

—— 4 tomos. Madrid y Argamasilla de Alba, 1863. 8vo.

Note.—This edition forms vols. iii.–vi. of the *Obras Completas.*

El ingenioso hidalgo, etc. Barcelona, 1864. 8vo.

———— 2 tomos. Barcelona, 1864. 8vo.

———— Nueva York, 1864. 8vo.

———— Paris, 1864. 4to.

———— Novísima edición, con notas históricas de la Academia Española, Pellicer, Arrieta. Aumentada del *Buscapié* anotado por Adolfo de Castro. Adornado con 300 grabados y el retrato del autor. Madrid, 1865. 8vo.

———— 2 tomos. Leipzig, 1866. 8vo.

NOTE.—This edition is included in the third and fourth volume of the *Colección de autores españoles.*

———— Madrid, 1867.

———— 2 tomos. Madrid, 1868. 8vo.

———— Madrid, 1868. 8vo.

———— Madrid, 1868. 8vo.

NOTE.—Only the first volume of this edition, apparently, has been published.

———— 2 tomos. Barcelona, 1869. 8vo.

———— La primera edición . . . reproducida en facsímile por la foto-tipografía, y publicada por su inventor el Coronel D. Francisco López Fabra. 2 tomos. Barcelona, 1871–1873. 4to.

———— 2 tomos. Valencia, 1872. 8vo.

———— [Edited by D. Ramón León Máinez.] Cádiz, 1877. 8vo.

———— Sevilla, 1879. 16mo.

———— 2 tomos. Madrid, 1880. 16mo.

———— Barcelona, 1881. 4to.

———— 2 tomos. Barcelona, 1882. 4to.

Don Quixote. Nueva edición, con notas sobre el texto, del puño y letra del autor, en el ejemplar prueba de corrección de la primera edición de 1605, etc. 2 tomos. Palencia, 1884. 8vo.

This is edited by D. Feliciano Ortego Aguirrebeña : he has been grossly victimised by some forger.

———— Novísima edición aumentado con El Buscapié. Adornado con 300 Grabados intercalados, láminas sueltas, etc. Madrid, 1887. 8vo.

ABRIDGMENTS OF DON QUIXOTE.

El Quijote de los niños y para el pueblo. Abreviado por un entusiasta de su autor. Madrid, 1856. 16mo.

z

El Quijote para todos, abreviado y anotado por un entusiasta de su autor. Madrid, 1856. 8vo.

DON QUIXOTE: BOHEMIAN.

Don Quijote de la Mancha. Ze španělského přeložil I. Boj. Pichl. Pt. i.–iv. Prag, 1864. 8vo.

Don Quijote de la Mancha. Ze španělského přeložil Kristian Stefan. Prag, 1868. 8vo.

DON QUIXOTE: CATALAN.

L' enginyos Cavaller Don Quixot de la Manxa compost por Miquel de Cervantes Saavedra. Traslladat á nostra llengua materna, y en algunes partides lliurement exposat per Antoni Bulbena y Tusell. Barcelona, 1891. 8vo.

DON QUIXOTE: CROATIAN.

Miguel de Cervantes Saavedra, život i djela glasovitoga viteza Dona Quixotta de la Mancha. Po francezkom, za mladež priredjenu izdanju hrvatski napisao Jos. Eugen Tomić. Zagreb, 1878. 8vo.

DON QUIXOTE: DANISH.

Den sindrige Herremands Don Quixote af Mancha Levnet og Bedrifter. Forfattet af Miguel de Cervantes Saavedra. Oversat, efter det i Amsterdam og Leipzig 1755, udgivne Spanske Oplag af Charlotta Dorothea Biehl. 4 vols. Kjöbenhavn, 1776–1777. 8vo.

Den sindrige Adelsmands Don Quixote, etc. Oversat af C. D. Biehl. Anden Udgan, revideret af F. L. Liebenberg. 2 vols. Kjöbenhavn, 1863–1869. 8vo.

Den sindrige Adelsmands Don Quixote af la Mancha, Levnet og Bedrifter. Oversat ved F. Schaldemose. 4 vols. Kjöbenhavn, 1829–1831. 8vo.

DON QUIXOTE: DUTCH.

Den Verstandigen Vroomen Ridder Don Quichot de la Mancha . . . uyt de Spaensche in onse Nederlandtsche Tale overgeset door L. v. B. [i.e. Lambert van den Bos]. Dordrecht, 1657. 8vo.

Reprinted at Amsterdam, 1669, 1670, 1696, 1699. Another edition at Hage, 1746, 1746, 1746, and 1802. 2 vols.

De oude en rechte Don Quichot de la Mancha, of de verstandige en vrome Ridder van de Leeuwen . . . uit de Spaansche in de Neder-duitsche Tale overgezet door L. v. B. 2 vols. Amsterdam, 1732. 8vo.

[This is the seventh edition of Lambert van den Bos' version.]

De Ridder Don Quichot van Mancha. 2 vols. Amsterdam, 1819. 8vo.

De vernuftige jonkheer Don Quichote van de Mancha, uit het Spaansch vertaald door C. L. Schuller tot Peursum. 4 vols. Haarlem, 1854–1859. 8vo.

Reprinted in folio at Haarlem, with Gustave Doré's illustrations, in 1870; at Leiden, 1877–1879.

Don Quichot van la Mancha, naar Miguel Cervantes de Saavedra, voor de Nederlandtsche jeugd bewerkt door J. J. A. Goeverneur. Leiden, 1871. 8vo.

Don Quichotte vertaal door Titia van Der Tuuk. Med 85 gravures. 2 vols. Amsterdam, 1889. 8vo.

DON QUIXOTE: ENGLISH.

Shelton's Translation.

The History of Don-Qvichote. The first parte. Printed for Ed : Blounte. [1612 ?] 4to.

Dedicated to the Right Honovrable, his verie good Lord, the Lord of Walden, etc., by Thomas Shelton.

The Second Part of the History of the valorous and witty Knight-Errant, Don Quixote of the Mançha. Written in Spanish by Michael Ceruantes : And now Translated into English. London, Printed for Edward Blount. 1620.

Dedicated to the Right Honourable, George Marquesse Bucking-ham, Viscount Villiers, Baron of Whaddon, Lord High Admirall of England, etc., by Ed : Blount.

See Arber's *Transcript of the Registers of the Company of Stationers of London* (vol. iii. pp. 204, 267).

The History of the Valorous and Witty Knight-Errant, Don Quixote, of the Mancha. Translated out of the Spanish; now newly corrected and amended. London, 1652. Fol.

—— London, 1675. Fol.

z 2

The History of the most Ingenious Knight Don Quixote de la Mancha. . . . Formerly made English by Thomas Shelton ; now Revis'd, Corrected, and partly new Translated from the Original. By Capt. John Stevens. 2 vols. London, 1706. 8vo.

The History of the Valorous and Witty Knight-Errant, etc. Translated into English by Thomas Shelton, and now printed ver-batim from the 4to edition of 1620. With cuts from the French of Coypel. 4 vols. London, 1725. 12mo.

Philips' Translation.

The History of Don Quixote of Mancha: and his trusty Squire Sancho Pancha. Now made English according to the Humour of our Modern Language, and adorned with several copper plates. By J[ohn] P[hilips]. London, 1687. Fol.

Motteux's Translation.

The History of the renowned Don Quixote de la Mancha. . . . Translated from the Original by several hands and publish'd by Peter Motteux. 4 vols. London [1701 ?]. 12mo.

NOTE.—Robert Watt's *Bibliotheca Britannica* states that the first edition was published in 1701, and Mr. Henri van Laun in his Life of Motteux repeats the statement. He tells me that he has not handled any edition earlier than the third ; nor have I.

———— Adorn'd with sculptures. The Third Edition. 4 vols. London, 1712. 12mo.

———— The Fourth Edition. Carefully Revised and compared with the Best Edition of the Original, Printed at Madrid. By J. Ozell. 4 vols. London, 1719. 12mo.

———— The Fifth Edition carefully Revised . . . by J. Ozell. 4 vols. London, 1725. 12mo. Also reprinted in 1733 and 1743.

——   4 vols. Glasgow, 1757. 12mo.

———— Revised a-new from the best Spanish Edition by Mr. Ozell. 4 vols. Edinburgh, 1766. 12mo.

———— Revised anew from the best Spanish edition by Mr. Ozell. 4 vols. Edinburgh, 1803. 12mo.

The History of the Ingenious Gentleman Don Quixote of La Mancha ; translated from the Spanish by Motteux. A New Edition with copious notes ; and an essay on the Life and Writings of Cervantes [by J. G. Lockhart]. 5 vols. Edinburgh, 1822. 8vo.

The History of Don Quixote de la Mancha. London, 1847. 8vo.

The translation of Motteux "has been principally adhered to in the present edition."

Adventures of Don Quixote de la Mancha. Translated from the Spanish . . . by Motteux. New and revised edition. London, 1877. 8vo.

This forms part of the *Chandos Classics.*

The History of the Ingenious Gentleman Don Quixote de la Mancha translated from the Spanish by P. A. Motteux. [With a Life of the Author and notes by J. G. Lockhart and etchings by A. Lalauze.] 4 vols. Edinburgh, 1874–1884. 8vo.

The History of Don Quixote of La Mancha translated from the Spanish by Motteux; edited with notes and memoir by John G. Lockhart; preceded by a short notice of the Life and Works of Motteux by Henri van Laun. With sixteen original etchings by R. de los Rios. 4 vols. London, 1880–1881. 8vo.

The Achievements of the Ingenious Gentleman Don Quixote de la Mancha. A Translation based on that of Peter Anthony Motteux, with the memoir of John Gibson Lockhart. Edited by Edward Ball, M.A. 2 vols. London, 1882. 8vo.

This forms part of *Bohn's Standard Library.*

Ward's Translation.

The Life and Notable Adventures of that renown'd Knight Don Quixote de la Mancha. Merrily translated into Hudibrastick Verse. By Edward Ward. 2 vols. London, 1711–1712. 8vo.

Jarvis' Translation.

The Life and Exploits of the ingenious gentleman Don Quixote de la Mancha. Translated from the original Spanish . . . by Charles Jarvis, Esq. 2 vols. London, 1742. 4to.

———— the whole carefully revised and corrected, with a new Translation of the Poetical Parts by another Hand. The Second Edition. 2 vols. London, 1749. 8vo.

———— The Third Edition. 2 vols. London, 1756. 4to.

———— 4 vols. London, 1766. 8vo.

———— embellished with new engravings [by Stothard], etc. 4 vols. London, 1801. 8vo.

The Life and Exploits of the ingenious gentleman Don Quixote de la Mancha. Translated from the original Spanish . . . by Charles Jarvis, Esq. To which is prefixed the Life of the Author [based upon that of Don Juan Antonio Pellicer]. 4 vols. London, 1809. 16mo.

——— 4 vols. London, 1819. 8vo.

The Life and Adventures of Don Quixote de la Mancha. A New Edition with engravings from designs by Richard Westall, R.A. 4 vols. London, 1820. 8vo.

The Life and Exploits of Don Quixote de la Mancha. 4 vols. London, 1821. 12mo.

——— 2 vols. London, 1824. 8vo.

——— Illustrated by Cruikshank. 2 vols. London, 1831. 12mo.

——— Illustrated by Tony Johannot. 3 vols. London, 1837–1839. 8vo.

——— 2 vols. London, 1842. 8vo.

Adventures of Don Quixote de la Mancha. 2 vols. London, 1852. 8vo.

——— Illustrated by John Gilbert. London, 1856. 8vo.

The History of Don Quixote by Cervantes. The Text edited by J. W. Clark, M.A., Fellow of Trinity College, Cambridge. And a Biographical Notice . . . by T. Teignmouth Shore, M.A. Illustrated by Gustave Doré. London, 1864–1867. 4to.

Note.—The English text adopted in this edition is that of Jarvis with occasional corrections from Motteaux' (*sic*) translation.

This edition has been reprinted in 1870–1872, in 1876–1878, and in 1880.

The Adventures of Don Quixote de la Mancha. Illustrated by Tony Johannot. 10 parts [incomplete]. London (1864–1865?) 8vo.

- – – London, 1866.

—— With one hundred illustrations by A. B. Houghton, engraved by the Brothers Dalziel. London, 1866. 8vo.

———— Carefully revised and corrected, London, 1870. 8vo.

This forms part of *Beeton's Boys' Own Library.*

———— London, 1879. 8vo.

- — London, 1880. 8vo.

— London, 1881. 8vo.

This forms part of the *Excelsior Series.*

Don Quixote; [Gulliver's Travels and Captain Cook's Voyages]. London, 1882. 4to.

Don Quixote from the Spanish. London, 1882. 4to.

El ingenioso hidalgo Don Quixote de la Mancha. Translated by Charles Jarvis. With an introduction by Henry Morley, LL.D. London, 1885. 8vo.

Vol. xxv. and xxvi. of *Morley's Universal Library.*

———— 2 parts. London, 1890. 8vo.

This forms part of *Routledge's Popular Library*, and is a reprint of the preceding edition of 1885.

———— London, 1892. 8vo.

This forms part of the series called *Routledge's Books for the People.*

NOTE.—The translations of Jarvis and Motteux have been frequently reprinted in the United States.

Smollett's Translation.

The History and Adventures of the renowned Don Quixote. Translated from the Spanish. . . . To which is prefixed some account of the author's life by T. Smollett, M.D. 2 vols. London, 1705. 4to.

NOTE.—Robert Watt's *Bibliotheca Britannica* mentions an edition of 1752. I am inclined to think that Watt is in error. I have failed to discover it in any collection.

———— 4 vols. London, 1761. 8vo.

———— 4 vols. London, 1765. 8vo.

———— 4 vols. London, 1782. 8vo.

———— The Fifth Edition. 4 vols. London, 1872. 8vo.

———— 4 vols. London, 1792. 12mo.

———— The Sixth Edition corrected. 4 vols. London, 1793. 12mo.

———— 4 vols. Dublin, 1796. 8vo.

———— Cooke's Edition. 5 vols. London, 1799. 12mo.

———— 4 vols. Glasgow, 1803. 8vo.

———— London [1837 ?]. 8vo.

Miscellaneous Translations.

The Delightful History of Don Quixot, The Most Renowned Baron of Mancha. Containing his Noble Atchievements, and Surprizing Adventures, his Daring Enterprises, and Valiant Engagements for the Peerless *Dulcinea del Toboso*, and the various and wonderful

Occurrences that attended his Love and Arms. Also The Comical Humours of his Facetious Squire Sancho Pancha. And all other matters that conduce to the illustration of that Celebrated History, no less pleasant than gravely Moral. London, 1689. 8vo.

The Epistle Dedicatory is signed *E. S.*

The History of the renowned Don Quixote de la Mancha. Written originally in Spanish . . .; and translated into English by George Kelly, Esq. To which are added notes of the more difficult Passages. 4 vols. London, 1769. 8vo.

Don Quixote de la Mancha. Translated from the Spanish [by Mary Smirke]. Embellished with engravings from pictures painted by Robert Smirke, Esq., R.A. 4 vols. London, 1818. 4to.

Don Quixote de la Mancha translated from the Spanish. . . . With fifty page plates by Sir John Gilbert, R.A. London, 1877. 8vo.

NOTE.—The editor's preface states that in this edition a free use has been made of preceding versions, but "too much has been either altered or re-written, throughout the whole, fairly to leave in the names of any of its former translations."

The Ingenious Knight Don Quixote de la Mancha. A new Translation from the originals of 1605 and 1608. The Second Part of the Ingenious Knight, etc., by Alexander James Duffield. 3 vols. London, 1881. 8vo.

Don Quixote, from the Spanish, with thirty Illustrations by Sir John Gilbert, Tony Johannot, and others. London, 1882. 8vo.

This forms part of *Routledge's Sixpenny Series.*

The Ingenious Gentleman, Don Quixote of La Mancha. A translation, with introduction and notes by John Ormsby. 4 vols. London, 1885. 8vo.

The Ingenious Gentleman, Don Quixote of La Mancha. A new edition; done into English, with notes, original and selected, and a new life of the author. By Henry Edward Watts. 5 vols. London, 1888. 4to.

ABRIDGMENTS OF DON QUIXOTE.

The much esteemed History of Don Quixote de la Mancha (contracted from the original). London, 1699. 12mo.

The History of the ever-renowned Knight Don Quixote. London [1700?]. 4to.

The much esteemed History of Don Quixote de la Mancha. 2 parts. London, 1721. 12mo.

The most admirable and delightful History of the atchievements of Don Quixote de la Mancha. London, 1721. 12mo.

The life and exploits of Don Quixote de la Mancha abridged. London, 1778. 8vo.

The history of Don Quixote; with an account of his exploits. Abriged [from Smollett's translation]. Halifax, 1839. 16mo.

The story of Don Quixote and his Squire Sancho Panza. By M. Jones. London, 1871. 8vo.

The Wonderful Adventures of Don Quixote de la Mancha. Abridged and adapted to youthful capacities by Sir Marvellous Crackjoke. With illustrations by Kenny Meadows and John Gilbert, London [1872]. 4to.

The Adventures of Don Quixote adapted for young readers, and illustrated with coloured pictures. London [1883]. 4to.

DON QUIXOTE: FINNISH.

Don Quixote de la Mancha eli ritari surullisen muodon ritaristosta. Kuopiossa, 1877. 8vo.

DON QUIXOTE: FRENCH.

Le Valevreux Don Qvixote de la Manche ou l'histoire de ses grands Exploicts d'armes, fideles Amours, et Aduentures estranges. Traduit fidelement de l'Espagnol. . . . Par Cesar Oudin. Paris, 1616. 8vo.

Note.—This contains the first part only. The third edition of 1620 is the earliest which I have seen.

Histoire du redoutable et ingénieux Chevalier Don Quixote. Traduite de l'espagnol par François de Rosset. Paris, 1618. 8vo.

Note.—The combined work of Oudin and Rosset, with a preface by E. Gebhart, has been reproduced in six volumes 16mo by the Librairie des Bibliophiles. Paris, 1884-1885.

Histoire de l'admirable Don Quichotte traduite de l'espagnol [par Le Sieur Filleau de Saint-Martin]. 4 vols. Paris, 1677-1678. 12mo.

Note.—A second edition appeared in 1679, and the third (the

earliest which I have seen) in 1695. The third edition consists of five volumes, in the last of which the adventures of Don Quixote are continued. A sixth volume was added by Grégoire de Chasles to the Amsterdam edition of 1715. Filleau Saint-Martin's version has been frequently reprinted. There are editions of 1696, 1700 (both published at Amsterdam), 1711–1713, 1732, 1741, 1750, 1752, 1757, 1768, 1773, 1795, 1825, 1826 (with a prefatory essay by Prosper Mérimée), and 1862.

Les Aventures de Don Quichotte, trad. l'Espagnol, par Florian. 6 vols. Paris, An VII. (1799). 18mo.

Note.—This version is still reprinted. There are editions of 1800, 1809, 1820, 1823, 1824, 1828, 1829, 1847, 1863, 1868, 1877, 1882, etc.

[Œuvres Choisies de Cervantes.] Le Don Quichotte. Traduction nouvelle par H. Bouchon-Dubournial. 8 vols. Paris, 1808. 12mo.

Note.—Reprinted in 1820 and 1852.

L'ingénieux chevalier Don Quixote de la Manche. Traduit de l'espagnol par de l'Aulnaye. 4 vols. Paris, 1821. 18mo.

Note.—A new edition with a prefatory life of Cervantes by Adrien Grimaux was issued in 1884.

L'ingénieux hidalgo Don Quichotte. Traduit et annoté par Louis Viardot. Vignettes de Tony Johannot. 2 vols. Paris, 1836–1837. 8vo.

Note.—Other editions were published in 1838, 1841, 1844–1845, 1853, 1857, 1858, 1859, 1863, 1864, and 1869.

L'ingénieux chevalier Don Quichotte. Nouvelle édition, revue et corrigée par M. l'Abbe Lejeune. Paris, 1844. 8vo.

Note.—Reprinted in 1845, 1847, 1849.

Histoire de Don Quijote de la Manche, traduite sur le texte original, d'après les traductions comparées de Oudin et Rosset, Filleau de Saint-Martin, Florian, Bouchon Dubournial et de l'Aulnaye par F. de Brotonne. 2 vols. Paris, 1837. 8vo.

———— 2ᵉ édition. 2 vols.

L'Admirable Don Quichotte de la Manche, traduction nouvelle par M. Damas-Hinard. 2 vols. Paris, 1847. 12mo.

Histoire de l'incomparable Don Quichotte de la Manche. Traduite par C. F. de Grandmaison y Bruno. 2 vols. Paris, 1854. 12mo.

Le Don Quichotte du Jeune Age, aventures les plus curieuses de Don Quichotte et de Sancho. Précédées d'une introduction historique . . . et suivies d'une conclusion morale par Elizabeth Müller. Paris, 1862. 8vo.

NOTE.—This is an abridgment.

L'ingenieux chevalier Don Quichotte traduction nouvelle, par Ch. Furne. 2 vols. Paris, 1858. 8vo.

Reprinted in 1866.

L'ingenieux chevalier de la Manche. Traduction nouvelle par Rémond. 2 vols. Paris, 1863. 12mo.

L'ingénieux hidalgo Don Quichotte de la Manche. Traduction nouvelle de Lucien Biart, précédée d'une notice . . . par Prosper Mérimée. 4 vols. Paris, 1878. 12mo.

L'ingénieux hidalgo don Quichotte de la Manche. Traduction par le docteur Théry. 2 vols. Paris, 1888. 12mo.

DON QUIXOTE: GERMAN.

Don Kichote de la Mantscha, das ist: Juncker Harnisch aus Fleckenland. Aus Hispanischer Sprach in hochteutsche übersetzt durch Pahsch Basteln von der Sohle. Köthen, 1621. 12mo. '

NOTE.—This incomplete translation extends only to chapter xiii. (pt. i.). A second édition was published at Hoffgeissmar in 1648 and a third at Frankfurt in 1669.

Don Quixote von Mancha: Abenteuerliche Geschichte. 2 vols. Basel und Frankfurt, 1682. 8vo.

Des berühmten Ritters Don Quixote von Mancha, lustige und sinnreiche Geschichte. Leipzig, 1734. 8vo.

———— Zweyte Auflage. Leipzig, 1753. 8vo.

———— Dritte Auflage. Leipzig, 1767. 8vo.

Don Quixote, vornehmste Begebenheiten. 4 vols. Leipzig, 1767. 8vo.

Leben und Thaten des weisen Junkers Don Quixote von la Mancha. Aus der Urschrift des Cervantes nebst der Forsetzung der Avellaneda von F. J. Bertuch. 6 vols. Leipzig, 1775. 8vo.

———— Carlsruhe, 1775 and 1785, Leipzig, 1781, and Wein, 1798.

Leben und Thaten des Scharfsinnigen Edlen Don Quixote von la Mancha von Miguel de Cervantes Saavedra, übersetzt von Ludwig Tieck. 4 vols. Berlin, 1799-1801. 8vo.

NOTE.—There are many reprints of this version—1810 (the

earliest edition which I have seen), 1817, 1831, 1860, 1866, 1872, and 1876.

Der sinnreiche Junker Don Quixote von la Mancha. Aus dem Spanischen übersetzt durch Dietrich Wilhelm Soltau. 6 vols. Königsberg, 1800–1801.

NOTE.—Reprinted at Leipzig in 1825 and at Vienna in the same year; also at Leipzig, 1837.

———— In völligneuer Bearbeitung von W. Lange. 2 vols. Leipzig, 1877. 8vo.

Leben und Thaten des edlen und tapfern Ritters Don Quixote von la Mancha. Zur Unterhaltung und Belustigung der Jugend neu bearbeitet von Louise Hölder. Ulm, 1824. 8vo.

Der scharfsinnige Junker Don Quixote von la Mancha. Aus dem Spanischen von L. G. Förster. Quedlinburg and Leipzig, 1825.

NOTE.—This forms part of the *Sämmtliche Werke.*

Leben und Thaten des sinnreichen Junker Don Quixote. Uebersetzt von Hieronymus Müller. Zwickau, 1825.

NOTE.—This forms part of the *Werke des Cervantes.*

Der sinnreiche Junker Don Quixote von la Mancha. . . . Aus dem Spanischen übersetzt. Mit dem Leben von Miguel Cervantes nach Viardot, und einer Einleitung von Heinrich Heine. 2 vols. Stuttgart, 1837. 8vo.

NOTE.—Reprinted in the *Sämmtliche Romane und Novellen* of A. Keller and F. Notter, Pforzheim, 1839. Other editions at Leipzig in 1843 and at Stuttgart in 1871. The Leipzig edition of 1843 does not include Heine's *Einleitung.*

Leben und Thaten des edeln und tapfern Ritters Don Quixote von la Mancha. Für die Jugend bearbeitet von Franz Hoffmann. Stuttgart, 1844. 8vo.

NOTE.—Reprinted in 1870 and 1875.

Der sinnreiche Junker Don Quijote von der Mancha. Aus dem Spanischen . . . von Edmund Zoller. 4 vols. Hildburghausen, 1867. 8vo.

Vols. liii., lvi., lxii., and lxv. of the *Bibliothek ausländischer Klassiker.*

Der sinnreiche Junker Don Quixote von la Mancha. Für die Jugend erzählt von C. F. Lauckhard. Leipzig, 1869. 8vo.

Leben und Thaten des bewunderungswürdigen Ritters Don

Quixote von la Mancha. . . . Frei fur die deutsche Jugend bearbeitet von Karl Seifart. Stuttgart, 1870. 8vo.

—————— Stuttgart, 1880. 8vo.

Der sinnreiche Junker Don Quijote von der Mancha übersetzt von Ludwig Braunfels. 4 vols. Stuttgart, 1884. 8vo.

Leben und Thaten des scharfsinnigen Edlen Don Quixote von der Mancha. Neu bearbeitet von Ernst von Wolzagen. Mit Illustr. von Gustav Doré. 2 vols. Berlin, 1884. Fol.

DON QUIXOTE: GREEK.

Δὸν Κισὸτ ἢ τὰ περιεργότερα τῶν συμβάντον αὐτοῦ. Athens, 1860. 16mo.

DON QUIXOTE: HUNGARIAN.

Don Quixote by Karady Ignácz. 1848. 12mo.

Note.—A Hungarian translation of *Don Quixote* is said to have been published at Pesth in 1813. I have not succeeded in tracing it.

Don Quijote, a hires manchai lovag spanyol eredeti mü Cervantestöl, Florian után francziából magyarva fordittota Horvath György. Kecskemét, 1850. 8vo.

Az elmes nemes Don Quijote de la Mancha, irta Miguel de Cervantes Saavedra. Spanyolból fordittota s bevezette Györg Vilmos. 4 vols. Budapest, 1873. 8vo.

Don Quichotte, a hires manchai lovag. Irta: Cervantes. Budapest. [1882?] 8vo.

DON QUIXOTE: ITALIAN.

L' ingegnoso Cittadino Don Chisciotte della Mancia . . . hora nuouamente tradotto con fedeltà, e chiarezza, di Spagnuolo, in Italiano. Da Lorenzo Franciosini (Fiorentino). Venetia, 1622. 8vo.

Note.—A translation of the first part only, the verses being retained in their original Spanish.

—————— Venetia, 1625. 8vo.

Note.—Navarrete says that in this second edition—which included both parts—the Spanish verses of the original were rendered into Italian verse by Alessandro Adimari (Fiorentino).

—————— Venice, 1629.

—————— 2 vols. Roma, 1677. 8vo

Dell' ingegnoso Cittadino Don Chisciotte della Mancia . . . hora nuovamente tradotto . . . da Lorenzo Franciosini (Fiorentino). 2 vols. Venezia, 1738. 8vo.

———— 4 vols. Venezia, 1755. 8vo.

———— 8 vols. Milan, 1816. 16mo.

L' ingegnoso cittadino Don Chisciotte della Mancia. Traduzione nuovissima dall' originale Spagnuolo, colla Vita dell' Autore [and with engravings by F. Novelli]. 8 vols. Venezia, 1818–1819. 8vo.

———— traduzione nuovissima di Bartolomeo Gamba con la vita dell' autore. 6 vols. Venezia, 1818. 12mo.

Le luminose geste di Don Chisciotte disegnate ed incise da Francesco Novelli in xxxiii Tavole con Spiegazioni. Venezia, 1819. 8vo.

Note.—It is stated at the end of the volume that only 102 copies were printed.

Don Chisciotte della Mancia. Milano, 1879. 4to.

Il Don Chisciotte della gioventù, avventure curiosissime di Don Chisciotte e Sancio, con istruzione storica sull' origine della Cavalleria di Elisabetta Müller. Milano, 1877. 8vo.

DON QUIXOTE: POLISH.

Don Kichot . . . przeklad z francuzkiego przez F. Podoskiego. 6 vols. Warsawa, 1786. 8vo.

Don Kiszot z Manszy przez Cervantesa. Przeklad W. Zakrzewskiego (z francuzkiego) illustracya slawnego Tonny Johannota. 4 vols. Warsawa, 1854–1855. 8vo.

Zabawne przygody Don Kiszota z Manszy. Krákow, 1883. 8vo.

DON QUIXOTE: PORTUGUESE.

O engenhoso Fidalgo Dom Quixote de la Mancha. Traduzido em vulgar. 6 vols. Lisboa, 1794. 8vo.

Other editions 1805 (Paris), 1830, adornada con 25 estampas finas, and Lisbon, 1853.

———— Traduzido por los Vizcondes de Castilho e d' Azevedo. Lisboa, 1876. 4to.

———— Traduzido por el Vizconde de Benalcanfor. 2 vols. Lisboa, 1878. 8vo.

DON QUIXOTE: PROVENÇAL.

L' enginous Signour Doun Quichoto dé la Mancho per Micheou de Cervantes Saavedra.

Porcien doou chapitre xlii. (2° partido). Dei counseou qué douné Doun Quichoto à Sancho-Pansa avan qu'anesse gouverna l'ilo, eme d'aoutrei cavo ben coumbinado.

NOTE.—A Fragment: Œuvres complètes de André Jean Victor Gelu. 2 vols. Marseilles et Paris, 1886. 8vo.

Vol. ii. p. 299 *et seq.*

DON QUIXOTE: ROUMANIAN.

Don Chişotu de la Manchia, din Florian, dupǎ Cervantes. Bucuresci, 1840. 8vo.

DON QUIXOTE: RUSSIAN.

Istoriya o Slavnom La Mankhskom ruitsarye Don Kishotye. 2 vols. St. Petersburg, 1769. 8vo.

Nesluikhannuii Chudodyei, ili . . . priklyuchenirga . . . ruitsarya Don Kishota . . . perevel c frantenzskago [by N. O., *i.e.* N. Osipov]. 2 pts. St. Petersburg, 1791. 12mo.

Don Kishot La Mankhsky, sochinenie Servanta. [By Vasily Zhukovsky.] Moscow, 1805. 16mo.

Other editions of 1815 and 1820.

Don Kishot La Mankhsky, sochinenie Servanta [by N. Osipov]. 2 vols. Moscow, 1812. 8vo.

Don Kishot La Mankhsky. 6 vols. St. Petersburg, 1831. 16mo.

Don Kishot La Mankhsky [by 'Konstantin Masalsky]. St. Petersburg, 1838. 8vo.

Second edition, 1848.

Don Kishot Lamankhsky [by A. Grech]. St. Petersburg, 1860. 8vo.

Third edition, 1868; fourth edition, 1881.

Don Kishot Lamankhsky [by V. Karelin]. 2 vols. St. Petersburg, 1866. 8vo.

Second edition, 1873; third edition, 1881.

Don Kishot dlya dyetia [by N. S. Lvov]. St. Petersburg, 1867. 8vo.

Don Kikhot Lamansky M. Servantesa [from Franz Hoffmann's German version, by N. Gernet]. Odessa, 1874. 8vo.

Don Kikhot Lamanchsky, ruitsar pechal'nago obraza. . . . Peredyelano . . . dlya russkago yunoshestva O. I. Shmidt-Moskvitinovoyu. [With six plates.] St. Petersburg, 1883. 4to.

Istoriya znamenitago Don Kishota Lamankskago [by M. Chistyakov]. St. Petersburg, 1883. 8vo.

DON QUIXOTE: SERBIAN.

Don Kiot Manashanin. Satirichki roman chuvenog shpan'olskog spisaotsa Servantesa. Belgrade, 1862. 8vo.

Pripovetka o slavnom vitezu Don Kikhotu od Manche. Panchevo, 1882. 8vo.

DON QUIXOTE: SWEDISH.

Don Quichotte af la Mancha, öfversatt efter Florian af C. G. Berg. Stockholm, 1802. 8vo.

Den tappre och snillrike Riddaren Don Quixottes af Mancha, Lefverne och Bedrifter . . . öfversatt af Jonas Magnus Stjernstolpe. 4 vols. Stockholm, 1818–1819. 8vo.

Don Quixote. För ungdom bearbetad efter Florian. Stockholm, 1857. 8vo.

Don Quixote af la Mancha. Öfversatt från spanska originalet af A. L. [i.e. Axel Hellsten]. Stockholm, 1857. 8vo.

Den beundrensvärda Historien om Don Quixote de la Mancha och hans vapendragare Sancho Panza.

Don Quixote de la Mancha. För ungdom bearbetad af A. Th. Paban.

Don Quixote från la Mancha. Bearbetad efter M. de Cervantes Saavedra af F. Hoffmann. Stockholm, 1876. 8vo.

NOVELAS EJEMPLARES.

Novelas | Exemplares | de Miguel de | Ceruantes Saauedra. | Dirigido a Don Pedro Fernan | dez de Castro, Conde de Lemos, de Andrade, y de Villalua, | Marques de Sarria, Gentilhombre de la Camara de su | Magestad, Virrey, Gouernador, y Capitan General | del Reyno de Napoles, Comendador de la En | comienda de la Zarça de la Orden | de Alcantara. | Año 1613. | Cõ priuilegio de Castilla, y de los Reynos de la Corona de Aragõ. | En Madrid. Por Iuan de la Cuesta. | Vendese en casa de Frãcisco de Robles, librero del Rey ñro Señor. | 4to. Ff. 274.

NOTE.—The *Aprovaciones* of Fr. Juan Bautista and Doctor Cetina are dated July 9, 1612. Those of Diego de Hortigosa and Alonso Geronimo de Salas Barbadillo are dated August 8, 1612, and July 31, 1613, respectively. The *Licencia* is dated November 22, 1612, and the *Privilegio de Aragon* is dated August 9, 1613. The *Fee de Erratas* is dated August 9, 1613, and the *Tassa* August 12, 1613. The Dedication is dated July 14, 1613.

——— Año 1614. En Madrid, por Juan de la Cuesta. 4to. Ff. 236.

——— Año 1614. Con licencia. En Pamplona, por Nicolas de Assiayn, Impressor del Reyno de Nauarra. 8vo. Ff. 391.

NOTE.—The *Aprovacion* is dated September 29, 1613, and the *Licencia* January 11, 1614.

——— En Brvsselas. Por Roger Velpio, y Hvberto Antonio, Impressores de sus Altezas, al Aguila de oro, cerca de Palacio, año de 1614. 8vo. Pp. 616.

NOTE.—The *Privilegio* is dated May 10, 1614.

——— Año 1615. Con Licencia. En Pamplona, por Nicolas de Assiayn, Impressor del Reyno de Nauarra. 8vo. Ff. 391.

——— En Milan. A costa de Iuan Baptista Bidelo Librero. M. DC. XV. 12mo. Pp. 763.

NOTE.—The Dedication of the publisher is dated August 1, 1615.

——— Venetia, 1616. 12mo.

——— Lisboa, 1617. 4to.

——— Pamplona, 1617. 8vo.

——— Madrid, 1617. 8vo.

——— Madrid, 1622. 8vo.

Novelas | Exemplares | de Miguel de | Ceruantes Saauedra.]
Dirigido a Don Pedro Fernandez de | Castro, Conde de Lemos, de
Andrade, y de Villalva, | Marquès de Sarria, Gentilhombre de la
Camara de su | Magestad, Virrey, Gouernador, y Capitan General
del | Reyno de Napoles, Comendador de la Encomien | da de la Zarça
de la Orden de | Alcantara. | Sevilla, 1624. 8vo.

———— Brvsselas, 1625. 8vo.

———— Sevilla, 1627. 8vo.

———— Barcelona, 1631. 8vo.

Salvá believes in the existence of a Barcelona edition of (about)
the year 1627 ; but he has not met with it.

———— Sevilla, 1641. 8vo.

———— Seuilla, 1648. 8vo.

———— Madrid, 1655. 8vo.

———— Madrid, 1664. 4to.

———— Sevilla, 1664. 4to.

———— Zaragoza, 1665. 4to.

———— Madrid, 1722. 4to.

———— Barcelona, 1722. 4to.

———— Añadido un indice de libros de novelas, patrañas,
cuentos, hecho por un curioso. Madrid, 1732. 4to.

———— 2 tomos. Haya, 1739. 8vo.

———— 2 tomos. Amberes, 1743. 8vo.

———— 2 tomos. Valencia, 1769. 8vo.

———— Nueva impression corregida, etc. 2 tomos. Madrid,
1783. 8vo.

———— 2 tomos. Valencia, 1783. 8vo.

———— Madrid, 1794. 8vo.

———— 2 tomos. Valencia, 1797. 8vo.

———— 3 tomos. Madrid, 1803. 8vo.

———— Nueva impresion, corregida y adornada con laminas.
2 tomos. Perpiñan, 1816. 12mo.

———— 2 tomos. Madrid, 1821.

———— 2 tomos. Lyon, 1825. 12mo.

———— 3 tomos. Paris, 1826. 16mo.

———— 2 tomos. Madrid, 1829. 12mo.

———— 5 tomos. Barcelona, 1831-1832. 32mo.

Note.—This includes *La Tia finjida.*

———— Coblenz, 1832. 12mo.

Novelas Ejemplares de Miguel de Cervantes Saavedra. Dirigido á Don Pedro Fernández de Castro, Conde de Lemos, de Andrade, y de Villalva, Marqués de Sarria, Gentilhombre de la Camara de su Majestad, Virrey, Gobernador, y Capitán General del Reyno de Nápoles, Comendador de la Encomienda de la Zarza de la Orden de Alcántara. 4 tomos. Barcelona, 1836. 8vo.

————— Paris, 1844. 4to.

————— 2 tomos. Barcelona, 1842. 8vo.

————— Madrid, 1842. 4to.

————— Madrid, 1842. 4to.

————— 2 tomos. Barcelona, 1844. 8vo.

————— Madrid, 1846. 8vo.

————— Nueva edición, con cuatro novelas de Doña María Zayas. Paris, 1848. 8vo.

————— 2 tomos. Málaga, 1852. 8vo.

————— 2 tomos. Toledo, 1853. 8vo.

————— Madrid, 1854. 8vo.

————— Barcelona, 1859. 8vo.

————— Madrid, 1864. 4to.

————— Madrid, 1866. 4to.

————— Madrid, 1869. 8vo.

————— Madrid, 1881. 16mo.

Rinconete y Cortadillo. Barcelona, 1831. 16mo.

La Señora Cornelia y la fuerza de la sangre. Mit Kritischen und Grammatischen Anmerkungen nebst einem Wörterbuche von P. A. F. Possar. Leipzig, 1833. 8vo.

El Amante liberal, La Señora Cornelia, El Casamiento engañoso. Barcelona, 1838. 16mo.

Isabela, ó la española inglesa : La Fuerza de la Sangre. Barcelona, 1842. 32mo.

La Fuerza de la Sangre (2 pts.). Madrid, 1842. 8vo.

El Licenciado Vidriera. Madrid, 1843. 8vo.

Rinconete y Cortadillo. Edición ilustrada. Madrid, 1846. 8vo.

Rinconete y Cortadillo : El zeloso extremeño y Las dos doncellas. Madrid, 1873. 16mo.

Tomo ix. of the *Biblioteca universal.*

Coloquio de los perros : La Señora Cornelia (pp. 9–103, *Joyas de la literature española* con artículos biográficos y bibliográficos . . . por Fernando Soldevilla). Paris, 1885. 8vo.

NOVELAS EJEMPLARES: DANISH.

Laererige Fortaellinger overs. af C. D. Biehl. 2 vols. Kjöbenhaun, 1780–1781. 8vo.

NOVELAS EJEMPLARES: DUTCH.

Vermaakelyke Minneryen. Delf, 1643.
——— Amsterdam, 1653.
——— Amsterdam, 1731.
——— Amsterdam [1750 ?]. 8vo.

NOVELAS EJEMPLARES: ENGLISH.

Exemplario Novells; in sixe books. . . . Fvll of variovs accidents both delightfvll and profitable. By Migvel de Cervantes Saavedra; one of the prime Wits of Spaine, for his rare Fancies and wittie Inventions. Turned into English by Don Diego Pvede-Ser. [*i.e.* James Mabbe]. London, 1640. Fol.

A collection of select novels, written originally in Castillian by Don Miguel Cervantes Saavedra. . . . Made English by Harry Bridges, Esq.; under the Protection of His Excellency, John, Lord Carteret, etc. Bristol, 1728. 8vo.

Instructive and entertaining novels. . . . Translated from the Original Spanish. By Thomas Shelton. With an account of the Work, by a Gentleman of the Inner Temple. London, 1742. 12mo.
——— Dublin, 1747. 12mo.

The Exemplary Novels of M. de Cervantes Saavedra . . . so called because in each of them he proposed useful example to be either imitated or avoided. 2 vols. London, 1822. 8vo.

The Exemplary Novels of Miguel de Cervantes Saavedra: to which are added El Buscapié, or, The Serpent; and La Tia Fingida, or, The Pretended Aunt. Translated from the Spanish by Walter K. Kelly. London, 1855. 8vo.
——— London, 1881. 8vo.

El Zeloso Estremeno: The Jealous Estromaduran. A Novel. Written by Miguel de Cervantes Saavedra, and done from the Spanish by J. Ozell. London [1710?]. 8vo.

A Select Collection of Novels and Histories. . . . Written by the most celebrated Authors in several Languages. 6 vols. London, 1722. 12mo.
——— 6 vols. London, 1729. 12mo.

The Dedication is signed S. C. Vol. i. contains *The Jealous Estremaduran*; vol. ii., *The Fair Maid of the Inn* and *The History of the Captive*; vol. iii., *The Curious Impertinent*, *The Prevalence of Blood*, and *The Liberal Lover*; vol. iv., *The Rival Ladies*; vol. v., *The Little Gypsy*; vol. vi., *The Spanish Lady in England* and *The Lady Cornelia.*

A Dialogue between Scipio and Bergansa, Two Dogs belonging to the City of Toledo. . . . To which is annexed, the Comical History of Rincon and Cortado. Both written by the Celebrated Author of Don Quixote; and now first Translated from the Spanish Original. London, 1767. 12mo.

The Force of Blood, a Novel. Translated from the Spanish of M. de Cervantes Saavedra. London, 1800. 12mo.

The Spanish Novelists. Translated from the Original with critical and biographical notices by Thomas Roscoe. 3 vols. London, 1832. 8vo.

Vol. i. (pp. 242–360) contains *Rinconete and Cortadillo*, *The Pretended Aunt*, and *El Amante Liberal.*

NOVELAS EJEMPLARES: FRENCH.

Les novveles, ov sont contenuës plusieurs rares advantures, et memorables exemples d'amour. . . . Traduictes d'espagnol en françois : les six premieres par F. de Rosset et les autres par le sr. d'Avdigvier. Avec l'Histoire de Ruis Dias, etc. Paris, 1620. 8vo.

Nouvelles de Miguel Cervantes. Traduction nouvelle [par Charles Cotolendi]. 2 vols. Paris, 1678. 12mo.

——— Traduction nouvelle. Paris, 1705. 12mo.

Nouvelles de Michel de Cervantes. Traduction nouvelle [par P. Hessein ?]. Amsterdam, 1705. 12mo.

Reprinted (Amsterdam) 1709, (Paris) 1723, (Lausanne) 1759, and (Paris) 1777–1778.

——— traduites par Mr. l'Abbé Saint Martin de Chassonville]. 2 vols. Lausanne, 1759. 12mo.

——— traduction nouvelle par Lefevre de Villebrune. 2 vols. Paris, 1775. 8vo.

——— imités de Cervantes etc. par le citoyen C[oste d'Arnobat]. 2 vols. Paris, An XI.—1802. 12mo.

——— [traduites par Claude-Bernard Petitot]. 4 vols. Paris, 1809. 12mo.

Nouvelles choisies de Cervantes ; par H. Bouchon-Dubournial. Paris, 1825. 32mo.

Les nouvelles de Miguel Cervantes Saavedra, traduites et annotées par Louis Viardot. 2 vols. Paris, 1836. 8vo.

Reprinted in 1838, 1841, 1844, and 1858 [omitting *La Tia Fingida* and substituting an adaptation of *El Licenciado Vidriera*].

L'illustre servante. Liège, 1706. 12mo.

Mélanges de poésie et littérature par J-P. Claris de Florian. Paris, 1787. 16mo.

Note.—This contains a version of *La Fuerza de la Sangre* entitled *Léocadie.*

L'illustre servante, nouvelle espagnole de Michel Cervantès. Traduite par M. de Villebrune. Lausaunne et Paris, 1793. 18mo.

Note.—The copy in the British Museum is believed to be unique.

Costanza où l'illustre servante. Traduction de L. Viardot. Paris, 1853. 16mo.

La Bohémienne de Madrid. Traduction de L. Viardot. Paris, 1853. 16mo.

Voyages à travers mes livres . . . par. M. Ch. Romey. Paris, 1862. 12mo.

Note.—Pp. 38–71 contain a translation of *El Licenciado Vidriera*, which the writer wrongly assumes to be the earliest in French.

Rinconète et Cortadillo, Nouvelle. Soixante-sept Compositions par H. Atalaya. Traduction et notes de Louis Viardot. Paris, 1891.

Le Licencié Vidriera. Nouvelle traduite en français avec une préface et des notes par R. Foulché-Delbosc. Paris, 1892. 8vo.

NOVELAS EJEMPLARES: GERMAN.

Satyrische und lehrreiche Erzehlungen des Michel de Cervantes Saavedra, Verfasser der Geschicte des Don Quischotts ; nebst dem Leben dieses berühmten Schriftstellers, wegen ihrer besondern Annehmlichkeiten in das Teutsche übersetzt (von Conradi). 2 vols. Frankfurt und Leipzig, 1753. 8vo.

Moralische Novellen . . . aus dem Original übersetzt von F. Julius H. von Soden. Ansbach, 1779. 8vo.

Kleinere Schriften (J. P. Florian). Zwickau, 1798. 8vo.

This contains a version of *La Fuerza de la Sangre.*

Lehrreiche Erzählungen . . . übersetzt von Dietrich Wilhelm Soltau. 3 vols. Königsberg, 1800. 8vo.

Spanische Novelle von Chr. Aug. Fischer. Berlin, 1801. 8vo.

Lehrreiche Erzählungen übersetzt von Fr. S. Siebmann. Berlin, 1810. 8vo.

Geschichte der schönen Theolinde, übersetzt aus dem Spanischen von Dr. Adrian. Frankfurt, 1819. 8vo.

Moralische Erzählungen (Sämmtliche Werke übersetzt von L. G. Forster). Leipzig, 1825. 12mo.

Lehrreiche Erzählungen (Werke übersetzt von H. Müller). Zwickau, 1825.

Musternovellen übersetzt von F. M. Duttenhoffer. (Romane und Novellen). Pforzheim, 1840.

Novellen übersetzt von A. Keller und F. Notter (Sämmtliche Romane und Novellen). Stuttgart, 1840.

Musternovellen. Aus dem Spanischen neu in's Deutsche übertragen mit Einleitungen und Erläuterungen von Reinhold Baumstark. 2 vols. Regensburg, 1868. 8vo.

Señora Cornelia. Novelle aus dem Spanischen . . . übersetzt von Carl von Reinhardstöttner. Leipzig, 1869. 12mo.

Vol. cli. of the *Universal-Bibliothek*.

Preciosa, das Zigeunermädchen. Novelle aus dem Spanischen . . . übersetzt von Fr. Hörleck. Leipzig, 1874. 16mo.

NOVELAS EJEMPLARES : ITALIAN.

Il Novelliere Castigliano di Michiel di Cervantes Saavedra . . . Tradotto dalla lingua Spagnuola nell' Italiana dal Sig. Gvglielmo Alessandro de Nouilieri Clavelli. Venetia, 1626. 8vo.

Novelli Esemplari, etc., da Donato Fontana Milanese. Milano, 1629. 8vo.

Again reprinted in 1629.

L'illustre sguattera: novella, la prima volta ridotta in lingua italiana per Ulderico Belloni. Pavia, 1879. 8vo.

Preziosa; Cornelia : racconti. Milano, 1882. 16mo.

Il matrimonio per inganno e il Colloquio dei cani: traduzione di G. A. Novilieri-Clavelli. Roma, 1882. 8vo.

NOVELES EJEMPLARES : PORTUGUESE.

Historia nova, famosa, e exemplar da Hespanhola Ingleza. Traduzida da Lingua Hespanhola no nosso Idioma Portuguez, e dado á luz por Bocache. Lisboa, 1805. 4to.

NOVELAS EJEMPLARES: SWEDISH.

La Gitanilla de Madrid por Miguel de Cervantes Saavedra. Spanskt original, Svensk öfversättning samt en inledande monografi öfver Cervantes. Akademisk Afhandling . . . af Victor Hjalmar Beronius. Upsala, 1875. 8vo.

VIAJE DEL PARNASO.

Viage | del Parnaso | compvesto por | Miguel de Ceruantes | Saauedra. | Dirigido a don Rodrigo de Tapia, | Cauallero del Habito de Santiago, | hijo del señor Pedro de Tapia Oy | dor de Consejo Real, y Consultor | del Santo Oficio de la Inqui | sicion Suprema. | Año 1614 | Con privilegio | En Madrid, | por la viuda de Alonso Martin. 8vo. Ff. 80.

The *Licencias* of Cetina and Joseph de Valdiuielso are dated September 16, 1614, and September 20, 1614, respectively. The *Tassa* is dated September 17, 1614; the *Priuilegio*, October 18, 1614; and the *Fee de Erratas*, November 10, 1614.

———— Milan, 1624. 8vo.
———— Madrid, 1736. 4to.
———— Madrid, 1772. 4to.
———— Madrid, 1784. 4to.
———— Madrid, 1865. 8vo.
———— Madrid, 1829. 12mo.
———— Paris, 1841. [12mo.]
———— Madrid, 1866. 4to.

VIAGE DEL PARNASO: DUTCH.

Cervantes reis naar den Parnassus overgeset door J. J. Putman. Amsterdam, 1872. 8vo.

VIAGE DEL PARNASO: ENGLISH.

Journey to Parnassus composed by Miguel de Cervantes Saavedra, translated into English tercets with preface and illustrative notes by James Y. Gibson. To which are subjoined the antique text and translation of the letter of Cervantes to Mateo Vazquez. London, 1883. 8vo.

VIAGE DEL PARNASO: FRENCH.

Le Voyage au Parnasse. Traduit en français pour la première fois avec une notice biographique, une table des auteurs cités dans le poëme et le facsimile d'un autographe inédit de Cervantes, par Joseph Miguel Guardia. Paris, 1864. 12mo.

DRAMATIC WORKS: COMEDIAS Y ENTREMESES.

Ocho | Comedias, y ocho | entremeses nvevos, | nunca representados. | Compuestas por Migvel | de Ceruantes Saauedra. | Dirigidas a Don Pedro Fer | nandez de Castro, Conde de Lemos, de Andrade, | y de Villalua, Marques de Sarria, Gentilhombre | de la Camara de su Magestad, Comendador de | la Encomienda de Peñafiel, y la Zarça, de la Or | den de Alcantara, Virrey, Gouernador, y Capi | tan general del Reyno de Napoles, y Presi | dente del supremo Consejo | de Italia. Los titulos destas ocho comedias | y sus entremeses van en la quarta hoja. | Año 1615. | Con privilegio. | En Madrid, Por la viuda de Alonso Martin. | A costa de Ivan de Villarroel, mercader de libros, vendense en su casa ¡ a la plaçuela del Angel. | 4to. Ff. 257.

The *Aprouacion* is dated July 3, 1615; the *Priuilegio*, July 25, 1615; the *Fe de las Erratas*, September 13, 1615; and the *Tassa*, September 22, 1615.

An edition published at Madrid in 1617 is alleged to exist.

Comedias y Entremeses . . . con una dissertacion, o prologo sobre las Comedias de España. 2 tomos. Madrid, 1749. 4to.

——— Madrid, 1784. 4to.

Ocho entremeses. . . . Tercera impresion. Cadiz, 1816. 12mo.

La Numancia. Tragedia. Berlin, 1810. 16mo.

El Teatro español. 4 tomos. Londres, 1817–1820. 8vo.

Tomo i., pp. 197–292, contains *La Numancia* and *El Trato de Argel.*

Tesoro del Teatro español . . . arreglado por Don Eugenio de Ochoa. Paris, 1838. 8vo.

Tomo i. contains *La Numancia, La Entretenida, La Guarda Cuidadosa,* and *Los dos Habladores.*

Teatro español. Colección escogida . . . por D. C. Schütz. Bielefeld, 1846. 8vo.

Pp. 1-24 contain *La Numancia.*

Las Entremeses de Miguel de Cervantes Saavedra.   Madrid, 1868. 8vo.

Comedias y Entremeses de Miguel de Cervantes Saavedra.   *Numancia, La Entretenida, El Juez de los divorcios, El Rufián viudo llamado Trámpagos, Elección de los Alcaldes de Daganzo, La Guarda Cuidadosa y El Vizcaíno Fingido.*   Precedidas de una introduccion.   Madrid, 1875.   4to.

DRAMATIC WORKS : ENGLISH.

Numantia : A Tragedy translated from the Spanish, with introduction and notes, by James Y. Gibson.   London, 1885.   8vo.

DRAMATIC WORKS : FRENCH.

Numance, tragédie [by I. B. d'Esménard].   Paris, 1823.   8vo.
Vol. xvi., *Chefs-d'œuvres des Théâtres étrangers.*
Théâtre de Michel Cervantès.   Traduit pour la première fois de l'Espagnol en Français par Alphonse Royer.   Paris, 1862.   8vo.
Le Gardien Vigilant (*La Guarda Cuidadosa*), intermède en un acte de Michel de Cervantès.   Traduit sur les éditions de Madrid 1615 et 1749, et de Paris 1826 par Amédée Pagès.   Paris, 1888.   8vo.

DRAMATIC WORKS : GERMAN.

Numancia, Trauerspiel.   Aus dem spanischen übersetzt von F. de la Motte Fouqué.   Berlin, 1810.   12mo.
Numancia, Trauerspiel.   (Ubersetzt von L. G. Förster).   Leipsig, 1826.   12mo.
This forms part of the *Sämmtliche Werke.*
Numancia, Trauerspiel.   Aus dem spanischen von R. O. Spazier Zwickau, 1829.   16mo.
Vol. ccxliv. of the *Taschenbibliothek der ausländischer Klassiker.*
Spanisches Theater.   Herausgegeben von A. W. von Schlegel.
Theater der Spanier und Portugiesen von F. J. Bertuch.   Dessau und Leipzig, 1782.
Magazin der Spanischen und Portugiesischen Literatur; herausgegeben von Friedrich Justin Bertuch.   3 vols.   Weimar, 1780.   Dessau und Leipzig, 1783.   8vo.
Vol. i. pp. 215–240 ; vol. iii. pp. 131–168.
Der Aufpasser.   Ein Zwischenspiel aus dem spanischen des Cervantes von Siebmann.   (*Pantheon.   Eine Zeitschrift fur Wissen-*

schaft und Kunst herausgegeben von J. G. Busching und K. L. Kannegiesser. 3 vols. Leipsig, 1810. 8vo.)

Vol. ii. pp. 23 *et seq.*

La Guarda Cuidadosa. Die wachsame Schildwach. (Vol. ii. pp. 287–315, 328, Spanische Dramen übersetzt von C. A. Dorhn. Berlin, 1841. 8vo.)

Zwischenspiele von Cervantes (Spanisches Theater. Herausgegeben von Adolph Friedrich von Schack). 2 vols. Frankfurt-am-Main, 1845. 8vo.

Cervantes Neun Zwischenspiele übersetzt von H. Kurz. Hildburghausen, 1868. 8vo.

Vol. lxxi., *Bibliothek ausländischer Klassiker.*

PERSILES Y SIGISMUNDA.

Los Trabaios | de Persiles, y | Sigismvnda, Histo | ria Setentrional. | Por Migvel de Cervantes | Saauedra. | Dirigido a Don Pedro Fernandez de | Castro Conde de Lemos, de Andrade, de Villalua, Marques de | Sarria, Gentilhombre de la Camara de su Magestad. Presiden | te del Consejo supremo de Italia, Comendador de la Encomienda de la | Zarça, de la Orden | de Alcantara. Año 1617. Con priuilegio. En Madrid. Por Iuan de la Cuesta. A costa de Iuan de Villaroel mercader de libros en la Plateria. Ff. 226.

The *Aprouacion* is dated September 9, 1616; the *Priuilegio,* September 24, 1616; the *Fee de Erratas,* December 15, 1616; and the *Tassa,* December 23, 1616. Cervantes' dedicatory letter is dated April 19, 1616.

——— Pamplona, 1617. 8vo.
——— Paris, 1617. 8vo.
——— Barcelona, 1617. 8vo.
——— Valencia, 1617. 8vo.
——— Lisboa, 1617. 4to.
——— Brucelas, 1618. 8vo.
——— Madrid, 1619. 8vo.
——— Pamplona, 1629. 8vo.
Historia de los trabajos, etc. Barcelona, 1734. 4to.
——— Barcelona, 1760. 4to.
——— Barcelona, 1768. 4to.
Trabajos de, etc. 2 tomos. Madrid, 1781. 8vo.

Trabajos de, etc.   2 tomos.   Madrid, 1799.   12mo.
———— 2 tomos.   Madrid, 1802.   8vo.
———— 2 tomos.   Madrid, 1805.   8vo.
———— 4 tomos.   Barcelona, 1833.   32mo.
———— Paris, 1841.   8vo.
Tomo xxvi., *Colección de los mejores autores españoles.*
———— Barcelona, 1859.   8vo.
———— Madrid, 1880.   16mo.

PERSILES Y SIGISMUNDA: ENGLISH.

The Travels of Persiles and Sigismvnda.   A Northern History.
Wherein, amongst the variable Fortunes of the Prince of *Thule*, and
this Princesse of *Frisland*, are interlaced many Witty Discourses,
Morall, Politicall, and Delightfull.   The first Copie, beeing written in
Spanish; translated afterwards into French; and *now, last, into
English.*   London, 1619.   4to.

Note.—The Epistle Dedicatory to Philip, Lord Stanhope, Baron
of Shelford, is signed *M. L.*

The Wanderings of Persiles and Sigismunda; a Northern Story.
[Translated by L. D. S., *i.e.* Louisa Dorothea Stanley.]   London,
1854.   8vo.

PERSILES Y SIGISMUNDA: FRENCH.

Les Travavx de Persiles et de Sigismonde, histoire septentrionale
. . . traduicte en nostre langue par François de Rosset.   Paris, 1618.
8vo.

Persile et Sigismonde, histoire septentrionale, tirée de l'Espagnol
. . . par Madame L. G. D. R. [*i.e.* Le Givre de Richebourg].   4 vols.
Paris, 1738.   8vo.

———— Nouvelle édition . . . avec quelques remarques du
traducteur, par le sieur D. S. L. (*i.e.* Pierre Daudé).   6 vols.
Amsterdam, 1740.   12mo.

———— par H. Bouchon-Dubournial (Œuvres complètes de
Cervantes).   Paris, 1820.

PERSILES Y SIGISMUNDA: GERMAN.

Persilus und Sigismunda.   Nordische Historie von dem berühmten Verfasser des Don Quixote Michael de Cervantes in

spanischer Sprache geschrieben, in's Deutsche übersetzt. Ludwigsburg, 1746. 8vo.

Abentheuer des Persiles und der Sigismunda . . . zum ersten Male aus dem Spanischen Originale verdeutscht durch Fr. J. H. von Soden. 4 vols. Ansbach, 1782. 8vo.

Leiden zweier edlen Lieben nach dem Spanischen des Cervantes . . . von Th. Fr. Butenschön. Heidelberg, 1789. 8vo.

Die Drangsale des Persiles und der Sigismunda. Aus dem Spanischen von Franz Theremin. Erster Theil. Berlin, 1808. 8vo.

Irrfahrten des Persiles und der Sigismunda übersetzt von L. G. Förster. Quedlinburg und Leipzig, 1825. 8vo.

This forms part of the *Sämmtliche Werke.*

———— übersetzt von J. F. Muller.

This is included in the *Werke von Cervantes.*

Die Leiden des Persiles und der Sigismunda. Aus dem Spanischen übersetzt von Dorothea Tieck. Mit einer Einleitung von Ludwig Tieck. 2 vols. Leipzig, 1837. 8vo.

Die Prüfungen des Persiles und der Sigismunda übersetzt von Cervantes sämmtliche Romane und Novellen. Aus dem Spanischen von A. Keller und Friedrich Notter. Stuttgart, 1839–1842. 16mo.

PERSILES Y SIGISMUNDA: ITALIAN.

Istoria Settentrionale de trauagli di Persile, e Sigismonda . . . di nvovo dalla lingva castigliana nella nostra Italiana tradotta, dal Signor Francesco Ellio (Milanese). Venetia, 1626. 8vo.

SUPPOSITITIOUS WORKS.

La Tia fingida, novella inédita. Mit Vorbericht von C. Franceson und F. J. Wolf. Berlin, 1818. 8vo.

Die betrügliche Tante. Stuttgart, 1836. 8vo.

Die vorgebliche Tante übersetzt von Bülow. Leipzig, 1836. 8vo.

El Buscapié. Opúsculo inédito que en defensa de la primera parte del Quijote escribió Miguel de Cervantes Saavedra. Publicado con notas históricas, críticas i bibliográficas por D. Adolfo de Castro. Cádiz, 1848. 8vo.

Comedia de la Soberana Virgen de Guadalupe, y sus milagros,

y grandezas de España [with a preface by D. José María Asensio y Toledo]. Sevilla, 1868. 8vo.

Issued by the *Sociedad de los bibliófilos andaluces.*

El Buscapié . . . With the illustrative notes of A. de Castro. Translated from the Spanish. With a life of the author and some account of his works by Thomasina Ross. London, 1849. 12mo.

The "Squib" or Searchfoot, an unedited little work which M. de Cervantes Saavedra wrote in defence of the first part of the Quijote. Published by Adolfo de Castro, 1847. Translated by a member of the University of Cambridge. Cambridge, 1849. 16mo.

The Troublesome and Hard Adventures in Love. Lively setting forth The Feavers, the Dangers and the Jealousies of Lovers. A Work very Delightful and Acceptable to all. Written in Spanish by that Excellent and Famous Gentleman, Michael Cervantes; and exactly Translated into English, by R. C[odrington?], Gent. London, 1652. 4to.

NOTE.—The translator in the Epistle Dedicatory states' that "the author was by birth a Spaniard, the same Gentleman that composed Guzman de Alfarache, and the second part of Don Quixot." There is, of course, no authority for identifying Mateo Alemán with Avellaneda.

The diverting works of the famous Miguel de Cervantes, Author of the History of Don Quixot. Now first translated from the Spanish. With an introduction by the Author of The London Spy [*i.e.* E. Ward]. London, 1709. 8vo.

NOTE.—This publication has not the remotest connexion with Cervantes. The originals may be found in the *Para Todos* of Juan Pérez de Montalván (Alcalá, 1661. 4to). The first story is a translation of *Al cabo de los años mil*; the last is a free rendering of *El Piadoso Bandolero.*

AVELLANEDA'S
CONTINUATION OF *DON QUIXOTE.*

Segvndo | tomo del | ingenioso hidalgo | Don Qvixote de la Mancha, | que contiene su tercera salida: y es la | quinta parte des sus auenturas. Compuesto por el Licenciado Alonso Fernandez de |

Auellaneda, natural de la Villa de Tordesillas. | Al Alcalde, Regidores, y hidalgos, de la noble | Villa de Argamesilla, patria feliz del hidal | go Cauallero Don Quixote | de la Mancha. Con Licencia, En Tarragona en casa de Felipe | Roberto, Año 1614.

The *aprobacion* of Doctor Rafael Timoneda is dated April 18, 1614; the *licencia* of Doctor Francisco de Torme y Liori is dated July 4, 1614.

Vida y Hechos del ingenioso hidalgo, etc. Nuevamente añadido por Isidoro Perales y Torres. 3 tomos. Madrid, 1732. 4to.

———— Nueva edicion. 2 tomos. Madrid, 1805. 8vo.

———— Madrid, 1851. 8vo.

Tomo xvii., Rivadeneyra's *Biblioteca de autores españoles.*

AVELLANEDA'S CONTINUATION OF DON QUIXOTE: DUTCH.

Nieuwe Avantuuren van Don Quichot, door Avellaneda. Amsterdam, 1718. 8vo.

AVELLANEDA'S CONTINUATION OF DON QUIXOTE: ENGLISH.

A Continuation of the Comical History of the most ingenious Knight, Don Quixote de la Mancha. By the Licentiate Alonzo Fernandez de Avellaneda. Being a third volume; never before printed in English. Translated by Captain John Stevens. London, 1705.

The History of the Life and Adventures of the famous Knight Don Quixote de la Mancha and his Humourous Squire Sancho Panca [*sic*]. Now first translated from the original Spanish. With a preface, giving an Account of the Work. By Mr. Baker. 2 vols. London, 1745. 12mo.

A Continuation of the History and Adventures of Don Quixote de la Mancha. Written originally in Spanish, by the Licentiate Alonso Fernandez de Avellaneda. Translated into English by William Augustus Yardley, Esq. 2 vols. London, 1784. 8vo.

The Life and Exploits of the ingenious Gentleman Don Quixote, de la Mancha ; containing his fourth sally, and the fifth part of his adventures : Written by the Licentiate Alonso Fernandez de Avelleneda, Native of the Town of Tordesillas. With illustrations and corrections by the Licentiate Don Isidoro Perales y Torres. And now first Translated from the Spanish. Swaffham, 1805. 8vo.

AVELLANEDA'S CONTINUATION OF DON QUIXOTE: FRENCH.

Nouvelles Avantures de l'admirable Don Quichotte de la Manche, composées par le Licencié Alonso Fernandez de Avellaneda. Et traduites de l'Espagnol en François, pour la première fois. 2 vols. Paris, 1704. 8vo.

NOTE.—This adaptation is, as every one knows, by Alain René Le Sage.

Le Don Quichotte de Fernandez Avellaneda. Traduit de l'Espagnol et annoté par A. Germond de Lavigne. Paris, 1853. 8vo.

BIOGRAPHY, COMMENTARY, CRITICISM, ETC.

REAL ACADEMIA SEVILLANA DE BUENAS LETRAS.—Certamen poético para conmemorar el aniversario CCLVII de la muerte de Cervantes. Sevilla, 1873. 8vo.

Conmemoración del aniversario CCLXI de la muerte de Cervantes en el dia 23 de Abril de 1877. Sevilla, 1877.

AGUILAR, PEDRO DE.—Memorias del Cautivo en la Goleta de Túnez el Alférez, Pedro de Aguilar. Madrid, 1875.

NOTE.—Published by the *Sociedad de bibliófilos españoles.*

El Alcides de la Mancha, el famoso Don Quixote. De un ingenio de esta corte. Comedia. Madrid, 1750. 4to.

ALMAR, GEORGE.—Don Quixote; or the Knight of the woeful Countenance. A Musical Drama in two acts. London [1833?]. 12mo.

NOTE.—Vol. xiv. of John Cumberland's *Minor Theatre.*

Aniversario de Cervantes. Fiesta literaria verificada en el Instituto de Cádiz para conmemorar la muerte del príncipe de nuestros ingenios. Cádiz, 1875.

Aniversario CCLX de la muerte de Miguel de Cervantes Saavedra. Álbum literario dedicado á la memoria del rey de los ingenios españoles: publícalo la redacción de la Revista Literaria *Cervantes.* Madrid, 1875. 8vo.

Aniversario CCLXII de la muerte de Miguel de Cervantes Saavedra Libro compuesto para honrar la memoria del príncipe de los ingenios españoles por sus admiradores de Chile. Santiago de Chile, 1878. 8vo.

ANTEQUERA, RAMÓN. — Juicio analítico del Quijote escrito en Argamasilla de Alba. Madrid, 1863. 8vo.

ANZARENA, CHRISTOBAL.—Vida y empressas literarias del ingenio-sissimo caballero Don Quixote de la Manchuela. Parte primera. Sevilla [1767?]. 8vo.

Aparición nocturna de Miguel de Cervantes á D. Fermín Caballero por el Corresponsal de los Muertos. Madrid, 1841. 8vo.

ARBOLÍ, SERVANDO.—Oración fúnebre que por encargo de la Real Academia Española y en las honras de Miguel de Cervantes y demás ingenios españoles pronunció en la iglesia de monjas trinitarias de Madrid el dia 24 de Abril de 1876, Servando Arbolí. Madrid, 1876. 8vo.

ARMAS Y CÁRDENAS.—El Quijote de Avellaneda, sus críticos. La Habana, 1884. 8vo.

ARMENGOL, A. C.—El Quijote en Boston. Madrid, 1874. 8vo.

ARNESEN-KALL, BENEDICTE.—Studie af : Den spanske Trilogi [Miguel de Cervantes, Lope de Vega, Calderon]. Kjöbenhavn, 1884. 8vo.

ARRIETA, AGUSTÍN GARCÍA.—El Espíritu de Miguel de Cervantes y Saavedra ó la filosofía de este grande ingenio, presentado en máximas, etc. Va añadida al fin de el una novela cómica intitulada *La Tia Fingida;* obra póstuma del mismo. Madrid, 1814. 8vo.

ASENSIO Y TOLEDO, JOSÉ MARÍA.—El Compás de Sevillas. Recuerdos de Cervantes. Seville, 1870. 8vo.

———— Cervantes inventor. Madrid, 1874. 8vo.

———— Cervantes y sus obras. Cartas literarias á varios amigos. Sevilla, 1870. 8vo.

———— El Conde de Lemos, Protector de Cervantes. Estudio histórico, etc. Madrid, 1880. 8vo.

———— Nuevos documentos para ilustrar la vida de Miguel de Cervantes Saavedra, con algunas observaciones. Madrid y Sevilla, 1864. 4to.

Les Auteurs espagnoles expliqués d'après une méthode nouvelle par deux traductions françaises . . . avec des sommaires et des notes. . . . El cautivo, histoire extraite de Don Quichotte. Paris, 1864. 12mo.

"Cet ouvrage a été expliqué littéralement, annoté et revu pour la traduction française par M. J. Merson."

Les principales Avantures de l'admirable Don Quichotte representées en figures par Coypel, Picart le Romain, et autres habiles maitres : avec les explications des XXXI Planches de cette magnifique collection, tirées de l'original espagnol de Michel de Cervantes Saavedra. La Haie, 1746. 4to.

The principal Adventures of Don Quixote engraved after designs by A. Coypel. London, 1775. Ob. 4to.

BARETTI, JOSEPH.—Tolondron. Speeches to John Bowle about his edition of Don Quixote ; together with some account of Spanish Literature. London, 1786. 8vo.

BAUMSTARK, REINHOLD.—Cervantes. Ein spanisches Lebensbild. Freiburg im Breisgau, 1875. 8vo.

BENAVIDES Y NAVARRETE, FRANCISCO DE PAULA (Bishop of Sigüenza and, afterwards, Cardinal Archbishop of Zaragoza).—Oración fúnebre que por encargo de la Real Academia Española y en las honras de Miguel de Cervantes y demás ingenios españoles, pronunció en la iglesia de monjas trinitarias de Madrid, el dia 23 de Abril de 1863, Francisco de Paula Benavides y Navarrete. Madrid, 1863. 8vo.

BENEKE, JUAN BASILICO VILELMO.—Colleccion [sic] de vocablos, y frases difficiles [sic], que occurren en la fabula del ingenioso hidalgo Don Quixote de la Mancha, en orden alfabético puestos para servir de notas y explicaciones. Leipsique, 1808. 16mo.

BEVILACQUA, MATTEO DI. See MELI.

BIEDERMANN, F. B. FRANZ.—Don Quichotte et la tâche de ses traducteurs. Observations sur la traduction de M. Viardot, etc. Paris et Leipsic, 1837. 8vo.

BOUTERWEK, FRIEDRICH.—Geschichte der Künste und Wissenschaften. 12 vols. Göttingen, 1801–1819. 8vo.

NOTE.—Vol. iii. pp. 328–361.

BRADFORD, CARLOS F.—Índice de las notas de D. Diego Clemencín en su edición de el ingenioso hidalgo Don Quijote de la Mancha. Madrid, 1885. 8vo.

BRAGGE, WILLIAM.—Brief Hand list of the Cervantes Collection presented to the Birmingham Free Library. Birmingham [1874?]. 8vo.

BRANDES, GEORG.—Æsthetiske Studier. Kjöbenhavn, 1868. 8vo. (To Kapitler af det Komiskes Theorie.)

1. Om Modsigelsen i det Komiske.
2. Om Lystfölelsen vid det Komiske. Pp. 71–143.

BURKE, ULICK RALPH.—Sancho Panza's Proverbs and others

which occur in Don Quixote; with a literal English Translation, Notes, and an Introduction. London, 1872. 8vo.

NOTE.—Only thirty-six copies were privately printed. A second enlarged edition was published in 1892.

———— Spanish Salt, a collection of all the proverbs which are to be found in Don Quixote. London, 1877. 8vo.

This is an abbreviated form of the preceding work.

CABALLERO, FERMÍN.—Pericia geográfica de Miguel de Cervantes demostrada con la historia de D. Quijote de la Mancha. Madrid, 1840. 12mo.

CALDERÓN, JUAN.—Cervantes vindicado en ciento y quince pasajes de texto del ingenioso hidalgo D. Quijote de la Mancha. Madrid, 1854. 8vo.

CARNOT, LAZARE NICOLAS MARGUERITE.—Don Quichotte. Poème heroï-comique en six chants. Paris, 1821. 16mo.

———— précédé d'une étude littéraire et historique par Georges Barral. Paris, 1891. 8mo.

CARRILLO DE ALBORNOZ, MAXIMINO.—Romancero de el ingenioso hidalgo Don Quixote de la Mancha, sacado de la obra inmortal de Miguel de Cervantes Saavedra por su admirador entusiasta Maximino Carillo de Albornoz. 2 tomos. Madrid, 1890. 8vo.

Carta escrita por Don Quijote de la Mancha á un pariente suyo, en que le hace saber varias cosas necesarias para la perfecta inteligencia de su historia : dála al publico un paisano y apasionado de ambos. Madrid, 1790. 8vo.

CASENAVE, JOSÉ MARÍA.—El Ayer y el hoy de Miguel de Cervantes Saavedra. Discurso pronunciado el 23 de Abril de 1877 en la casa de Cervantes en Valladolid. Valladolid, 1877. 8vo.

CASTRO, FEDERICO DE.—Cervantes y la filosofía española. Sevilla, 1870. 4to.

Catálogo de varias obras y folletos referentes á Miguel de Cervantes Saavedra que ha logrado reunir la constancia de un Cervantista. Sevilla, 1872. 4to.

Cervantes as a novelist; from a selection of the episodes and incidents of the popular romance of Don Quixote. In two parts. London, 1822. 8vo.

CHASLES, EMILE.—Cervantes, sa vie, son temps, ses œuvres. Paris, 1867. 8vo.

CLEMENCÍN, DIEGO.—See BRADFORD.

COLERIDGE, SAMUEL TAYLOR.—Notes and lectures upon Shakespeare and some of the old poets and dramatists; with other literary remains. 2 vols. London, 1849. 8vo.

NOTE.—Vol. ii. pp. 56-73.

COLL Y VEHÍ, JOSÉ.—Los refranes del Quijote ordenados por materias y glosados. Barcelona, 1874. 8vo.

The Cornutor of Seventy-five. Written originally, in Spanish, by the Author of Don Quixot, and translated into English by a Graduate of the College of Mecca in Arabia. London, 1748. 8vo.

DELGADO, JACINTO MARÍA.—Adiciones á la historia del ingenioso hidalgo Don Quixote de la Mancha, en que se prosiguen los sucesos ocurridos á su escudero el famoso Sancho Panza, escritas en arábigo por Cide-Hamete Benengeli, y traducidas al castellano con las memorias de la vida de este por Don Jacinto María Delgado. Madrid [1770 ?]. 8vo.

DÍAZ DE BENJUMEA, NICOLÁS.—La Estefeta de Urganda, etc. Londres, 1861. 8vo.

———— El Correo de Alquife ó segundo aviso de Cid Asam-Ouzad Benenjeli sobre el desencanto del Quijote. Barcelona, 1866. 8vo.

———— El mensaje de Merlín ó tercer aviso de Cid Ouzad Benengeli sobre el desencanto del Quijote. Londres, 1875. 8vo.

———— La verdad sobre el Quijote. Madrid, 1878. 8vo.

DIEULAFOY, MICHEL.—Le Portrait de Michel Cervantès, Comédie en trois actes, et en prose. Représentée pour la première fois le 21 Fructidor, An X, sur le Théâtre Louvois. Paris, An XI. 8vo.

Dom Quixote de la Mancha. Comédie. Paris, 1640. 4to.

Dom Quichot de la Mancha. Comédie. Seconde partie. Paris, 1640. 4to.

NOTE.—The *Priuilege du Roy* for both parts is dated May 28, 1639. The first part was printed October 25, 1639; the second part was printed July 15, 1640.

Don Kikhot. Balet v. 5 dyeistviyakh. St. Petersburg, 1875. 8vo.

DOREN, EDMUND.—Cervantes und seine Werke nach deutschen Wirtheilen. Mit einem Anhange: Die Cervantes Bibliographie. Leipzig, 1881. 8vo.

DROAP, M.—Epístolas Droapianas. Siete cartas sobre Cervantes y el Quixote dirigidas al muy honorable Doctor E. W. Thebussenn. Publícalas con notas y apéndices Mariano Pardo de Figueroa. Cádiz, 1868. 8vo.

DROAP, M.—Droapiana del año 1869. Octava carta sobre Cervantes y el Quijote . . . publicado por Mariano Pardo de Figueroa. Cádiz, 1869. 8vo.

DUFFIELD, ALEXANDER JAMES.—Don Quixote, his Critics and Commentators with a brief account of the minor works of Miguel de Cervantes Saavedra, and a statement of the aim and end of the greatest of them all. London, 1881. 8vo.

DUNLOP, JOHN COLIN.—History of Prose Fiction. 2 vols. London, 1888. 8vo.

NOTE.—Vol. ii. pp. 313-323.

D'URFEY, THOMAS.—The Comical History of Don Quixote. Parts I. and II. London, 1694. 4to.

Part III. London, 1696. 4to.

E. T. [*i.e.* VALENTÍN FORONDA].—Observaciones sobre algunos puntos de la obra de Don Quixote. [Londres, 1807.] 8vo.

EMMERT, J. H.—Las Donquixotadas mas extrañas. Oder die abentheuerliche Rittenthaten des den Quixote von la Mancha, etc. Tübingen, 1826. 8vo.

ESPINO, ROMUALDO ÁLVAREZ. — Miscelánea literaria. Burgos, 1886. 8vo.

NOTE.—Pp. 189-205, 207-227.

El espíritu de Miguel de Cervantes y Saavedra, ó la filosofía de este grande ingenio presentada en máximas, reflexiones, moralidades y agudezas sacadas de sus obras, y distribuidas por orden alfabético de materias, etc. Madrid, 1814. 8vo.

———— Nueva edición. Madrid, 1885. 12mo.

EXIMENO, ANTONIO.—Apología de Miguel de Cervantes sobre los yerros que se le han notado en El Quixote. Madrid, 1806. 8vo.

FERNÁNDEZ, CESÁREO.—Cervantes marino. Madrid, 1869. 4to.

FERNÁNDEZ, CAYETANO.—Oración fúnebre que, por encargo de la Real Academia Española y en las honras de Miguel de Cervantes y demás ingenios españoles pronunció en la iglesia de monjas trinitarias de Madrid, el 29 de Abril de 1867, el Padre Don Cayetano Fernández. Madrid, 1867. 8vo.

FERNÁNDEZ Y AGUILERA, MANUEL DE.—Cervantes viajero con un prólogo del Excmo. Señor Don Cayetano Rosell y un mapa con las viajes de Cervantes formado por Don Martín Ferreiro. Madrid, 1880. 8vo.

FLÖGEL, C. F.—Geschichte der komischen Literatur. 4 vols. Liegnitz und Leipzig, 1784–1786. 8vo.

Vol. i. pp. 307 et seqq.; vol. iii. pp. 280–296; vol. iv. pp. 165–169.

FORONDA, VALENTÍN.—See E. T.

FEUILLERET, H.—Le Captif, ou Aventures de Michel Cervantès. Paris, 1859. 8vo.

GALLARDO Y VICTOR, MANUEL.—See Muley Roviedagor, Nallat.

GAMERO, ANTONIO MARTÍN.—Recuerdos de Toledo, sacados de las obras de Cervantes. Toledo, 1869. 8vo.

——— Jurispericia de Cervantes. Toledo, 1870. 8vo.

GAYTON, EDMUND.—Pleasant Notes upon Don Quixote. London, 1654. Fol.

——— Festivous Notes on the History and Adventures of the Renowned Don Quixote. Revised, with corrections, etc. London, 1768. 12mo.

GIBSON, JAMES YOUNG.—The Cid Ballads and other Poems and translations from Spanish and German. . . . Edited by Margaret D. Gibson. With memoir by Agnes Smith. 2 vols. London, 1887. 8vo.

NOTE.—The poetry of *Don Quixote* occupies pp. 165–215 of the second volume.

GILES, HENRY.—Illustrations of Genius. Boston, 1854. 8vo.

NOTE.—Pp. 7–65.

GONZÁLEZ, M. F.—El Manco de Lepanto. Madrid, 1874. 8vo.

Le Gouvernement de Sancho Pansa. Comédie. Paris, 1642. 4to.

NOTE.—The *Privilege du Roy* is dated May 3rd, 1641.

GRAVES, RICHARD. — The Spiritual Quixote: or the Summer's Ramble of Mr. Geoffry Wildgoose. A Comic Romance. 3 vols. London, 1773. 12mo.

——— 2 vols. Dublin, 1774. 12mo.

HAGBERG, CHARLES AUGUSTE.—Cervantès et Walter Scott, parallèle littéraire soumis à la discussion publique l'avant midi du Novembre, 1838. Lund, 1838. 8vo.

HAY, JOHN.—Castilian Days. Boston, 1871. 8vo.

NOTE.—Pp. 282–312.

HEINE, HEINRICH.—Nachricht über das Leben und die Schriftes des Verfassers. Stuttgart, 1837. 8vo.

NOTE.—Pp. i.–xliv.

HERNÁNDEZ MOREJÓN, ANTONIO.—Historia bibliográfica de la medicina española, obra póstuma. 7 tomos. Madrid, 1842-1852. 4to.

NOTE.—Tomo ii., published in 1843, pp. 166-180, contains the *Bellezas de Medecina práctica descubiertas en la obra de Cervantes.*

―――― Etude médico - psychologique sur l'histoire de Don Quichotte. Traduite et annotée par le Docteur Joseph Miguel Guardia. Paris, 1858. 8vo.

Historia del mas famoso escudero Sancho Panza, desde la gloriosa muerte de Don Quixote de la Mancha hasta el último dia y postrera hora de su vida. 2 pts. Madrid, 1793-1798. 8vo.

HUGO, VICTOR.—William Shakespeare. Paris, 1864. 8vo.

NOTE.—Pp. 101-105.

IGARTUBURU, LUÍS DE.—Diccionario de tropos y figuras de retórica, con ejemplos de Cervantes. Madrid, 1842. 8vo.

INGLIS, HENRY DAVID.—Rambles in the footsteps of Don Quixote. London, 1837. 8vo.

Instrucciones económicas y políticas dadas por el famoso Sancho Panza, Gobernador de la ínsula Barataria á un hijo suyo. Madrid, 1791. 8vo.

JIMÉNEZ, FRANCISCO DE PAULA, Bishop of Teruel.—Oración fúnebre que por encargo de la Real Academia, y en las honras de Miguel de Cervantes y demás ingenios españoles, pronunció en la iglesia de monjas trinitarias de Madrid, el dia 23 de Abril de 1864, Francisco de Paula Jiménez, etc. Madrid, 1864. 8vo.

KARELIN, V.—Don-Kikhotizm i Demonizm . . . Po poroda Don Kikhota Servantesa. St. Petersburg, 1866. 8vo.

KING, ALICE.—A cluster of lives. London, 1874. 8vo.

NOTE.—Pp. 58-82.

KLINGEMANN, AUGUST.—Don Quixote und Sancho Panza, oder die Hochzeit des Camacho. Dram. Spiel. mit Gesang. Leipzig, 1815. 8vo.

LANGFORD, JOHN ALFRED. — Prison books and their authors. London, 1861.

NOTE.—Pp. 58-82.

LATOUR, ANTOINE DE.—Etudes sur l'Espagne. 2 vols. Paris, 1855. 8vo.

NOTE.—Vol. i. pp. 252-291.

―――― Espagne : traditions, mœurs et littérature. Paris, 1869. 8vo.

NOTE.—Pp. 246-292.

LATOUR, ANTOINE DE.—L'Espagne contemporaine. Paris, 1864. 8vo.

NOTE.—Pp. 340–369.

———— Valence et Valladolid. Paris, 1877. 8vo.

NOTE.—Pp. 68–118, 175–212.

LEMCKE, LUDWIG.—Handbuch der Spanischen Litteratur. 3 vols. Leipzig, 1855–1856.

NOTE.—Vol. i. pp. 371–392 ; vol. ii. pp. 112–115.

LOCKHART, JOHN GIBSON.—Life of Cervantes. Edinburgh, 1822. 8vo.

NOTE. — Prefixed to an edition of Motteux' version. Pp. v.-lxiv.

LOUVEAU, E.—De la manie dans Cervantès. Thèse présentée et publiquement soutenue à la Faculté de médecine de Montpellier le 9 Juin, 1876. Montpellier, 1876. 4to.

LOWELL, JAMES RUSSELL. — Democracy and other Addresses. London, 1887. 8vo.

NOTE.—Pp. 159–186.

MÁINEZ, RAMÓN LEÓN.— Cartas literarias por el bachiller Cerrántico. Cádiz, 1868. 8vo.

———— Vida de Miguel de Cervantes Saavedra. Cádiz, 1876. 8vo.

Manual alfabético de Quijote ó colección de pensamientos de Cervantes en su inmortal obra, ordenados con algunas notas por Don Mariano de R[ementería y Fica?]. Madrid, 1838. 8vo.

MAYANS Y SISCAR, GREGORIO.—Vida de Miguel de Cervantes Saavedra. Briga Real, 1737. 8vo.

———— Vida de Miguel de Cervantes Saavedra. Londres, 1738. 4to.

NOTE.—This life is prefixed to the edition of Don Quixote prepared at the request of Lord Carteret, pp. 1–103.

———— Vida de Miguel de Cervantes Saavedra. Quinta impresión. Madrid, 1750. 8vo.

MELI, GIOVANNI. Poesie Siciliane. 4 vols. Palermo, 1787. 8vo.

NOTE.—Vols. iii. and iv. contain *Don Chisciotti e Sancio Panza. Poema*, xii. Cantos.

———— Don Chisciotte e Sancio Panza nella Scizia. Poema originale in dialetto siciliano del celebre Giovanni Meli, tradotto in lingua italiana del Cavaliere Matteo di Bevilacqua. 2 vols. Vienna, 1818. 4to.

Merimée, Prosper.—Mélanges historiques et littéraires. Paris, 1855. 8vo.

Note.—Pp. 239–263.

Michaëlis, Carl Theodor.—Lessings Minna von Barnhelm und Cervantes Don Quijote. Berlin, 1883. 8vo.

Moja y Bolivar, Federico.—Alegorías, etc. Madrid, 1868. 8vo.

Molins, Marqués de.—Sepultura de Miguel de Cervantes. Memoria escrita por encargo de la Academia española. Madrid, 1870. 8vo.

Monnier, Marc.—Histoire générale de la littérature moderne. 2 vols. Paris, 1884–1885. 8vo.

Note.—Vol. ii. pp. 341–403.

Montégut, Emile.—Types littéraires et fantaisies esthétiques. Paris, 1882. 8vo.

Note.—Pp. 45–92.

Morán, Jerónimo.—Vida de Miguel de Cervantes Saavedra. Madrid, 1863. 4to.

Mor de Fuentes, José.—Elogio de Miguel de Cervantes Saavedra. Paris, 1835. 8vo.

Note.—Prefixed to an edition of *Don Quixote.* Pp. i.–xxxix.

Muret, Théodore César.—Michel Cervantès, drame en cinq actes en vers. Paris, 1858. 12mo.

Nallat, Muley Rovicdagor [*i.e.* Manuel Gallardo y Victor]. —Memoria escrita sobre el rescate de Cervantes. Cádiz, 1876. 8vo.

Navarrete, Martín Fernández de.—Vida de Miguel de Cervantes Saavedra. Madrid, 1819. 8vo.

Ni Cervantes es Cervantes ni El Quijote es el Quijote. Santander, 1868. 12mo.

Noriéga, F. de Paule.—Critique et défense de Don Quichotte, suivies de chapitres choisies de l'ingenieux Hidalgo, etc. Paris, 1846. 18mo.

Oliphant, Margaret Oliphant.—Cervantes. Edinburgh, 1880. 8vo.

Note.—This forms part of *Blackwood's Foreign Classics for English Readers.*

Pardo de Figueroa, Mariano.—See Droap, M.

Pellicer, Juan Antonio.—Vida de Miguel de Cervantes Saavedra. Madrid, 1797. 8vo.

Note.—This life, prefixed to the Academy edition, occupies pp. lv.–ccxviii.

PELLICER, JUAN ANTONIO.—Examen crítico del tomo primero de el Anti-Quixote por Nicolás Pérez. Madrid, 1806. 12mo.

PEREZ, NICOLÁS.—El Anti-Quixote. 1805. 12mo.

PI Y MOLIST, EMILIO.—Primores del Don Quixote en el concepto médico-psicológico y consideraciones generales sobre la locura para un nuevo comentario de la inmortal novela. Barcelona, 1886. 8vo.

PICATOSTE Y RODRIGUEZ, FELIPE.—La casa de Cervantes en Valladolid. Madrid, 1888. 8vo.

PIERNAS Y HURTADO, JOSÉ MANUEL.—Ideas y Noticias económicas del Quijote. Ligero estudio bajo este aspecto de la inmortal obra de Cervantes. Madrid, 1874. 8vo.

PIGUENIT, D. J.—Don Quixote, an entertainment for music. London, 1774. 8vo.

———— Second edition. London, 1776. 8vo.

PINELLI ROMANO, BARTOLOMEO.—Le azioni più celebrate del famoso cavaliere errante Don Chisciotte della Mancia, inventate ed incise da B. P. R. Roma [1834 ?], obl. fol.

PRESCOTT, WILLIAM HICKLING.—Biographical and Critical Miscellanies. London, 1845. 8vo.

NOTE.—Pp. 108-154.

A los profanadores del ingenioso hidalgo Don Quijote de la Mancha. Crítica y algo mas, por El Diablo con antiparras. Madrid, 1861. 16mo.

Remarks on the proposals lately published for a new translation of Don Quixote. In which will be considered the design of Cervantes in writing the original and some new lights given relative to his Life and Adventures. In a letter from a Gentleman in the country [Colonel W. Windham] to a friend in town. London, 1755. 8vo.

REMENTERÍA Y FICA, MARIANO DE.—Honores tributados á la memoria de Miguel de Cervantes Saavedra en la capital de España en el primer año del reinado de Isabel II. Madrid, 1834. 8vo.

RENHOLM, G.—Spansker Berättelser. Miguel Cervantes med inledande studie öfver Spaniens skönliteratur. Stockolm, 1877. 8vo.

RÍOS, VICENTE DE LOS.—Vida de Miguel de Cervantes Saavedra y análisis del Quixote. Madrid, 1780. 4to.

NOTE.—This precedes the Academy Edition of 1780, pp. iii.-ccii.

Roscoe, Thomas.—Life and writings of Miguel de Cervantes Saavedra. London, 1839. 8vo.

Saint-Victor, Paul de.—Hommes et Dieux. Etudes d'histoire et de littérature. Paris, 1867.

Note.—Pp. 441–456.

Sainte-Beuve, Charles Augustin.—Nouveaux Lundis. Paris, 1885.

Note.—Vol. iii. pp. 1–65.

Sbarbi, José María.—El Refranero general español. 10 tomos. Madrid, 1874–1876.

Note.—Tom. v. (Instrucciones ecónomicas y políticas, dadas por Sancho Panza á su hijo, Respuestas de Sanchico Panza); Tom. vi. (La intraducibilidad del Quijote).

——— Cervantes téologo. Toledo, 1870. 8vo.

Schack, Adolf Friedrich von.—Geschichte der dramatischen Literatur und Kunst in Spanien. 3 vols. Berlin, 1845–1846. 8vo.

Note.—Vol. i. pp. 310–365.

Scherer, Edmond.—Etudes critiques de littérature. Paris, 1876. 8vo.

Note.—Vol. vii. pp. 84–97.

Schlegel, August Wilhelm von.—Sämmtliche Werke. Leipzig, 1846. 8vo.

Note.—Vol. i. pp. 338–343 ; vol. iv. 189–203.

Schueller, J. Carl.—Voorlezing over den Don Quijote gehonden . . . te Utrecht den 10 Feb., 1842. Utrecht, 1842. 8vo.

Segovia, Antonio María.—Cervantes. Nueva Utopia. Monumento nacional de eterna gloria imaginado en honra del príncipe de los ingenios. Madrid, 1861. 8vo.

Sentencias de Don Quijote y agudezas de Sancho. Máximas y pensamientos mas notables contenidos en la obra de Cervantes, Don Quijote de la Mancha. Madrid, 1863. 16mo.

Siñérez, Juan Francisco. — El Quijote del siglo XVIII. 4 tomos. Madrid, 1836. 8vo.

——— El Quijote de la Revolución o historia de la vida, hechos, aventuras y proezas de Monsieur le grand-homme Pamparanuja, héroe político, filósofo moderno, caballero errante y reformador de todo el género humano. 2 tomos. Méjico, 1862. 8vo.

SIMONDE DE SISMONDI, JEAN CHARLES LÉONARD.—De la littérature du Midi de l'Europe.   4 vols.   Paris, 1813.   8vo.

NOTE.—Vol. iii. pp. 329-436.

Stories and Chapters from Don Quixote versified.   The Novel of the Curious Impertinent.   London, 1830.   12mo.

TUBINO, FRANCISCO MARÍA.—Cervantes y el Quijote : estudios críticos.   Madrid, 1872.   8vo.

———— El Quijote y La Estafeta de Urganda : ensayo crítico. Seville, 1862.   8vo.

URDANETA, AMENODORO.—Cervantes y la crítica.   Carácas, 1877. 8vo.

VALERA, JUAN.—Estudios críticos sobre literatura, política y costumbres de nuestros dias.   2 tomos.   Madrid, 1864.   8vo.

———— Sobre el Quijote y sobre las diferentes maneras de comentarle y juzgarle.   Madrid, 1864.   8vo.

VIDAL Y DE VALENCIANO, CAYETANO.—El Entremés de refranes ¿ es de Cervantes ?   Ensayo de su traducción.   Estudio crítico-literario. Barcelona y Madrid, 1883.   8vo.

VIDART, LUIS.—Algunas ideas de Cervantes referentes á la literatura preceptiva.   Madrid, 1878.   8vo.

———— Cervantes, poeta épico.   Apuntes críticos.   Madrid, 1877. 8vo.

———— El Quijote y la clasificación de la obras literarias.   La desdicha póstuma de Cervantes.   Madrid, 1882.   8vo.

———— El Quijote y el Telémaco.   Madrid, 1884.   8vo.

———— Los biógrafos de Cervantes en el siglo XVIII.   Madrid, 1886.   8vo.

Der Spanische Waghalsz oder des vom Liebe bezauberten Ritters Don Quixote von Quixada.   Gantz Neue Auschweiffung auf seiner Weissen Rosinanta.   Nürnberg, 1696.   8vo.

WINDHAM, W.—See Remarks on the proposals lately published, etc.

Wit and Wisdom of Don Quixote.   New York, 1867.   12mo.

———— With a biographical sketch of Cervantes by Emma Thompson.   Boston, 1882.   8vo.

WOLOWSKI, ALEKSANDER.—Cervantès, poète dramatique.   Mémoire lu à la séance de l'Institut historique le 4 novembre, 1849.   Batignoles, 1849.   8vo.

Y. T.—Don Quijote de la Mancha en el siglo XIX.   Cádiz, 1861.   8vo.

THE CRITICISM AND COMMENTARY OF PERIODICAL LITERATURE.

Cervantes Saavedra, Miguel de. *Semanario Pintoresco*, by J. de la Revilla, 1840, pp. 329–332 ; *Bentley's Miscellany*, vol. xxiv. (1848), pp. 626–627 ; *Dublin University Magazine*, vol. lxviii. (1866), pp. 123–138 ; reprinted in the *Catholic World*, vol. iv. (1867), pp. 14–28 ; *Month*, vol. vii. (1867), pp. 50–62 ; *Argosy*, by Alice King, vol. vii. (1869), pp. 117–122 ; *La Ilustración Española*, by F. M. Tubino, 1872, pp. 250–251 ; *All the Year Round*, vol. xxxvii., New Series (1886), pp. 534–539.

Cervantes and Beaumont and Fletcher. *Fraser's Magazine*, vol. xci. (1875), pp. 592–597.

Cervantes and his Writings. *American Monthly Magazine*, vol. vii. (1836), pp. 342–354.

Cervantes and Lope de Vega. *Sharpe's London Journal*, by F. Lawrence, vol. xi. pp. 228–236.

Cervantes en Valladolid. *Revista de España*, by Pascual Gayangos, vol. xcvii. (1884), pp. 481–507 ; vol. xcviii. pp. 161–191, 321–368, 508–543 ; vol. xcix. (1884), pp. 5–32.

El Buscapié. *Dublin Review*, vol. xxvi. (1849), pp. 137–152.

Caractère historique et moral du Don Quichotte. *Revue des Deux Mondes*, by Emile Montégut, vol. l. (1864), pp. 170–195.

¿Cervantes fué ó no poeta? *Semanario Pintoresco*, by Adolfo de Castro, 1851, pp. 354–355.

La Cocina del Quijote. *La Ilustración española* (1872), pp. 533–539, 554–555, 566–570.

Comentarios filosóficos del Quijote. *Crónica hispano-americana*, by Nicolas Díaz de Benjumea, Nov. 14, 15, 16, 17, 18, 19, 20.

Conjeturas sobre el fundamento que pudo tener la idea que dió origen á la patraña de el Buscapié. *Revista de Ciencias, Literatura y Artes*, by Cayetano Alberto de la Barrera, vol. ii. (1856), pp. 731–741.

Los continuadores del ingenioso hidalgo. La obra de un Avellanedo (*sic*) desconocido. *Revista de España*, by José María Asensio y Toledo, xxxiii. (1873), pp. 451–469.

Crónica de los Cervantistas. Cádiz, 1871, etc. 4to.

NOTE.—This magazine, established under the editorship of D. Ramón León Máinez, is issued at irregular intervals.

Don Quixote. *Blackwood's Edinburgh Magazine*, vol. xi. (1822), pp. 657–668 ; *North American Review*, by W. H. Prescott, vol. xlv. (1837), pp. 1–34 ; *Revue française*, vol. vii. (1838), pp. 299–327 ; The *Knickerbocker*, by R. J. de Cordova, vol. xxxviii. (1851), pp. 189–203 ; *Westminster Review*, vol. xxxiii., New Series, 1868, pp. 299–327 ; reprinted in the *Eclectic Magazine*, vol. viii., New Series, pp. 909–925 ; *Cornhill Magazine*, vol. xxx. (1874), pp. 595–616.

Don Quixote and Gil Blas. *Penn Monthly*, by C. H. Drew, vol. iii. (1872), pp. 555–564.

The Drama of Cervantes. *Gentleman's Magazine*, by James Mew, vol. ccxlv. (1879), pp. 446–470.

Duffield's Translation of Don Quixote. *Blackwood's Edinburgh Magazine*, vol. cxxx. (1881), pp. 469–490.

Educación científica de Cervantes. *El Museo Universal*, by Nicolás Díaz de Benjumea, vol. xiii. (1869), pp. 19–22, 38–39.

Episodes of Don Quixote. *London Magazine*, vol. vi., New Series (1826), pp. 557–566, and vol. vii., New Series (1827), pp. 11–19.

The Entremeses of Cervantes. *Gentleman's Magazine*, by James Mew, vol. ccl. (1881), pp. 451–469.

Estatua de Cervantes. *Semanario Pintoresco*, 1836, pp. 249–253.

The Galatea of Cervantes. *Gentleman's Magazine*, by James Mew, vol. ccxlvi. (1880), pp. 670–690.

Hamlet et Don Quichotte. *Bibliothèque Universelle et Revue Suisse*, by Ivan Turgenev, vol. iii. (Troisième période), pp. 56–79.

Heine on Don Quixote. *Temple Bar*, vol. xlviii. (1876), pp. 235–249.

Huellas de Cervantes. *Revista de España*, by Enrique Cisneros, vol. xi. (1869), p. 58.

Jarvis's Translation of Don Quixote. *Monthly Review*, vol. iii., New Series (1837), pp. 230–240.

Library of Don Quixote. *Fraser's Magazine*, vol. vii. (1833), pp. 324–331, 565–577.

Life of Cervantes. *United States Review and Literary Gazette*, vol. ii. (1827), pp. 415–427 ; *Monthly Review*, vol. ii., New Series (1834), pp. 383–395 ; *North American Review*, by E. Wigglesworth, vol. xxxviii. (1834), pp. 277–307 ; *North American Review*, by W. H. Prescott, vol. xlv. (1837), pp. 1–34.

Nota de las personas que intervienen en la historia del Ingenioso Hidalgo Don Quijote. *Semanario Pintoresco*, by Remigio Salomón, 1850, pp. 129–134.

Notas á la Vida de Cervantes. *Revista de Ciencias, Literatura y Artes*, by Cayetano Alberto de la Barrera, vol. iii. (1856), pp. 468–478.

Cervantes' Novels. *Gentleman's Magazine*, by James Mew, vol. ccxliii. (1878), pp. 358–372 ; vol. ccxliv. (1879), pp. 95–110.

Observaciones sobre las ediciones primitivos de Don Quijote de la Mancha. *Revista de España*, by José María Asensio y Toledo, vol. ix. (1869), pp. 367–376.

Ormsby's Translation of Don Quixote. *Quarterly Review*, vol. clxii. (1886), pp. 43–79 ; *Saturday Review*, vol. lix. (June 13, 1885), pp. 794–795 ; *Nation* (New York), vol. xli. (1885), pp. 513–514, 535–537.

El progreso de la crítica del Quijote. *Revista de España*, by Nicolás Díaz de Benjumea, vol. lxiv. (1878), pp. 474–488 ; vol. lxv. pp. 42–59, 450–466 ; vol. lxvi. (1879), pp. 158–172, 329–348 ; vol. lxvii. pp. 519–538.

Un Paseo á la patria de Don Quijote. *Semanario Pintoresco*, by José Jiménez-Serrano, 1848, pp. 19–22, 35–37, 41–43, 109–111, 131–133.

Le Portrait de Cervantes. *Revue germanique*, by J. M. Guardia, vol. xxxviii. (1866), pp. 300–314.

Découverte du véritable Portrait de Cervantes. *Revue britannique*, by Antoine de Latour, vol. ccxxxvii., 9ᵐᵉ série (1865), pp. 471–485.

Rambles in the Footsteps of Don Quixote. *Dublin University Magazine*, vol. xi. (1838), pp. 574–581.

Recuerdos de Cervantes. *Semanario pintoresco*, by José Jiménez-Serrano (1848), pp. 161–163.

Resumen por orden cronológico de las principales aventuras del Ingenioso Hidalgo Don Quijote. *Semanario pintoresco*, by Remigio Salomón, 1850, pp. 148–151.

Significación histórica de Cervantes. *Crónica hispano-americana*, by Nicolás Díaz de Benjumea, vol. iii. (1859), pp. 8–9.

Théâtre de Michel Cervantes. *Revue des Deux Mondes*, by Charles de Mazade, vol. xxxviii. (1862), pp. 255–256.

La Tia fingida. *El Criticón*, by B. J. Gallardo, No. 1, 1835.

Una traducción del Quijote. Novela original. *Revista de España,* by Florencio Moreno Godino, vol. vi. (1869), pp. 397–437, 547–567; vol. vii. pp. 54–75.

Viaje de Cervantes á Italia. *El Museo Universal,* by Nicolás Díaz de Benjumea, vol. xiii. (1869), pp. 102, 103, 110.

Cervantes' Voyage to Parnassus. *Gentleman's Magazine,* vol. ccxlvi. (1880), pp. 81–95.[1]

---

[1] The volume of the *Gentleman's Magazine* for the months January–June, 1880, is numbered ccxlvi.; the volume for July–December, 1880, is numbered ccxlix. I have followed this numeration, without endeavouring to correct it.

INDEX.

2 c

THE END.

CHARLES DICKENS AND EVANS, CRYSTAL PALACE PRESS.